ISBN 979-8-9864995-9-8

Edited by Represent Publishing

Cover Design by Brittany Evans

COURT OF OF LIES

COURT OF LIES

NICOLE MOORE

RP Represent Publishing

Shout out to my "Writing" playlist for helping me write this book. I couldn't have done it without the support of Paramore, Taylor Swift, and Harry Styles.

CHAPTER 1

DOWN IN THE DUMPS

I can't believe that just happened. I seriously can't believe it. I, Raven Montclair, will NEVER date another human again.

Until about twenty minutes ago, I was the happiest I had been in a while. I pretty much had everything going for me: a running car, a great boyfriend, and a pretty good control on my powers. Now, I have none of those things.

Let me take you back to when life decided to rain on my happy parade. Literally. I was on my way over to my boyfriend Kyle's house to celebrate our one-year anniversary. That is, until my car had other plans. Now, don't get me wrong. I love my beat up, sandstone-colored, 2002 Jeep Liberty. Me and Libby the Liberty, as I like to call her, had some great times together but today she decided it was her last day and there were no ifs ands or buts about it.

About five miles from Kyle's house, smoke started coming out of the hood of my car. I made it about three more blocks and that's when it all went to hell in a handbag. Black smoke started billowing out from the hood of my car. Apparently, Libby was making her last stand.

I pulled over to the side of the road and jumped out just in case she decided she wanted a Viking burial. At this point, I popped the hatch on the trunk and grabbed the only two things I care about in the car: my overnight bag and my purse.

I reached into my purse to find my phone so I could call Kyle to tell him I was going to be late, but he didn't answer. No big deal, right? Wrong. I haven't heard from Kyle since this morning when we talked on the phone after breakfast. Normally, he texts me every hour or so, but today, it was radio silent. That should have been my first clue.

Once I put my phone away, I began the five-mile trek to Kyle's. Now, for me, five miles is nothing. As a witch, living in the human world is as plain as it gets for someone like me. I look like every other human, besides my gray eyes. But it turns out, I'm not too plain after all. Witches can normally control one or two elements. I can wield all four elements: earth, water, air, and fire. I also have heightened endurance, which helps me control my powers . . . most times.

As I strolled down the sidewalk, I received plenty of over-long looks from the passing cars, but I didn't let it bother me since they probably thought I was just some dolled up sorority girl from the university heading to a party. I did spend almost two hours getting ready for this night and not even a little car trouble was going to stop me from celebrating.

Finally, as I rounded the corner to Kyle's house, I saw my best friend's car in the driveway, which I found rather odd. I waved the thought away and figured she must be helping Kyle set up for a romantic dinner in the house. As I approached the door, my heart sped up with each step and butterflies started to build in my stomach from the anticipation.

Trying to be as quiet as I could, I opened the front door and put my bags on the floor. I didn't see anyone in the living room or the kitchen, but that's when I heard voices coming from down the hall.

Wait, not the hall, Kyle's bedroom. I slipped off my shoes and tiptoed down the hallway. I peeked inside the cracked bedroom door, only to find Bree Taylor, my supposed best friend, in Kyle's bedroom. Not only in his bedroom, but in his bed, with them both naked. Unfortunately, that image will be burned into my memory.

One can only imagine what they were doing under those satin sheets, which were, in fact, a birthday present from me. I didn't intend to stick around and find out. That is, until my phone rang, interrupting the moment.

I quickly silenced my phone, but it was too late. Kyle's face suddenly spun around while Bree's eyes revealed that deer in the headlights look.

"Oh shit!" Kyle yelled as he and Bree peeled themselves off each other.

"Raven, wait!" Bree called.

In a matter of seconds, Bree jolted out of the bed, half wrapped in the satin sheet, bursting out of the door behind me. It was too late. There was nothing either of them could say to clear up this situation.

I raced for the front door and ignored what both of my "used to be boyfriend" and "used to be best friend" had to say about what just happened. I grabbed my bag and opened the door to leave, but before I stepped out the door, I turned to face them. Both still half naked from their afternoon delight, I just shook my head.

I looked up, plastering a fake smile on my face.

"Don't worry, you two are perfect for each other," I said. Then I slammed the door behind me.

CHAPTER 2

RAIN CHECK

BACK TO PRESENT:

I take off in a dead sprint down the street as a sudden surge of power hits me that I haven't felt before. Suddenly, the sky has turned from a perfect sunny day to a scene from Twister. A loud, thunderous roar comes from the black clouds above. My mood worsens as I realize the hold I once had on my powers is long gone and the sky opens like a water hose.

"I'M NOT EVEN THAT UPSET!" I shout into the rain above me. My powers shouldn't be going haywire over something like this.

Trying to find any piece of dry land I can, I seek shelter from a random stranger's front porch. It does a good job of protecting me from the pounding rain, but the house is old and every so often I feel a trickle of water fall through the ceiling.

Mostly safe from the elements, I pull out my phone and call one of the four people I have on speed dial.

"Hello? Raven? I thought you would be devouring your

boyfriend right now?" Leah says, and I hear the devilish grin through the phone.

"I would be, but Bree got to him first," I say, almost cutting off Leah mid-sentence.

"No. Effing. Way!" Leah yells into the phone. "I knew that little slut wouldn't be able to resist. No offense, Raven, but you know I never could forgive Bree after what happened last year when you almost got kicked out of college. She always wanted what she couldn't have, and, most of the time, it was usually things you had."

In some ways, I always had a gut feeling about Bree being a shady friend, but she was the second friend I made, besides Leah, when I first moved to the human world back in middle school. It's always been Raven, Leah, and Bree. The three best friends. That is, until Bree decided to sleep with my boyfriend.

"Who needs her, anyway? Her head is bigger than her boobs now and all she does is talk about the next guy she's going to hook up with. Good riddance!" Leah pipes up on the other end of the phone.

"I just wish I saw the signs sooner. Maybe I was too naïve since we have been friends for so long." There's a long pause. It hits me that I have no car, my clothes are soaking wet, and my feet are starting to hurt from my little track race. "Hey, can you pick me up?"

"Um, where's your car?" Leah asks, a little skeptical.

"Probably still smoking on the side of the road. I was on my way to Kyle's, and Libby decided to take a left turn to Death Valley. I need a ride. I was headed back to my apartment until the sky decided to grace us with this lovely little storm. I'm currently held up under someone's covered porch around the corner from Kyle's. Do you mind picking me up?" Hoisting my bags over my shoulders again, I wait for Leah's response.

"Of course I'll come get you! Tell you what? I'll pick you up and we can hang out at your apartment, and you can tell me all the gross details of what happened at Kyle's. Deal?"

I sigh in relief. I know I can always count on Leah to be my knight in glittering, kick ass armor.

"Deal. I'm ready to get out of this soaking wet dress and put some dry clothes on and forget this even happened."

"See you soon!" Leah sings into the phone as she hangs up.

Just like that, as I think about having a relaxing night, the sky turns back into a picture-perfect day.

"Really? The thunderstorm should not have happened in the first place. He wasn't that great of a boyfriend," I mumble to myself.

Ten minutes later, my best friend, Leah Collins, pulls up to the curb beside me in her storm blue, 2017 Toyota Rav4. Her shoulder-length, sandy blonde hair is in a tight bun on top of her head, which makes her face look even more slender. She pulls her sunglasses down enough for me to catch a glimpse of her blue eyes scanning the street, making sure no one is going to sideswipe me as I cross the street to her car.

I reach the passenger door only to find my other best friend, Asher Beaumont, already occupying the passenger seat. Asher has alway been a part of our friend group, blending in seamlessly with us and never minding that he was the only boy in the group. I didn't mind either because ever since I can remember, there has been something I just can't put my finger on about him and the way I feel when I'm around him. There is a definite attraction, that's for sure, but with us being so close as friends, I never wanted to ruin the dynamic of the group by getting involved with him.

I stare into Asher's dreamy green eyes, and that familiar, unknown pull he has on me tries to reel me in as he throws out his typical greeting.

"Hey Witch," he says, flashing me one of his knockout

smiles. "Heard you finally dumped that loser boyfriend of yours."

Asher is one of those guys who you could just drool over. He's your typical college athlete with a good-looking body to back him up. His shirt clings dangerously to his biceps, and I can see the outline of his toned abs under his white shirt.

Leah must have picked him up right after cross country practice because his short, wavy light blonde hair is still damp from his shower. Even in the middle of September, he somehow maintains his shimmering tan skin. He looks like he should be lounging on an island somewhere instead of driving back to my apartment in the suburbs of Arkansas.

As I walk past the passenger side window, I fire back, "Well, Shifter, you sure are quick to step in for my rebound." And I wink at him before I get in the back seat.

"That's enough, you two," Leah says as she chucks an empty water bottle toward the passenger. "Asher, I didn't pick you up so you could try to flirt with her right after the mess she's been through."

We all laugh as the light turns green. I'm glad that I have these two to keep me company tonight.

We pull into the modern apartment complex and I instantly relax, seeing the familiar black and white buildings in neat little rows. My apartment sits on the second floor and thankfully my upstairs neighbors are an elderly couple who barely make a peep. Leah is the first one out of the elevator and we follow her lead, taking a left and finding my door at the end of the hallway. My one-bedroom apartment isn't much, and it's definitely nothing like home, but does the job. As we walk in the front door, I can still smell the aroma of the vanilla candle I had lit just a few hours ago.

"Dibs on picking the Netflix show!" Asher yells, as he and Leah get settled on the couch.

Leah groans and throws a pillow at him. "It better not be *The Office* again. You've made us watch that show five hundred times."

I roll my eyes and holler back, "I'll decide what we are watching after I'm done changing. Give me five minutes."

Once in my bedroom, I throw my overnight bag in the corner.

Guess I won't be needing you tonight after all.

I should be feeling sad, but honestly, I think I'm glad Kyle and I are over. Deep down, I knew the relationship wasn't going to end up anywhere special.

Shaking away the thoughts, I peel off my wet clothes and change into my favorite t-shirt and leggings. After I discard my clothes in the laundry, I head toward the bathroom to look at what's left of my makeup.

"Not bad," I whisper to myself.

My freckles have peeked through what little foundation I had applied, revealing my clear olive skin. My hip length dark brown hair has become a mess of flattened curls due to the rain and is practically glued to the sides on my cheeks, bringing out my gray eyes even more.

Forgoing any hope of salvaging my curls, I tie my hair back in a loose braid and head back out to the living room to make sure my friends haven't destroyed my apartment yet. "I've decided we're sticking with *New Girl* tonight. Who's hungry? I'll order take out!"

CHAPTER 3
TURNING THE TABLES

I'm woken up early the next morning by a single annoying beam of light that has found its way through my blinds. I growl and reach for the extra pillow on my bed to shield my eyes. After five minutes of tossing and turning, I give up all hope of going back to sleep.

I quietly roll out of bed and peek my head around the corner to see what kind of mess awaits me in the living room. Leah is sprawled out on the love seat, face smashed into a pillow to block out the morning light, and Asher is asleep on the floor with one leg draped over the chase lounger in the corner, with one of my throw blankets covering him like a toga.

I pull out my phone to document this terrific scene when my phone rings yet again in the worst situation.

I really should learn to put my phone on silent.

Careful not to wake the sleeping lions, I turn toward my room to answer the call.

"Hi honey! How did last night go? I tried to call you before you left for dinner, but you didn't answer."

"Hi Mom," I whisper as I step back into my room, closing the door.

Thinking back to last night, I decide it's better to spare her the major details and just let her know I'm now newly single and Asher and Leah spent the night helping me forget the whole ordeal.

Little did she know, I headed over to Kyle's early and SHE was the one who interrupted all the fun last night.

"Oh, Raven. I'm so sorry. I'm glad Leah and Asher were there for you last night. Speaking of Asher . . . " I cut her off before she can even begin.

"Mom, don't even start. How many times do I have to tell you? Asher and I are just friends. He may be super dreamy, good-looking, and he's always got my back, but we are just friends."

I'm pretty sure I say that last bit to convince myself more than my mom. Have I thought about the idea of dating Asher? Oh yeah. Is it a good idea? Probably not. I don't want to be the one to cause a riff in our group if something goes wrong.

"Alright, Raven. I'm just saying. Not to change the subject, but you should come down for the weekend. Grandpa Artie is coming into town, and I know he would love to see you."

I haven't seen my Grandpa Artie in almost a year. Every year, he tries to come back from the Realm of Shadows to see me for my birthday. Looks like I'll be getting an early present this year!

I agree to come down the next weekend and stay on the phone long enough to learn that Mom has recently turned our old barn by the lake into her new workshop for young witches. Her old shop was caught in the middle of a preteen break up and a few minutes later the shop was up in flames. I don't believe that insurance will cover "untrained witch fire" as a reason for an insurance claim, as humans don't know supernaturals exist

but then one thing led to another, and we just couldn't keep our hands off each other."

As I'm wondering if I just overlooked the fact that Bree has always had this sour personality her whole life or what I did to her to ever deserve something like this, she takes two steps closer and whispers in my ear.

"How does it feel having things ripped from your grasp?"

I step back, turning my puzzled eyes to meet her mischievous grin as she continues, "Ever since we were kids, you always took what wasn't yours. First Leah, then Asher, and now Kyle. Enough is enough. Now, it's about time that I take things back for myself."

Suddenly, it hits me! I must have shaken ties between her friendships with Leah and Asher when I moved into town, but I never considered how it would affect her.

"Bree, I'm sorry. I had no idea you felt that way, but what you did to me isn't something a friend would do. It's downright evil."

Looking at her, I thought I would feel sorry for her, but something feels off.

"Oh, this is only the first of many things to come. Just you wait."

And somehow, I know she's not lying as goosebumps rise up my arms at her warning. Ready to be done with this conversation, I turn to leave, but Bree grabs my arm, halting my escape.

Her lips are mere inches from my ear as she whispers another ominous warning, "There are worse things coming for you than me, Raven." She smirks as she continues, "You better get those powers of yours under control, or you might not make it very much longer."

Puzzled by not only how she knows about my powers but also by the fact that I swear I just saw her brown eyes turn golden yellow for a split second, I break free of her hold and

walk away. All I hear is her sinister laugh fading into the background as I try to put as much space as I can between us.

Bree and Leah don't know about the supernatural world, and they especially don't know Asher and I are a part of that world. We haven't told them because, most times, humans tend to freak out when you tell them the monsters and stories they were told about as children are real. They think the nicknames Asher and I have for each other came about the year after we all met because that year, Asher and I dressed up as what we really are for Halloween. I dressed as a witch, but not with the broom because we don't use those to fly, and Asher's mom found the cutest dog costume. She even painted his face to pull the whole look together.

After walking two blocks to get off campus, I call the only person I can trust with what's been on my brain since the second I broke free from Bree's grip.

It only takes two rings before the call is answered.

"What's up, Witch? Did you miss my dreaminess?" Asher says playfully.

"Are you alone?" I ask with a little too much suspicion in my voice.

"No, I'm at cross country practice. Why, what's up?"

"I need you to come by my apartment when you're done. I can't talk about this over the phone."

My eyes dart around, making sure no one is following me as I wait for Asher's reply.

The playfulness vanishes from Asher's tone. "Okay, that sounds ominous. Are you sure you don't want me to come now?"

"No, it's okay. Just come after practice." Sounding a little too serious, I try to lighten the mood. "I'll make you dinner since you're coming straight over. Wouldn't want you to miss out on all those calories."

Instantly, his playfulness returns. "Hey, whatever the news is,

it can't be that bad since you offered me dinner. This is practically a date now."

I roll my eyes, becoming less tense with Asher on the phone. "Just don't be late or the food will get cold."

Asher gasps. "I wouldn't even dream of being late for our first date."

"It's not a date!" I try to say, but it's too late, Asher already hung up the phone.

My nerves from meeting Bree morph into a different set of nerves from Asher mentioning this being our first date. Having only about an hour and a half to prepare for dinner, I head straight home and hope I have all the ingredients to make one of Asher's favorite dinners that I remember from our childhood.

CHAPTER 4
ALWAYS CHECK THE PEEPHOLE

Even though it's the middle of September, I pull out all the stops to make Asher's favorite dinner. The aroma from the brown sugar and spices fills up the room enough to remind me of winter nights cuddled up by the fire back home. My homemade chili is ready in record time, just as I hear a knock at the door.

Wiping my hands on the kitchen towel, I start to open the door. "Asher, I will have you know you're ten minutes late for —" My sentence is cut short as I stare at the person standing in my doorway.

"Hey Raven. What is Asher late for?" Kyle says coolly.

"Dinner," I grumble, as I hesitate to open the door anymore. Leave it to me the one time I don't check the peephole, it's someone I don't want to see. I was home free all week and now I see both Bree and Kyle within two hours of each other.

Just. My. Freaking. Luck.

"How nice of you to make him dinner. Looks like you've moved on quickly then."

"Asher and I are just friends, Kyle, you know that. Besides, I

don't have to explain anything to you." I lean up against the door frame, placing one of my feet behind the door as a stopper. "Seems to me that it's you who should be doing a little explaining. Don't you think?"

Staring at him, all I think is how badly I want to shut the door right in his smug-looking face. Any feelings I had for him are long gone.

Kyle tries to wedge the door open as he attempts to smooth talk me, but my foot is holding the door in place like I planned.

"Well, why don't you let me in so I can explain things clearly for you, Raven."

Kyle is a good six inches taller than me, which forces me to look up to face him. I try to sound convincing as I stare into his chocolate eyes. "I don't think so. Whatever you have to say can be said in the hallway," I say as I point out the door. "Besides, Asher will be here any minute, so I suggest you make it quick."

"Come on, Raven. Just hear me out," Kyle pleads, pathetically.

"There really isn't anything I need to hear that Bree hasn't already told me. All those supposedly late-night study sessions you had with her were you two hooking up behind my back. We are over, Kyle. No sense in trying to explain the obvious."

This time, I try to slam the door in his face, but he catches it with his hand.

"I'm not done talking about this. Now, you either let me in, or I will let myself in. What do you say, Raven? Which one is it?"

"Neither! Now, get out of my apartment!" I give him one more chance before I use my witch wind to help close the door.

"Wrong answer." With one big shove, Kyle catches me off balance and pushes me back into my apartment, but not until I see Asher in the hallway, marching toward us.

"Is everything alright here, Raven?" Asher asks, popping his head into the room, trying to calm the situation.

"Get lost, Asher. This is between Raven and I," Kyle says, as he steps farther into the room.

Asher strolls in, positioning me behind him in a protecting way. Which would be sweet for anyone else, but I don't need protection.

"I believe I heard Raven say that you weren't welcome here. Isn't that right, Raven?"

"You are absolutely correct, Asher," I say, stepping beside Asher.

I catch a movement in the corner of my eye; Asher clenches his fists, clearly not happy with the situation. I can't have things escalate to the point where I need to use my powers to pull these two apart if they decide to duke it out in my entryway. Not that I wouldn't enjoy watching Kyle get his ass handed to him, but I'd rather not have the neighbors snooping around my business.

Asher zeros in on Kyle. "That's what I thought. Now, I suggest you leave before things escalate."

Asher grabs the edge of the door and holds it open as he waves his hand in front of himself like he is escorting Kyle out.

Kyle heads for the door and leaves me with one final warning. "This isn't over. I'll be back when you don't have other people around to fight your battles."

"I think I am more than capable of fighting my own battles, Kyle. But if I were you, I wouldn't want to find out just how capable I am." I wink at Kyle, and Asher shuts the door in his face.

Asher walks over to the window to make sure he left. After Asher is sure he's gone, he turns to face me with a quizzical look on his face. "First, what the heck was that about?" he says as he points toward the door. "Second, do I smell chili?"

"Who knows! I was going to open the door to rip you a new one for being ten minutes late for dinner, and I forgot to look through the peephole. Next thing I know, Kyle is trying to push his way inside my apartment for some unknown reason."

Part of me wonders if he showed up to apologize, but the other part of me questions why he became so aggressive. He was always the one to stay away from fights and confrontation. That whole situation can wait and be filed under my "Shit Raven doesn't have time for" folder.

I refocus my attention on Asher. "I spent all afternoon cooking your favorite meal and you show up almost thirty minutes late! Remind me never to call you if I'm dying." I turn away from him and start fixing both our bowls for dinner.

"Oh, please," Asher teases, as he comes up beside me and hops up on the counter. "You had what, an hour and a half tops to prepare dinner?" He stretches his hand out and taps me on the nose. "Besides, I had the worst time trying to pick out the perfect outfit for our first date tonight."

"It's not a date," I say, as I wave my spoon in his face. I quickly take note of his washed out blue jeans and tight black university shirt. I mean, he does look good, but that's besides the point. "If you keep calling it that, you're not going to get any of this delicious chili. Now, get your butt off my counter and get the Fritos."

Asher beats me to my chair, pulling it out for me. "Ladies first." He smiles brightly at me, patiently waiting for me to accept the gesture.

I glare at him but decide to play along. As he goes to sit, I wave my hand and his chair scoots out from under him. Just before he's about to hit the floor, there's a shimmering bright light, then Asher is gone. Replacing my best friend is now a white owl hovering above my table. Another brilliant white flash and Asher is back to his human form.

He wags his finger at me as though scorning me as he grasps his chair with his other hand. "Very funny, Raven, but you have to be quicker than that if you want to catch me."

"Next time then, Shifter." I promise, smiling sweetly at him.

"Next time then, Witch." He promises right back with a wink.

As we finish dinner, Asher finally asks about what brought him over tonight. "So, what was with the phone call today? Why couldn't you talk about whatever it was over the phone?"

I swirl my spoon around in what is left of my chili for a moment before saying, "Do you know anything about dragons?" I ask, a little suspiciously.

"What? You and I both know that dragons are one of the more rare supernatural beings in the Human Realm. I've never actually seen one in person. I've only heard stories from my parents. Why do you ask?"

I end up telling Asher what happened today after class with Bree. When I tell him about how I saw her eyes flash golden yellow, he looks at me puzzled.

"So, let me get this straight," he says, leaning over the table, perplexed. "You're overlooking the fact that somehow Bree knows about you being a witch because you think you saw her eyes turn golden yellow, which means she could be a dragon?" Asher asks, a little shocked.

"I'm not overlooking anything, Asher, but her eyes really did turn yellow and the one thing I know about dragons that's true is when they're about to transform, their eyes turn yellow."

I pick up both of our dinner bowls and start washing them in the sink.

"The main issue here is that if Bree really is a dragon, how did neither of us pick up on her aura?"

"I have no idea." Propping his elbows on the counter, he rests his face in both of his hands and ponders the question. "Dragons are supposed to give off a golden hue. Just as witches have purple, vampires have gray, and shifters have a green hue. How have we never seen Bree's aura? We've known her for more than ten years."

"I don't know, but I don't like the feeling of not knowing

what's going on." I finish washing the dishes and walk back around to sit next to Asher. "Dragons typically don't leave the Realm of Shadows unless they're cast out. We know how territorial they are of the treasure troves they keep hidden, and besides, they can't shift freely here into their dragon form."

There is a beat of silence while we both think through the possibilities. Could her family have been cast out, or did they truly just up and leave the Realm of Shadows on their own accord, like most of the other supernaturals who are in search of a better life in the Human Realm.

I sigh, leaning into Asher's side, hoping it'll take the edge off the next topic I'm about to bring up. "I'm going home this weekend since Grandpa Artie is coming back for my birthday."

Asher throws me a fake smile.

"You should come home with me. That way you can see your family and we can also ask Grandpa Artie what he knows about dragons and see if he can help us figure this out."

"I don't know, Rave. Dad and I haven't been as close as we used to be ever since Brandon died. You know it's like walking on eggshells with him."

Brandon was Asher's older brother. He died five years ago, protecting Asher and another shifter from a rogue vampire attack. Brandon was always selfless and put everyone else first, especially his family. He was his father's favorite child and after his death, Asher's father kept his distance, blaming Asher for Brandon's death.

Sighing, I lay my head on Asher's shoulder to comfort him.

"Tell you what. Just stop in and say hello to your mom and then you can crash at my house for the weekend. My mom would love to have you over to show you the new witch training barn."

Asher turns and gives me a confused look. "She turned the barn into a witch workshop for her classes? What happened to the old shop?"

"Oh, a teenage break up and a little bit of uncontrolled witch fire. The whole place went up in flames." I motion my hands to explode like a bomb.

"Dang. What a bummer." After a few seconds, he lets out a sigh. "All right, fine, I'll come down, but only to see Mrs. Montclair and Grandpa Artie."

"Perfect!" I hop up and head to my room to start packing my bags. "I hope you don't mind skipping class tomorrow because I told my mom I would leave tomorrow morning."

Asher is studying to be an elementary teacher, which makes sense because he is amazing with kids, but he hates taking what he calls "unnecessary classes" to fulfill his degree. From my room, I hear Asher bark out a small laugh. "Are you kidding? I will be more than happy to miss my calculus class."

"Great. Pick me up tomorrow morning around eight."

Asher's almost out the door and I snap my fingers to hold him in place. "Oh, and Shifter? Don't be late again." I snap my fingers and release him.

He turns to me and holds the door halfway open. "Wouldn't dream of it, Witch." He grins, shutting the door behind him.

CHAPTER 5
ROAD TRIP

I set my alarm a little earlier than normal so I can finish packing the rest of my bag. I make sure all my homework for the weekend is done and turned in, and then I head toward the kitchen to fix some breakfast. Reaching into the fridge, I pull out a couple eggs and begin to make scrambled eggs and French Toast. I figured this was a good start to repaying Asher for driving us home for the weekend.

About halfway into cooking breakfast, I hear my front door open and close quietly. Only four people have access through my protection ward, so I let my guard down. With my small apartment, it's easy enough to encase my area with a small protection ward by myself. I pop my head around the corner of the kitchen and watch Asher stroll into my apartment.

"Did you miss me that much?" I ask, glancing at the oven clock. "You're twenty minutes early."

"I figured being the little miss goody two-shoes you are, you'd be up already making sure you had all your assignments submitted before we left."

I stick my tongue out and give him the finger before transferring a few slices of French Toast to a plate and slide it over to Asher as he sits on one of the bar stools at the counter.

"And besides, I knew you would have breakfast cooking," Asher says, adding syrup over his food.

"Well, of course. We can't take a road trip on an empty stomach."

We finish eating our breakfast and Asher insists on carrying my bags as we make our way down to his navy two door pickup truck in front of my apartment building. After Brandon died, Asher tried not to ask his dad for much of anything. So, he worked two jobs one summer to save up enough money to buy this truck. It's his prized possession.

"You ready?" Asher asks, as he starts the truck.

"Ready."

After some small talk about classes, track practice, and what we have been up to the past weeks, the conversation gradually dies down and we sit in silence for a few minutes just listening to the radio.

Asher startles me as he clears his throat, clearly wanting to break the silence. "All last night, I couldn't stop thinking of what we could have missed with Bree and her possibly being a dragon. I honestly couldn't think of anything. Her family seems normal. I mean, from what I could always sense, they were normal. What do you think?"

I think for a couple minutes, my mind running in circles. I don't believe I have seen anything out of the ordinary with Bree or her family. Her parents seem perfectly normal and nice, but now that I am starting to realize Bree isn't the person I thought she was, my ideas of her family start to make me wonder if everything was all a lie.

"Honestly, Asher? I have no idea. You and I don't know a lot about dragons, so I really don't know what else we should be looking for. The one thing I know is if Bree and her family are

dragons, we would have seen their aura and felt their power. But we don't have either of those hinting at us."

We sit in silence for a while longer and the lull of the radio pulls me into a light sleep. By the time I wake up, we are just outside Ridgedale, Missouri.

"Jeez, how long have I been asleep? I can't believe we're almost home."

"Just about ten minutes from your house," he says.

We turn off the highway onto the road that leads to my house. As we wind down the driveway, I peer out at the giant trees shading the road on either side. It's my favorite time of year when the leaves start to melt into the signature yellow, orange, and brown fall colors.

It feels like ages since I've been home, but it has only been a couple of months. Though we live in the Human Realm trying to hide our powers and fit in with society, I'm happy to come home and finally be able to be my true self. Even though Asher dreads coming back to his home, I know he feels better being able to shift freely around our small town, which is made up of mostly supernaturals, besides the sprinkle of a few human families that don't have a clue we exist.

Knowing how excited I am to see my family, I remember Asher feels the complete opposite way. "Hey, do you want me to come to your house? I can wait outside for you."

"No, I'll be okay. Mom and I are going to meet at the coffee shop down the street after I drop you off, so I don't have to worry about running into Dad."

I open my mouth to comfort Asher, but he cuts me off before I can even start.

"Really, Raven, I'm okay. It's probably better this way, so I don't cause any unneeded stress on my mom. I'll drop you off, go have coffee with Mom, and be back to your house around suppertime."

I don't push the matter any further. Asher knows what he is

doing at this point. We finally pull into the driveway and my mom waves as we approach. As soon as the car is in park, I open the heavy door and run to give her a big bear hug.

"I've missed you, my little witch."

I bury my face in her maroon sweater. Her familiar citrus perfume wraps around me as she holds me closer.

"I've missed you too, Mom."

Realizing that I left Asher to tend to my bags, I unfold out of her embrace and we both walk toward Asher's pickup.

Asher turns to find us looking at him taking out my bags. After he sets the bags down, he lowers himself into a gentle-man's bow.

Oh boy. Here we go.

"Mrs. Montclair. So nice to see you again."

My mom blushes and swats the air in front of her with her hand. "Asher, how many times do I have to tell you that it's just Moriah."

Asher rises and flashes her a dazzling smile. "About a dozen more, Mrs. Montclair. I'll be back a little later around supper-time, if that's okay? I am going to visit with my mom for a while."

"Of course, Asher. Do tell her I miss her and that we need to get together soon."

"Will do, Mrs. Montclair," Asher says, climbing back into the pickup. He vanishes down the long road back to the highway. As soon as his truck is out of sight, Mom and I turn to each other in unison.

"I have so much to tell you!"

"Wait, you go first," I tell Mom.

My dragon inquiries can wait until we are all settled in for the night. Besides, I want my grandfather's input on the situation as well. As we walk through the front door, I can feel Mom's excitement rolling off her body. Not to mention her aura is almost blinding me right now.

"SURPRISE!!"

As I look around the room, dozens of presents fill up our sitting room in the front of the house. The amount of presents is somewhat daunting since I know for a fact I don't have this many friends.

"Um, Mom, what is all this?"

I can't keep myself from wondering where all these presents came from.

Before Mom can answer, a familiar voice comes from around the corner. "From your family back in the Realm of Shadows, of course."

"Grandpa Artie!"

"Hello, my dear. I've missed you very much."

I run into my grandpa's embrace and smell the familiar scent of pine needles coming from his sweater. As I look up, his purple hue is as radiant as ever and he has more silver strands peppering his hair than I remember. However, his gray eyes that match mine are still sharp. Pulling apart, we turn and look at all the gifts.

"You brought all these back from the Realm of Shadows for me? But who are they all from?"

I begin to make my way around the room, looking at the tags on the gifts, not recognizing half of the names attached.

"Twenty-one is a big birthday for witches, my dear. Most of these people are family friends, but all who want to wish you a magical birthday."

Mom stops all the fun before it can even start. "We can start opening presents after dinner. Come on, Raven. You can help me make dinner tonight. It will be like old times."

Grandpa and I share the same uneasy look, but follow Mom to the kitchen, anyway. Whenever Mom asks anyone to help with cooking, it usually means we can't use our magic, making the process twice as long. When I step into the kitchen, our twelve-foot island is completely covered in different foods for dinner.

"You and Grandpa can start peeling the potatoes. I'll start on the kabobs. And no magic. Let's see if you both still remember how to peel potatoes properly."

"Jeez, Mom, you're no fun," I say, as I give her a little hip bump. Looking around at the island full of food, I grab a potato, sit next to Grandpa, and start peeling.

"You could feed a small army with all this food," I say to my mom.

"Raven, you know as well as myself that kabobs make the best fajitas the next day. Now, keep peeling."

As Grandpa and I peel potatoes, he tells me of all the new things happening in the Realm of Shadows. Before my family left the Realm, my dad had been named the next successor to the Mage Court, which meant my grandfather would be stepping down.

However, Dad didn't agree with what the Alliance was trying to accomplish, so he packed up everything we had and moved Mom and I to the human world. When my dad denounced his claim to the throne, my grandpa had no choice but to remain as the leader since my dad's sister was still at the university.

Although he will never admit how much of a burden it was to stay on the council when my dad left, I have no doubt my grandfather is doing an excellent job ruling. The bad thing is, I can start to see more wear on him throughout the years. Aunt Melody never wanted to rule the Mage Court, she wanted to be a schoolteacher, just as my mom is here in the Human Realm, and my grandpa would never force her into the role.

Growing up, I always assumed Grandpa would want me to take over as the Mage Court leader, which is why I made my mom a bargain. I would agree to be the next ruler of the Mage Court after having a human college experience. She eagerly agreed, noting that it would help make me a well-rounded leader. All I want to do is make my mom and grandpa proud.

As if he can sense me staring at him, Grandpa turns toward

me and smiles. "My little Raven, you have grown into such a beautiful woman. I wish your father was here to see this."

"Oh, Artemis, you stop that right now! You're going to make me cry and no one needs to see that!"

"Sorry, Moriah, you're right. Let us keep the happiness for tonight going."

Sensing Asher's presence through our protection barrier, I use my powers to open the front door before he can knock. His fist drops from the air as he shakes his shaggy blonde hair.

"Hey, for once, can you let me have the element of surprise?" He pouts.

"Never," I say, as I turn to see Asher walking in with a small pink box complete with a white bow on the top of it. No doubt his coffee date with his mother turned into a shopping spree. I'm just happy Asher and his mom had a couple of hours of catching up.

"Asher, my boy! So good to see you, lad!"

Scrunching my nose at their odd but friendly banter, I finish peeling my last potato. Asher and my grandpa have always had a close relationship since my dad died, but I figured it's because Grandpa Artie considers Asher part of our family since he hangs around so much.

"As to you, sir. It's been a while. You look like you've not aged a day."

"Don't try to flatter me, Asher. You know it won't work." Grandpa points at my mom. "But you know, Moriah is always a sucker for your charms."

Asher and I turn and laugh to each other, knowing full well how true that statement is.

"Artie!" my mom yells, snapping the towel in my grandpa's direction, playfully scolding him.

"Nice to see you again, Asher. You're just in time for supper. Go ahead and leave your gift in the sitting room with the rest of the presents. We'll open them after we have all had a nice meal together. Raven, can you please set the table? The food is almost ready."

"I'll help you, Rave."

As Asher and I make our way into the sitting room to grab the nice dinner plates out of the hutch, I nudge him with my elbow.

"I thought we agreed on no presents?"

"No, YOU said no presents. I never agreed to such a thing. Besides, it's nothing special."

Before I know what has come over me, my words are already out of my mouth and there is no way of taking them back. "Don't say it's nothing special. It's from you, so it has to be something special."

Asher turns toward me to say something but is cut off by my mom yelling down the hall; something about us getting lost on our way to get the plates. Thankfully, Mom unintentionally bails me out of a sticky situation again. I hand Asher the plates, grab the silverware, and we head back to the kitchen.

I mentally kick myself for the comment that came out of my mouth. What the heck was I thinking?

Grandpa gives us both a look and asks, "What took you two so long? I've waited almost a year for your mom's cooking. Let's dig in!"

CHAPTER 6

After eating enough food to put me into a four-day food coma, I reluctantly stand and help my mom clear the dishes. Asher and Grandpa start dividing the leftovers into separate containers, so we have all the ingredients for fajitas the next day. Once we get the kitchen cleared, we head into the sitting room to go through all the presents.

Most of these people I've never even heard of; however, Grandpa has a name and title for each person I don't know. I guess that's the good thing about him being the Mage Court leader.

He knows literally everyone.

As I go through each present, Mom is taking notes of who sent what gift, which can only mean I will be spending most of tomorrow night writing "thank you" cards to people I have never met.

I slump back against the small lavender sitting chair and throw my arms in the air.

"Finally! Thirty gifts later and I think I have about seven paper cuts. Only one present left!"

I face Asher, giving him the sweetest smile. "Asher? Can I have my present now?" I ask, as I bat my eyelashes at him.

Asher reaches a nervous hand up to rub the back of his neck, trying to avert my gaze.

"Oh, well, I, uh, actually wanted you to open this in private."

"Why not now?" I try to catch his gaze, but it's no use.

He shifts his body uncomfortably in a way that I haven't seen before. "Because it's meant for you, so I figured you should enjoy it by yourself."

Now he has my attention. What could this gift possibly be? Before I can push for further details, I catch movement in the corner of my eye as my mom pulls a manila envelope from behind her.

My mom stretches the envelope out toward me with a shaky hand. "Here, sweetie, it's from your father."

And just like that, my attention has shifted. They have a gift from Dad? My mind starts to think of all the different things that could be in the envelope as I reach out and take it from my mom.

"Well, what is it! How did it get here?" I ask anxiously. Inspecting the envelope, I turn it over to show Dad's perfect cursive writing. On the front is a little white note card that reads:

Dear Raven, please forgive me, but you cannot open this until the day after your 21st birthday. Moriah and Artemis were both sworn to keep this a secret until that date.

Love, Dad.

With tears filling my eyes, I see Mom is as emotional as I am. I look at Grandpa, but he just shrugs his shoulders.

"I'm sorry, Raven. We swore to your dad that we wouldn't give this to you until your birthday," Mom says, wiping her eyes.

"You still cannot open it tonight." Grandpa continues, "Your dad was a powerful warlock, Raven. He enchanted the envelope to open on the exact date after your twenty-first birthday. Not even your mother or I know what is inside."

I know Dad was a powerful warlock, since he was the one who put all the protection wards on our house and around our property. Which is no small feat since we own a little over fifteen acres. Normally, when the person who places the protection ward passes away, the spells dissipate over time, but Dad's has been locked in and secure since his passing.

Leave it to Dad to leave me an enchanted envelope for my birthday.

Why the heck would Mom and Grandpa tease me like this if I can't open it for another four days?

Looking up at them, I express just that. "You both are really too cruel. Giving me something you know I can't open for another four days. This is going to drive me mad!"

"At least you have four days. Your grandfather and I have waited nine years to find out what is in that envelope. Imagine how we feel."

Her words hit me hard. She's right. I have no idea how she feels. She lost her mate and on top of that, she had to carry the burden of looking at the last piece he left of himself every day until my birthday. I walk over to both my mom and grandpa and sit in between them. I wrap my arms around their shoulders and bring them in for a hug.

"You're right, Mom. I'm sorry you both had to carry this around for so long. I'm sad Dad isn't here, but I am also happy I have this last piece of him here with me."

And with that, my mom loses it . . . I mean, full on ugly

crying. She excuses herself out of the room so she doesn't embarrass herself any more than she feels she has already. I wait a few moments and follow behind her. I look at the boys before I leave the room.

"I'll be right back. I need to check on the emotional mess that is now my mother. You two catch up while I'm gone."

I follow Mom into the kitchen and grab the box of tissues we keep in the corner. I hand her one and wait for her to take it.

"I really am sorry, Mom. I didn't mean for you to cry."

"It's okay, honey. I just wish your dad was here to see you grow up. He sacrificed so much for both of us."

We sit in silence for a few minutes, waiting for her to collect herself again.

"I'm sorry, Raven. Why don't you go back into the sitting room and grab the boys? I made your favorite cake for dessert."

"Oh, Mom, you didn't have to go to all this trouble for me!"

"It's no trouble at all for my favorite daughter."

"I'm your only daughter," I remind her.

"Exactly," she says with a wink.

I head back into the sitting room and overhear my grandpa saying something about the gift Asher got me. I halt mid step and wait on the other side of the wall to listen.

"Are you sure you want to give this to her now? She doesn't even know anything about this yet."

"I'm sure, Artemis. I've never been more sure in my life. Even if she doesn't know now, eventually she will, and I want her to have this when she knows."

Piquing my interest in what Asher is keeping from me, I try to get a little closer, but my foot slips, and I nearly fall into the sitting room. Hoping to recover from this horribly failed spy mission, I wave my hand in a welcoming manner.

"Howdy, boys. Mom has some dessert in the kitchen when you're ready."

With both men looking puzzled, Grandpa finally answers for both. "Thank you, Raven. We will head in there now."

As I follow them into the kitchen, I can't help but kick myself.

Really, Raven? Howdy, boys? I think to myself.

Nice recovery.

Everything fades from my mind when I see the most amazing double decker, vanilla cake with strawberries scattered on top.

"I hope that is my favorite strawberry shortcake recipe from Grandma Elaine!"

"Yes, the one and only."

And in unison, the three people I care about most in the world wish me a happy early birthday. After devouring two pieces of cake, I finally tap out.

"If I eat any more, I am pretty sure I will turn into a strawberry shortcake myself."

Looking at the clock, it is almost midnight. Mom must realize how late it is as well, because she tries to shove us off to bed.

"Asher, I made up the guest bedroom across from Raven's for you. Raven, why don't you take your things upstairs and help Asher settle in?"

I roll my eyes behind her back. I swear this woman loves playing matchmaker even more than cupid.

Asher understands the hint and takes me by the arm, leading me to the stairs.

"Come, my darling, show me to my chambers," he says, loud enough for my mom and grandpa to hear. All I hear is their laughter from the kitchen echo into the hall.

"Really?" I turn to him and smack his arm off mine. "Was that necessary?"

"Of course, my darling. How else would your family know we are madly in love after our first date?"

I try to trip him up the stairs, but with a quick flash of light, he quickly shifts into my favorite dog from when we were kids. As I chase the black and white collie up the stairs, I can't help but feel like things are so simple with Asher.

Stuck in my head, I don't even realize Asher has shifted back into his human form and has hidden around the corner. As I round the corner, he nearly scares me out of my own skin.

Standing too close to the stairs, I take one step backward, but don't feel the stair beneath me. Asher catches me by the waist and pulls me toward him. He yanks a little too hard because, the next thing I know, we are both falling the opposite way and I find myself laying on top of his body in the hallway.

His very chiseled body that I may or may not have just melted into. His spicy cinnamon scent wraps around me, and I almost forget my near-death experience. Almost.

Lifting my head to meet his eyes, I pound my hand into his chest. "You scared me to death! Literally! I could have fallen to my death on those stairs!"

"But you didn't, did you? I saved you." His lips curl into a seductive smirk as he tilts his head, looking into my eyes. "Now, how are you going to thank me?"

I'm still laying on Asher, so I roll off him and start to stand up.

"I'm thanking you by not throwing you down the stairs myself after that little incident."

I flick my hair over my shoulder and lead us to our rooms as Asher stifles a laugh. My hand still tingles from the contact of touching his rock-hard abs and my heart is nearly breaking free from my chest from the way he was looking at me on top of him. Breaking free from my daydream, I open his door and welcome him into his room.

"As you know, you have your own bathroom. The TV remote is in the nightstand and there is an extra phone charger cord if you need it. If you need anything, you can text me or just knock on my door."

I turn to leave, but Asher grabs my hand. Before I can pull away, he lays a soft kiss on the top of my hand, bringing the fire right back where his lips met my skin.

"Thank you for everything, Raven. You really make my life a heck of a lot better."

Our eyes connect and the temperature skyrockets, not only in my body, but in the space between us. He releases my hand, and it takes all my strength to leave the room and make it safely into my own room.

After shutting the door, I jump onto my queen size bed and smother my face into one of my pillows.

What are we even doing?

Can I really be falling for my best friend?

And why is he suddenly Mr. Smooth Talker?

Having too many questions running through my mind, I roll over, heading to my own bathroom to shower for the night. A glimpse of something pink catches my eye, stopping me dead in my tracks. I take a step back into the bedroom, finding the pink box with the white bow sitting on my nightstand.

"Sneaky little shifter," I say under my breath.

CHAPTER 7
SCOOT OVER

I leave the gift on the table for the time being and unpack my things. After finishing, I head toward the bathroom to get ready to shower, but all I can think about is what just happened on the stairs. Trying to clear my mind, I let the water heat up before stepping in, hoping the warm water will ease my thoughts.

With the water gently massaging my skin, I close my eyes and let today's events wash away. Suddenly, the water temperature drops, forcing me to open my eyes. Something is wrong. This isn't my shower. A familiar cinnamon scent weaves around my body, causing me to turn my head slowly.

Oh shit. What did I just do?

I scream while Asher quickly covers his eyes, but not without giving a snarky remark. "I knew you were always thinking of me and this just proves it. But why are you naked and in my shower, and more importantly, how the hell did you get in here?"

"I don't know!" I cry into my hands. "One second, I was in my shower and the next I'm in here with you!"

Oh god, this cannot be happening. Not now.

Turning my face, I peek through my fingers to make sure Asher has his eyes closed, which he does. Then I take a moment to take in his body. Thankfully, Asher has the sense to cover himself with his other hand, but I take a quick second to mentally save this image in my mind.

I must be quiet for too long because Asher starts to smile, shifting his weight to one side. "You like what you see?"

"Ugh, you're so gross!" I groan, trying to hide my embarrassment from being caught checking him out. "Get out!"

"Hey, you interrupted my shower, so I think it's you who needs to leave."

He tries to move his hands from his eyes, but I turn, reaching out to cover his hand with mine, holding them firmly in place.

"Fine, but keep your eyes closed or I'll keep them closed for you."

After grabbing Asher's towel from the hook next to the shower, I quickly cover myself and head straight for my room. I switch out the towel for my robe and take a few deep breaths, trying to calm down before anything else out of the ordinary happens. I fall on the edge of the bed and cover my eyes with my arm.

Great, a brand-new power just decides to show up at the absolute worst time. It's hard enough trying to keep the powers I already have under control these past weeks, and now I have to figure out how the hell I can teleport and what triggers it?

Nope.

Not happening.

Not today.

My "Shit Raven doesn't have time for" folder just keeps getting bigger.

At this moment, I think my embarrassment outweighs my

shock of finding out I can teleport. The last witch that could tele-port was the one who created the barrier between the Human Realm and the Realm of Shadows. She was practically the savior for both realms.

With this knowledge, my mind starts racing about what this means for me. I'm already a target, being able to wield all four elements, but now if people find out I can teleport, that means I'm twice as valuable.

Taking a few more deep breaths, I finally seem to have calmed down enough to feel in control of my powers again. I stand and reluctantly head back to Asher's room to face my embarrassment head on. I hear him turn off the faucet to the shower just as I open the door to the bathroom.

"Before you open the curtain and tease me about what just happened, just know that I took your only towel," I say, hoping it will lessen the harassment.

I can hear the smile in his voice as he tries to sound convincing. "I promise not to tease you if you bring me a new towel."

I sigh as I place the new towel on the hook. As soon as I leave the bathroom, I yell across the bedroom, "Okay. You're safe to get out of the shower now."

A short time later, Asher emerges from the bathroom. His hair is still damp, leaving a few wet spots on his white shirt, but I quickly look away, wishing this moment was already over. I feel the bed dip as he sits next to me, his cinnamon scent threatening me closer.

"Soooo, can we just forget this whole thing happened?" I say nervously, playing with the sleeve of my robe.

"There's no way. You were obviously thinking of me in some way and teleported to where I was, which happened to be the shower," he says jokingly.

"Okay, I teleported to your shower. We get it."

I smile weakly up at Asher, but he seems to understand I am

silently freaking out in my head. He slides his arms around me, forcing me back to reality with his comforting touch.

"Raven, calm down. We will figure this out, okay? Is this the first time it has happened?" Asher asks in a low whisper.

"Yes, and I am scared out of my mind. Recently, my powers have started to go haywire, and I don't know why. Every time I get emotional about something, it's like the control I have on my powers weakens and something unexpected happens."

"So, the rainstorm last weekend, that was you, wasn't it?"

I nod my head, not wanting to talk about that right now. Asher clearly got the hint about not talking about "the incident" and lays his head against mine.

"Don't worry, Rave, we will figure it out. Just go get some rest. I'll talk to you in the morning." I nod and stand, but when I'm halfway out the door, Asher calls out, "Hey, Rave, don't think of me too much while you sleep."

I flip him the bird and close his door. As I lie in bed, I can't help but think there's something that my mom and grandpa aren't telling me. Something is happening to me, and I can't explain it. The only people I can count on right now are me and Asher. With that knowledge, I crawl under the covers and hope tomorrow will be a better day and I can try to figure out what is going on.

Waking up the next morning, I feel like I've been hit by a truck. It seems the whole teleporting incident is not recommended for someone overly stressed already. My body aches from head to toe as I throw my covers off. Every little movement brings another ache to my body.

I gently slide my legs to the edge of the bed, sitting in painful silence for what seems like an eternity. It takes me two minutes to finally rise to my feet and another five minutes to get dressed.

My whole body feels like it's working in slow motion. I trudge my way downstairs and, about halfway down, I catch the most amazing smell. With this delicious scent wafting around me, my body starts to move somewhat quicker, but still not fast enough as I hear my stomach rumble when I make it to the last step.

Rounding the corner to the kitchen, I'm surprised to see Asher and my mom cooking breakfast. Not only cooking, but dancing and cooking, and honestly, I think it's more hilarious to watch my mom try to keep rhythm with the music. Of course, Asher is a natural dancer.

I mean, come on. Is there anything this man isn't good at?

"Not to interrupt this dance party, but whatever you are cooking smells delicious."

"It's one of Grandma Elaine's recipes and Asher is knocking it out of the park." Pointing her batter-filled spoon toward Asher, Mom raises her eyebrow and looks me dead in the eyes with a full smile on her face. "Who knew this boy could cook. Better snag him before some other girl does, Raven."

"Mooom," I draw out as I cover my eyes in embarrassment. I swear it is Mom's goal to have Asher and I paired up by the end of this trip, and unfortunately, this isn't the first time she's tried.

"Come on, Raven," Asher beckons. "Help me over here and give your mom a rest. I know how good of a cook you are."

"Fine," I say, as I slowly make my way to take over Mom's spot. "What do you need help with?"

I'm exhausted by the time Asher and I finish making breakfast. I didn't want them to worry about my dwindling strength this morning, so I did my best to push through, hoping neither of them would find anything amiss.

When I plop onto the kitchen chair with my plate full of food, Mom informs us Grandpa had to run some errands in town and he will be back for supper. As we eat, I ask if Asher and I can sit in on her classes for the day. I used to love watching her work with students and teaching them how to control their powers.

"That would actually be perfect! The Mage class starts at noon, and Asher, I am glad you're here. Andrew couldn't make the shifting class today and I won't be able to find a sub this last minute. I was going to cancel today's lesson, but would you mind filling in? It's just a simple shifting lesson today. I have no doubt you would be the perfect substitute."

"Of course, Mrs. Montclair," Asher says, with a nod of his head. "I would be honored."

"Kiss ass," I say under my breath.

Mom elbows me as a sign of caution. "Why don't you two go upstairs and get ready for class. I'll clean the rest of this."

As we head upstairs, I turn back to Asher, who is following close behind me.

"You really could have said no."

"What? I think it'll be fun to show off a little," he says, as we reach our rooms. "Besides, you're really the only one who I get to show off in front of. It'll be fun to watch the class, and you, be in awe of my awesomeness," he jokes, as he poses in front of his door.

"Yeah, yeah. Just keep it under control. I don't want some teenage shifter drooling all over you."

"Oh, is someone already jealous of my mad skills?" he says, slowly approaching my door.

"You wish," I say, as I challenge him and take a step forward.

Now inches from each other, I'm caught off guard when Asher cups my cheek with his hand and lowers his mouth to my ear sending goosebumps down my body.

"You're the only person I am concerned with showing off for. No one else matters to me."

As he turns his face back to mine and our eyes lock, I quickly realize he meant every word. Before things can go any farther, I back away into my room.

"We'll see about that," I joke. "Now, get ready and meet me downstairs in fifteen minutes."

I shut my door and lean my back into the door's cold wood, hoping it will give me some clarity, but the only thing I can think about is what Asher just said.

Could that really be true?

Come to think of it, I've never seen Asher date anyone or be remotely interested in anyone, and now within the last few days since "the incident", Asher seems to be more persistent in winning my affection. He always flirts with me, but I chalk that up to his personality, not him actually being interested in me. But what if I read the situation all wrong all these years?

I try to convince myself I don't need to be wrapped up in another relationship right now, but it falls flat when I think about Asher. For some reason, the idea of being with him sounds nice.

Shaking the thought from my head, I change and head downstairs, beating Asher down to find my mom getting some things ready for the classes.

"Can I help with anything, Mom?" I ask, walking into the kitchen.

"Sure! Can you grab ice packs from the freezer?"

"Oh, fun! Are you teaching fire lessons today?" I say with excitement.

"You bet! We will need a couple of those ice packs, so make sure you stock up. Just bring those down to the barn, and I'll meet you there in a few minutes."

"Okay. Can you tell Asher to meet me at the barn?"

"You got it," she says and gives me a thumbs up.

Heading down to the barn with my arms full of ice packs, I take a moment to let my eyes wander around the property. Today is a perfect September day. The air is still warm, but I can feel fall is just around the corner. The leaves are starting to shift into soft yellow and orange and there are even a few trees starting to shed their leaves.

I approach the barn and take in the beauty of my mom's hard work of updating the exterior. The old, chipped brown paint has been upgraded to a stunning white, with dark blue shutters on each side of the two windows. The front door has been replaced with one of those split doors where you can open the top and have the bottom closed. She really outdid herself.

Shortly after reaching the front door with my arms full of ice packs, I remember an old trick I learned from Grandpa. I shift the ice packs and wiggle my nose, then tap my foot twice. The door gently cracks enough for me to open it the rest of the way with my foot.

As I fumble for the light switch, a sharp tingle races up my spine as though I am being watched. Quickly turning, I worry I'm not alone in the darkness. I swear I feel a gust of wind brush past me, causing a pang of fear jolt through me. Panicking even more, I finally find the light switch and bring my arm back, ready to hurl the ice packs at the intruder, only to see Asher leaning against one of the wooden cabinets in the corner, smirking at me.

"Jeez, Asher, don't sneak up on me like that. I almost threw these ice packs at you!"

"Well, I wouldn't want that, would I?"

Strolling to meet me halfway, Asher takes a few of the ice packs and unloads them in the freezer in the back of the room.

"Besides," he says, "I'm pretty sure you throw like a girl."

"I am a girl, but you know I can kick your ass," I say as I throw one of the ice packs at him. I place the rest in the freezer and admire the barn.

"Your mom did an amazing job with this place. I hardly recognized it when I flew over."

"I knew it was you. I felt someone watching me."

"Don't flatter yourself too much, Rave," Asher jokes. "I was just making sure you were safe. And besides, it was faster to fly so I could beat you here."

"Why would you need to make sure I was safe?" I ask, skeptically. "It's just us out here."

"Just double checking everything. It's always better to be safe than sorry," he says, holding the door open for me.

That comment catches me a little off guard as we exit the barn. I feel as though there might be more than what Asher is saying, but I don't get the chance to ask before he turns to me.

"Where did you learn that little trick with the door?"

"Grandpa Artie showed me a couple of easy tricks when I was a kid. Not a lot of people know that one, though. Most people believe with witchcraft we use spells all the time, but for small things it just takes little movements in the body and to think of what you want to happen."

"Dang, that's pretty cool," Asher says, as we turn to walk back up the path.

We walk up to the house to collect the rest of the items we need for class, and I hear cars pulling into our driveway before I can see them.

"The kids are here!" Mom joyfully announces. "Hurry down to the barn. We will start in about ten minutes."

After we collect the rest of the supplies, we make our way back down to the barn and I quickly realize that this day is about to turn into a very long day of lessons.

CHAPTER 8
ELEMENT OF SURPRISE

My mom, Asher, and I were the first to head into the barn. After that, a steady stream of teenagers followed suit. The class has twelve witches, which is a decent size considering when I went through witching school, there were only six of us. Our tight knit supernatural community seems to have gained new families recently.

I recognize some of the teens from working at the docks on the lake throughout high school. I would see their families out on the lake frequently, but some of the kids must have come from neighboring towns or must have moved here recently.

The class starts to settle into their workstations, preparing their items for the lesson. Asher and I help Mom with the remaining items for class, then we both take a seat at the side of her desk and wait for her to start the class.

"Welcome, everyone. I want to introduce my daughter, Raven. She will be helping with today's lesson. Asher is here as well, but he will help with the next class. Now, if everyone could take out their tinder and set it in their pottery bowls, we will get started."

Mom starts by showing everyone how to set the tinder on fire with a short verse, then she explains how it was done. Placing her new tinder in her pottery bowl, she starts the lesson. "First, one must know what we want the fire to do. Spells were created thousands of years ago by our ancestors."

Dropping tinder to my pottery bowl, I add, "Derived from the Latin language that most of our spells were formed in, we ask 'Fire ignite with light'."

In unison, both of us translate the fire spell.

"Ignite lumine ignis."

With that phrase, both of our tinders spark and a small fire appears in our pottery bowls.

I smile at the class, watching their hopeful expressions. "As everyone knows, magic and spells are about asking the elements what we want. To put the fire out, we ask, 'Extinguish all flames before us'."

With the wave of both of our hands over our bowls, we both say, "Ante omnia extinguit incedium."

In Mom's bowl, the fire twirls for a moment, then suffocates itself in a mini smoke tornado, only to be left sending up a thin smoke line. In my bowl, the fire is slowly extinguished with a water cyclone.

"Now, I want you all to try this for yourself. Once you think you have it down, please sit at your workstation so either Raven or I can come observe."

After the demonstration, the teens eagerly stand to work on their fire creation. Before the class can get too far, Mom adds, "Now, not everyone will be able to create fire. Most witches can only conjure two elements. Most of you already know what elements those are, but we are here to work on strengthening our skills. If you cannot create fire, but you can use the wind or water element, have a neighbor light your tinder and you practice putting it out."

My mom can control the fire and air elements. Dad had the ability to control water and earth. Grandpa Artie can control air and water. Only these people, plus Asher, know I can control all four elements.

To keep me safe, I tend to use fire and water around our kind because the last witch and warlock that could control all four elements were hunted down and used to start wars against the other supernatural races. That was a thousand years ago and if someone could control all four elements like myself, they would be smart to keep that hidden. I chose fire and water because it's a mix of both my parents. Fire, representing my mom, and water, representing my dad.

Right off the bat, a girl with short brown hair has her fire started and extinguished within minutes, and I head over to see her progress.

"Hi, Anna, was it? Do you mind showing me the spell one more time?"

"Sure!" Anna says, standing from her stool. "It was pretty easy, actually."

Anna shows me her spell and I can tell she is gifted with the fire element more than any of the other students here. Her air element could use more practice, but overall, she has it under control. "Very nice, Anna!"

As I walk over to the next student, I can see he is struggling a little. "Hey, what was your name?" I ask, smiling tenderly. "I haven't seen you around before."

He looks up, and I am hit with a sense of water elements just by looking into his eyes. His blue eyes almost seem to dance like waves. I have a certain sense about someone's powers just by looking at them. It's like whichever power suits them seems to manifest itself in some way in their appearance.

"My name is Shane. My family just moved here recently."

He looks down again and sighs. "I just can't seem to get the hang of making fire."

"Well, Shane, I think that's because you're more suited to water elements."

He looked up at me in amazement. "Really? How can you tell?"

I take the tinder out of his pottery bowl and replace it with some water from his water bottle.

"I have a little bit of a gift for sensing what elements best suit someone. Here, try this." I take his hands and place them above the bowl of water. "Repeat after me. Aquae fluxus mihi."

"Water flow to me?" he asks.

"Yes, very good. It looks like someone has been studying their Latin homework. Now, you try."

"Aquae fluxus mihi."

We both look and the water starts to move—just a little.

"Shane, you have to feel the water. You have to want the water to move where you need it. Try again."

Shane takes a deep breath and tries again. "Aquae fluxus mihi." Shane lifts his hands from the bowl and the water has flowed into his palms and split between his two hands. "Woah! This is awesome! What do I do now?" he asks excitedly.

"Move your hands back and forth and the water will follow." I guide his hands back and forth and the water shifts between both his hands. I draw the water from his hands and start to move it up my wrists.

He stands there and watches in awe.

I move the water to my right hand and flick small droplets toward Shane. He catches them and throws them right back. "This is so cool. Thank you, Raven."

"No problem. Everyone should know what elements are better suited to them so they can work on bettering those skills."

I maneuver the water and swirl it back into the bowl. "How

long have you known about your powers?" I ask, setting his station back up.

"I only came into my power recently. That's why we moved here. My parents weren't witches, but my great grandfather was. My great grandparents migrated from the Realm of Shadows for a new start with their family, and somehow the magic gene skipped two generations. When my powers manifested, my parents were thrilled, but they didn't know how to teach me, so we sought out your mom."

That makes sense why he didn't know what element he was familiar with. "Tell you what? You keep working with this water spell today and I'll let my mom know that we need a couple of extra classes to find out what your second familiar element is."

He smiles at my words and turns back to his bowl to work on his water spell. I then move on to the other students, but before I can reach the next student, Mom catches me in the aisle.

"That was a really nice thing you did for Shane. His family insisted he join my class because he had no other teacher since his parents weren't witches."

"He seems like a really nice kid. I'm glad I could help him out. He will need a couple of extra sessions to find his second element, though. Maybe talk to his parents after class and see if that's okay."

Before we can finish our conversation, a brief scream from the back of the class has Mom and I both rush to see what is happening.

"It was an accident, I swear! One minute, I had my tinder in my bowl, the next moment my whole desk was on fire!"

"That's not true," someone said from behind us.

Mom and I turn to see a short blonde-haired boy with freckles on his face. He can't be older than thirteen.

"That's not true, Mrs. Montclair. I watched her set her desk on fire to get Raven's attention."

I spin around to face the girl. "Mine? Why would you want my attention?"

The girl drops the innocent student act and replaces her persona with something sinister. Her face is void of any emotion when she finally speaks again. "Because, you stole something you weren't supposed to."

That sounds oddly familiar to something Bree said earlier, but I push the thought to the back of my mind and refocus. Holding my ground, I look her right in the eye. "And what would that be exactly?"

The girl points one long finger at Asher.

"What are you talking about? I didn't steal him."

And just like that, the girl grabs a handful of fire and throws it right at Asher. I quickly step in front of him, grab the fire myself, and douse it with water in my hand.

"Alright, that's enough," I say, a little pissed off.

"No!" the girl yells. "Not until you let them go!"

Them?

"Look, I don't know what you're talking about, but this is ridiculous."

Again, she grabs a handful of fire, and this time sends it flying at me. At this point, I'm more than a little angry.

Who does this girl think she is?

The angrier I become, the more the control over my powers slip away. With the fire still in my hands, I let it snake up my arms and creep to my chest, down my whole body until suddenly I am engulfed in fire. I should be freaking out at this moment, but all I care about is hurting this girl for trying to hurt my mom and Asher. Also, for the fact of putting the rest of the students in harm's way.

As if someone else has taken over my body, I shut out the rest of the world. I lock eyes with her, and the fire creeps toward her. When the fire starts to surround her, I hear my mom trying to get my attention. I shut her out, trying to focus my attention on this random girl who was about to hurt two people I care deeply about . . . that is, until I hear Asher's voice calling to me.

At first, the sound is distant, then slowly it gets clearer. His voice is like a lullaby, calming me out of my trance.

The fire starts to slowly retract from my body, and it feels like I'm in control again. Finally realizing what I am doing, I quickly put the fire out. Once it's out, we all notice the girl disappeared from the barn and vanished into the forest.

My mom is at my side in an instant, grabbing both of my shoulders. "Raven, what just happened?"

"I'm fine, Mom, really," I assure her, as I look over to Asher.

"How could I hear you in my head?" I ask, totally baffled.

"What do you mean? I was right here calling out to you to stop," Asher says, taking a step closer.

"No, you weren't. You were in my head. I didn't see your lips moving at all."

"Rave, I don't know what you're talking about. You clearly weren't in control of yourself, so you might think you saw something different."

He is probably right. But how did I lose control like that? I have never felt that angry before.

And what did this girl mean about I stole Asher? That sounds even crazier than the fact I almost just burned down my mom's new workshop. With everyone still staring at me, Mom saves the day by cutting classes short.

"Alright, everyone, I think we have all had enough excitement for one day. Why don't we end class early and I will see you all next weekend?"

As the teens clear out, I have some questions I need answered; before I can ask, my mom beats me to it.

"Raven, what the hell was that!?" she says, stopping me from leaving the barn.

"I don't know! One second, everything was fine and then that girl tried hurting you guys. The only thing I could think about was hurting her in return. Who was that girl, anyway?"

"I don't know," she answers hesitantly.

"What? What do you mean you don't know?" My voice raises as I panic.

"I mean, she's not in my class. I have never taught her before, and I don't know how she got in here."

Sitting in silence for a second, I wonder how she could have possibly gotten past our protection ward. Nothing is adding up, especially since what she said was almost a dead ringer to what Bree said earlier.

"Well, what do you think she meant about me stealing Asher? Obviously, I haven't stolen him. He is sitting right here, and no one is looking for him."

There is no mistaking the glance between Asher and my mom. Obviously, there's something they're not telling me. Before I can open my mouth to ask what the heck is going on, the next set of students arrive for their shifting class.

Great, just what I needed after all this. I get to watch teenage girls drool over my best friend.

CHAPTER 9

DON'T BE SHIFTY

The shifters' class consists of four girls and three boys. Typically, shifters don't come into their power until after the age of eight. Two of the boys look like they couldn't be older than ten and the other boy must be at least old enough to drive. Two of the girls are twins, who are about nine, and the other two girls, I would assume, are in their early teens.

The class starts out like the witch class. My mom introduces Asher and pretty much lets him take over from there. I sit next to my mom and watch the show in front of me.

Before Asher even starts his demonstration, I can sense him calm down. He's comfortable around these kids because they are just like him. Here, he can be himself without the repercussions of living in a human world. All of them can.

Looking around, I feel a sense of pride. Not only to be a part of teaching the younger generations, but for what my mom has done and is doing. She works so hard to help our kind not forget who we are or where we came from.

I watch my mom and I can see how proud she is of Asher.

He's in full teacher mode now and there is no doubt he will make a wonderful teacher once he graduates. The first task he explains to the kids is to start small. "Start small, think small," he would say when he was younger.

The next thing I know, a bright flash has Asher transformed into a small white mouse on the floor. As he scurries across the floor, there's another bright flash and then the beautiful black and white collie from my childhood is running around the room. Finally, another flash of light and there sits the king of the jungle. A massive lion is looking around the room and lets out a tremendous roar.

Asher finally shifts back, and all the kids erupt in applause.

I swear I saw the two teenage girls almost faint in the front row.

I sit back and roll my eyes. I must admit, seeing him like this, comfortable being his true self, really makes me happy. Asher dismisses the class to give them a short break before they all come back and attempt to shift themselves. As the students make their way out of the barn, Asher walks toward me and my mom.

"How about the show, huh? Pretty awesome, right?"

"I think you've just proved your 'super awesomeness'," I say, air quoting the last part.

"Oh, that was nothing. That was just the warm-up!"

"Asher," my mom's sweet voice cuts in. "You're doing great! That was a marvelous demonstration."

"Thank you, Mrs. Montclair. I'll have the students start off with shifting into a mouse, then I was thinking maybe a small bird to end the class?"

"That sounds great," Mom says, as she moves to prepare the stations.

I should give him some credit. He's doing amazing with the kids. Sighing, I hop off the stool and nudge his shoulder, reluctantly giving him a compliment. "You look like a natural."

"Woah, is that a compliment?" he feigns surprise, making me laugh.

"Don't get too used to it," I tease back. "It's just nice to see you relaxed like this. You seem so peaceful when you shift, and it seems so effortless to you," I say, with a hint of jealousy.

"It didn't just come overnight. I had to practice constantly." Asher turns away from me as he continues, "And after my brother died, I needed to prove to my dad that I wasn't worthless. So, I thought if I could be a great shifter, he would finally forgive me. Obviously, I was wrong."

"Asher, how could you even think that?" I say as I grab his hands. "Your dad is the one who is missing out on the amazing person you grew up to be."

He just looks at me. Like, really looks at me.

I swear he can see into my soul, and strangely enough, I feel as though there's some force pulling me toward him. Before I can figure out what this feeling is, the students make their way back into the barn. Breaking the connection, Asher smiles at me, then returns to his spot at the front of the class.

The mouse lesson goes smoothly, with Asher walking around and making sure every student is shifting properly. Halfway through the small bird lesson, I notice we are one student short. The teenage boy is nowhere to be found. I calmly scan the room to not ruin Asher's lesson.

A few seconds go by, and I still don't see the boy. I'm about to use one of my location spells when I feel something small hit my shoulder. Turning my head calmly, I can only assume the mouse perched on my shoulder is the missing student.

I reach up to grab the mouse, but an eagle swoops down, snatching the mouse before I can. A quick burst of light and Asher is holding the missing teenage boy by the ear.

"Ow, ow, ow! You're hurting me!"

"What do you think you are doing?" Asher says, as he flicks the student in the head.

"I just wanted to scare her; I swear!" the boy says, trying to break free from Asher's hold.

"Don't ever do that again. Besides, Raven isn't someone who scares easily," he says, as he smirks at me.

I roll my eyes and walk to the front of the class. "Class is dismissed for today. You all did a wonderful job. Check in with Mrs. Montclair on your way out for your next assignment."

Asher releases the boy, and he scurries out of class, but not before stopping to apologize to me.

"Sorry, Raven. It was just a joke," he mumbles, clearly embarrassed.

"It's alright. Just don't let it happen again. To me, or anyone, because you never know how others will react," I say to warn him.

The boy practically sprints out of class, and I look up to see the two teenage girls have Asher pinned in the back of the room. Both have a lock of hair wrapped around their fingers and are twirling it uncontrollably. Apparently, Asher seems to enjoy this newfound attention.

When I walk out of the barn, I flick my hand and create a gust of wind that pushes the girls to the front of the room, causing them to hightail it out of there. Luckily, no one saw me use another element.

After all the students are gone, Mom and I head back to the barn to clean up. It's been a while since I had this much fun with my own kind. I can tell she is just as happy as I am since she hasn't stopped smiling the whole time.

"Thank you for today. I really had a good time." I wipe down another table before continuing. "Sorry about losing control. I really don't know what came over me."

"It's alright. I had a great time with both of you today. We'll figure out what is going on with you. Don't worry," she promises, planting a kiss on my head.

Asher strides back into the barn, helping collect the rest of the bowls from the back counter. "Mrs. Montclair, do you mind if Raven and I walk down to the boathouse before dinner?"

"Of course not! You two go ahead. I'll finish cleaning."

Asher hands my mom the bowls, smiling sweetly at her. "Thank you, Mrs. Montclair."

I look between Asher and my mother and wonder what is going on here. The look they share seems like some sort of inside secret I'm not allowed to know and they have been acting way too suspicious for my liking.

As I stand up, Asher grabs my hand. "Shall we then?" he asks.

Looking at my mom, she nods slightly with approval. "I suppose," I reply, letting Asher lead the way.

What am I getting myself into?

CHAPTER 10
NEON MOON

I t only takes about three minutes to walk the path to the lake and when we pass through the tree line, it makes me miss being home that much more. This time of year, the leaves reflect off the lake, creating a picture-perfect scene.

"Wow," Asher says. "I almost forgot how amazing it is down here."

"Me too. Let's go open the hut and put some music on for a while."

When I open the door, I'm shocked. My present from Asher is on the table along with a fruit tray, Caesar salad, angel hair pasta with my favorite sauce, and a bottle of champagne to top it off.

"Happy birthday, Raven," Asher whispers in my ear as he walks past me, leaving his cinnamon scent lingering around me.

"Asher, this is amazing. You didn't have to do all this."

"Of course, I did. You deserve all the happiness in the world. I'm just making sure you get that little slice of happiness today. Especially after the day we had."

He's right. This is exactly what I need after today. I had a great time teaching until my powers swelled out of control and I wasn't looking forward to explaining everything just yet to my mom and grandpa. Besides, they get to enjoy more fajitas now.

With a smile, I haul two chairs from the hut to set the table for dinner on the deck. Asher quickly follows with the champagne and the full meal he prepared. He really outdid himself this time.

He offers me a glass of champagne and we both relax into our chairs, watching the sun paint its fading colors across the calm water. With music softly playing in the background, I can't think of a more perfect night.

"When did you have time to do all of this?" I ask as I take a sip of champagne.

"Earlier this morning. Instead of going on my morning run, I went downstairs and made everything. Then, when you were talking to your mom in the kitchen before you left for the barn, I snuck past you and set everything in the hut and even beat you back to the barn."

Asher has always done something special for me on my birthday, but I think this one takes the cake.

"Wow. That's pretty sneaky."

Asher leans back in his chair and takes a sip from his champagne. "Yeah, I don't want to brag, but I think I'm pretty cool."

"I think those two shifters would agree with that statement."

He laughs and then pins me with a quizzical look. "I wondered where that random gust of wind came from that practically shooed them out the door."

I take another sip of my drink and roll my eyes. "Those girls were way too young for you, anyway. They hardly know the basics of shifting safely. I was just trying to help you out."

I stand, grabbing my drink, and head for the end of the dock. Asher follows closely behind me, and we both peel our socks off and ease our feet into the cold water. I close my eyes, taking a deep breath as a gentle breeze flows through my cascading hair.

"You know, I miss being around here. We had so many fun memories at my house."

"Yeah, remember that one time when you, me, Leah, and Bree came down here and camped on the dock in the tent?" Asher asks. "Bree got so scared and tried to squeeze in between our sleeping bags and Leah yelled at her for waking her up."

I internally cringe when Asher brings Bree's name up, but the memory is too funny to forget. "Oh my gosh. Yes, how could I forget? Leah acted like the world was ending because Bree woke her up and I thought Bree was going to cry."

After reminiscing on more childhood stories, I bring my glass to my lips, only to realize I finished the last of my champagne and the bottle in between us is empty.

"Hey, did you bring more champagne or wine down here?"

"Of course. I prepared fully for this night. Hang on."

Asher collects my glass and saunters back to the hut. Waiting for him to return, I look at the little remaining lights of the sunset peeking through the trees.

Feeling a tap on my shoulder, I turn to see Asher's hand extended.

"May I have this dance?" he asks with a devilish grin on his face.

I smile as the pulsing intro of the music spreads around us on the dock. "How did you know to play this song?" I ask, taking his outstretched hand.

Asher's emerald eyes glisten as he pulls me closer. "I'm very observant. You should know this by now."

He's right. Every little thing that most people miss, Asher picks up on. And it's not just things about me. It's about everyone.

With Kasey Musgrave's reboot of "Neon Moon" playing in the background, I rest my head on Asher's shoulder. He draws me in tighter and it feels like our hearts beat in sync as we dance, watching the final colors of the sunset fall below the shoreline to the west. Hardly noticing the song ending, Asher lifts my chin.

I peer into those green eyes, feeling the warmth coming from his body. My heart rate quickens, and something inside me clicks into place. I want to ask how he got inside my head today, but instead, without thinking, I stretch up on my tiptoes and bring my face closer to his. As though he reads my mind, Asher lowers his head down to mine, confirming this isn't a one-sided crush.

Before our lips can meet, Asher snaps his head up in high alert. With a quick burst of light, he shifts into his hawk form and vanishes into the tree line. Just as quickly as he left, he returns and shifts back into human form.

"We need to go."

"What the hell was that?" I ask, utterly confused.

"We need to go. Now!" he repeats as he grips my hand and tows me toward the house.

"Asher, what the hell is going on?" I ask, digging my heels into the ground, hoping it'll do some good to stop him.

"I'll tell you once we are safe inside the house. Please, Raven. Let's go."

His eyes catch mine and the panic is evident. I stop protesting and follow him up to the house. Whatever is out there has Asher on high alert. My argument can wait until we are safely back up at the house. With my hand in Asher's, he drags me back toward the house.

When we reach the outside fence of the pool, the sound of my mom's panicked yell has me on edge. I release Asher's hand as we are ushered inside.

"Okay. I'm safe. Now, one of you is going to tell me what the hell is going on," I say, turning to face them both.

My mom speaks up first, calming her tone. "Honey, I was just worried about you two. It's dark now, and it's not safe outside the grounds after the sun sets."

I look at her, puzzled. "We have the boundary spell all the way down to the lake. No one who isn't welcome is able to get inside. We were fine."

"Of course you were. It's just that we have had some unwelcome guests around here in the past week, and I just want to take extra safety steps." Mom looks at Asher as though they both are keeping something from me.

I'm done with the secrets and the not-so-subtle looks that everyone but me is cued in on. "Okay. Enough. What is really going on here?"

It's Asher who finally breaks the silence. "I heard a noise when we were out on the dock. When I shifted, I saw a gray aura toward the end of the boundary."

"A gray aura? That means it was a vampire," I say, sounding a little more concerned than I meant to.

"Yes, honey." Mom walks around me and locks the patio door. "We have had a few vampires wandering around the town the last couple of days. That's where your grandfather went today. He went to go meet with one of the vampires to see what they were up to."

Becoming more upset with all the lies being kept from me, I start to raise my voice. "So, when were any of you going to tell me we had vampires wandering around town?"

Asher notices my temper rising and steps closer, reaching out for me. "Rave, we didn't want to make you think you were unsafe."

"Unsafe?" I laugh pathetically, taking a step back from him. Normally, his touch has a soothing effect on me, but I don't want him anywhere near me right now. "The only thing that is unsafe right now is me and my powers."

As if on cue, the floor starts to shake. Barely noticeable at first, but the angrier I become, the more the ground starts to move. Asher tries to take another step forward, but I stop him, holding my hands up. "Both of you lied to me. Why can you not trust me with the truth? I'm almost twenty-one. I can handle these things. I can protect myself."

"Honey," Mom pleads, "you need to calm down."

Backing away from the two of them, I try to think of something to calm myself. I think back to the first few months we moved to this house. Dad and I would go down to the lake and float in the boat he made. We would make jokes and pretend we were back in the Realm of Shadows.

Sometimes, he would row us to a secret cove near our house and let me work on my other elements that I had to keep hidden. He always encouraged me to control all four, in case one day I needed to use them.

Those were my favorite memories of him.

After a few moments, the ground slowly stops shaking.

Not wanting to talk about what just happened, or anything that happened today, I turn and make my way up to my room, leaving my mom calling after me as I close the door. Collapsing on my bed, I stuff my pillow over my head in an attempt to shut everything and everyone out.

Vampires roaming the barriers is a big deal, and I'm upset I wasn't made aware. Sure, Mom says it's probably nothing, but what if it isn't? And Asher, of all people, knew and kept this hidden from me.

A soft knock breaks me from my thoughts. "Hey," Asher sighs. "Can you open the door so we can talk? I'm sorry for not telling you about the vampires. I just wanted to keep you safe. Please, Raven. Open the door," he pleads.

I roll over, but stay on the bed. I need time to think about everything on my own. Asher must realize this, because he gives up and I hear him close his door. I know Asher and Mom had good intentions, but I can handle myself, even with my powers going haywire.

I tell myself that I will talk to my mom, grandpa, and Asher with a clear mind in the morning. Right now, all I want to do is lay here and have just one night of peace before I must face the reality of my powers.

Remembering all the presents from the family and friends in the Realm of Shadows, I sit up and reach for the "thank you" cards my mom left on the nightstand and start writing to clear my head. With about four cards left, I drift into sleep.

The last thing I think of is the almost kiss with Asher. For some reason, the feeling wasn't me wanting to kiss him, but it felt like a need to kiss him? Something strange is happening and I need to figure it out before it gets me into trouble.

CHAPTER 11

AND IN THE MORNING, I'M
MAKING WAFFLES

The next morning, I take my time getting ready. Mostly, I'm thinking of how to approach everything I need to discuss with everyone. I finally make it down for breakfast and when I walk into the kitchen, I am met with my favorite meal. Nothing in my family says "I'm sorry" like a mountain of waffles smothered in whipped cream, syrup, and topped with strawberries.

"Hi honey, hope you brought your appetite! I made your favorite breakfast."

"Yes, I can see that," I say to Mom, as I eye the plate she hands me.

It's taking all my strength not to show how happy I am that she made waffles for me. I look over to Grandpa Artie and Asher and they both give me a small, apologetic smile. Asher pats the seat next to him to invite me to sit and join them, and yet, another part of me wants to just stay in this moment and not talk about everything that has been going on lately.

Wait, I can't forget I came down here on a mission to get

information out of these people. C'mon, Raven, I tell myself. *Keep it together and keep a straight face on. You got this.*

I recompose myself and sit across from Asher, making him give me a challenging look. I eat in silence while secretly enjoying every bite as the conversation flows around me. After everyone has finished their breakfast, I clear the table and start cleaning up the kitchen. This gives me just enough time to figure out how I want to start my interrogation.

I figure there's no better way than to just dive in. Grabbing the coffeepot, I refill everyone's mugs, then walk back and return the coffeepot to its home. It's now or never.

Here goes nothing.

"So, I hope none of you have anything planned the rest of the morning because no one is leaving until we get this all straightened out."

Everyone exchanges glances, so I continue.

"First off," I say, as I turn and face my mom. "When were you going to tell me that we had vampires in town?"

"Raven, I'm sorry. I really thought it was just a few vampires passing through town. I told your grandpa when he got here that I've been noticing more vampires recently, and he looked more into it."

Looking guilty, she stares out the window and continues, "Your Grandpa Artie found something didn't add up, so he said he was going to meet with them to ask questions, and I knew something more was happening. We weren't going to tell you until we knew for sure what the vampires wanted."

I turned to face my grandpa now. "Okay, now it's your turn to fill in the blanks. What happened when you met with the vampires?"

As if none of this fazes him, he picks up his mug, takes a long sip of coffee, and smiles at me.

"Well, since you want to know so badly, I shall tell you.

When I met with one of the vampires, she said that they were just passing through town trying to locate someone."

"What? That's it?" I say, confused. "You just believed her and let her leave?"

"There is no sense in arguing with a vampire when I already have the facts of why they are here. I heard from the Alliance that the Vampire Court sent out hunters to find a certain person. We are uncertain of the identity of the person, but we are working to find out. Which means the vampire I met with wasn't lying, so I had no reason to detain her any longer."

"So," Asher finally says, "it makes sense that when I shifted last night, I caught the aura of the vampire on the outer edge of the barrier spell. One of them was just passing by."

"Most likely," Grandpa Artie replies.

"Am I really the only one who is a little unsettled about who they're looking for?" I ask nervously.

"We have double and triple checked the protection ward. You're safe here," Mom assures me.

"Besides, no one knows about your powers besides us, and none of us would ever tell anyone. They were probably sent to look for an escaped vampire," Grandpa Artie adds.

I have no reason not to believe my family, but going forward, I'll try to keep my hidden powers in check. "Okay, well, now that's all settled, I have another issue Asher and I both want to discuss with you two. What do you know about dragons?"

"Dragons?" they both question at the same time.

"Yes, dragons. Asher and I have never met one, and we want some information on them. Could either of you help us?"

"Sorry, honey," Mom says as she looks at Asher and me. "I don't really know a lot about dragons. They live on the other side of the realm. Even though the borders between the courts are open, we hardly saw any in our territory."

"Okay, well then, Grandpa, do you know anything about

dragons? I mean, you must, since two dragons are in the Alliance with you."

"Why do you want to know about dragons, my little Raven?" Grandpa asks, a little suspiciously.

"In all honesty, do you remember Bree? She used to hang out with me, Asher, and Leah when we were younger." I take a deep breath and continue, "I think she is a dragon."

Suddenly, my mom spits her coffee out all over the island.

"What?" she says, wiping her mouth. "Bree can't be a dragon. We would have noticed already."

"I know, Mom, but I am asking, is there a chance we missed something? Can dragons hide their auras?"

"No. No creature can hide their aura." Mom looks at Grandpa for reassurance. "Right, Artie?"

"Technically, no, but I have heard of a spell that can alter a creature's aura to be almost human-like. It hasn't been done in many years, though, because it's reserved for undercover creatures that work for the Alliance, doing recon in the human world."

"Well, I can tell you Bree certainly is NOT working for the Alliance."

Mom asks a little suspiciously, "Honey, why do you think Bree is a dragon?"

Okay. So, do I tell her about the whole break up debacle, or do I just skip the bad parts and tell her about the conversation Bree cornered me to have? Well, crap, everyone is being honest, so I guess it's only fair I keep up the honesty party.

I tell everyone what happened with the breakup and Bree cornering me. I also explain how her eyes shifted colors and her ominous warning. Once the whole story is out in the open, leave it to my mom to focus on the part where Bree was caught sleeping with my now ex-boyfriend.

"Oh god, I had no idea, Raven," Mom says gently.

"Yeah, it's not exactly something I want to be sharing with

you all, but since we are in a sharing mood this morning, there you go."

I glance over at my grandpa to find him sitting silently. I can practically see the wheels turning in his mind, trying to process everything.

"I'll investigate Bree and her family and see what I can dig up. I will be returning to the Realm of Shadows later tonight, but I will call you both with anything I find."

With the conversation pretty much over, I thank everyone for finally being honest with me. I make my way upstairs as Asher catches me halfway up the stairs.

"Sooo, that went well?" he questions as we reach the landing.

"I actually think so. Hopefully, now you and my family will trust me a little more," I say, a little annoyed.

"Raven, come on. It's not that we didn't trust you. We just want to protect you."

"I can protect myself just fine, thank you very much." I turn to my room to pack my things and close the door. I grab my suitcase and set it on the bed, reaching for my clothes and shoving them inside.

Why does everyone think I'm some delicate flower? Sure, my powers aren't totally under control right now, but that doesn't mean I can't defend myself if it comes down to it. Frustrated, I finish packing and head out my bedroom door.

Just as I reach the bottom stair, my mom and grandpa are waiting for us in the living room. We say our goodbyes and Asher and I head to the truck. Grandpa and Asher load our belongings into the truck and with one last goodbye hug, we depart from my home.

The drive home is uneventful. I'm too into my thoughts to make conversation with Asher, and thankfully, he lets me be. Hopefully, the vampires leave town soon and peacefully. From what Grandpa said, he has no reason to believe they will be a threat and I believe him when he says this, despite being lied to previously. I'm optimistic my family learned their lesson and all their secrets have been revealed.

We finally make it back to school and Asher drops me off at my apartment right at three o'clock. Just enough time to unpack, shower, and snuggle up to catch up on all my shows.

Before Asher leaves, I pull him over the center console of the truck and into a bear hug. I feel bad about giving him the silent treatment on the way home, but I hope this helps make up for it. I sit back and thank Asher for a great weekend.

"You know, even though it might have been rudely interrupted by you shifting in my face, it was still a very sweet birthday dinner," I tease him.

"Well, you forgot one gift," he says, as he pulls out the small pink wrapped present.

I reach for it, but he places it on the dashboard in front of him, out of my reach.

"Now, you'll have to wait for Tuesday. Don't worry, I'll keep it safe."

Sliding out of the truck, I close the door and watch him disappear around the corner.

"Stupid shifter," I whisper to myself as I head up the stairs to my apartment.

I finally get all my clothes unpacked, shower, and make myself some dinner before flopping on the couch to start my Hulu marathon. I shoot off a quick text to my mom saying that I made it back in one piece and text Asher, once again thanking him for a great weekend. After what feels like hours of catching up on my missed shows, I grab my phone and see Asher's reply.

ASHER

Can't wait for Taco Tuesday birthday / extravaganza!!

I smile as I plug my phone in for the night. I can't wait either.

CHAPTER 12
ONE TEQUILA, TWO TEQUILA, THREE TEQUILA

Monday and Tuesday afternoon go by in a blur. Six o'clock rolls around and as I finish getting ready for the night, Leah opens the door and announces her presence.

"Sup, sloot! You ready for your twenty-first birthday or what??" Leah says, as she throws a handful of confetti into the air above my head.

"Yeah, I'm ready to peel your drunk ass off the floor at the end of the night from too many margaritas," I shoot back, plucking multi-colored confetti out of my shirt.

Leah's dressed in a sage green crop top with a black skirt. She's also got these amazing knee-high black boots to complete the outfit. Her hair is pinned in two Miley Cyrus buns on the top of her head with her smokey eye makeup to pull off the look.

We are practically opposites in our outfit choices because I'm dressed in a black, long sleeve crop top with an army green pencil skirt and black heels. My makeup is modestly done to bring out my gray eyes.

Leah always tells me, "Less is more when it comes to your

beautiful face" and every time she says it, she squishes my cheeks together and shakes my head back and forth. I swear she does it to push my buttons.

"Alright, birthday girl, you ready to get your drink on?" Leah asks excitedly as she tosses me a fireball shooter.

"You mean, legally?" I say as I catch the shot. "Hell yeah! On three?"

We count down together. "One. Two. Three."

We down our shots and a surge of warmth runs through my whole body.

"Damn! That will never get easier, will it?" Leah exclaims, tossing her shooter at me as she blows her cinnamon breath in my face.

"I don't believe so," I say, shooing the air away from me.

We grab our purses and make our way out of the apartment to find Asher waiting for us in his truck. He rolls down the window and yells, "Get in, losers, we're going shopping."

Leah and I turn toward each other and burst out laughing.

"Wow, Asher, never pegged you for a *Mean Girls* type of guy," Leah says, wiping the tear from her eye as she climbs into the truck.

"You go, Glen Coco!" Asher yells.

We all crack up as he pulls out of the complex. Once downtown, we find our typical parking lot close to the strip of bars on Main Street. The strip is just starting to fill up with a steady stream of college kids heading out for a night on the town for Taco Tuesday, usually known around here as "Margarita Tuesday". In any case, we follow most of the crowd down the street and start our night at the Tipsy Taco.

The Tipsy Taco has the best margaritas, which I can now have legally. As we enter the retro themed Mexican bar, the smell of tequila and tacos bombard my senses. It's a little busier than usual, but I figure that's because fall break is next week, and students are trying to go for one last HOORAH! before they go home for the weekend.

Asher heads to the bar to buy the first round as Leah and I fight our way through the growing crowd for a standing table near the stage. When Asher finally makes his way back to us, Leah gives Asher an exacerbated look and reaches out like a toddler for a sippy cup as he sets the drinks down on the table.

"Dang, dude, what took you so long! I almost died of thirst."

"Sorry, but the bar is packed, and they only have three bartenders right now." He slides both of us our drinks. "One pink jalapeño margarita for Leah, and for the birthday girl, one regular margarita."

"Thanks!! Cheers to you two goons for not kicking me out of the cool kid club way sooner," I say as we raise our glasses. We're about to take our first drink when we're interrupted by the bartender.

"Three tequila shots?"

"Yep! That's us!" Asher says and hands her a tip. She hurries and sets the shots down with three limes and extra salt before scurrying back to the busy bar.

I give Asher a sidelong look.

"What?? You don't really think we would toast without shots, did you?" he pleads with his puppy dog eyes.

Leah pats him on the back. "Alright! Way to go, Asher!"

"I hate you both," I groan as I look at my shot.

Leah hugs me from the side, her lavender perfume quickly replaced by the smell of tequila as she slides my shot closer. "No, you don't."

"Yeah," Asher says as he licks his salt from his hand. "You'd be lost without us."

I roll my eyes. "Yeah, something like that."

With that, we down the first shot of the night.

The night flies by as we hop from bar to bar. Crazy 80s is our final stop of the night and let me tell you, the bar is absolutely packed with intoxicated college kids trying to party it up. I mean, would you really expect anything else from an 80s throwback bar? Of course, all the college kids end the night here to dance their drunkenness away to some 80s bangers before last call.

I holler at Asher over the pounding music to take Leah and her guest up to one of the booths next to the stage. At the last bar we were at, Leah pulled me aside and told me, and I quote, "Raven, I think I just found my future husband."

Apparently, Leah and this fella named Colby ran into each other at the bar and he bought Leah her last drink. They got to talking and found out they both love traveling, spicy food, horror films, and they have both been to the Villisca Axe Murder House in Iowa.

Asher and I instantly tensed up when Leah brought Colby over to make the introductions. We could clearly see his gray aura, letting us know he is a vampire. Since humans can't see the auras that supernaturals emit, I quickly reigned in my surprise and made sure Asher composed himself as well.

With all the pleasantries out of the way, Leah towed him along to our last stop. Which is fine with me. That girl deserves a little happiness in her life, but Asher and I will still be cautious for her without giving anything away.

As I make my way up to the bar, I try to wiggle my way through the crowd. I make it almost to the front when a huge, and I mean huge, as in six foot six-ish, two hundred thirty pounds of solid muscle huge, guy cuts in front of me. I tap him on the shoulder and yell over the music.

"Hey, I was actually next in line and you just cut me off. Do you mind?" I gesture as I try to squeeze by him.

"Actually, I do mind," the muscle guy says, pushing me back.

"Are you serious? Everyone just saw you cut in front of me,

and it's my birthday, so you should be a little more courteous." I eye him as I cross my arms over my chest.

"Look, chick, I don't care if it really is your birthday. I'm bigger and stronger than you, so what are you going to do about this situation? Push your way past me? I don't think so." He turns back to face the bar, completely ignoring me.

Just as I am about to draw up some witch power, someone grabs the muscle guy by his arm and swings him around. "I do believe the girl said she was next. So, you can just make your way right behind her."

"Hell no. What are you going to do, move me?" the muscle guy says.

I turn to my savior, seeing his gray aura. With one quick flash of fangs, the muscle guy looks like he just wet himself and cowers past my newfound friend back to the end of the line. Leave it to a vampire to scare the piss out of a human.

The vampire turns toward me and hands me two drinks as he carries three more. "So, I overheard it was your birthday," he says in an Italian accent. "Happy birthday. These are on me."

I give him an odd look, but dang, this guy is good-looking, and I am pretty sure he knows it. Gazing up at him, since I only make it to about his shoulders, I notice his black hair is tousled lazily, making me want to run my fingers through it. His eyes are the color of a glacier. Icy blue and hiding some deep secrets, but his body. Oh lord, his body is chiseled and toned. His shirt hugs his biceps and his jeans fit perfectly on his hips. I quickly peel my eyes from him and decide to thank him for helping me.

"Thanks. But you didn't have to buy my drinks for me and my friends."

Oblivious to me not-so-subtly checking him out, he offers, "Oh, it's no problem at all. Let me help you to your table."

I point in the direction of where I left my friends, and he steps in front of me, heading toward the table. I follow close behind as he parts the Red Sea of bodies. Once we reach the table, we set the drinks down and I'm surprised I haven't spilled a drop on our way back through the jam-packed bar.

Leah and Colby are too involved with each other to notice, but Asher quickly stands up and puts a possessive arm around my shoulder, also taking note of the gray aura from the man in front of him.

"Who's your friend, Rave?"

"Kieran," the vampire says before I have the chance to even ask what his name is. Kieran notes the possessive hold Asher has on me and I gracefully shimmy out of Asher's arm and turn to Kieran.

"My name is Raven, and thanks so much for the help up there. Would you like to sit and have a drink?"

"No thanks. I have to return to my friends before they send a search party for me." Kieran grabs my hand and lays a soft kiss on my knuckles. "I hope we meet again, Tesoro."

I blush, knowing I'll have to look up the nickname later. Smiling, he releases my hand and turns and disappears into the crowd. Rage radiates off Asher when I face him.

"What?" I say, as I scoot into the booth.

"Really? Who the hell was that and what happened at the bar?" Asher questions.

"Nothing really. Some guy tried to cut in front of me and Kieran sent him to the back of the line. That's it."

"Stupid vampires," Asher mumbles.

"Oh stop, Asher. Finish your drink and take me for one last dance on the dance floor before the bar closes."

Asher's mood instantly changes as he takes a sip from his drink, grabs my hand, and leads me to the dance floor. We join the other club patrons as Madonna's song, "Crazy for You", comes on. We dance around the floor. I can't help but feel a sense of wholeness. Leah and Asher have made my birthday one for the books. As the song comes to an end, Asher leads me back to the table to collect our things.

CHAPTER 13

DIAMONDS ARE A GIRL'S BEST FRIEND

Leah says her goodbyes and she and Colby walk off in the opposite direction—I can only assume to his car—leaving Asher and I to walk back to his truck together. As we head down the street to the lot, I intertwine my arm in Asher's. Asher looks down at me and gives me one of his signature smiles, which melts my slightly tipsy brain.

"You look stunning tonight, Raven."

"Hey, you don't look so bad yourself," I say, as I hip bump him.

"I hope you had a good birthday."

"Definitely one for the books. I'll have to get the details from Leah tomorrow. Colby seems like a nice guy." I whisper to myself, "For a vampire."

"Remind me again why we let Leah go off with him?" Asher asks, worried.

Apparently, he heard me whisper under my breath.

"What if she gets hurt? Seriously, what are the chances of us running into not one, but two vampires tonight?" He turns to question me, and I just shrug my shoulders.

"You know we can't tell Leah about the supernatural world and besides, the bracelet she wears has a protection spell on it, so if she's in any danger, my own bracelet will alert me. I wouldn't leave our girl defenseless."

"Okay, fine," Asher concedes. "But if he hurts her emotionally, we can both kick his ass," he jokes, pretending to punch the air, making me laugh.

We make it to Asher's truck and as I reach for the door, Asher beats me to it. He opens it and sitting there is the mysterious pink present. I turn to him and he inclines his head to say, "go ahead."

I grab the present and gently unwrap the bow. I take a deep breath before lifting the lid off the box. Inside is a stunning necklace. I gently take the silver chain from the box and stare at the most beautiful black diamond. I turn to Asher, finding him already blushing.

"This is beautiful, but I can't accept this."

"Of course you can," he says as he looks down at his hands and nervously rubs his wrists.

"You know my grandmother and I were close after my brother died. She shielded me from a lot of my dad's anger. Before she passed away, she wanted me to have this necklace and said to give it to someone who means the most to me." Asher finally looks at me and my breath catches. The air between us shifts, almost turning electric. He steps forward and takes the necklace out of my hands.

"I really can't take this, Asher."

He gently places his hands on my shoulders and turns me around. "Just try it on and see how it looks, please?"

I close my eyes and sigh; in this moment, I'd do anything he asks. "Fine."

His strong hands gently drape the necklace over my neck. I

move my hair so he can clasp the hook. As he finishes, he closes the door so that I can see my reflection in the window.

I'm at a loss for words when I see myself. Not only myself, but Asher behind me as well. We look so perfect together and I don't want it to end. He turns me around to face him, one hand lingering on my shoulder, the other hand caressing the diamond.

"What do you think?" he asks, looking at the necklace.

"I think it's amazing. You're amazing," I say as I reach to lift his face to meet mine. Something shines in his eyes as he leans down.

This is it.

This is the moment that will change our relationship forever. Just as our lips are about to meet, we hear a car alarm go off behind us, bringing us out of our trance.

We turn to see Kieran and two of his friends strolling down the parking lot. Kieran's icy blue eyes catch mine and I can't help but feel a little embarrassed. He winks at me, stirring up a strange feeling in my chest, as he gets in the car and pulls out of the lot with his friends.

Asher grinds his teeth behind me. "I really hate that guy," he says, opening my door.

"Hate is a strong word, and you don't even know him," I say, getting into the car.

Asher quickly gets in the driver's seat and starts the car. I know our moment was interrupted yet again, but I try to smooth things over.

"Asher, thank you so much for the present," I say as I lean over and place a gentle kiss on his cheek.

Asher blushes just a little as we leave the lot, sliding his hand in mine as we head for my apartment. With our hands inter-twined together on my thigh, my mind races a million different directions. What does this mean for us? What did Asher mean when he said his grandmother told him to give this necklace to someone special?

All too soon, we arrive back at my apartment. Asher parks outside the front door and releases my hand, taking the heat with him. Not ready to define what this could be, I bid Asher a quick, and probably awkward, goodnight and flee the vehicle. Being the gentleman he is, Asher waits until I get into my apartment before driving off.

While getting ready for bed, I can't help but smile when I think about the car ride home with Asher's hand holding mine.

Am I ready to see what our relationship could turn into?

My mind instantly shifts to Kieran. His icy blue eyes, dark tousled hair, and ridiculously charming Italian accent. Before I think about him too much, I drift into sleep and let the dreams take me away for the night.

I wake up startled with tingling in my fingers. Normally, I get this feeling when someone uninvited is passing by my protection ward near my apartment. Realizing it's probably some drunk college kid returning to their room, I roll over and pull the covers back over my head. I close my eyes and nearly drift back to sleep when I hear a noise on my patio.

I throw my covers off my head, only to see a shadow standing in the corner of my patio. I flick my hands to bring the lights on and as soon as the lights are on, the shadow is gone. Relief finds me and I tell myself I must still be half asleep. When I turn the lights back off, I swear I see two icy blue eyes staring at me before I close my eyes and fall asleep again.

Waking up Wednesday morning, I feel as though I'm in a daze. Snippets from last night flow through my mind and I reach down to run my thumb over the diamond at my neck. Acknowledging the banging in my head, all I can think about is chugging a nice cool glass of water when the image of two icy blue eyes staring at me from my patio bombards my thoughts.

I slowly get up to inspect the patio. The door is locked, thank goodness, so I turn and head for the kitchen. Class doesn't start until one today, so I have plenty of time to mope around. I fix myself breakfast and grab my phone to find out about Leah's night.

RAVEN

How did last night go? Give me all the deeeeets!!!

LEAH

Still sleeping.

RAVEN

It's 9am! Get your lazy butt up!

LEAH

Not sleeping . . . sleeping. 😉

RAVEN

OMG STOP REPLYING THEN!

Okay, gross. Thank goodness I was done eating because I don't think I would have much of an appetite left. Although, I no longer have to wonder how the night went. I'm sure Leah will never let me hear the end of this, especially since she doesn't know Colby is a vampire. She probably just thinks it was the best sex of her life, which it most likely was. Vampires are notorious lovers, or so I've heard from the gossip back home.

I grab my plate and head back to the kitchen to clean up my mess. Just as I finish wiping off the counter, my phone dings. Hoping it's not Leah again bragging about her sex life, I check my phone to see a text from Asher.

ASHER

So, what was in the envelope?!

Realizing I can now open the present from my dad, I drop my phone on the counter and run to my room. My heart pounds with anticipation as I race inside, only to find my desk in the corner, void of any envelope.

"That's weird," I say to myself, my heart now pounding with fear. "I left it right here."

I drop to my knees to inspect under the desk. Maybe I dropped it by accident. Finding nothing but cords, I turn to my bed and rip the sheets off. I head to the closet next and go through every inch, trying to find the missing envelope. Panicking, I run back to the kitchen and grab my phone. Asher picks up on the second ring.

"Hey, Rave, did you find—" but I cut him off as I yell into the phone.

"I can't find it! It's gone!" Trying to hold it together, I take a deep breath and whisper into the phone. "The envelope is gone, Asher."

"Hey, don't worry, I'll be over in five minutes, and we can look together. I'm sure it's not gone."

I squeeze my eyes closed, but the vision of icy blue eyes flashes into my mind again.

Stop. I tell myself. *It's just your head playing games. Focus.*

I hang up and tear my apartment to shreds looking for the envelope. Panic fills my body as I search every nook and cranny. The envelope was magically sealed until today, so whoever has it now can read whatever my dad worked hard to hide.

Just thinking about the endless possibilities of the envelope makes me sick. Feeling absolutely defeated, I fall to my knees on the hardwood floor, wrapping my arms around my body. As my body starts to shake, so does my furniture, telling me my control over my power is fading. I hear the shatter of glass and look up to find a picture of me, Leah, and Asher laying cracked on the ground.

I hang my head, squeezing my eyes shut and willing myself to get a grip on my powers before the whole apartment starts shaking. I can't hear anything but the roar of my blood in my head. Thankfully, when I feel a tingle up my arm, I know Asher has entered the protection ward. I hear him slowly close the front door, but I can't bring myself to face him.

"Raven," Asher whispers as he approaches my crumpled body on the floor. He reaches out and places a comforting hand on my shoulder, stopping the shaking in my apartment. I don't know how his touch calms me, but I'm truly thankful for it at this moment.

"It's not here. I looked everywhere, Asher. It's not here."

Asher gently scoops me up and brings me to the couch. He sits with me in his lap and brushes a fallen strand of hair from my face. I finally look at him and can't hold it in any longer. I bury my head in his chest and let all the anger and sadness out. He just sits there and strokes my hair until I raise my head and face him.

"It's gone, Asher. I had it on my desk last night and when I woke up this morning, it was gone. How does something just vanish like that?"

He slides his thumb over my cheek to brush a falling tear. "I don't know, Raven, but we will find it. I promise."

I unfold myself from his lap and we search the apartment one last time. After trying to clean the mess I made the best we could, we end in the kitchen and I feel nothing but defeat. I know it was here. I saw it last night before we went out to the bars.

"Is there anything strange that happened last night after you got home?" Asher asks.

"No, I went home and went right to bed."

I don't tell Asher that I saw a pair of eyes staring at me when I woke up in the middle of the night because that sounds ridiculous and I don't even know if it was real. That's something I will investigate on my own. I want to prove to not only myself, but to my family that I can handle things on my own.

Leaving it at that, he pulls my hand and brings me in for a hug. "We will find it. I promise."

"I hope so." I squeeze him back and step out of his embrace.

"But I have to get ready for class. Do you mind dropping me off at campus? If I walk, I'll be late."

"No problem! I'll meet you down at the truck so you can get changed."

Asher lets himself out of the apartment as I go back to my room to change. With one last sweep of the room, I know the envelope is gone. Shedding my pajamas shorts, I slide on a pair of jeans, grab my flannel, and head out the door. I sling my backpack into Asher's pickup, and we head to campus.

Thanking Asher for the ride, I step out and before I shut the door, Asher grabs my hand.

"Hey. Chin up. We will find it even if it means tearing this city apart."

"I know, and thank you for your help this morning."

I shut the door and start walking to class, a plan formulating in my brain. First, I've got to somehow find Kieran. Second, I need to find a non-creepy way to ask him if he knows where my apartment is, because I swear it wasn't a dream I was in when I saw those eyes peering back at me. No, it was real. It had to be.

After about six missed calls from my mom, I finally answer the seventh time my phone rings. Between the incident at her house and not picking up the phone after my birthday night out, my mom's voice rings with panic.

"Honey! I have been so worried about you! Are you okay?"

"I'm fine, Mom. Just a little hungover from last night."

I use the hangover excuse because I can't face telling my mom I lost the envelope from Dad. The envelope that Mom had for nine years and I ended up losing after four days.

Mom exhales a sigh of relief on the other end of the phone. "Oh, it was that kind of night, huh?" She giggles.

"Yeah, it was great. I got this beautiful necklace from Asher. It was his grandmother's before she passed."

"I bet it's stunning," Mom says.

She pauses and I know what she's going to ask me next, and my heart literally can't bear it. I feel the tears coming before she even asks the question she really called for.

"So, what was the gift from your father?" she asks excitedly.

I can't lie to her, not after everything she's done for me.

"I lost it, Mom. We went out for drinks, and I swear I saw it when I came home and when I woke up the next morning, it was gone. Poof. Vanished." I sob into the phone.

There's more silence, and I know I have royally messed up.

"I'm sorry, Mom. I feel like a horrible daughter right now. You can yell at me all you want."

"Now that's enough. You are not a bad daughter." I try to cut her off, but she silences me. "Zip it, child."

I stop crying and try to compose myself.

"Now listen, I'm sure it's just misplaced. It'll show up, Raven, I know it will."

"I really hope so, Mom."

We stay on the phone for a few more minutes, but before I hang up, I apologize again.

"No more apologizing. It will turn up. Now, go drink a cup of tea to relax yourself before bed. I love you, little witch."

I try not to cry again. "I love you too, Mom."

I hang up the phone and throw my pillow over my head to muffle my screams. I really feel like a crap daughter, but her and Asher are so sure the envelope will show up. I hope they're right.

CHAPTER 14

COINCIDENCE? I THINK NOT

Friday morning is filled with nothing but lectures. Two classes down, one to go and my last class happens to be my absolute favorite as it pertains to my major. World History of the 1700s. When my mom let me apply for college, I knew I wanted to pursue a major involving history. Hence why I'm working toward my Bachelor's degree in World History.

I stroll into class ten minutes early and pick my usual spot by the window that overlooks campus. As the class slowly fills in, my arm hairs suddenly stand to attention and I lift my head to see Kieran striding into class. Our eyes meet for a brief second before I quickly look back out the window.

My curiosity gets the best of me and I turn and find him sitting in the row behind me on the opposite side of the room, which is strange because I never noticed him in this class before. Now that I think about it, I haven't come across one vampire on campus yet this year, besides running into him and Colby at the bars this week. Coincidence? I think not.

Just before my mind starts running over every possible

reason he could be in my class, Mr. Simmons, our professor, walks in. Thankful for the brief distraction, I turn my attention back to the front of the room. For the next hour and a half, I feel wandering eyes glance my way. Their intense gaze slices into my skin, giving me goosebumps.

After the longest class in the history of classes, Mr. Simmons finally dismisses us to start working on our next assignment, Italian culture of the 18th century.

As I look over to a certain sexy Italian, I find said Italian staring back at me. Frozen in my seat, all I can do is watch Kieran smirk and rise from his chair. He exits class, and that's when I'm finally able to move. Determined not to let him affect me anymore, I muster up all my courage and hightail it out of class after him.

Step one: find Kieran, complete.

Nearly sprinting out of class, I round the door and run right into a brick wall. A brick wall of muscle.

"Ciao, Tesoro." His soft Italian voice makes me look up.

"Oh, hello." I smile up at him, tucking my hair behind my ear, and take a few steps back. "If I were a betting woman, I would think you were stalking me."

He readjusts his bag and cools his expression. "How much would you win on this bet, then?"

I think back to Tuesday night and remember those icy blue eyes staring at me from the patio. I remember walking back to my apartment on Thursday and seeing Kieran's car drive by with his friends in the back seat. Breaking me from my trance, Kieran reaches out and lightly pushes my shoulder.

"I was kidding. Guess I need to work on my sarcasm. I must be a little rusty."

Laughing nervously, I try to save the conversation. "Right, yeah, you were being sarcastic and so was I. I know you're not stalking me."

I turn and internally kick myself.

Step two: ask Kieran if he was stalking me, failed.

I'm surprised when I turn to see him walking by my side.

"So," I start, "how long have you been attending the university? I haven't seen you in my class until today."

"I just recently transferred. The Vampire Court knows the president of the university and they let me start late since I was held up in Italy on business."

"Ah, the mysterious Vampire Court, huh?"

He smiles and we continue walking out of the building in silence. As we make it to the parking lot, he faces me suddenly.

"Would you care to join me for some coffee? I can drive us to the little shop down the street."

Taken aback by the sudden movement from him, I step back.

He notices and creates some space between us. "Sorry."

"No, it's fine! I just forgot how fast vampires can move sometimes. I haven't chatted with a vampire lately."

He eyes me suspiciously. Of course, he doesn't need to know that the last time I spoke to a vampire face to face was at my mom's Christmas party six years ago. Mrs. Valentino was the only vampire in town at the time, but she made a mean cinnamon shortbread and everyone loved her until she moved away.

"Hey now! I've broken plenty of vampire hearts in my days."

I'm frozen in my tracks by the sound of his laugh. The warm sound vibrating from his chest has me transfixed. "I'm sure you have, Tesoro."

He starts to walk to his car and looks back after a couple steps. "You coming?"

Unfreezing my feet from the concrete, I move toward his car. He walks to my side and opens my door for me.

"So apparently chivalry isn't dead then."

He laughs again as I slide into the front seat. We make it to the coffee shop in a few minutes and when we arrive, Kieran's phone rings. "I apologize. I've got to take this. Do you mind finding us a table? I promise I'll be right in."

I nod and start toward the coffee shop. As I walk away, I hear Kieran start speaking to someone in Italian, which makes me curious as to who could be on the other end of the line. I select a corner table toward the front by the big bay window, but before I slide into my seat, I hear a familiar voice.

"What's up, babe?" Leah says, walking toward me with two cups in her hand.

"I should be asking, what's up with you? Are those both for you?" I ask, placing my bag down and motioning for Leah to sit with me.

"No, silly, one is for Colby." She wiggles her eyebrows. "Remember him? The gorgeous man from your birthday?"

So that means Colby didn't drink Leah's blood since he is still out in the sun. If a vampire drinks from a human, they can erase the human's memory of the event. However, vampires can't go in the sun until the blood runs its course through their body after they drink human blood, which typically takes up to two days.

"I do and I hope your night was amazing, if you know what I mean," I say, wiggling my eyebrows back at her. She giggles and Kieran enters the coffee shop. I wave at him, and Leah turns and gasps.

"Is that the sexy savior from your birthday? Ooo la la, Raven."

"Oh my god," I plead, "please don't be weird. I'll introduce you, then you can leave, and I'll give you the details later."

"Oh, you better, babe." She winks at me, then turns toward Kieran. He walks up to the table and I stand to introduce the two, but Leah beats me to it. "Raven, who is this tall glass of water?"

She reaches out and takes Kieran's hand. Kieran smiles, takes her hand, and places a kiss on her knuckles.

"The pleasure is mine. I'm Kieran Evers."

He rises and Leah shoots me a look that says, "TELL ME EVERYTHING".

"Yes, Leah was just leaving." I rise and start to shoo her away. "Weren't you, Leah?"

She winks and turns back to Kieran. "Yes, I was just leaving. So nice to meet you, Kieran."

He releases her hand and nods. "The pleasure is all mine."

Kieran takes his seat as Leah leaves and I see her fake faint behind him. I shake my head and start apologizing to Kieran.

"I am so sorry about her. I usually don't let her out in public as she doesn't have a filter when it comes to good-looking men."

Kieran fakes a gasp. "You think I'm good-looking?"

I internally reprimand myself for the comment and try to recover. "I mean, objectively speaking."

He smiles and reveals what I had already put together. "So, that's the woman Colby won't shut up about."

"Oh, you know Colby?" I question, but obviously they know each other since they are the only two vampires I have met within the last three years, and they happened to show up at the same time.

The waiter comes to check and see if we would like to order. Since I know the menu by heart, I order my usual, but it takes Kieran a couple minutes to decide what he wants. I can tell by the way he grimaces at the menu that he isn't used to American coffee customs yet. Once he orders, he answers my question.

"Colby and I have known each other for a long while. Some would say we are as close as brothers." The waiter arrives with our drinks as Kieran continues, "He came with me from Italy to the States."

He pauses to take a drink and I try to hide my smile as he makes a dissatisfied face when he swallows, trying to push through it.

"That's why I had to take the phone call earlier. My old supervisor back in Italy had some questions about the archives I was studying."

"You were studying archives in Italy? Why on earth would you leave Italy and come to the States?" I ask, confused.

"I was summoned by the Vampire Court to come and study some interesting findings out here." Kieran leans in toward the middle of the table, forcing me to do the same as if we were sharing sacred secrets.

"I'm the historian for the Vampire Court and we received a tip that something we've been searching for was discovered around the university. We don't know what our target is yet, but they want me to help with the retrieval because, as it so happens, I'm very good at finding things that have been hidden."

My first instinct is to retreat and run for the hills. There's no way he knows about my powers, right? Trying to hide my growing anxiety, I plaster a challenging look on my face while I silently freak out on the inside. "I guess we'll find out how good you are at your job, won't we?"

CHAPTER 15
STALKER STATUS

The conversation flows naturally as Kieran and I finish our drinks. Everything about a vampire is supposed to draw humans in, from their striking features to their mysterious personas. Other supernaturals are slightly less inclined to be drawn in, yet I feel myself wanting to know more. It's odd how comfortable I feel around him.

I glance at my phone and notice it's almost six. "Thank you for the coffee and for sticking around, even after meeting my crazy best friend."

I pick up my bag and start to stand when Kieran gently grabs my hand.

"I know you might find this hard to believe, but I do enjoy your company," he teases.

I laugh and Kieran smiles back, releasing my hand. He stands and grabs my cup for me and tosses it into the trash as we walk out. "Do you need a ride home?" he asks, as we approach his car.

"No, I think I'll walk and enjoy the night. It's almost October and I don't know how many nice nights we will have left. Besides, I just live down the block. But thank you for the offer."

As he turns to walk to the driver's side, I know it's now or never. It's been a while since I engaged in conversation with a vampire, let alone sat down and had coffee with one. Why not take advantage of the situation?

"Hey, Kieran? Are you free for dinner tomorrow night?" I ask nervously.

He turns to me with a sly grin. "Oh, I think I could pencil you in."

"Oh really? Pencil me in, huh?" I joke back.

"Yeah, I think so. How about we meet back at the coffee shop around five?"

I nod, but remember vampires don't really eat regular food. "Wait, what can you eat?" I ask, genuinely curious.

"Anything. Just pick your favorite restaurant and I'll be here at five to pick you up."

"Okay," I wave to him, "see you at five."

After he pulls out of the parking lot, I rummage for my phone and instantly dial Leah's number. She picks up after only one ring and I don't even get a hello.

The first words out of her mouth are, "Are you seeing him again? Because if not, I'm hanging up."

"Well, hello to you too, Leah. Yes, I had a good day. Thanks for asking."

"Stop. You're seriously killing me." Leah groans into the phone. I laugh and drag her on a little more.

"Were you referring to the tall, sexy Italian I was having coffee with? Because if you were, then yes. I asked him to dinner tomorrow night."

I extend my phone away from my ear, so her shriek doesn't blow my eardrum.

"Girrrrl," she says after she calms down. "He is one fine human."

I laugh silently to myself. If only she knew he WASN'T human.

"So, what are you going to wear? Where are you going for dinner?" Her barrage of questions continues, but all I can focus on is the redhead walking toward me.

"Hey, Leah. I'm going to have to call you back. You'll never guess who I just ran into."

"WHO?!" Leah asks, as I narrow my eyes and stare at the girl in front of me.

"Bree," I say as I hang up before I can hear any more string of curse words and threats coming from Leah.

"Oh, hi Raven," Bree coos. "Was that Asher on the phone? Or was it that yummy Italian fellow from the coffee shop?"

I'm taken aback how she even knows that I was with Kieran, but I try to keep a straight face. "That's none of your business," I scoff. "You lost the right to ask questions after you slept with my boyfriend."

Bree steps in front of me, stopping me from continuing my way home. "Ex-boyfriend, and Kyle told me he went by your apartment after I saw you last week."

She reaches and grabs a piece of my hair, swirling it around her finger. "He informed me that you finally moved on," she narrows her eyes, "with Asher."

I slap her hand away and take a step back.

"Asher and I aren't together," I say, but it sounds more like a question. I don't know where Asher and I stand after the almost kiss at the lake and the almost kiss in the parking lot. Him almost kissing me confirms that he feels something for me too, but now isn't the time to dive into that mess.

She takes my silence as a win.

"You know, it's pathetic how you string him along. The boy is clearly in love with you, and you just don't see it." She takes a step forward and continues, "And now, it looks like you've moved right along to this new fellow. What's his name?" She taps a finger to her lips, pretending as if the name slipped from her mind. "Oh, Kieran," she says, looking right at me.

I'm baffled. "How do you know his name?"

"Like I said, Raven, watch your back. I'm not the only scary thing out here anymore." She steps to the side and walks right past me. "Toodles," she says, as I turn to watch her walk away.

I grab my phone back out of my pocket and fire a text to Leah.

RAVEN

Meet me at my place ASAP.

Rounding the street corner, I see the familiar rows of apartments and spot Leah's Rav4 in the parking lot. I meet Leah outside her car, and she instantly hugs me.

"What the hell did the little cockroach want this time?" she asks, pulling away. We walk into the main apartment and head for my door.

"She knows about Kieran. She even knew his name, Leah." I shake my head, not believing what I'm about to say. "I think Bree is following me."

I grab my keys and unlock the front door.

"Oh, hell no!" We step inside and Leah slams the front door. "She's not getting away with this. This chick is straight up asking for my fist in her face."

I laugh, knowing she is trying to make light of the situation, but I also know she's serious. "Calm down, tiger."

I take my bag to my room as Leah stretches out on the couch. When I come back, I curl up in the chair beside her.

"She said some other things, too." I turn to Leah because I need to see her face for what I'm about to ask her. "Leah, do you think Asher is in love with me?"

She looks away and I know that's her tell when she doesn't want to reveal something.

"Be honest. Am I just that blind?"

She looks at me and smiles. "I mean, yeah. Yeah, you are Raven." I fold my arms over my eyes, and she continues, "That boy worships the ground you walk on. He would do anything for you."

"Okay, what if I said I might have feelings for him also, but am too afraid to act on those feelings in case we don't work out?" I peek out between my arms and Leah is smiling like a schoolgirl. "And what if we almost kissed," I hear her gasp and clap her hands together, and I continue, "twice."

She slaps my leg. "You almost kissed TWICE?? When were you going to tell me?"

"Well, things were a little crazy after my birthday and I wanted to tell you in person and not over the phone or text. So, surprise?" I laugh.

"Listen," Leah says, placing her hand on my knee. "That boy has been in love with you from the moment you two met. If you want to explore what this could be, I say go for it."

I blink a few times, not believing what she just said. "But what if we don't work out and things get weird between us three?"

Leah waves her hand in a nonchalant manner. "We'll cross that bridge if we get there, babe. But if you want to explore this thing with Kieran, I also support that."

With no idea what to do at this point, I turn the tables, trying to steer the conversation away from me. "Since you left me on my birthday, tell me all about Colby. Did you do it? Was it amazing?"

She shoots me with a look.

"Okay, you're right. It was, otherwise, you wouldn't still be seeing him."

"You're not wrong," she counters. "For your information, we didn't 'do it'," she air quotes. "He was a perfect gentleman."

"Speaking of gentleman, that reminds me, did you know Colby and Kieran know each other?"

Leah deadpans. "Shut. Up."

"I know. Weird, isn't it?" I wiggle my eyebrows and tease her. "Kieran mentioned it after you walked away. He said, and I quote, 'So that's the girl Colby won't shut up about'."

I look at Leah and can see the wheels turning. I fake a gasp. "Don't tell me you're smitten with him?"

Leah has never really had a serious boyfriend. Just casual flings lasting about a week. She always said she wasn't "wife material", which is a lie. She watched her mom get her heart broken when her dad left when she was eight. Her mom always held on to a sliver of hope that he would come back, but Leah knew the truth.

Even at eight-years-old, she knew he wasn't coming back.

So, she hid her heart away where no man could find it. It makes me sad because Leah is the person someone would want fighting in their corner, and I am damn lucky I have her as a friend fighting in mine.

Finally, after a few minutes, she turns back into her bubbly self. "You think they would do a double date?"

We both fall into a laughing fit. And that's why I'm lucky to have her: even though she doesn't know that there is a whole other world out there filled with supernatural beings, she still accepts me as I am. Boy drama and all.

After a couple episodes of *New Girl*, Leah leaves after I promise to fill her in on Sunday about my dinner with Kieran. I lock the door behind her and head in my room to get ready for bed. I think back to my conversation with Leah and realize I do have feelings for Asher, but question myself when I get excited thinking about dinner with Kieran tomorrow.

With Asher being out of town this weekend at a cross country meet, I figured it wouldn't hurt to enjoy my time with Kieran tomorrow. If the interest I have in him fizzles out, no harm done. We can remain friends.

I turn off the light and bury myself under the covers. I tell myself that I'm just excited about the chance to get to know a vampire for the first time. At least, I hope that's the reason and not this mysterious pull I feel toward him.

CHAPTER 16

SORRY, I'M NOT LEWIS AND CLARK

Two hours before I'm supposed to meet Kieran, I'm sitting here overthinking the whole situation. I have gone through every outfit, and nothing seems right. Now I have a pile of discarded clothes occupying the corner of my room.

It's supposed to be casual, but I also want to look cute. It's not a date. Just two people—a witch and a vampire—going to dinner to get to know each other . . . *which is the definition of a date*, I say to myself in the mirror.

Finally, I give up and settle for casual/cute with a pair of black jeans with a white V-neck and my favorite pair of vans. After taking nearly all afternoon worrying over what to wear, I actually ended up in something I felt most comfortable wearing. I still have Asher's necklace on, which reminds me to call him tonight after dinner to see how his cross-country meet in Florida is going.

I decide to keep my makeup simple and just apply my tinted moisturizer, which reveals some of my freckles, but mostly gives me more comfort rather than going full coverage. I also apply my mascara and my favorite nude lipstick. I glance in the mirror one more time and am happy with the result. On my way out of the apartment, I grab my jacket in case it gets colder toward the end of the night.

Walking to the coffee shop, I'm thankful it's turned out to be a beautiful evening. The temperature gives the perfect amount of warmth while the sun is still out, but chilly once it goes down. The sunset is a mix of pinks, yellows, soft oranges, and deep blues.

While admiring the sunset, I catch a movement toward the left of my shoulder. Thinking nothing of it, I keep walking. I pull my air pods out of my jacket and listen to music the rest of the walk. When I turn the corner to the coffee shop, I feel eyes staring at my back. The hairs on my arms stand at attention; someone is following me.

I quicken my pace to make it to the coffee shop door and turn around swiftly, but find nothing, only an empty sidewalk on both sides of the street. Whoever was following me must have abandoned their pursuit after I made it safely to the front of the building. When I face the door again, Kieran is standing in front of me.

"Holy hell!" I scream and nearly topple over backward.

Kieran grabs my elbows to steady me.

"You nearly scared me to death!"

"Sorry," he says, letting go of my elbows. "I saw you out the window and you looked panicked, so I came to meet you at the door. You must not have seen me."

"I guess I didn't, but it's kind of hard NOT to miss you."

Kieran chuckles and leads me to his car. "Are you sure you're alright?"

I pull my air pods out and tuck them back into my jacket. "Well, besides the fact that my soul left my body for two seconds, yeah, I'm fine."

I plaster a winning smile on my face and follow him to his

car. I'm not going to mention I thought I was being followed. Not a good way to start off a date that's not really a date.

After he enters the car, I notice how small the car is and how tall he is. However, once we are inside his car, he seems to fit perfectly. I guess I didn't notice the first time since it was a short drive and my mind was preoccupied.

"You know, I was wondering how all of that fit inside this small car," I tease.

"What do you mean 'all of that'? You just motioned to my whole body." He pouts.

"Exactly. In case you haven't noticed, you're not exactly a normal-sized person."

He pulls onto the road and smiles. "So, where is the restaurant you selected?"

I put the address into his phone, because let's be honest, I'm not exactly Lewis and Clark when it comes to giving someone directions. I'd rather have Siri take care of the instructions instead of me trying, and ultimately failing, to distinguish between my left and right under pressure. It's only a fifteen minute drive, and the time passes quickly.

As we pull into Stanlee's parking lot, I feel a little emotional. My dad and I used to come here every time we came to a Saturday football game. We used to drive up the night before and have dinner. It was our spot.

In all honesty, I could have chosen any place to eat, but something deep within me chose to come here and bring Kieran. I don't know what that says about me, but I'm a little scared to find out why.

I lead Kieran into the funky burger joint and I'll never forget the look on his face when we walk into the building. His face is a mixture of awe and confusion. He turns to see the side wall painted to look like a comic book.

"You've got to be kidding, right?"

"Absolutely not!" I say with a straight face. "This place has the best burgers around."

We are greeted by an older gentleman, dressed in Spider-Man shirt, who instantly comes to life after seeing me. "Do my eyes mistake me or is that my little Birdy?!"

Thomas embraces me as I look at Kieran, trying to hold back laughter. I shoot him a look that says, "Call me Birdy and let's see how well vampires can fly."

I return my attention to Thomas. "Thomas! It's so good to see you! This is my friend Kieran."

Kieran extends his hand and shakes Thomas' hand. Thomas gives me a look and I can't help but laugh. "You old goat, he's just a friend. I'm here to show him how a real burger is made. Think you can still do that, or do I have to go somewhere else?"

Thomas just laughs. "It's good to see you haven't lost your spunk, Birdy. Have a seat. I'll be right out."

Kieran leads us to a table by the comic book wall. His expression gives nothing away, but I can tell he is curious about the nickname. "So, Birdy, huh?"

"Thomas is the only one allowed to call me Birdy. I dare you to try and call me that," I challenge sweetly, lacing my fingers together under my chin.

Kieran smiles and takes in the scene around him. There are old comic books everywhere. Some in glass cases and some lay on tables for customers to read. There are even little action figures dangling from the ceiling.

"Can I ask just how you know this place exists?"

"My dad knew Thomas from when I was little. He owns this place, and we used to come here every time we could make it up for a football game. It was kind of our thing. Thomas is like family to me. He helped a lot after my dad died."

Kieran gently places his hands over mine. "I'm sorry to hear that. You must have been close to your dad."

I smile through a stray tear. "I was. He was my best friend."

Kieran reaches over to wipe the tear away. "I can tell. He raised a hell of a daughter, from what I can see."

I'm taken aback by the sweet gesture, but thankfully, I don't have to say anything in return because Thomas is back with our food. My mouth is practically watering when he sets the tray down in front of us.

"Enjoy, you two."

As Thomas leaves, Kieran grabs his burger and takes a bite.

Then another.

Then he does the most Italian thing I've ever seen. He kisses his fingers. You know, in the way Italians do when something is delicious.

"I have to say, Raven, this truly is the best burger I think I have ever eaten. Although, burgers weren't around when I was human, so my taste might be a little skewed."

"Ahh, so you're like, really old then," I say as I point one of my fries at him. That earns me a smirk.

"I guess you could say that."

"So how does this work then with you being, well, you know. Doesn't eating human food mess up your stomach or something?"

"Not as much as myths and legends make it out to be. We mainly survive off blood. It's our primary food source and it's what keeps us strong. But if we must, we can eat human food. It just doesn't satisfy our hunger the way that blood does."

"Huh. I guess you really do learn new things every day."

After we finish our food, I take our trays up and find Thomas behind the counter.

"Thank you, old man. The food was as delicious as ever!" I tease.

"I wouldn't want to disappoint my girl now, would I?" Thomas pulls me in for a hug. "Don't be a stranger. It's been too long since you've been by."

"Yeah, yeah, don't go getting all emotional on me," I say,

shoving him playfully away. "You know I'm still your best customer."

After I promise to bring Leah next time I come, I finally make my way back to Kieran. As we head out the door, I can't help but want to spend more time with him.

He must read my mind because before we reach the car, he speaks up. "So, I was thinking we could go walk around the city park to the pedestrian bridge?" He hesitates. "If you're up for it?"

"Yes!" I say, a little too quickly. Trying to recover, I add, "I mean, if you don't have any other plans tonight. Sure."

Kieran chuckles and we start walking down the path. We walk in silence for a couple minutes, listening to the subtle breeze sweeping through the trees. "So, what's your story, Raven?" he asks, his icy blue eyes peer into mine.

I try to deflect and turn it back on him. "Oh no, let's hear about you first because you are by far the more mysterious one here."

"You know mine already. I was peacefully studying archives in one of the most beautiful places in the world when I was summoned by the 'dreaded Vampire Court', as other supernaturals like to call them, to help with their investigation."

I smile at the mocking tone he uses to describe the "dreaded Vampire Court".

"And how exactly did you end up working for the Vampire Court?" I ask. It's known that most vampires who work for the court are sought out for a specific skill they possess.

"Well, I told you that I am particularly good at finding lost things. I was working as an archivist when they summoned me. Apparently, when you find the location of the Rosetta Stone, you become very valuable to people."

I stop in my tracks. "Wait. You mean to tell me you uncovered the location of the Rosetta Stone?"

Kieran looks at me, unfazed. I quickly do the math in my head from what I remember from my history classes.

"Kieran. You mean to tell me that you found the Rosetta Stone? But that was uncovered in the 1800s!" I exclaim.

"Actually, it was 1799, to be exact." He smirks and continues walking.

If my head could explode, it would have at that moment. Not only because he found the most coveted item in all modern history, but also the fact he was alive at that time. I quickly catch up to him after my mini freak out session.

"So, how old are you, exactly?" I inquire.

Kieran only glances at me. "Isn't that a rude question. I don't go asking you how old you are, Raven," he jokes.

We eventually reach the bridge and he leans over the railing, staring out at the water, seeming to be torn over something. I'm surprised when he breaks the silence, his voice sounding so sad.

"I was born in 1605 in a small town near Tuscany. At that time, a major plague swept through our country. I was one of the unlucky ones to fall victim to the plague. Fortunately for me, Colby's father, Antonio Benevito, the ruler of the Vampire Court, found me and saved my life. I was only twenty-seven when he turned me."

I try to keep an even face as realization strikes me, putting two and two together. After all the complaining I did when my grandpa insisted I learn the names of all the rulers of each court, his lessons are finally paying off. Colby is Antonio's son, and the next in line to rule the Vampire Court. *Oh hell. What has Leah gotten herself into?*

Kieran takes a deep breath and continues, "He took me to the Vampire Court, and I was raised with Colby learning to control my blood lust. Once I could do that, I was free to roam about the Vampire Court or lead my own life. Little did I know that I would be forever tied to Antonio to do his bidding."

Trying to make light of the situation, I point out, "So you

mean to tell me that you're stuck in this perfect, twenty-seven-year-old body forever?" I let out a slow whistle. "Dang, dude. Must be hard being this good-looking for the rest of your life. You must get ALL the ladies."

Kieran turns toward me, and I am rewarded with his warm laughter. "Leave it to you to point out my age again when I just shared my whole life story."

"And you're also the best friend of a prince. How demoralizing." I fix my eyes on Kieran as I teasingly pout at him, but he quickly grabs my hand and pulls me close to him. He smells like rain on a summer night, and I find myself being drawn more to him.

"Does it bother you that you're on a date with an older man?"

Date. Did he just say date? As in, we are on a date right now?

My mind is running a million miles an hour to the idea that Kieran thinks this is a date.

"Hey," he says, bringing my chin up to face him. "We don't have to take this fast. I just thought that when you asked me to dinner, that was what this was. A date."

He's right. Any normal person would consider someone asking them to dinner, a date. My excitement got the better of me at the opportunity to hang out with a vampire to notice my mixup. Trying not to think too much about it, I decide to go with and see where the rest of the night takes us.

"You're not old, you're ancient. But no, I suppose I don't mind."

Kieran's smile returns as he turns us to face the river with his arm still around me. Suddenly, a chill invades my body and I let out a small shiver.

"Here. Take my jacket." Kieran removes his arm from me, shakes his jacket off, and places it around my shoulders. "I suppose we better get back to the car and get you warmed up."

"I suppose," I say, starting to walk away. I don't get too far before Kieran takes my hand and interlaces his fingers in mine. I look up at him and he graces me with the sweetest smile. For being a vampire, his hands don't feel cold at all. Instead, they almost feel warmer than mine.

Hoping that I dodged my backstory, I am sorely mistaken when Kieran brings it up on the walk back to the car.

"So, now that you know my pitiful story, don't you think I am owed a little peek into the life of Raven?"

I glance up at Kieran, hoping to charm him into forgetting that he asked when I see his face fall as he looks forward. I hear her before I see her standing in front of us.

"Hello, Kieran. Lovely night, isn't it?"

CHAPTER 17
INTERROGATION SKILLS: NONE

I'm in shock. There is no way that Bree is standing in front of us right now. Right? I must be dreaming. This is all a dream. At least that's what I think until she starts talking again.

"What a pretty picture. Although, I'm a bit surprised to see you with Kieran instead of Asher. But who am I to judge?" She shrugs. My heart constricts as I think of my feelings for Asher. Being caught by Bree almost feels like a betrayal to him.

She leans a little closer, like she's trying to tell me a secret.

"Although, between you and me, Kieran does have that little extra mystery around him. Am I right?" She winks.

Kieran is the one who finally breaks me out of my trance when he releases my hand. "What are you doing here?"

Wait. They know each other?

I have a hundred questions running through my head, but they are going to have to wait. I need to play this cool and try to put the pieces together later. I look at Kieran and he looks pissed. Although, I do have to say he still looks super sexy, even staring Bree down.

Bree takes a couple of steps closer. Just enough to reach out and run her fingers across Kieran's arm. "I was sad to see you out here with another girl." She looks me up and down and continues, "Especially her."

Kieran yanks her wrist. "First off, don't touch me. Ever." He releases her wrist and Bree grabs it; it's already starting to bruise. "Second," he continues, "I can do whatever I want with whoever I want. You're not my babysitter."

Bree throws her head back and laughs. "Oh, if you only knew. You're cute when you're mad."

Kieran grabs my hand and side steps Bree. "We are done here."

Bree turns to face our backs as we walk away. "You won't be able to protect her for long, Kieran."

I don't know if I was taking mental notes or having a mental breakdown, but I didn't say anything through that whole exchange. Actually, I don't say anything the whole way home until we pull into my apartment complex. I run through the scene over and over in my head. Why is Bree suddenly making it her mission to ruin my life? How does she know Kieran? And why does it feel like everyone is keeping secrets from me?

As Kieran parks, he shuts the car off and we sit there in silence for a few seconds.

Kieran turns to me, but I speak first.

"I need answers. Now." I turn to face him, and he looks at me with his piercing blue eyes. "First, how do you know Bree?"

"We are acquaintances," he says, trying to avoid the whole truth.

"Do NOT lie to me. If you have any intentions in seeing me again, I suggest you tell me the truth, or I will walk out of this car and never see you again."

Kieran sighs but continues, "We met a couple weeks ago before I started at the university. Colby and I were moving into the house that the Vampire Court rented for us and Bree happened to be jogging past. She saw both of us and obviously decided to stop to talk to us. Colby didn't want to be rude, so he invited her up to the porch to talk. After a couple minutes, Colby got a phone call that he had to take so he stepped inside, leaving Bree and I alone on the porch."

He grips the steering wheel before continuing, like what he is about to say makes him want to punch something. "The second Colby went into the house, she asked me on a date."

"You're kidding, right?" He pauses to look at me. "I mean, don't get me wrong, I can see the appeal, but she literally just stole my ex-boyfriend from me. And now she's asking you on a date?" I huff and sit back in the passenger seat with my arms crossed over my chest.

"Well, you should be happy to know that I politely declined her invitation."

"Oh?" I ask and peek over at him.

He has a big smile on his face. "Yeah. But she didn't take it very well. She said I would regret it. But I figured I would never see her again, so it didn't bother me."

"Well, obviously you don't know Bree."

"And you do?" he asks.

"Yeah, well, she used to be my best friend until she slept with my ex-boyfriend. Apparently, they were seeing each other for two months before I found out."

Kieran looked at me like he wanted to pity me. Instead, I cut him off before he could talk and gave him a winning smile.

"Hey, no biggy. Turns out she did me a favor. Looking back, she wasn't that good of a friend, and I figured Kyle and I weren't going to work out, anyway."

I'm surprised at myself for revealing such a personal thing about myself with someone I practically just met, but there's something about Kieran that makes me want to trust him.

We sit in silence for a couple more minutes until Kieran asks, "What's the second question."

Oh, right. I was in the middle of an interrogation. "Ah yes, well, what did she mean by 'You won't be able to protect me'. In case you haven't noticed. I'm pretty good at protecting myself. You know, being a witch and all."

Kieran gasps, "What? You're a witch? I had no idea."

A small laugh escapes me, but I quickly smother it. "I'm serious. I can protect myself."

Kieran nods, seeming to mull over his answer. "I don't know, Tesoro. It could be that since I'm close to you, it could lure unwanted attention while I'm here."

His answer seems sincere, but my gut tells me there is something he's hiding. Before I can ask him what the actual reason is, my phone rings.

It's Asher.

My heart rate quickens, and it's evident Kieran seems to notice, since vampires have super hearing. He offers for me to take the call, but I decline.

"No, it's fine." I know he saw who was calling because his mood seems to shift. He almost seems jealous. And I guess I was right because the next thing I know, Kieran gently grabs my hand, turning me toward him.

"I'm sorry that our night got ruined, but if you'll let me, I would like to make it up to you. Would you be willing to give me another chance and go out with me on Thursday?"

I hesitate. Obviously, I want more answers so it would make sense for me to use this date. But I also have a pull to Kieran that I can't deny. The logical part of my brain says not to go on the date. One date was enough and I should end it there. But the other side of my brain says I need to investigate not only what other things Kieran is hiding but also why I feel this pull to him.

"Fine. But you're picking the place this time." I smirk.

"Thank you, Tesoro." He kisses my knuckles and looks at me with those icy eyes.

Before I can say anything stupid, I open the door. "Goodnight. I'll see you Monday in class."

He waits until I get inside the building to leave. Once his car pulls out of the complex, I head toward my door. When I get inside, I slip my shoes off and slide down the door. There are so many questions, but all I want to do is crawl into bed and process everything tomorrow. I shoot Asher a text that I will call him tomorrow and get ready for bed. As soon as my head hits the pillow, I'm out.

CHAPTER 18
SPILL THE TEA

I wake up to the sound of the front door closing. I don't have to be on alert because only Asher and Leah have keys to my apartment. I roll over to see it's nearly eleven in the morning. Footsteps approach my bedroom, and I sit up in time to see Leah peek her head around my bedroom door.

"Good morning, sleepyhead!" she sings, as she throws my door open. "I thought we could take a walk to the coffee shop," she says cheerfully. I give her a look and she adds, "And you could tell me about your date."

"I have a better idea. Let's not." I throw my covers back over my head and pretend I can't hear her gasp in shock, like I just told her Santa isn't real.

Suddenly, Leah grabs the comforter and rips it off the bed. "Not a chance. Get up."

As if I didn't think she was serious, she gets into her super-hero stance with her hands on her hips. "We're talking about this."

Well, that doesn't sound good.

Wait a second.

Could Leah be talking about what I think she's talking about?

"Leah," I ask casually, giving up and getting out of bed. "Why do you want to talk about my date so badly that you showed up at my apartment to bribe me with coffee?"

She looks at the ground. She doesn't want to reveal how she knows about last night. So, I decide to play her little game and start asking my own questions.

I walk to my closet and open the door. "So, I assume you were over at Colby's last night?"

"I was."

"And . . . " I wait for her to continue. I finish changing and make my way out of my closet. She still hasn't divulged any more information.

"Did you happen to hear Kieran and Colby talking about the date?" I question, as I tie my hair in a messy bun.

"Maybe," she says casually, looking at her nails as if she just got them done at the nail salon and is deciding if she likes the color or not. She's waiting for me to tell my side of the story, but I'm not that easy to break. If I keep asking questions, Leah will finally give up.

"So, were you eavesdropping, or were you a part of the conversation?" I grab my jacket and we head out the front door.

"Well, it's kind of hard to eavesdrop when Kieran was practically yelling at Colby."

"Gotcha!" I yell, turning to her.

She realizes her mistake and decides it's better to come clean. "Yes, I was eavesdropping, but it's not my fault I could hear them through the door."

We exit the apartment complex and make our way to the coffee shop as she continues, "I went over to Colby's to hang out. When Kieran came back from the date with you, he was acting weird. At least, that's what Colby told me."

I remember learning that vampires could sense each other's

emotions by listening to their breathing patterns. Even though a vampire's heart doesn't beat, they still breathe like humans. Which was probably how Colby could tell something was off about Kieran. Obviously, I keep this information to myself and let Leah continue her account of last night.

"Colby went to find Kieran, and I heard something about someone showing up with a warning about not keeping someone safe anymore. When Colby came back into the room, I could tell he was thinking about something, but he turned to me and kissed me and asked if I could check in on you this morning. So here I am!"

I have to admit, Colby seems to be very sweet on Leah and I appreciate him asking if she would check in on me. However, that makes me even more suspicious of Colby and Kieran. A tiny part of my brain is happy that Kieran came home and talked about our date, but the majority of my brain tells me it's only because Bree ruined the date. I tally this as another question to ask Kieran on our date this week.

After we make it to the coffee shop and order our drinks, we sit at our usual table next to the stained-glass window. Leah gives me this look like, "Okay, now it's your turn to tell me what happened".

Our drinks arrive just in the nick of time. I take a sip to delay the inevitable. I'm hoping that once I get to the part about Bree showing up, Leah won't make a scene since we are in public. But one never knows with Leah.

I take a deep breath and dive right in.

"The date was great. I took him to Stanlee's and Thomas knocked it out of the park with the food. Also, side note, Thomas practically threatened me to bring you with me next time." Leah laughs and agrees to accompany me next time.

"After we ate, we walked around the city park and over to the pedestrian bridge." I left out the part when Kieran shared his past with me and how he became a vampire. "When we were on the bridge, I got cold and Kieran gave me his coat, then we started walking back to the car when we ran into a little bit of an issue."

Leah almost choked on her coffee. "Please. Please do not tell me that you ran into Bree."

"Yep," I take a drink of my coffee, "the one and only."

Leah clenches her coffee, and I swear I see the ceramic cup crack. I have a feeling that if we were at my apartment instead of in public, Hurricane Leah would be a Category 5 instead of a Category 1 right now.

"Hey," I say, taking her hand off her mug and holding it in mine. I give her a reassuring smile. "It's fine. Kieran handled the situation perfectly."

I also left out the part about Bree's warning about keeping me safe because Leah doesn't need any more to worry about.

Leah squeezes my hand and smiles back at me. "I'm glad Kieran was there to handle the situation," she pauses, and her face reveals all the emotion she is feeling right now, "because if I ever see Bree, you can bet you'll be bailing my ass out of jail."

I crack up laughing. "You know I got you if it ever comes to that."

We finish our coffee and Leah tells me more about Colby on our walk back to my apartment. It makes my heart happy to hear her talk about him. He makes her happy and he seems like a genuinely nice guy from what Leah tells me. Most of Colby's backstory matches up with what Kieran revealed to me. It's just the major details of being over one hundred years old and growing up in another realm he decided to leave out.

The walk from the coffee shop is quick and I watch Leah pull out of the complex before heading inside. Once I get to my apartment, my phone rings. I look at the caller ID to find Asher FaceTiming me. I quickly unlock my door and jump on the couch before answering.

"Hello?? Oh, good. You're alive," Asher jokes, wiping pretend sweat from his forehead.

He looks good. The team must have hung out at the beach because he is more tan than usual, which brings out his eyes. Before I get too distracted, I refocus and engage in the conversation.

"Yes, I'm alive and well," I quip. "How was the meet? Let's see the medal."

Asher smiles and holds up his first-place medal. "How did you know I won?"

"Just a feeling. And because you win almost every meet you go to. Pretty sure your closet is going to have a whole wall dedicated to your medals."

"Too late," he shrugs.

We laugh and talk about the competition and how his other teammates did. Asher asks how my weekend was and I graze over the subject, saying it was good and that I went and visited Thomas.

I omit the date with Kieran and the run in with Bree because if I told Asher he would be upset about the Bree situation. I'm not entirely sure how he would handle me hanging out with Kieran, but I know there would be some reprimanding about me hanging out with a vampire alone and I would rather avoid that whole conversation. Especially since my feelings for Asher and Kieran have yet to be worked through.

Before we say goodbye, Asher asks about my grandpa. "Have you heard any news about Bree and her family?"

"No, but he is probably busy with other council matters. I'm sure he'll reach out when he finds something," I assure Asher.

He nods, but his smile doesn't quite reach his eyes, making me wonder what's going on in that head of his. Seeming to hide his disappointment, he shifts gears, gracing me with his mischievous grin.

"Hey, let's get together with Leah and go out for margaritas on Tuesday before you leave to go home for fall break."

"Hell yeah! I'll reach out to the group chat. Turnt Tuesday round two!" I shout, as I fist pump obnoxiously.

"Alright, Pauly D, cool it with the fist pumps. I'll pick you up Tuesday. Asher out."

Asher ends the FaceTime call and I fire off a text to the group chat that includes Asher and Leah. Leah instantly replies.

LEAH

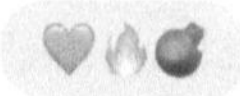

I assume that means she's in.

I spend the rest of the afternoon finishing my assignments, but since I only have class on Monday and Tuesday this week, there's not much to do.

My night ends by selecting a random movie on Netflix, but halfway through, I end up drifting off. I wake up with my arm wrapped around my jacket as a pillow and one of my legs is hanging off the side of the couch. I check my phone to see it's around two in the morning and head to my room.

After plugging my phone into the charger, I don't even bother changing into my pajamas. I flop onto my bed, grab the edge of the comforter, and roll into a cozy Raven burrito.

CHAPTER 19
BOMBS AWAY

Walking into my history class Tuesday, I find my typical seat by the window occupied. I nearly drop my textbook in surprise when Kieran looks up and waves me over to the spot next to him. Feeling anxious about seeing him, I tuck my book tighter against myself and pretend like he has no effect on me.

"You haven't even been in this class for a whole week and you're already taking my spot?" I hang my bag on the back of the chair next to Kieran. I make a point to sit and cross my arms over my chest as if I'm throwing a tantrum. "How rude."

"Do you always act like a child when you don't get your way?" Kieran asks, leaning closer to me. "It's kind of cute."

I playfully slap his shoulder and unzip my bag to grab my pen and notebook for class. Kieran does the same, but turns to face me as he takes out his own supplies, forcing me to look at his face. He winks at me, and I quickly turn back toward the desk.

Halfway through the lesson, Kieran passes me a folded note.

I have no idea when he would have written it since I didn't see him write anything but his notes in his notebook. Okay, yes, I did sneak a couple glances his way, but that's beside the point. I look at him curiously and he points to the folded sheet of notebook paper.

I unfold the note to find Kieran's adorable handwriting laid out on the paper. One problem. It's written in Italian. I bump his elbow and point to the note.

"You do know that I don't speak Italian, right?" I whisper to him.

He nods and passes me another note. I take this one and find I can read this note.

If you want to know what the first note says,

join me for a hike tomorrow.

-K

When I turn to look at him, he's ignoring me by pretending to pay attention to the lecture. However, there's a smile on his lips.

Thirty minutes later, our professor ends the lecture and releases the class early. I instantly grab the letter and shake it in Kieran's face.

"You're funny. You know I could just Google this, right?" I figured as soon as class ended, I would have Google translate the note for me.

Kieran leans back in his chair and shrugs. "You could. But it isn't Italian."

My face falls. There goes my plan. "It isn't?"

"No, it's an ancient language from the Vampire Court. So, unless you know Iydren, I doubt you'll decipher this," he says, pointing at the unknown language sitting in front of me.

"That's not fair," I pout, as I shoulder my bag and start heading out the door.

Kieran catches up to me; he knows he has me. I'm not going to pass up the chance to get more answers and learn an ancient language from the Realm of Shadows. I sneak a look at him through the side of my hair and he catches me looking.

I let out a sigh of defeat. "Fine," I say, pretending to be mad. "What time are you picking me up tomorrow?"

He stops me in my tracks by pulling me into a hug. I look up at him, surprised by the gesture, only to find him smiling sweetly at me.

"I'll pick you up at noon." Then, without warning, Kieran places the softest kiss on my cheek. He releases me before I even know what's happening and turns to walk away.

"Ciao, Tesoro!"

I stand at the fountain in the middle of the campus square in a daze.

Did he just kiss me? His lips were so soft. How did I get to the fountain? How long have I been standing here with my hand on my cheek?

I finally come to my senses, but not quick enough as I see Colby smiling at me through the water on the other side of the fountain. I really haven't talked to Colby all that much, but as he makes his way toward me around the fountain, I figure now is probably the best chance I'll get without Leah or Kieran around.

"I know that look." Colby smiles.

I plead the fifth. "What look? I don't have a look. This is just my face," I say, pointing at my face.

Colby laughs at that, which I was hoping he would. "Leah and Kieran were right; you're funny."

"Why thank you, sir," I say, turning to bow to him. "Care to take a walk? I'm on my way home from classes."

Colby nods and falls into step beside me as we walk toward the edge of campus.

"So," I start, "I have heard raving reviews from Leah. You two must enjoy each other's company," I say, giving him a knowing look.

"I know what you're thinking and no, I have not charmed her or drank any of Leah's blood."

I want to push and say more, but what Colby says next has me rethinking everything.

"What Leah and I have is organic. It's fun and pure, and I honestly believe that she's my mate."

I halt in my tracks. If anyone had been observing us, you would think I just ran into an imaginary wall with how hard I stopped. It's not uncommon for two different species to be mated. However, I haven't personally met anyone with a mate of a different species, especially not having a human mate.

"I know this is a lot to take in, but I told Kieran and I wanted to tell you since you're her best friend."

So, Kieran knows. One more question to add to the list of things to ask on our hike tomorrow.

"Does Leah know?" I panic. "She doesn't even know the supernatural world exists."

"No, she doesn't know," Colby reassures me.

We are almost to the edge of campus, but I need more answers. I pull him over to a shaded bench on a path not a lot of people take.

"So, now what?" I ask as we both sit. "You're the heir to the Vampire Court. Do you really think it's a good plan to take her, a human, to the Vampire Court?"

Colby is quiet for a while.

"I plan to see how this goes. If we can make it a couple months, I'll reveal everything to her, but I would like to stay here in the Human Realm. I won't reveal you being a witch and Asher being a shifter. I figure that maybe you would like to tell Leah yourselves."

Colby looks at me and I can't help but think I am damn lucky this man is Leah's mate. Vampires aren't typically known for their loving and compassionate side, but it's nice to know that some vampires still have a heart.

Well, you know what I mean.

"I think it would mean more coming from you rather than me." He nudges my shoulder playfully, trying to lighten the mood. "Plus, it might freak her out a little less to start with a witch, rather than a vampire." We both crack a smile because he's not wrong.

"Alright," I say, extending my hand. "You have a deal. Just give me some time to figure out how to break the news?"

Colby takes my hand and gives it a quick shake. "Of course."

I make it home in what feels like record time. I was so in my head the entire walk home that when I made it into my apartment, I questioned how I even got here safely. I clearly don't remember barging into the apartment building and unlocking my door. I fling my bag into the corner of the couch and flop down on the other end.

I finally let the emotion of everything I just learned sink in. How am I going to reveal to my best friend, someone who is practically my sister, that there is a whole other world out there filled with supernatural beings. Oh, and by the way, I'm a witch. I've been lying to you since day one.

I don't realize I'm crying until Asher walks through the front door and stops when he sees me.

"Raven, what's wrong?" He closes the space between us in four strides and sits next to me on the couch.

I wipe my face, pretending like he didn't just see me crying yet again. Can't a girl catch a break lately? Asher pulls me into a side hug and tucks me under one of his arms.

"Hey, you know you can tell me about whatever is going on." He smiles down at me.

Little does he know he just got sucked into this whole mess, considering he has also been lying to Leah. At least now I can have some support when we tell Leah. I sit up and face Asher, crossing my legs underneath myself. I decide it's better for the direct approach on this one. Time to rip off the band-aid.

"Colby told me that Leah is his mate," I watch, as Asher's face falls, but I continue before he can cut in, "and Colby wants me," I pause, then motion between ourselves, "us, to tell Leah about the supernatural world. He realizes that this is going to be a lot, and he is kind enough to let you and I reveal it to her first, since we have known her longer."

I pause for dramatic effect and to let Asher process all this. "And I agree with him." I hold up my hand to stop Asher from interrupting. "Listen to me, Asher. I would prefer to come clean to her rather than have Colby break the news. She grew up with us. She knows our fears and has been there for us through everything. Will she be mad, pissed even? Absolutely. Will she forgive us? I freaking hope so."

I take Asher's hands in mine and force him to look at me. "But we have to do this for her. We have to do this so she can finally be loved the way a person deserves and dammit, Leah deserves to be loved like that. She deserves to be happy. Colby is a good guy. I can tell because he was thoughtful enough to let us tell her. He knows how much we mean to each other, and he is willing to put his feelings on the back burner for us to do this."

I feel like one of the bricks holding me down has been removed from my chest and it's a little easier to breathe. We never had a time frame to tell Leah about the supernatural world. Asher and I agreed it was on a "need to know" basis for us to reveal our secrets. I know in my heart this is the right decision to tell her now and I hope Asher agrees. My only validation that he is on board with the plan is when he says, "She's gonna be soooo pissed."

I exhale a sigh of relief and release his hands, falling back against the couch. "Yeah, but at least now she will know why we call each other our nicknames."

We both laugh and after the laughter dies down, it goes quiet with both of us thinking of the best way to go about this.

"You know what?" Asher asks, as he gets up from the couch. "I think we should just go out tonight, have a great time, and keep pretending a little longer we don't have to have this conversation. We can go on fall break and then figure out when to tell her. Sound good?"

Leave it to Asher to make everything better when I need it.

"Deal." We shake on it when both our phones ding at the same time. Asher's phone is out first, since mine is still in my bag. He opens his phone and quickly shoves it back in his pocket.

"What was that?" I say skeptically.

"Nothing," Asher says.

"I don't believe you," I say, already diving for my bag on the other side of the couch. Asher dives for me instead and pulls me off the couch, away from my phone.

"PUT ME DOWN!" I yell, jokingly poking him in the chest.

"Okay! Okay!" he concedes. "But don't look at your phone right now. Get ready and then I'll let you have your phone."

Now I'm even more curious. I could fight him on this, but the look on his face when he read the message tells me I should just comply for once.

"Fine," I say as I walk down the hallway. I turn around just as I make it to my bedroom door. "You promise you'll let me have it when I'm done getting ready?"

He crosses his fingers over his heart and smiles. "I promise."

I get ready in record time. After sunset, the chill of the crisp evening air will begin to settle in and my light blue, oversized sweater and ripped black jeans will be perfect to defend me from the slightly cooler weather. I apply my minimalist make-up and grab my black ankle boots and head out to meet Asher.

Eyeing Asher's outfit of light blue jeans and a form-fitting black shirt, I know even he won't be safe from feeling the late night chill.

"You're going to be cold at the end of the night without a jacket," I tease.

He pulls a sweatshirt from behind the couch. "Don't worry. I've got this."

Damn him. That sweatshirt is my weakness. I bought it for him a couple years back for his birthday and it fits him like a glove, which unfortunately for me, draws extra attention from the ladies. Coming back to reality, I get down to business.

"Okay, am I able to have my phone now?" I ask sweetly.

Trying to distract me, Asher walks up to me and holds me at arm's length. "You look really good tonight, Witch."

I play into this little act by running my fingers up his chest. "Why thank you. You don't look too bad yourself. However," I say, taking a big step backward, "what's the deal? Why can't I have my phone? You promised, remember?" I say, frustrated as I put my hands on my hips.

Asher hangs his head in defeat. "I know I promised, but please don't get upset." He pleads as he hands me my phone. I check the group chat with Leah and Asher and my mood instantly shifts.

I look up at Asher. "She's not coming?"

"I'm sorry, Rave. I called her when I went to get my sweatshirt out of the truck. She said that Colby invited her to a fancy dinner downtown with his dad. She said we would understand, and that she owes us a date night."

That got my attention. "Antonio is here?"

I thought I questioned it in my head, but apparently I didn't, because it was Asher's turn to question me. "Who?"

Shit. "Antonio is Colby's dad," I say as I walk toward the kitchen. "Colby mentioned it when I spoke with him earlier," I add, hoping Asher believes me enough. Asher never had to study important things about the Realm of Shadows like I did, so he doesn't know who Antonio is. I grab two shooters from the fridge and toss him one, hoping to distract him.

"Well, looks like it's just you and me tonight, Shifter." I unscrew the top of my Fireball shooter and wait for Asher to do the same. He wants to dig for more information, but thankfully, he chooses to leave it for now. He steps closer and unscrews his shooter.

"Let the night begin," he cheers as we tap our plastic bottles together.

"Let the night begin," I echo.

CHAPTER 20

BFF? MORE LIKE BF

I don't remember leaving the bar or the drive home. I vaguely remember being carried through the front door of my apartment and being set down on the couch. It's quiet for a while, but then somewhere in the background I hear the fridge open and shut. A few seconds later, I feel my boots being gently unzipped. The soft touch of a large hand sends an electric shock up my leg, causing me to stir.

I look up to find Asher in his sweatpants. No shirt. Just sweatpants, kneeling on the ground and carefully taking my boots off.

I'm dreaming, right? This has to be a dream. I've only had one intimate dream about Asher and we didn't get farther than kissing in my room before my alarm went off. Even in my dreams, the kiss felt electric.

"Hey, drunky pants. Welcome back." His smile is so sweet that if I wasn't already melted to the couch, I would be a puddle on the floor.

Drunky pants?

Nope.

Not dreaming.

He sits back against the couch and hands me a glass of water. I immediately finish the glass and as I peel myself off the couch for a refill, my legs wobble and I start to fall. Asher quickly catches me over his lap and laughs.

"How about you go lay down and I'll get the water?"

Before I can protest, Asher cradles me to his chest and stands up. I've got to admit, I'm impressed. I could probably fight him off, but honestly, it feels nice to be so close to him and I'm too intoxicated to care. I let him carry me to my room and apparently once we enter the room, all my senses go out the window. As Asher sets me down on the bed, I pull him down with me.

I caught him off guard; his eyes widening at our compromised position when he lands on top of me. He sucks in a breath, holding it for what feels like eternity as his eyes soften, a small smile playing at his lips. We stay there for a moment, the air crackling with anticipation, before I reach up and try to kiss him. Asher quickly pulls away and sits up, leaving me wishing this truly was a dream, because if it were, I wouldn't be sitting here feeling absolutely embarrassed and rejected.

I plaster my hands on my face and begin my apologies. "I'm sorry! I don't know what came over me!" Asher doesn't say anything, so I keep babbling on. "I had way too much to drink, and then you were taking my shoes off, and you carried me to my room, and you didn't have a shirt on, which distracted me even more."

Asher pulls my hands off my face and shakes his head. "Raven, stop apologizing. I do want to kiss you, but I want you to remember our first kiss." He slides to the side of the bed and stands up before continuing, "Also, I can put my shirt on if I distract you that much." He smirks.

I mentally kick myself for letting that slip, but he really does look good. I take my pillow and smash it over my face. Asher pulls my covers up and removes the pillow from my face. I can tell he is debating whether to leave or not.

"Asher, will you stay with me?"

His face softens as he looks at me. "Always."

He strides over and turns the light off, and I scoot over so he has enough room. As I settle into my new spot on the far edge of the bed, I'm surprised when Asher wraps his arms around me and slides me closer to him. The feel of his arms around my body has my head spiraling. I heave a sigh of relief as I settle into his strong arms.

He wanted to kiss me. I didn't read the signs wrong.

His warm breath tickles my ear when he leans his head against mine and I feel a smile on his lips when he kisses my hair and says, "Goodnight, Witch."

"Goodnight, Shifter." I smile into my pillow as I fall asleep in his arms.

I wake up feeling like I'm trapped in a sauna. Half asleep, I realize I still have on last night's clothes, besides my shoes. I wiggle myself out of my jeans and take off my sweater, throwing it in the corner of the room. I snuggle back into the warmth radiating from the other side of the bed.

Without opening my eyes, I reach out and feel an arm in my bed.

An arm that's connected to a body.

A very nice and sculpted body.

It takes me a second, but everything from last night comes crashing into my brain. I open my eyes to find Asher staring right back at me.

"Well, good morning to you too," he says, with a slow, sensual smile forming on his face.

I scream and throw my pillow at him because, well, what else am I supposed to do . . . die in shame?

I wish.

Asher catches the pillow with ease and laughs. I try to roll my way out of bed, but then remember I just stripped off my clothes.

In front of him.

Dear lord, strike me now.

I stay frozen in place. Maybe if I don't talk, he'll just go away.

As if he can hear my thoughts, Asher taps me on the forehead, forcing me to open my eyes. "I'm not going away."

I put on my best annoyed face, but Asher sees right through me.

"Alright. What's wrong?" he asks, propping his head on his arm, looking at me.

"Nothing." I shake my head. "What could possibly be wrong?" I pause. I'm probably still drunk because suddenly, all my suppressed emotions come tumbling from my mouth. "Besides the fact that everyone I love always ends up leaving me." I hold up my index finger. "My dad."

"He died. He didn't choose to leave," Asher points out.

I continue and hold up a second finger, pretending not to hear him. "Now Leah. She's found her mate, even though she doesn't know it yet. Soon she'll be off frolicking with her vampire boyfriend leaving us in the rearview."

I turn and point at Asher.

"Soon you'll leave me too. You'll find your mate and leave me behind, just like everyone else. Then who will I have left?" I wipe a stray tear from my face and continue.

It's a rhetorical question, but of course, Asher replies. "Your mom? You two could really do some damage teaching young teenage witches," he jokes.

I shove his arm out from under his head, watching it hit the pillow. "I'm serious, you jerk. One day, you'll leave me too. You won't be able to control it."

In one swift movement, Asher has me pinned to the bed below him. I try to wiggle away, but he presses his hips into mine, tightening his grip on my wrists pinned above my head. My mind fizzles at his touch and my stomach clenches in a way that I've never experienced around Asher before.

"Look at me," he says tenderly. When I refuse, he asks again. This time, the sound of him begging makes my heart break. "Raven, please look at me."

I slowly turn my head. Looking at his face, I realize what I have known all along but never wanted to face.

"Someday," I say in a whisper, sliding one hand from his grip and cupping his cheek, "someday, I'll have to let you go when you find your mate and I'll be utterly alone with no one by my side. That's why I never tried to be anything more than friends. It would make the heartbreak easier. At least that's what I told myself."

Holding my gaze, Asher says something that will resonate with me forever. "I will never leave you. No matter where you go, I'll find you. I'll be there. I will always protect you, Raven."

Before I know what's happening, Asher leans down and lays a soft, feathery kiss on my lips. When our lips meet, it's like an explosion of colors in my mind until one color remains. He releases my hand and slips his hand under my head, deepening the kiss.

His cinnamon scent wraps around us, invading my senses and making me want more of him. The sensation in my stomach moves lower as I arch my body into his and he releases a low, sexy moan. The sound has my body reacting in ways I never knew could be possible. Asher slowly unwinds his hand from my hair and gently brushes his knuckles down my face, trailing down my arms, then to my stomach. Excitement zips through my body as I wind my fingers through his soft, shaggy hair.

Suddenly, a hundred snippets of us flash through my head and it feels like time stops as I see them. Asher and I when we were kids when we first met. If you can believe it, I was the shy one at the time. Us as kids playing in the pool in my backyard while our parents socialized on the back deck. Me chasing Asher in his collie form in my backyard.

As the images progress in age, most images are of me, carefree and smiling ahead, looking out at the distance, while Asher looks at me. In that moment, he looks at me like I'm someone he can't live without.

The last image shows us now, lying in bed facing each other, holding hands. The picture zooms in and that's when I see a single magenta string coming from both of our chests. Curious about the glowing string, I reach out and gently tug it.

Suddenly, I'm thrust back into the moment. I soften the kiss and Asher pulls away, leaving just inches between us. That kiss put my dream kiss to shame.

"Do you believe me now?" Asher says, placing a gentle kiss on my lips. "I will never leave you."

"I believe you," I whisper. I saw the mating bond. I even felt it. It's real. "How did you know?" I ask as he rolls onto his side, facing me just like the last image in my head. I reach out and touch his chest, right over his heart where I saw the string.

He smiles, taking my necklace in his hand and running his thumb over the black diamond. "I've always known. It's always been you."

I avoid his eyes as shame begins to eat away at me. How has he always known, and it took this long for me to realize it? How could he be so patient with me? Before I can get too far into my self-pity, Asher slowly and delicately places soft kisses on my temple, whispering in my ear.

"It's okay," he assures me.

He continues down the side of my face until he reaches my

neck, where I let out a satisfied sigh. I place my hand under his chin and bring his lips to mine.

Just as quickly as the kiss started, Asher pulls away.

Frustrated, I sit up and face him. I feel myself starting to lose control of my powers. The night stand next to my bed starts slowly shaking, causing the lamp that's settled on top to wiggle its way toward the edge. "How can it be okay? How could you know I was your mate and be okay with watching me go out with other guys?"

Asher sits up and takes my hands. "First of all, I need you to look at me."

Asher holds my gaze and I feel myself starting to calm down as the table stops shaking next to us.

"Second, I wasn't okay with you dating other guys. However," he flashes me one of those brilliant signature smiles, "I knew you were my mate, and it would never work out with them."

I burst out laughing. "Okay, Mr. Know-It-All."

And just like that, my powers are back in check and my mood is relatively brighter. When I was a little girl, I always dreamed of the day I found my mate. I figured we would be strolling down a busy street, lock eyes, and instantly know we belonged together. Even though it didn't happen the way I imagined, a part of me always hoped I would be mated with Asher. I know it sounds so cliché, but he feels like my safe place.

I hop out of bed and run out to the living room, leaving Asher in bed.

"Hey! Where are you going, my little witch?!" he calls after me.

I pull his hoodie over my head as I enter my room.

"Well, I suppose this is officially mine now, right?"

CHAPTER 21

After reluctantly letting Asher leave to get ready for practice, I head back to my room and grab my phone from the charger. I swipe through my missed notifications and find I have a text from an unknown number.

UNKNOWN

> It's Kieran. I hope you don't mind, but I asked Leah for your number. Do you mind if we push things back until four? I'm sure you heard, but Antonio is in town, and he has requested to meet with me.

I instantly freeze. How am I supposed to go on this date with Kieran, knowing Asher is my mate? I take a couple of deep breaths to calm myself down and mentally make a pros and cons list in my head.

Cons: Asher would be livid if he found out I went out with Kieran.

Pros: I still have questions I need answers to, and Kieran is the best source for this information right now. I could also let him know that the only thing I have to offer is my friendship, nothing more.

Well, it looks like the pros outweigh the cons here. If it comes down to it, I can justify to Asher the reason I went on the hike with Kieran.

RAVEN

No problem! I'll see you at four!

I swear time is crawling by. When four rolls around, it feels like I've been waiting for ten hours. I just finished getting dressed when my phone dings.

KIERAN

I'm outside. Want me to come up?

I almost reply, letting him know the front door is open, but then I remember vampires have a very good sense of smell. Kieran would be able to tell that Asher was here merely hours ago and somehow it makes me nervous. It shouldn't, but it does. Kieran knows that Asher is one of my best friends. Of course, his scent would be all over my apartment. Hopefully, even though I showered, Kieran shouldn't be able to pick up Asher's cinnamon undertones on me. I quickly lace up my hiking boots and fix my message before heading out the door.

RAVEN

No need. I'll be down in a second.

Kieran is leaning on the hood of his car when I make my way out the main door. I catch a glimpse of him scowling at his phone, but when he sees me, his face warms into a small smile. He stands and walks over to the passenger side to open my door.

"I hope everything went okay with Antonio," I say as I slide into the seat. Kieran doesn't say anything as he closes my door, so I know that's not a good sign.

Kieran picked the place where we are hiking today and doesn't say a word the whole thirty-minute drive out of the city. The only sound is the radio and sometimes a sigh from me as I watch us climb into the foothills of the mountains. I have a whole list of things I need to talk over with Kieran, but I let him have his quiet time in the car to work through whatever happened with Antonio. It'll probably be better to bring up my questions while we hike.

Kieran finally speaks when we pull into the small parking lot and he shuts the engine off. "I'm sorry," he says, placing his head on the steering wheel. "I wanted today to be fun and exciting. My meeting with Antonio did not go as I planned."

Uh duh. I wanted to tell him. I figured that was the case when we had a silent car ride up here. Instead, I turn on my charm and try to cheer him up.

"Hey, forget that jerk. I'm sure whatever you two are arguing about will pass, and one day you'll both have a good laugh about it."

He pins me with the most adorable "Oh really?" looks I've ever seen.

"You don't even know what it was about, and you certainly don't know Antonio."

"You're right. I don't," I say, getting out of the car, making Kieran do the same.

"But I do know two things."

I wait until Kieran locks the car and meets me at the start of the hiking trail.

"One," I say as we start the hike, "I know that you're a great guy and you won't let it affect you for too long."

Kieran just rolls his eyes.

"And two. You're both old as dirt and live forever, so someday it'll work itself out."

"Again, with the age thing. I secretly think you're obsessed with me," he jokes.

"Yeah, yeah. You wish."

We hike about a half mile in silence, which gives me enough time to formulate the order in which I want to ask my questions. Before I'm about to ask my first question, there's rustling in the trees behind us. This trail isn't a hot spot for hikers, and we haven't seen anyone else on the trail yet, so I figure it's just my imagination.

Not even a minute later, I hear rustling behind us again. This time, I turn to Kieran and grab his arm.

"Okay," I whisper, "tell me you heard that."

Kieran stops walking and bends down as he whispers back to me. "I didn't hear anything."

I push him away and continue walking. "Oh, come on. You're a vampire and have super hearing. You really didn't hear that?"

"What did it sound like?" he asks.

I look around skeptically as we continue to hike. "Like soft footsteps in the fallen leaves."

"I didn't hear anything, but I'll tell you what?" He takes my hand and interlocks our fingers. "I'll hold your hand so nothing can happen to you, okay?" My body immediately stiffens under his touch, but there's something inside me that softens when his thumb brushes over my hand. I can't put my finger on what it is, but whatever feeling it may be makes this whole situation even harder.

Yes, I can admit that I might have some small feelings developing for Kieran, but nothing compares to what I feel about Asher. I'm about to pull my hand away and explain about Asher and I when Kieran continues.

"Thank you for giving me another chance at our date. After the meeting with Antonio, I was really looking forward to seeing you."

I look up at him; he is genuinely happy I'm here with him.

His stone cold expression in the car has melted away to reveal his goofy and playful personality again.

"Somehow, when I'm around you, I feel like everything that clouds my mind gets washed away when I see you smile or hear you laugh."

I mentally kick myself.

How the heck am I supposed to break it to him that we can only be friends when he shares things like that?

I smile back at him and drop his hand, giving him a short side hug. "I'm glad I could be of assistance to you."

It was meant to be sarcastic, but somehow it felt genuine. I promise myself once we get back to the car, I'll tell him everything.

We finally arrive at our destination, and it's like a scene from a postcard. Nestled on the hillside is an enormous waterfall. The main waterfall extends far above our heads and it's at least five feet wide, with a few smaller streams to either side. The water glistens in the sun, giving the illusion of tiny rainbows cascading down with the water.

On the opposite side of the waterfall is the most amazing view. Stepping close to the edge reveals the valley we hiked up to get here. The trees have just started to change colors, giving way to a tie dye of colors below us. I wish I could capture this moment and save it forever.

Next to me, Kieran suddenly stiffens. "Get behind me," he growls as he steps in front of me.

When I peek around Kieran, I don't see anything. I'm about to step around him when I hear laughter coming straight ahead from where we entered the clearing.

"What a sight to behold; am I right?"

Stepping out from the covering of the trees is a man I've never seen before and thank goodness for that, because this man is intimidating. He clearly works out every day, otherwise the steroids he's taking are definitely working.

I catch a glimpse of Kieran. He must know this guy, because he clenches his jaw.

"What are you doing here, Sven?" Kieran asks, repositioning me behind him.

Sven casually strolls forward like he came here to enjoy the hike and nothing else. "You didn't think Antonio would let you stall forever, did you?"

Wait, hold the phone. Antonio sent this Arnold Schwarzenegger looking mofo here? What does he mean by Kieran stalling? Before I can ask any questions, Kieran beats me to it.

"So, Antonio sent a lowly dog after me? How sweet."

Sven releases the most sinister laugh and looks straight at me. "Give me the girl and I'll think about letting you live. We all know you're Antonio's favorite, so I don't think he'd take it well finding out I had to kill you."

Now, wait a damn minute. I know the Terminator did not just say that he was here to kidnap me, right? They can't know about my powers, can they? As if to confirm my fear, Kieran starts to push me backward.

"Raven, I need you to run. I need you to keep running no matter what you hear," he says, not taking his eyes off Sven.

My stomach twists as I look between the two vampires in front of me. My anger starts to flare as I come to terms that Kieran is here for me and my powers. He was never here for anything more than that.

I summon my fire element and force my arm to heat up. Kieran quickly releases my hand and turns to face me.

"I can handle myself. Even though I'm pissed at you, I'm not leaving you here to fight this guy on your own. I can help. I'm a witch, remember?" I say, as I wiggle my fingers in his face.

"Oh, that's cute. C'mon, Kieran. Let her stay and show me just how powerful she is."

I sidestep Kieran and throw a fireball at Sven's head. For as massive as he is, he quickly tucks and rolls out of the way right before it makes contact with his annoying face. I smile and mentally pat myself on the back, but regret my choice of action when I see the murderous look on Sven's face as he barrels straight toward us.

CHAPTER 22

CALL ME THOR

Kieran launches himself at Sven before he can reach me. Just as Kieran grabs him, Sven lands a powerful punch to Kieran's face, throwing him off balance. As Sven reaches to grab Kieran, I take that opening to hurl another fireball at Sven.

This time, it hits him in the back, catching his jacket on fire. He's taken by surprise and stumbles forward a few steps toward the edge of the cliff. He quickly sheds his jacket, throwing it over the edge. The distraction gives Kieran enough time to fade to where Sven is near the cliff.

The next thing I know, it's a tangled mess of bodies. They quickly fade side to side as they fight, making it impossible for my eyes to keep up with the movement. I've never seen vampires fight before. Their speed is incredible. There's no way I can compete with them and the thought has me second guessing why I stayed.

Suddenly, Sven is thrown against the rock wall behind the waterfall. While Sven is recovering, Kieran takes a quick moment to yell over at me. "Raven! You need to leave. NOW!"

I mean, it doesn't sound like a bad idea . . . but I can't just leave him. Even though I'm angry at Kieran, that small, annoying feeling I can't shake keeps me rooted in place. Just as I'm about to tell him I'm staying, Sven runs straight at me. I channel the water from the waterfall and thrust it at him, wrapping him in the vortex. He fights to make his way out of the vortex, but I twist the water and throw him back at the wall, releasing him into the pool below.

I don't see the knife flying toward me until it's too late. I cry out in pain when the knife lodges into my thigh. As I fall to the ground and clutch the knife, Kieran fades to my side but not before Sven rams into him mid fade.

Kieran yells in agony as Sven takes another knife and slashes it across his chest. Nothing too deep, but enough to make him falter. Sven takes advantage of that opening and grabs Kieran, twisting him around so Sven has him in a choke hold.

All I can do is stare in horror. Kieran is trying his best to get out of the hold, but it's not working. Sven reaches into his back pocket and takes out another knife, this one smaller than the rest, and plunges it into Kieran's chest.

Time seems to slow down.

I think I scream as Kieran's body falls to the ground.

His body goes stiff, and his face is starting to lose its color, but all I see is red. I watch as Sven laughs and steps over Kieran's body, stalking toward me. My powers come to life like they never have before. The sky instantly turns black as we hear one loud, thunderous roar come from above.

The wind picks up enough for Sven to have a hard time closing the distance between us. I use the rage inside me to summon the power I've just unleashed and start to levitate two feet off the ground, giving me the advantage over Sven. He's still a few feet away from reaching me when I summon the water from the waterfall to freeze his feet to the ground. He looks down at his frozen feet, and when his eyes meet mine, I can almost feel the fear radiating from him.

He's never seen a witch do what I'm about to do.

I spare a quick glance over at Kieran, and he's still not moving. I reach down and whimper as I pull the knife from my leg. I can't see the blood as it trickles down my thigh, but the wet sensation hints that I'm losing a lot of blood. I ignore it for now, raising the crimson stained knife above my head as the sky swirls above me.

Channeling all my energy from the storm above, I conjure a single lightning bolt and wrap it around the knife. I fix my gaze back on Sven and his face falls.

"This is going to hurt," I sneer.

I throw the lightning encased knife right at Sven's heart. He doesn't even have time to blink before the lightning bolt helps the knife cut clean through his heart, pinning it to the tree behind him. I watch Sven look down and grab at the hole where his heart used to be right before he falls forward, his lifeless body hitting the ground hard.

I instantly drop to the ground and crawl to where Kieran's body is still laying, unmoving. The wind has now picked up, thanks to my panic, and when I finally reach Kieran, I nearly pass out from the pain and from how much blood I've already lost. The only thing keeping me upright is when I turn Kieran's body over, he slowly opens his eyes. I sigh in relief but know he is still barely holding on.

Kieran tries to reach for my injured leg but is too weak to even pick up his hand. I assess him up and down; his body slowly turning gray. The knife in his heart didn't completely pierce through, which slows down the dying process for vampires.

I need to remove the knife before it's too late.

I look at Kieran's face, and he nods. He is too weak to remove the knife himself. I grab the handle of the knife with one hand and place my other hand on his shoulder to steady his body for when I pull the knife out. I take a deep breath and let it out.

I can do this.

I count to three and slowly remove the knife. Once the knife is out, I throw it to the side and focus on Kieran. I assumed that when I took the knife out of his body, he would miraculously get better, but nothing happened.

"I don't get it. Taking the knife out was supposed to heal you. Why aren't you healing?"

I'm starting to panic when Kieran's hand brushes my leg. Kieran turns his face toward me, and I can tell it takes a lot for him to speak.

"The knife," he pants, "was coated in poison."

I look over at the knife and see the remnants of a green substance on the end. I know enough about the supernatural world to know that the only thing capable of slowing down a vampire is Hartsbane. Once it's in the bloodstream of a vampire, it slowly neutralizes their nervous system until they can't move.

"How can I help?" I beg. I don't have much time until I pass out from my own blood loss. Suddenly, I realize what will help Kieran. "Drink from me," I demand.

Kieran's face drops. This is the only way I know how to save him. He slowly shakes his head, as it's now the only part of his body still able to move. Even as he tries to argue with me, his fangs start to extend.

I use my earth element to move a boulder closer to us. Kieran already knows who I am and what powers I possess, so there's no need to hide anymore from him. I grab Kieran's shoulders and help him sit up, resting his back against the boulder.

"This is the only way to save you," I plead, as I brush my hair away from my neck.

Kieran turns his head, refusing to drink from me. A bloody tear slides down his cheek as he turns back to face me. "I'm sorry," he whispers.

His breathing is becoming shallower. I don't have a lot of time left to save him.

Realizing this, something inside me breaks. "I won't accept your half ass apology!" I yell in his face. I can hardly hear myself as the wind whips between us. "You're going to drink from me and you're going to get better. And when you do, I'm going to kick your ass for whatever you're keeping from me." I tilt my head, revealing my neck to him. "Now drink."

Kieran reaches up and brushes a soft kiss to the side of my neck. I shudder as his fangs scrape across my skin. Suddenly, the wind stops and creates a small funnel around us. Everything becomes still inside our little circle, but outside the circle, the wind is still howling.

There's a quick pinch, then everything inside me explodes. Kieran takes his first pull of my blood, causing me to reach out and grab his shoulders to steady myself. I close my eyes and even though my body is cold from the wind and the blood loss, I feel like I've been lit up inside. My body is burning up, but in a good way.

Kieran must be getting his strength back because he shifts my body, so I'm cradled in his lap. I lean up against him to give him better access, but mostly because I'm too weak to hold myself up.

He drinks deeply and I start to drift away, but before I do, there's a flutter in my chest. I force one eye open to see a stunning dark blue string appear from Kieran's chest. I follow the string and realize that the other end is connected to me.

That's the last thing I see before I pass out.

CHAPTER 23

HELLO MATE(S)

Is this what dying feels like, because if so, I'm loving it. My body feels weightless as I fall back into a giant white fluffy cloud. Obviously, clouds aren't made of silk, but when I reach out, my hands run over the most amazingly soft material. Someone should be offering me champagne in a glass flute and feeding me grapes off a vine.

Laying with my back on the cloud, I hold my hand up and examine it. Taking a closer look, little bolts of electricity run under my skin, illuminating my hand slightly. I sit up and examine the spot on my thigh where the knife hit me, thinking there would be a hideous scar staring back at me. Instead, it looks as though there was never a trace of a wound. The skin is perfectly intact, beside a faint line where the skin was mended back together.

The last thing I remember is losing a decent amount of blood and passing out. I try to remember what happened after that, but I come up with nothing. The only remnants of the event is the metallic taste still lingering in my mouth.

I roll over onto my stomach and peer down at the vast blue sky below me. Ever so softly, a low voice whispers above me. I roll back over toward the sound and find nothing but more endless blue sky. Then I hear the voice again, except this time there's a second voice. The voices start getting closer and it sounds like they are arguing over something, but I can't make out any words.

Out of nowhere, a strong gust of wind blows through my cloud, disintegrating it. Panic fills me as I start to fall, making my powers surge. I throw my hands out in front of me, trying to slow my fall, but it's no use. My wind element can't catch me as fast as I'm falling. My hands start to brighten and I channel the surging energy I feel building inside myself.

Realizing I have seconds to use this new energy before I hit the ground, which is rapidly approaching, I throw my hands back out with as much force as I can muster and aim it right at the ground, hoping something will slow me down. A bright flash of light expels from my hands, blinding me briefly before I'm about to slam into the ground.

I jolt up in bed, throwing a super energy ball right through the wall in front of me, silencing the two voices that were just arguing. My eyes slowly adjust when the light fades from the room, revealing Asher and Kieran staring at me, clearly surprised by what I just did.

I look between each of them, wondering what the heck is going on, but before I can process anything, it feels as though all my energy left my body with the energy ball. Unable to hold myself up any longer, my body instantly collapses back against the bed. Asher is the first one to come back to reality. However, it's Kieran who catches me, gently laying me down on the bed.

With his hand still under my head for support, Kieran leans down and lays his forehead against mine.

"I thought I lost you. Don't ever scare me like that again."

I look up to reassure him I'm okay, but before I can speak, Asher cuts in.

"Kieran. Take your cold, dead hands off my mate. Now."

That brings me back to reality.

Asher and I are mates.

I was attacked by another vampire and gave Kieran my blood because he was dying.

Oh god, Kieran and I are mates, too.

And he fed me his blood?

I'm not sure about the last part, but I'm pretty confident since that's why I taste a metallic substance lingering on my tongue.

WHAT THE HELL IS GOING ON?!

Kieran slowly stands and turns to face Asher. "What did you say?" Kieran questions in a deadly tone.

Asher takes a step forward, challenging Kieran. "You heard me."

I don't have time for these two to duke it out. My head is pounding, and I think I almost died?

Yep.

Pretty sure I almost died.

"Alright, listen," I say, trying to sit up. That was a huge mistake because both men practically dive toward me, trying to help. I hold out a hand to keep them both frozen in place with my powers.

"Rave, unfreeze me so I can help you," Asher begs.

"No," I shoot back. I slowly sit up and readjust the pillow behind me so I can lie up against the headboard.

Wait. Whose bed is this??

Just another question to tally on the list. Once I'm comfortable and my head has stopped spinning, I pin both men in front of me with a look that says "I mean business".

"It's my turn to demand answers. I'm going to let you two go now, but if either of you move an inch, I will freeze you in place again. Is that understood?"

Kieran and Asher both nod reluctantly. I lower my hand, unfreezing them.

"First of all, where the hell am I?"

"You're in my house," Kieran answers.

"And why is that?" I ask, hoping to fill in the gap from after I passed out.

"Well, after you passed out, I had to take you somewhere and I figured the safest place to let you heal would be at my place."

"And why did she pass out?" Asher asks skeptically.

I answer for Kieran, knowing Asher is less likely to kill me than Kieran at this point.

"Kieran and I went for a hike and ran into another vampire. He attacked us and I was hit in the thigh with a knife and Kieran was poisoned. I killed the vampire that attacked us by pulling the knife out of my leg and running it straight through his heart."

I take a deep breath to prepare myself for the next part. "When I pulled the knife from Kieran's chest, we noticed that it had traces of Hartsbane on it. He wasn't going to survive unless . . . "

I don't get to finish the rest of the sentence before Asher's fist flies into the side of Kieran's jaw. Kieran could have easily caught the punch, but he let Asher hit him.

"Tell me you didn't feed off her!"

"Asher, stop!" I plead, freezing him in place again.

Asher looks at me, his face distraught. "Raven, please tell me you didn't let him feed from you."

I grab the sheet and wring it with my hands, trying to calm myself down. I don't need my powers going haywire again. Not after everything that has already happened.

"He would have died, Asher. He would have died if I didn't help him."

"I don't care!" Asher yells, startling me.

I have never seen Asher so upset before. Especially with me. We've always had our little arguments, but he's never raised his voice like this. His words cut straight to my heart, making me feel like I'm the bad person for saving Kieran.

"Why would you save him?" Asher asks, throwing a disgusted look over at Kieran.

This time, Kieran answers for me, "Because I'm her mate, too."

CHAPTER 24
THE TRUTH HURTS

I swear if I wasn't holding them in place, Asher would have passed out. His face falls, and he looks as though he's about to collapse. Feeling guilty, I release him from the hold and reach for his hand.

"I'm sorry," I say, as he takes my hand in his.

"How?" he asks, settling beside me on the bed.

I turn to Kieran for answers. "You're the oldest here. You must know something, right?"

"Again, with the age thing," Kieran teases. I give him a small smile as he walks around the bed and settles on my other side.

"Yes, I've been around for a long time, but I've never come across someone with two mates. I would have to search the archives at the Seneca Library back in the Realm of Shadows to see if this had ever happened."

"Well, that doesn't do us any good now," I say, leaning back against the headboard. I just found out that Asher is my mate less than a day ago, and now I've come to find out I have two mates? My mind literally cannot comprehend right now. Oddly enough, with them both so close to me, I instantly feel relaxed. My headache begins to fade and my energy feels like it's starting to come back.

Another question pops into my head. "Asher, how did you even find me?"

Asher squeezes my hand and meets my gaze. His green eyes soften; his little outburst of emotion is far behind him.

"I felt your fear. I tried calling you, but you wouldn't answer. I called Leah, and she said that Colby mentioned something about you going on a hike with Kieran."

He shoots a look of disgust over at Kieran. "Just as I was about to shift and fly to where you were, I felt a sharp pain, and then nothing. I didn't know what happened. One minute, I could feel you through our bond, then the next, it was like a curtain came down and I couldn't feel anything."

I reached over and put my other hand on Asher's leg. "I'm sure that must have been scary."

"You have no idea. I didn't know what to do, so I did the only thing I could do. I asked Leah for Kieran's address, and I came straight here. When I walked in and found him leaning over you, I lost it, but then you woke up and threw that energy ball." He sighs in relief. "I was just glad that you were alive."

"How did I throw that energy ball, anyway?" I turn, directing the question to Kieran.

Kieran thinks for a second, then shrugs his shoulders. "I don't know. It has to do with the energy you absorbed when I fed you my blood."

"I knew it!" I shout, as Asher reaches for Kieran.

Asher looks murderous. "You did what?!"

Kieran reaches over and slides me closer to him, trying to protect me as I try to wrangle Asher back down, but it's no use and I end up freezing Asher in place again. I understand why he's upset. If I were to die with vampire blood running through my system, I would come back as a vampire. My magic would be gone; just as if a dragon or shifter were turned into a vampire, their powers would die along with their supernatural powers. Typically, it takes anywhere from two to three days for human bodies to cycle through vampire blood.

"I had to. She lost enough blood with the knife in her leg, but it would have killed her if I didn't after she gave me her blood."

"You mean YOU would have killed her," Asher seethes.

"It was the only way to save her! She would have died if I didn't give her my blood."

"She wouldn't be in this situation if you weren't here in the first place! So why are you really here, Kieran?"

Kieran's arms tighten around me, which makes Asher push more.

"Let me guess, you saved her so you can hand her over to the Vampire Court? You figured out she could wield all four elements and now she's a bargaining chip," Asher accuses.

As I turn my head to look at Kieran, his face has gone completely blank. When we were on the mountain, the idea did cross my mind that Kieran could be here to capture me, but I somehow couldn't get myself to believe it. And now? Looking at Kieran's closed off face, I know Asher's right. The last week has been a setup; a trap from the very beginning that I played right into.

"Tell me that's not true," I whisper, holding onto a tiny sliver of hope that this is all just a misunderstanding.

"He's right," Kieran says in the softest voice.

I use what is left of my strength to create a gust of wind to push Kieran up against the wall.

"Raven, please let me explain!"

Kieran tries to break free, but it's no use. I use the rest of my energy to keep him in place. After a few more minutes of fighting, he finally stops, realizing I'm not letting him go.

"I was sent here on a mission from the Vampire Court. We received a tip that someone in the city might be able to possess all four elements, and I was sent here to investigate. I didn't know why at the time, but I kept getting drawn to an area near Victor Street. The first time I saw you, you looked like you were running from something. Then, out of nowhere, the skies turned nearly black, and it started raining."

"Yeah, that was when I found Kyle and Bree together. I didn't know where else to go, so I just ran."

Kieran looks at me with sadness in his eyes. "I knew it was you. I knew in that instant it was you I was sent to find. I sent word to Colby, and we formulated a plan. The night of your birthday, we were supposed to capture you and bring you in for questioning at a warehouse on the outside of the city, but then Colby saw Leah and he knew instantly that she was his mate."

"So, what then?" I counter, slowly getting out of bed. "You were supposed to take over and do it instead?"

"Yes, I told Colby I would get close to you instead. Colby was having second thoughts on bringing you in because it meant hurting his mate by taking away her best friend. I couldn't let Colby jeopardize his happiness. The plan was to see if you were a danger to yourself or others around you."

"We tried to stall long enough to figure out a plan to throw off people from looking for you. However, I didn't anticipate Antonio would grow impatient and send someone else to bring you in. They must have been spying on my movements and figured out you were the target. I genuinely care for you and didn't want you to get hurt because of me. That's why I told you to run."

Kieran lowers his head, avoiding making eye contact with me. "I didn't know we were mates until you healed me."

"Oh, so I was just a mission to you until you found out we were mates?" I throw my hands in the air. "Then what? Were you even going to tell me all of this? How am I supposed to hide from the Vampire Court now?!"

Asher lays a comforting hand on my shoulder and I ease into

his touch, trying to rack my brain around what I just heard. I thought the worst was behind me until Kieran looked up, his eyes blazing.

"You want to know about deception and lies?!" Kieran asks. "At least I'm willing to tell you the truth. Asher has been lying to you for years."

Asher tightens his grip on my shoulder.

"What are you talking about?" I accuse Kieran.

"Go on, Asher. Tell her how you were selected to be her personal protector. Antonio had one of his minions dig up your little family ties to Raven."

"Enough!" Asher shouts at Kieran.

They both start to argue, but I can't make out the words they're saying. My head starts to pound again. I feel woozy and drop to a knee, losing my hold on Kieran. They both reach out, trying to help me.

"DON'T TOUCH ME!" I scream, throwing my hands over my head.

Suddenly, there is no more arguing. It's completely silent and when I open my eyes, I know why. Looking down from my kneeling position, I push fallen strands of hair out of my eyes to see concrete and painted yellow lines.

Confused, I look up at the building in front of me and realize where I am. I just teleported right outside the coffee shop.

Shit.

This is just freaking perfect. Not only did I use the last of my strength to teleport, unwillingly, but it's also barely five in the morning and I look like I just stepped out of a zombie movie. My leggings have a hole in the thigh from the knife and my shirt has zig zagging burn marks spread all over, which makes it look like it's been hit by lightning.

Well, technically it was.

As I toss my long, dark, tangled, braided hair back over my shoulder, I stand up from the curb of the coffee shop and start the journey back to my apartment. I only get two steps from the building when I feel a sharp object prick the side of my neck.

A second later, a stream of black dots swarm over my vision. My eyelids flutter and I'm barely able to keep them from closing. My body is so numb I don't even feel the pain as I slam into the concrete.

My cheek meets the curb of the sidewalk with a sickening crack, but I can't make a sound. I'm completely paralyzed. My racing heart starts to slowly beat back in rhythm and my vision fades as whatever drug I was injected with takes hold of me, plunging me into a dark abyss.

CHAPTER 25

THEN THERE WERE TWO

ASHER

Kieran and I reach for Raven. Suddenly, she's gone, leaving the two of us falling to the floor on top of each other.

"Get off me!" I yell, pushing him off me. I scramble to my feet and shove him out of my way.

"What the hell was that?" Kieran questions, pulling himself up.

Not wanting to spend another minute in the same room with him, I head toward the bedroom door, but Kieran fades in front of me, halting my departure. "Get out of my way, vampire. I have to go find Raven." I try to sidestep him, but he matches my moves.

"Asher, what the hell was that? Where is she?" Kieran pleads.

I grab the bridge of my nose, shaking my head. Not even ten minutes ago, we were at each other's throats. When I walked into

Kieran's room and found him leaning over her, I thought the worst. But then Raven sat up, and I felt her pulse in her wrist. He hadn't turned her into a blood-sucking monster.

Even though I snapped at Raven for feeding Kieran her blood, I could never truly be mad at her. She would never willingly let someone die if she could help it. Unlike me. I was ready to snap Kieran's neck just for touching her.

"I need answers first before I can decide to trust you," I say, leaning against the doorframe.

Kieran nods and pulls a chair from the desk in the corner of his room. "Okay, sure."

"Great. Who is Antonio, and how did he know I'm Raven's protector?" I vaguely remember Raven saying something about Antonio, but I can't remember what it was right now with my mind in shambles.

Kieran purses his lips, weighing his answer. "Antonio is the leader of the Vampire Court and also happens to be Colby's father."

My mind shifts into overdrive as I remember Raven telling me that Antonio is Colby's father. I nearly have a heart attack with what this means. Colby is the heir to the Vampire Court and is mated to Leah.

Over my dead body.

There's no way I'm going to let Colby take Leah to the Vampire Court.

As if Kieran knows what I'm thinking, he continues, "Colby doesn't plan on taking Leah to the Vampire Court. It's far too dangerous, and I agree."

"Well, at least we agree on one thing," I mumble. "And how did he know I'm her protector?"

Kieran stands, taking a cautious step forward. "Antonio has spies everywhere. He's been keeping tabs on Artemis Montclair for years. Personal vendetta or something. I overheard Antonio in one of his briefings saying that there was a shifter assigned to protection duty over Artemis' granddaughter. At the time, it seemed like nothing, but when I arrived in town and figured out Raven was Artemis' granddaughter. Well, the pieces started falling together."

Kieran raises one perfectly trimmed eyebrow. "I'm assuming you never told her?"

I grit my teeth, clenching my fist behind my back. I swear I'm not a violent person, but Kieran makes me want to change that. "No, she was never meant to know. All I was told was that with her powers, she would be hunted and Artemis needed people he could trust to protect her."

Kieran smiles, putting the pieces together. "And he trusted you because you're her mate."

"Yes. I eventually told Artemis that I believed Raven was my mate. From then on, I've been silently playing the role of protector."

"Don't underestimate Antonio," Kieran warns. "His network of spies runs deep. You need me to help keep Raven safe, and deep down, you know it."

I hate that he's right. My options are very limited and I don't want to involve Raven's mom in this. Artemis made me swear that if things were ever to get bad, not to involve Moriah. He didn't want something to happen to Moriah and for Raven to lose both parents.

With no other viable options presenting themselves right now, I have no choice but to trust Kieran. He did go against Antonio after all and tried to save Raven in his own way. I hate that I'm about to reveal this secret to him, but since he seems to genuinely care for Raven, it's better to have him on our side. The more people on our side, the more protection for Raven. Her safety is my top priority.

"Listen. I don't like you. I probably never will, BUT Raven's safety is my number one priority. I need your word that you're serious about her. About her being your mate and that you will do everything you can to keep her safe." I pin him with a look, trying to see any sign that he's lying to me.

"I just saved her from a vampire attack. Do you think I would have done that if I didn't care? And that was without knowing we were mates."

I internally wince at his admission of them being mates as I cross my arms over my chest, waiting for him to answer my question. I waited YEARS, trying to cover my feelings the best I could until Raven finally figured out we were mates. I don't know why it took her so long to realize. When I first laid eyes on her, I knew she was the one for me. Hearing another man, let alone a vampire, admit that he is her mate too makes me want to punch through a wall. Again, I swear I'm not violent.

"I swear," he says, placing his hand over his chest, "I will never put her in harm's way. You have my word."

"Okay. Well, as you can see for yourself, Raven has the ability to teleport, and she doesn't know how to control it yet."

Something must click in Kieran's head, because his eyes go wide. He tries to turn and leave, but I grab him, pinning him against the door.

"What do you know?" I growl in his face. "Unfortunately, we are in this together now. If you know something," I say, letting him go, "spill it."

He brushes his chest like I may have wrinkled his shirt, which somehow annoys me more.

"I remembered something Antonio said about when the barrier was first created. He said the witch who created it had power like he's never seen." Kieran steps around me and grabs his phone from the bedside table, quickly firing off a text to someone. "She could control all four elements and teleport, just as Raven can. The only way the barrier could be dissolved was with someone just as powerful as the one who created it."

Well, shit.

"By now, I'm sure Antonio has figured out that Raven is his

key to bringing down the barrier." He looks down at his phone again and cusses. "Asher, I need you to go out and see if you can find her."

"Why the hell aren't you coming to help?" Who is this guy? He thinks he can just boss me around. No way.

He looks at me and raises an eyebrow. "Did you forget? I have human blood in my system. I can't go out during the day for at least two days."

Yep. I hate him.

"Fine," I sigh. I dig into my back jean pocket and pull out my phone and toss at him. He catches it with ease and looks at me, confused. "Put your number in my phone in case I find anything." I swear if I find Raven before he does, first, I'm going to kiss the hell out of her. Then, I'm going to give her shit for being mated to a dumb ass vampire.

Kieran tosses my phone back at me; he already sent a text to himself so he will have my number. I roll my eyes as I notice his contact's name, "The Better Mate", and storm out of the house on a mission. It's a little past five in the morning, which tells me Leah won't be up for at least another two hours. I don't want to call and freak her out if I don't have to, so I decide to get a head start on searching where Raven could be, heading toward her apartment first.

From what I know about her teleporting last time, she didn't teleport very far, and she said her mind was preoccupied. When she teleported into the shower with me, we were both completely caught off guard. When I joked and told her I knew she was thinking about me, I embarrassed her a little, but the truth is, I couldn't stop thinking about her either.

The time had finally come for me to step up my game if I had any chance of winning her over after her breakup with Kyle, but I hadn't meant for her to fall on top of me in the hallway when she chased me up the stairs at her mom's house. When her body fell against mine, I thought my heart was going to beat out of my chest.

Her touch had lit me up like a firework and everywhere her hand roamed, I felt a trail of heat left behind. All I wanted to do was wrap my arms around her slender body and taste her lips. I tried to play it cool, but in all honesty, I was freaking out. From that moment on, I made it my mission to break out of the permanent "friend zone".

From the first moment I saw her, I knew we were mates. When I was five, my mom told me her good friends from the Realm of Shadows were moving to our town and they had a little girl around my age. I knew how tough moving realms could be since my family had just moved to the Human Realm two years prior, so I wanted to help her navigate hiding her powers in the Human Realm.

What I didn't anticipate was that even as a child, the mating bond would take hold. When my mom introduced us, I'm sure I must have come off as a complete weirdo. I couldn't take my eyes off her. Her fair skin seemed to shimmer in the light, and her dark hair brought out her incredibly beautiful eyes. I wanted to reach out and take her hand to see if she could feel the bond heating her body like it did mine.

The first two times our parents wrangled us all together for a backyard barbecue, she was so shy she didn't even talk to me. I tried a few times to approach her, but every time I said hello, her face would turn red and she'd run off toward the lake. Finally, the third time our families met, she grabbed my hand and led me to their backyard, past the privacy fence that houses their pool. When she dropped my hand and turned around, she had a small smile on her face. Her gray eyes found mine and I couldn't help but stare at the tiny freckles that peppered her face.

I was released from my trance when she asked me what my powers were. I blinked a couple times, then showed her my best smile. "I'm a shape shifter." I was so excited she was finally talking to me that I didn't even wait for her reply. In an instant, she covered her eyes at my flash of light from shifting. When she peeked through her fingers, her shock dissolved into a huge grin.

I barked and ran up to her, licking her fingers while she laughed. The sound of her laugh was like music to my ears, and I would do anything to hear it again. I remember nudging her hand with my head so she would run her fingers through my black and white collie fur. Instead of petting me, she bent down and wrapped her arms around my belly, burying her face into my neck as she hugged me. At that moment, I knew I would do anything in my power to keep her safe.

My whole body felt a pull to her and when I wasn't around her, it felt like a part of my soul was missing. Sure, I questioned why Raven didn't mention the mating bond, but when I finally had the guts to tell Artemis I thought Raven was my mate, he was ecstatic. He told me that sometimes the bond doesn't click for both people at the same time. I just needed to give her time to come around to her feelings for me.

So I did. I waited and watched her date the most awful men. I mean, don't get me wrong. I'm sure they were nice guys. But to me, they had stolen something precious away. When she finally dumped Kyle, I knew that was my moment to see if the feelings she felt for me were true. When she tried to kiss me after our night out, I was so surprised I nearly let her do it. But then, my sanity came back, and I wanted her to remember our first kiss in case this was the missing link in our mating connection. Thank goodness I was right.

So here I am, on my way to her house to search for the woman who makes my heart skip a beat with her laugh. The girl who had my heart from day one. My mate. My Raven. I know she said she's also mates with Kieran, but all that matters is finding her and making sure she's safe. Once I know she's okay, we can worry about everything else later.

I approach Raven's apartment and make my way to the

entrance of the building. Her curtains are still closed and there doesn't seem to be any light on the inside. Once inside the building, I make my way to her door, fumbling to retrieve the key from my pocket. Before I unlock the door, I place my ear against the door, trying to hear if anyone is inside. Without hearing a sound, I place my key in the lock and enter the apartment.

Her vanilla apricot perfume wraps around me, but not as intensely as it usually does, which tells me she hasn't been here since I was with her yesterday. Still, I search her apartment from corner to corner, making sure she's not here. I pull my phone to check the time again; 5:32 a.m. I fire off a text to Kieran, letting him know she isn't at her apartment before calling Leah.

The line rings four times before she finally picks up, her groggy voice tiny and angry. "I swear to all things mighty, you better be dying, Asher. Do you have any idea what time it is?"

"I do," I tease. "How's your beauty sleep coming?"

"Oh, for heaven's sake. What do you want, Asher?"

I hesitate for a moment. If things go sideways, I'm going to be responsible for telling Leah about everything. The supernatural world, how Raven and I are both supernatural, and how she might have been taken by an old, crazy vampire trying to enslave humans again.

Let's just hope it doesn't come to that.

I try to make my voice sound light and airy, instead of scared shitless. "Have you heard from Raven by chance?"

"No. It's not even six in the morning. Did you already mess this up?" she asks, yawning halfway through the sentence.

"Mess what up?" I ask, confused.

"Seriously, Asher? She told me she has feelings for you, you big dummy. If you screw this up, you're kicked out of the best friend trio."

I laugh, knowing full well that Leah isn't joking, but it also makes my heart happy that Raven told Leah she has feelings for me. I'm assuming Raven hasn't had time to tell Leah about what happened yesterday morning between us and I'm not going to be the one to tell her.

"Yeah, yeah," I joke. "I was just wondering if you heard from her in the last hour."

"The last hour?" Leah pauses for a few seconds and it's like I can hear the wheels turning in her head. "Asher, what are you talking—"

"Okay, thanks anyway! Gotta go! Bye!"

I press the end button on my phone before Leah can ask any more questions. I can't involve her in this. As I turn to lock up Raven's apartment, my phone buzzes like crazy. I leave the apartment as text after text comes through from Leah. Most of them threaten to cut off my manly parts if I ever hang up on her again, but some seem genuinely worried about the questions I was asking.

I fire off a quick text, telling her I'll call her when I get back to my place, which seems to slow the barrage of messages for the time being. Her last message said that Colby had to leave and go meet with Kieran at the house over something important. I wonder if the text was from Colby that Kieran looked at when I was at his house earlier.

CHAPTER 26
Too Much Testosterone in One Room

KIERAN

I have to wait for Asher to leave before I can call Colby and demand answers. The text he sent me was vague and left my mind in complete chaos. The phone rings once, then goes straight to voicemail. Before I can leave a nasty message, the front door to the house opens. I fade to the living room to see Colby hanging up his jacket.

"What the hell, Colby?"

"Sorry, I couldn't risk talking over the phone." He opens his overnight bag on the floor and rummages through it before pulling out the small, round, black encrypted hologram device we use to communicate with his aunt. He sets it down on the coffee table in the middle of the room and scans his thumbprint on the top of the device. "I received this from my aunt twelve minutes ago. You need to see this."

The device turns on with a flash of blue light emanating from the center and shining on the wall like a movie screen, revealing his aunt. "Hello boys, I don't have much time, but I have information on the target that you were sent after. A girl was just brought in and thrown into the holding cells on the lower level of the court, and by the sounds of it, it seems to match the description of the girl Antonio was looking for. I will try everything in my power to protect her from harm." She pauses at the knock at her door and yells over her shoulder. "Kieran, if this girl is really your mate, you need to think of a plan of action soon. I must go now. Please be safe, my lovely boys."

The hologram shuts off and I'm left speechless and furious. I take a deep breath, trying to calm my growing anger. I've waited over three hundred years to find my mate, only for her to be taken away from me within hours. I understand why Asher is frustrated. I really do. He's pined over Raven his whole life only to find out she's mated to two men. I don't mind sharing. Being around as long as I have, I've seen it all.

The thing that upsets me is Colby going behind my back to enlist his aunt's help. "Colby, how does your aunt know that Raven and I are mates?"

Colby walks over to collect the hologram and places it in his pocket. "I might have sent a message to her after I saw you kiss Raven's cheek at the fountain before your date. The way you two looked at each other is the way that I look at Leah."

"But you didn't know for sure?"

"No, not for sure. But when you called me yesterday after you brought Raven here and told me you saw the mating bond, I knew I was right in enlisting my aunt's help."

"Yeah, but she can only help her if she's still alive. And if that isn't bad enough, your father now has what he needs to bring down the barrier."

I sit on the couch and bury my hands in my hair, trying to think of the best way to retrieve Raven safely. The couch cushion next to me sinks down as Colby takes a seat and pats my knee.

"It's going to be okay, Kieran."

I turn to Colby and let out a deep sigh, hating what I'm about to say. "Colby, I think it's time for you to take over. We can't keep living in fear of Antonio and his plan to take down the barrier. Especially now that he has Raven. I can't make any promises that I won't tear him limb from limb when I see him."

Colby stands up and paces the living room. I give him the time he needs to think about what has to be done. Antonio needs to be handled, and if we succeed, Colby will take his father's place as the Vampire Court leader. Which also means he has to tell Leah about the supernatural world and that means Asher and Raven will be outed in the process.

"Uffa," I grumble.

"I know, brother," Colby says, halting his pacing. "This does not bode well for either of us."

The silence that stretches between us while we think of a way to overthrow Antonio is deafening. The past hundred years, Antonio has really stepped up his tactics to bring down the barrier. Colby and I have been putting up a fight behind his back with his aunt's help, but I don't know how much longer we can last now that he has Raven. I don't want to kill him because he's Colby's father, but he also can't be free to roam about to gain supporters again. Colby mumbles something, but I can't make out what it is until he says it again. This time, louder with more confidence.

"I'll do it. I'll kill my father."

I stand and make my way around the coffee table to my oldest friend. My blood brother. "Are you sure?" I ask, placing my hand on his shoulder. "I can do it if it'll be too much for you."

Colby flashes me a small, tight smile. "No. It has to be me. If I'm going to take over, I have to show the Vampire Court what happens to people that try to overthrow and disrupt the home we have built for ourselves in the Realm of Shadows."

I squeeze his shoulder and give it one last pat. "I'm proud of you, Fratellino."

"Thanks, brother. Now, let's go get your woman!"

It's my turn to pace the living room. "Yeah, about that," I say, rubbing the back of my neck. "After I called you, Asher showed up at our house."

"What? Why?" Colby asks.

"So, funny story, but apparently, Raven and Asher are also mates." I watch as Colby's eyes nearly pop from his face and his mouth hangs open. As much as I would love to be the sole hero of Raven's story, I know I'm not the only one who matters to her.

"Yeah, so if we make any decisions to save Raven, we have to include Asher."

"Wow. I did not see that coming." Colby laughs.

"I know, I know," I say, pulling out my phone. I quickly send Asher a text informing him I have information on Raven. My phone pings before I even have the chance to shove it back in my pocket.

"Asher will be here in five," I say to Colby.

"Do I need to play referee for you two, or will you be able to get along?" Colby jokes.

"Might not be a bad idea to nonchalantly place yourself in between us when he gets here."

Colby's laugh fills the hall as he takes his overnight bag back to his room. Five minutes later, the front door bursts open.

"Jeez, don't you know how to knock?" I ask sarcastically.

"I can only assume the worst from the text you sent. So no, I didn't see the need to knock," Asher says, strolling into the living room. "What info do you have on Raven?"

Before I can answer, Colby emerges from his room and greets Asher. "Asher." Colby nods, sliding in place between us. He takes out his hologram and places it on the table like before.

"Colby." Asher nods back, watching Colby unlock the device with his thumb. "What's this?"

"This is an encrypted hologram device from the Realm of Shadows. We've been using it to communicate with Colby's aunt at the Vampire Court." Skepticism forms on Asher's face. "Don't worry, she's on our side. She hates Antonio more than Colby and I combined. She just sent us this message."

Colby hits play as we watch the hologram relay the same message as before, but Colby cuts it off right after the knock at her door. I subtly nod in appreciation for him cutting out the part about his aunt knowing Raven and I are mates. When it's over, Asher cusses from the other side of the room.

"What's the plan?" he asks no one in particular.

"We thought we could discuss this with you," I say, hoping to earn his trust with my willingness to include him in the plan.

Asher shoves his hands in his jean pockets as he leans up against the wall. "I think Colby should go back to the Vampire Court and check in on his father," Asher says. "Alone."

"What!" I shout, taking a step toward Asher. Colby pins me with a look and places his hand on my chest to stop me from taking any more steps.

"Hear him out," Colby says, turning back toward Asher.

"If we all go, Antonio will know that we know Raven is there and we will have no chance of freeing her. But if Colby goes alone, he can act like he is just checking in with things at the court. Not bringing too much attention and trying to free Raven. He can leave his encrypted hologram with us. That way when he finds his aunt, he can use her device to fill us in on what's going on. Hopefully, by that time, you'll be able to go in the sunlight and we can go save Raven."

Colby and I look at each other and back to Asher. Colby already knew I had to feed on Raven in order to survive the Hartsbane, but his jaw flexes, telling me he's shocked Asher knew.

"That's actually a really clever plan, Asher," Colby says. When I don't agree, Colby nudges me in the ribs.

"Yeah," I grumble. "It's pretty good." It's brilliant actually and I'm upset I didn't think of it myself. I hate that we have to stay here and play the waiting game, but unfortunately, that's the hand we were dealt. Colby turns to retrieve his travel talisman from his room when Asher grabs his arm.

"What about Leah?" Asher asks, dropping his arm. "Do you plan on telling her where you're going or what's happening?"

Colby clenches his fist and rolls his shoulders back. I know this is a tough subject for him. He never wanted to involve Leah in any of this, especially his father drama.

Asher takes a step closer to Colby, a brave but stupid choice. "We have to tell her, Colby. We can't just leave her here unprotected. What if the same people who were tracking Raven noticed you were spending time with some human girl? What if they come after her, too?"

I don't have time to react before Colby has Asher pinned against the wall with his forearm up against Asher's throat.

"You don't think I haven't thought of that?" Colby shouts. "I don't want to leave her here unprotected. If something were to happen to her while I was gone, it would be because of me."

I fade to where Colby has Asher pinned against the wall, but Asher's glare stops me. I back off, but I'm still close enough in case I have to pull Colby away. I have to hand it to Asher; the guy can hold his own. Maybe this whole sharing a mate won't be as bad as I thought.

"I know how you feel," Asher says, glancing at me. "We both do. Raven has been kidnapped and we're stuck here playing the waiting game, but we have to tell Leah. Unfortunately, she is a part of this world now that you two are together and I think it's time she hears the truth from me."

Colby drops his arm from Asher's throat, and I sigh in relief. I grab Colby's shoulder and pull him back a few steps, giving Asher room to breathe.

"I'll tell her about Raven being kidnapped and why she was kidnapped, but it's up to you to tell her about you and Kieran."

"Deal," Colby agrees.

I clap my hands together and point my fingers at Colby. "Alrighty then, Colby, text Leah to meet us here ASAP." I then point my fingers at Asher, but he cuts me off before I can give him instructions.

"I'll prepare for Hurricane Leah," he sighs. "Can you take any sharp items out of the living room? I know you two heal quickly, but I don't, and I do NOT want to be fed either of your blood when Leah decides to break a vase and stab me with the sharp, shattered end."

Colby and I share a look, then burst out laughing.

"You think I'm kidding?" Asher complains. "Just wait. You'll see."

After we finish laughing, we help Asher take any item that might be turned into a weapon out of the living room.

"Colby, when Asher is done breaking the news to Leah, we will give you space to tell her about you and me. But after, we need you to leave for the Vampire Court. Asher and I will protect her while you're gone. I promise."

Colby nods in agreement just as the doorbell rings.

"Oh hell, here we go," I hear Asher say from the living room.

CHAPTER 27

FREAK OUTS ARE OVERRATED

LEAH

When I was woken up this morning by Asher's call, I was surprised, to say the least. After Asher hung up on me, leaving me fuming in bed, I rolled over to find Colby missing. Jumping out of bed, I shoved my feet into my fuzzy slippers and made my way through my one-bedroom apartment only to come up empty. The only hint that Colby was here was a note on my kitchen island letting me know Colby had to meet Kieran for some sort of emergency. Not even twenty minutes later, my phone dings with a text from Colby asking me to come over as soon as I can.

The drive over has done nothing to soothe my temper. If anything, it gives me time to become angrier as I replay the events this morning. I know Asher and Raven joke that I turn into Hurricane Leah when I'm angry, and I don't really blame them. I'm quick to anger, but easy to calm down. However, something's going on with Raven, and Asher was concerned enough to call me and ask if I've seen her but gave no context as to why he was calling. Then, he had the audacity to hang up on me! Waking up in bed was probably icing on the cake.

Parking on the street, I march my way up the front steps, ready to lay into Colby for leaving without a goodbye, then demanding I come over, as if I'm some push over he can walk all over. Well, I'll show him. I bang my fist on the front door, hoping to make my anger apparent.

I didn't know what to expect when Colby answered the door, but it definitely wasn't this. Colby gently takes my wrist and pulls me in for one of his amazing hugs. To my complete and utter shock, all my anger vanishes under his touch and I sigh, leaning into him as he kisses my head.

"I missed you," he whispers into my hair.

I take a step back and cross my arms. "It's hardly been twenty minutes since you vanished on me and you're already missing me?" Colby just shrugs, shoving his hands into his pockets. "So, this can't be good since both of you are together," I say, waving my hand between Asher and Kieran. They both share a look, and Kieran gives Asher a quick slap on the back.

"You're up, bud," Kieran says, backing away into the kitchen, laughing. "Scream if you need help."

Before I can ask what Kieran means, Colby comes up behind me and hugs me again. He leans around to one side of my head and kisses my ear. "You and Asher need to have a quick chat. Kieran and I will be in the kitchen if you need anything, sunshine." He squeezes me, then releases me to join Kieran in the kitchen.

When I turn to face Asher, he looks like he's going to be sick, and a little afraid. I move to approach him, but he holds a hand up. "I think it's better if you sit," he says.

Oh boy. This can't be good.

I watch Asher stuff his hands in his pockets and pace behind the coffee table. He's working himself up to tell me something, and every time he's about to talk, he stops pacing, looks at me, then starts pacing again.

"Oh, for the love, Asher!" I shout at him, halting his pacing. "Just tell me whatever it is you have to say."

He takes a deep breath, then comes to sit beside me, taking my hands in his.

"You know you're the best part of the best friend trio, right?" he says, catching me completely off guard.

"Well duh," I joke, recovering my wit. "Who would keep you two in check if I wasn't there?"

"Exactly. You're the glue that holds us all together." He smiles. It's one of his famous Asher smiles that melts Raven's heart. "Raven and I would never do anything to hurt you or put you in harm's way." His grip tightens slightly on my hands. "We can't lose you as a friend, Leah."

"Ohhhh kaaay . . . " I say, a little lost in this conversation. Asher's always the goofy one, not the serious one, so this new version that I'm seeing is really freaking me out. Asher takes another deep breath and his emerald green eyes hold mine.

"Do you believe in supernatural beings?" he asks cautiously.

I can't help it, but I laugh right in his face. He rears back as Colby rushes into the room. I'm lost in a fit of giggles when Asher drops one of my hands and holds his palm to the back of my forehead.

"She doesn't have a fever," Asher announces. "She must have finally cracked and is in full on Hurricane Leah mode."

I gasp for air, trying to calm myself down. I pull my other hand from his and wipe the tears from my eyes. "I'm not in Hurricane Leah mode, Asher." I gasp, trying to catch my breath in between laughs. "It's just that you looked like you were about to tell someone that you forgot to feed their pet fish while they were on vacation and you accidentally killed it."

I keel over as another fit of laughter takes over. Colby comes to sit next to me, rubbing my back. "But instead," I sit up, finally getting control of my laughing fit, "you ask me if I believe in supernatural beings."

"Leah," Asher says, looking at Colby and Kieran for guidance, "you're scaring me."

His admission makes me laugh even harder before Kieran shrugs his shoulders. "So, is that a yes?" Kieran asks from the kitchen counter.

"Yes. Yes, I believe in supernatural beings. I know for a fact that Raven's a witch. I was just waiting for her to buck up and tell me."

"What?!" Asher shouts, practically falling off the couch. "How do you know?"

I lean back into Colby and kick my feet up on the coffee table. "Remember the summer Raven's dad died?" Asher nods his head; I know neither of us would ever forget that summer. "The day you and I brought her down to the lake and had the whole dock decked out in her dad's favorite things, I saw her use her powers. When I left to go up to the house to grab extra towels, I forgot my shoes to take a shortcut through the forest to her house. When I came back down, I saw you help her into her dad's little boat. There weren't any paddles in the boat, and I was about to yell at you guys that the paddles were in the shed, but then Raven extended her hands out and a gust of wind carried her away on the lake."

I shrug my shoulders as Asher sits in front of me, speechless. "I didn't think much of it at the time, but then things kept happening that I couldn't explain. Like the next summer when we didn't have any matches for the bonfire in my backyard. I went inside to ask my mom to go to the store, and when I came back out, Raven was standing by the fire pit, placing her hands back in her hoodie with a raging fire in the fire pit. Just little things that I couldn't explain kept happening."

"Why didn't you ask her about it?" Asher questions.

"She was hiding her powers for a reason, and I didn't want to ask her and risk you guys laughing in my face. Am I mad that you both kept this from me? Hell yeah, but there must be a good reason for keeping this a secret. So, I waited until she felt comfortable enough to tell me, which is my next question. Why are you telling me instead of her?"

"Oh, um, well," Asher hesitates.

Kieran picks up Asher's slack and finishes his sentence. "Raven has been kidnapped."

"What?!" If Colby wasn't holding me in place, I would have jumped through the roof. "You're asking me if I believe in supernatural beings while my best friend has just been kidnapped instead of going to rescue her?"

"Yes," Kieran answers.

I glare at Kieran but appreciate his directness.

"There's more you need to know, Leah," Asher says. Bringing my attention back to him as he stands and moves away from the couch. "Raven isn't the only supernatural being. I have also been keeping a secret."

"You're a witch too?" I ask.

"Technically, a male is a warlock, but no. I'm a shapeshifter."

"A WH–?" My sentence is cut off by a bright flash of light in the living room. When the light fades, it reveals a familiar black and white collie. "No. Freaking. Way."

"Really," Kieran laughs, "he could have turned into anything, and he chose a dog?"

"It's not just a dog," I say, standing to pet the collie. "Anytime Raven or I were sad, a black and white collie would appear and play with us and make us feel better. Sometimes, we would sit outside for hours playing fetch and having him chase us. I never noticed, but Asher was never present during those times." I smile down at the dog and pat his head, making his tail wag as he licks my hand. "You were the dog."

The dog, I mean, Asher barks, and there's another brilliant

flash of light and Asher is standing back in front of me. "I told you. We would do anything to protect you and keep you safe and happy."

With tears threatening my eyes, I close the space between Asher and I and wrap him in a tight hug. "Thank you," I whisper into his chest.

He pulls back but keeps me at arm's length. "So, does that mean you're not mad?"

"Oh, no. I'm pissed." I smile, seeing his face fall. "But," I say, stepping back, punching his shoulder, "thank you for telling me. Now, do we know who took Raven?" I catch the look Asher gives Colby. I spin around and face him. "Who took Raven?" I demand.

It's Kieran that speaks up. "Well, we know where she is and why, but we don't know who did it."

"I bet I can guess and if I'm right, that little red-headed bitch—"

"Down kitty," Asher laughs, patting my shoulder.

"There's one more thing you should know," Colby says, walking toward me. "My father has Raven back at the Vampire Court."

His father? The Vampire Court? So that means . . .

"So, let me get this straight," I say, shaking my head. "Your father has my best friend held hostage at the Vampire Court?"

"Yes," he says, taking another step closer.

"And I'm assuming he's a vampire?"

"Yes," he answers, taking another step forward. I refuse to back away and show that I'm afraid of him, no matter how much my brain tells me to run. Vampires are a thing of myths and legends. Or so I thought.

"Which makes you?" I question, knowing the answer.

"A vampire," he says, closing the last step between us.

I turn my head to look at Kieran smirking from his spot in the kitchen. "And what does that make you? A dragon?" I tease.

Kieran laughs and shakes his head. "I wish, but no. I'm just a lowly vampire like your boyfriend."

Colby brings his hand to my chin and turns my face toward him. "Are you really not afraid?"

"Ha, I'm freaking terrified! But I'm more worried about saving my best friend to back down and go hide under a rock. So, what's the plan to save Raven from daddy dearest?"

The guys laugh as Colby takes a step back and heads toward his room. Asher fills me in on the plan and I agree not to be a nuisance for my two babysitters while Colby is gone. While Kieran and Asher try to avoid each other in the house, I head back to Colby's room and knock on the door.

"Come in."

I open the door to see Colby packing clothes I've never seen before into his overnight bag. I plant myself on the end of his bed as he finishes packing.

"Sooo . . . you're really a vampire, huh?"

Colby turns and flashes me a smile. His canines are extended into sharp pointed teeth, just like in the movies. I'm highly frightened, but I have to admit, those fangs make Colby look ten times more attractive. "Are you sure you're okay?" he asks, retracting his fangs.

"I think so. I mean, don't get me wrong. I always fantasized about dating Edward Cullen, but to have it be real is a little freaky."

Colby laughs and sits down next to me. "I don't give off Edward Cullen vibes, do I?"

"That depends." I lean in and whisper, "Do you sparkle in the sun?"

He gasps as I fall into a fit of giggles. In all seriousness, I'm still hurt that everyone waited so long to tell me, but it sounds like they have their own messes to take care of, too.

"So, where are you going?" I ask, placing my hand in his.

"The Vampire Court back in the Realm of Shadows."

"Realm of Shadows?"

"Yes, a long time ago, humans and supernatural beings once lived together until rogue vampires and dragons started enslaving the humans. Long story short, a witch with immense power created the barrier that separates the Human Realm from the Realm of Shadows." He holds up what looks like a large ancient coin. "This talisman is the only way to travel between worlds. Only high-ranking supernatural beings have access to these to keep everyone safe."

"Wow. So, you're a high-ranking official then?" I tease.

Colby sighs and places a kiss on my hand. "My father is the leader of the Vampire Court. When we take him down, I will be the next leader."

Oh.

That means he'll live in the Realm of Shadows, and I'll be here in the Human Realm. My heart tightens and I stand before any other emotion threatens to sneak up on me. "You'll make a great ruler."

"Leah," Colby says, grabbing my hand. "We can talk about our future when I get back. Okay?"

I give him my best smile, even though my head is spinning with this new information. "Okay. Now go save my best friend."

He leans down and kisses my cheek before exiting his room. I don't want to watch him go, so instead, I grab the covers and tuck myself in his bed, hoping that everything will be okay.

CHAPTER 28
DADDY ISSUES

COLBY

I exit my bedroom, leaving Leah behind. I was already forced to have Leah meet my father, but there is absolutely no way in hell I will ever bring her to the Vampire Court with him ruling. No matter how much my body screams to keep her close, I know it's safer for her here with Kieran and Asher. When I emerge into the kitchen, Kieran is sitting on the island and Asher is laying on the couch in the living room.

"Are you two going to be okay here by yourselves?" I ask Kieran. "I don't want to come back to a mess," I joke.

"You forget that you're leaving your lady in charge of us. I'm sure she won't hesitate to keep our asses in check."

"You're right," I laugh, taking out the talisman and holding it up against the wall.

Kieran steps down to meet me, placing his hand on my shoulder. "Good luck, Fratellino."

"Thanks," I say, opening the portal to the Vampire Court. "I'll contact you as soon as I can."

I step through the portal and remove the talisman from the stone wall in the docking hall. Normally, the docking hall is busy with supernatural beings coming and going, but right now, I'm the only one in the room, which sets my internal alarm bells ringing. I quickly shove the talisman into my bag and head to the giant wooden door that leads to the receiving hall.

Before I open the door, my vampire hearing picks up on three or four sets of heavy footsteps quickly approaching the door. I drop my bag and prepare to fight whoever is about to enter through the door. The doorknob turns and standing before me is my father, with four guards behind him. I don't drop my guard; something is very wrong here.

Once, I used to look up to my father, but that was a very long time ago. My father is a very cruel man who stops at nothing to get what he wants. After Kieran was brought to the Vampire Court, I thought things would be different and that the beatings would stop. They didn't. In fact, they seemed to get worse and I wasn't the only one behind his unprompted attacks. My mom and Kieran were also beaten.

Soon after my father started hunting down mages, Kieran and I took it upon ourselves to try and stop him. My aunt found out, and bless her heart, started helping us in any way she could. Now, all I see when I look at him is nothing. It's pointless to feel anything after a while.

"Welcome home, son." My father smirks. "Seize him," he commands the guards behind him.

I quickly immobilize the first guard that attacks, throwing him into the second that approaches. Unfortunately, I'm not quick enough when the third and fourth guard approach. The third guard lands a heavy punch to the back of my head before the fourth guard kicks me hard in the stomach, sending me sailing backward into the white stone wall.

My body slams on the white marble floor as I watch the two remaining guards approach me.

"Put him in the tower," I hear my father command, before watching him turn to leave.

"Why are you doing this?!" I shout as the two guards haul me to my feet, slapping magic siphoning shackles on my hands.

My father pauses and stretches his neck before turning to face me. He walks up to me, and the two guards sweep my feet out from under me, making me kneel. My father looks down at me with disgust.

"I can't have you ruining my plans. I thought you would eventually join me in bringing down the barrier and enslaving the humans again, but instead, you found yourself a human mate."

My face must reveal my shock because my father continues. "Oh, you didn't think I was just going to let you complete this mission by yourself, did you? I had my spies follow you to make sure the plan went smoothly," he says, tucking his hands behind his back and walking around me. "Imagine my shock when you decided to let Kieran take over instead. So, I did a little digging myself and when you brought that human to dinner with me, I knew you had betrayed me."

I'm too shocked to react when he spits in my face. "You disgust me." He turns heads toward the door. "Now, if you'll excuse me. I have to meet the little witch who is going to help me bring the barrier down."

"NO!" I shout at his back as he disappears down the hall. I fight against the shackles, but it's no use. The cuffs prevent me from using my vampire strength.

As the two guards haul me back to my feet and lead me through the servants' hall to the tower, I silently pray Asher and Kieran are able to protect Leah from whatever my father has in store for her and I hope Raven is strong enough to face my wicked father.

CHAPTER 29
BARGAINING CHIP

For the second time today, I wake up not knowing where I am. Except this time, I'm not resting on a lavish bed with satin sheets.

This is completely different.

I try to move, but my body still feels numb from whatever I was injected with. I know I should be freaking out right now, but honestly, with everything that has happened to me in the last twelve hours, I think I'm still in shock. Things really couldn't get worse, right?

Laying on the hard, cold ground, I roll over to find I must be in a holding cell because there are two walls made up of bars. The wall in front of me where the door is, and the side wall, which divides mine from another cell. There is another door on the outside of our cells, which I assume is also locked.

The only light in the whole room comes from two windows on the back side of each cell. If people thought prison was bad, they should see this place. It's straight up medieval.

With barely any light illuminating the room, I don't even

notice the man sitting in the other cell until he whispers my name.

"Raven."

I would know that voice anywhere. Finally able to at least move my limbs, I scramble to crawl over to the man, reaching for him through the bars that separate us.

"Grandpa! What happened and why are we here?"

My grandpa takes a second before answering me, hugging me as best he can even as the bars separate us.

"I'm just so relieved you're okay."

I tighten my grip around him and can tell he's lost weight by how easily my arms wrap around him. Reluctantly, I pull back slightly and take a good look at him. Even with hardly any lighting, I can tell he's in bad shape. Fresh purple and blue bruises cover his arms, and he's got one mean looking black eye that he can barely see out of because of the swelling.

The longer I look at him, the angrier I become. I may be weak right now, but my rage is building the longer I look at him and when I unleash it, it's going to burn this place to the ground.

"Who did this to you?"

"It doesn't matter."

"How can you say it doesn't matter? Look at you!"

"Raven, listen to me. It doesn't matter now. We have to find a way for you to escape before they come back."

Okay, so there is more than one person who took him. Which is going to make escaping harder, but we can cross that bridge when we get there. Just as I'm about to ask who he is talking about, the main door outside our cell opens.

"Oh good, you're awake!"

I slump back against the bars, shaking my head. "You've got to be kidding me?"

"Is that any way to treat your best friend?" the fiery redhead asks sweetly.

"Ex-best friend."

Bree steps up to our cells, looking us both over before a sinister smile appears on her face.

"Bree, what the hell is going on and where are we?"

"Oh, I see you didn't have much time to catch up before I so rudely entered. You're at the Vampire Court, silly."

"The Vampire Court? But that means . . . "

"Yes. That means we are in the Realm of Shadows. I'm sure you're very excited to be back, right, Raven?"

My grandpa reaches for me through the bars, setting a warning hand on my shoulder.

"Don't listen to her, Raven."

"Are you the one who kidnapped me?"

Bree scoffs, as though I offended her. "Of course, I kidnapped you. Kieran couldn't finish the job and I saw an opportunity and took it."

I flinch as she mentions Kieran's name.

"Ahh, so I take it he told you everything then?" Bree fake pouts, walking up to my cell. "Such a shame Antonio was tipped off that Kieran was slacking on his mission."

"Wait. You were the one who ratted Kieran out? He was almost killed by that lackey Antonio sent!"

Bree flips her red hair behind her shoulder and pins me with a look. "Uh duh. That was the plan."

"How did we even get here? You can't cross over the barrier without a talisman."

Bree pulls an ancient-looking talisman from her jacket, holding it up in the dim light. "Oh, you mean this? Antonio lent me his spare. He also loaned me a few of his vampire guards to help track you down. After you teleported from Kieran's, it only took the guards three minutes to track you down. I had one of the guards fade me to where you were. You looked so pathetic sitting on the curb outside the coffee shop and you were so dazed that you didn't even hear me approach you from behind."

I take a step back, letting everything sink in. Bree was the one following Kieran. She was the one who tipped off Antonio. And now, she's turned me into the Vampire Court, but something in this doesn't add up.

"Why? How does doing any of this benefit you?"

"For this, of course." Bree holds her hand up; I watch as her perfectly black, manicured nails extend into giant claws. Her brown eyes flashing golden yellow.

"So you can become a dragon?" I say, confused.

"No," Bree says, walking over to take a seat in the chair next to the door.

"Not to become a dragon, but to reinstate my dragon."

I turn to Grandpa for some sort of clue as to what's going on, but his face gives nothing away.

"I can see you're confused, so let me tell you a little story. Long ago, my family once lived in the Realm of Shadows. As you already know, dragons are very prideful creatures when it comes to their treasure. My parents were approached by the Vampire Court and given an offer of treasures so vast they wouldn't dare refuse.

"They were hired to find a warlock that possessed all four elements, just like yourself. Luckily for my parents, they were able to capture the warlock and bring him to the Vampire Court. However, once my father found out what Antonio was going to use him for, he helped the warlock escape from these very cells that you're in."

Bree motions in the corner, which reveals remnants of a fire and charred bars that I didn't notice before.

"Well, as you can imagine, Antonio was furious when he found out. Our whole family was brought to the throne room and stripped of our dragons. I was only two, but I remember the pain as though it happened yesterday."

Listening to her story, I can't help but feel sorry for Bree. She didn't do anything to warrant her dragon to be taken away, but it doesn't warrant the behavior she's been displaying recently.

Bree's face looks haunted as she recounts what happened, her face turns into a look of disgust. "We were then cast out of the Realm of Shadows, forced to live as humans for the rest of our lives. That is, until I found you. I waited nine years. Nine long years to finally feel my dragon again."

I quickly do the math and my stomach drops. This can't be true. My face falls and Bree releases a sinister laugh, leaning forward in her chair.

"That's right. The night your dad died, we saw your powers in full effect. My dad and I were on our way to your house to comfort your family when we were stopped by your parents' force field around your property. We were about to turn around, but then we saw you running toward the road. You were a mess and so blinded by your grief you didn't even notice us.

"My dad was about to get out of the car and approach you, but then you summoned a lightning bolt and sent it straight through the forest, shattering half of the trees. When we looked back at the road, you were just gone. My dad was silent the whole way home, but I knew you were my ticket out of that terrible world.

"So, I waited, and bided my time, until I could figure out a way to contact Antonio. And just by luck, I ran past two good-looking vampires moving into their house off campus. Imagine my surprise when I found out one of those vampires was none other than Antonio's only son, Colby. And imagine their surprise when I ran into Colby, Antonio, and Leah at dinner a few nights ago."

My feelings of sadness for Bree quickly dissolves as she keeps talking.

I can't imagine what Leah did. Actually, I can. And I hope she was able to throw one good punch to Bree's face before Colby could hold her back.

"Too bad Leah was in the ladies' room. I would have loved to see my old bestie. Alas, all I had to do was wait until Colby and Leah left and I made my move. As Antonio was waiting for his car, I revealed to him that his little protégé was keeping you away from the Vampire Court on purpose. I was then awarded the opportunity of a lifetime. Bring you to Antonio, and my dragon would be reinstated. How could I say no to that?"

Bree stands and claps her hands together. "So here we are!"

"Go to hell," I spit at Bree through the bars.

Bree grabs me by the shirt, pulling me harshly up against the bars. I grip her wrist and try to use my witch fire on her, but nothing happens.

"Think again before using your powers. See that little shackle on your wrist? It's a siphon for your powers, essentially rendering you useless. Now you'll see what it's like to be human and be absolutely powerless," she sneers in my face.

Bree uses her newfound strength and throws me, then turns toward my grandpa. My body slams against the wall and falls into a crumpled pile on the cold floor.

CHAPTER 30

PAYBACK'S A BITCH

"Let her out of here, Bree! You don't need her," my grandpa shouts from his side of the cell.

Bree laughs and stalks toward him. "Oh, really? And why is that? You've done nothing for her but keep secrets. Go on, tell her how you ended up here."

Grandpa turns his head toward me, and I see the shame in his face.

"Fine then. I'll tell her," Bree says excitedly. "One of Antonio's spies caught your grandfather snooping around in the restricted section at the Seneca Library, which is only accessible to the High Families of the Vampire Court. When he was imprisoned and taken to the throne room for questioning by Antonio, your grandfather said he was merely doing harmless research and got lost on the vampire's side of the library. Well, I did a little bit of research myself and look what I found."

Bree struts back to her bag she set down next to the chair and takes out a familiar manila envelope. I instantly realize what it is before she even turns it around to reveal my dad's handwritten note on the front.

Rage continues to fill me, reaching each and every part of my body. I use the cell bars for support to pull myself up, trying to look intimidating. I grab each bar to support my weight as I make my way slowly to the front of the cell. However, Bree must have dislocated my arm when she threw me against the wall because with every move I make, pain radiates down my arm.

"I found this in your room while you were out for your birthday. And lucky for me, I didn't have to wait long to open the envelope. As you can see here," Bree turns the envelope toward me so I can see my dad's note, "all I had to do was wait a couple hours until after your birthday was over."

I grit my teeth, fighting through the pain. "Give me the envelope."

Bree laughs and shakes the envelope in my face. "Oh, you're cute when you're mad, you know that?"

I finally reach the front of the cell and my body is screaming at me to stop moving. It feels like I've been set on fire from the inside and there is no escaping the red-hot flames trapped within me. I wedge myself in the corner of mine and my grandpa's cell so I can support myself, taking some of the weight off my injured leg, which cools the flames for the time being.

Bree steps closer, running the envelope across the bars. I reach for it, but she snatches it away with a wicked grin.

"You know, your dad really has a way with words. His letter was so heartfelt."

I slam my hand onto the bar, stoking the fire inside me once again. "I said, give me the damn envelope!"

"You know what, I think my birthday gift to you will be reading this to you. How does that sound? Hmm?"

I've had enough of her shit. I push myself off the bars that were supporting me and grab the two bars closest to her. "GIVE. ME. THE. ENVELOPE."

Bree reaches out and slaps me across the face, her elongated nails slashing my cheek. I stumble back from the force and my injured shoulder slams into the dividing cell bars. Luckily, Grandpa reaches through and braces most of my fall.

"You ungrateful piece of trash," Bree spits toward me. "Now, you're going to listen as I read you this letter because it falls quite nicely into my final plans for you."

Bree slides a soft blue piece of paper out from the envelope. The blue paper represented important documents that were used to correspond with The Alliance. Even looking at the letter, my heart constricts in my chest.

Bree clears her throat and reveals a sly grin before she starts reading:

"My dearest Raven, by the time you read this letter, I will most likely be long gone. I was hoping to tell you this all myself in person, but fate had other designs. I wish I could be there to see you grow up and be there for every new discovery of your powers. I know your mother and grandfather will do their best to help you through the most difficult times.

"There is so much I wish I could tell you, but unfortunately, I'm on borrowed time, so I will say this: Listen to your heart and don't be afraid to embrace your powers. I know it can be scary, but trust your instincts. If you ever feel like you need more answers, go to our special place at the edge of the river. The answers will come. I love you, Raven. Forever and always, Dad."

Silent tears fall down my face as Bree finishes reading the letter. The fire inside me is gone, replaced with a wave of sadness and despair. I release the breath I didn't know I was holding as Grandpa tries to comfort me as best he can through the bars. Feeling his touch relieves some of the pain, but I don't feel like any amount of comfort will ever be enough. Especially knowing the last remaining thing I have from my dad is now in enemy hands.

Bree slips the letter back into the envelope, then reaches into her back pocket and pulls out a small lighter. With all the energy left in my body, I lunge toward Bree.

"NO! BREE, STOP!" I scream as she flicks the lighter, holding it under the envelope. In mere seconds, the envelope is up in flames.

I drop to my knees, utterly defeated.

Bree kneels on the other side of the bars and clenches my chin in her hand. Her eyes blazing golden yellow. "Ask me the real reason your grandfather is still kept in his cell."

I shake my head, forcing my face out of her hands. "Why? You've already taken everything from me."

"Not everything," she warns. Bree stands and grabs my grandpa by his collar through his cell.

"What are you doing? Let him go!" I race over to his cell, but I can't reach him. Bree has him on the far side of his cell.

Bree flares her nostrils. "Tell her what you did, Artemis."

Grandpa shakes his head, refusing to tell me.

Bree takes her other hand and digs her claws into the back of his neck. "Tell her!" she commands.

"I . . . I . . . created the spell to strip away someone's dragon!"

"What?" I say, taken aback. "You told me it was for dragons doing undercover work in the Human Realm?"

"He lied," Bree says through gritted teeth. "Tell her what it was really for."

"The Alliance was made aware of a possible revolt coming from a rogue group of dragons. Your grandmother and I were tasked with making a spell that could strip a person of their dragon. It was never meant to be used!"

"But it was!" Bree screams. "I was only two years old, and it felt like I was being torn in half!"

Bree closes her eyes and takes a deep breath to reign in her anger. When she opens her eyes, she pins me with a murderous glare. "I want you to suffer like I suffered, Raven. An eye for an eye, as the humans say. Your grandfather took my dragon away, so I'm going to take your grandfather away."

Before I can even comprehend what is happening, Bree releases her hand holding my grandpa's shirt and uses it to slash her claws across his neck.

I'm frozen in place with shock.

I feel like I'm trapped in my body.

I can hear myself screaming in my head, but no sound is coming out.

I watch as she releases him, and his body falls limply to the floor. It only takes seconds for the floor to be covered in his crimson blood. The blood reflects off the little sliver of light in the room, forcing me to witness the leaking fluid pooling around his lifeless body.

Bree's sinister laugh breaks me free from my shock. I turn and face her, silent tears streaming down my face.

"What have you done?"

She turns to leave, grabbing her backpack from the chair. When she reaches the outer door, she turns back to me; she's won.

"Payback's a bitch," she mutters, slamming the door behind her.

CHAPTER 31

THIS IS GOING TO HURT

I don't know how long I sit in silence, clutching the cell bars. Right now, it's the only thing holding me up because if I let go, I don't know if I will be okay. They are the only thing keeping me from slipping into the farthest pits of despair.

What little light that is filtered into my cell starts to fade again, letting me know I've been in this spot for almost a whole day.

Immobile.

Unwilling to face the reality that in the cell next to me is my grandpa's corpse. I briefly glance at his body; the blood still staining his face. He wouldn't want me to sit here and fall apart.

No.

He would want me to fight.

Fight my way out of this prison I find myself in.

And that's exactly what I intend to do. Closing my eyes, I touch my heart, hoping his spirit can hear my vow.

"As soon as the opportunity arises, I will escape this place. I promise."

Then the steel door in front of me creaks open, revealing a brute of a man. Fear races through me as I take in his chilling features. He has a scar that runs the length of his face with mismatching eyes. His body is pure muscle, and he is so tall he has to duck to make it through the door. I promised I would put up a fight, but it looks like it won't last long if this is who I have to go up against.

He takes another step into the room, practically sucking the remaining life from the room, but then he steps aside and a kind-looking woman appears. She's half his size and looks to be about my mother's age. Her skintight, black clothing shows me that even though she's tiny, she's fit. Her soft brown hair is pinned in a top-knot bun, but her face is like a beacon in a storm.

As soon as she lays her eyes on me, she smiles brightly and in the darkness of my cell, I'm almost burned by the warmth it brings to my frozen heart. Two gray auras appear around them, letting me know they're vampires.

When she speaks, I'm caught off guard by her thick British accent. "Vail, open the cell and let's get this girl some proper housing."

The man, who must be Vail, reaches into his jacket and takes out the key to my cell. I scramble backward as he swings open the cell door. My first instinct is to use my powers and blast these two into next week, but I remember the shackles on my wrists and think twice before bolting. Even if I somehow escape them, I won't be able to run far.

Leisurely, the mystery woman steps into my cell. Her smile reaches her eyes and somehow my nerves settle a little. Slowly, she kneels, addressing me on my level.

"Hello, dearie. My name is Amera. Let's get you out of here and into some new clothes, shall we?"

She holds out her hand for me and I stare at her for a second, weighing my options. I could try to overpower her with what little strength I have left, then try to make it by Frankenstein.

Most likely ending up with me being caught not even a minute later. Or, I can go with them and hope that I'm not their next meal. Against my better judgment, I cautiously take her hand as she helps me to my feet.

She squeezes my hand in encouragement. "Atta girl."

As she leads me out of my cell, I remember that my grandpa is still occupying the cell next to mine and I come to an abrupt stop. Amera turns back to face me and her happy demeanor is replaced with empathy.

"I can't leave him," I whisper, looking over at his lifeless body.

Amera's soft hand turns my face away from my grandpa as she steps forward, pulling me into her warm embrace. She smells like fresh lilacs, and I melt into her arms.

"Don't worry, darling," she whispers into my ear. "I will take care of him, understand?"

I nod my head that's nuzzled in her shoulder.

I believe her.

She pulls away from the embrace and takes my hand again. With one last look at Grandpa Artie, I send up a silent prayer for him. As we exit the cell, Amera whispers something to Vail. He nods and turns to lock the steel door as we exit.

I only make it fourteen steps until my body gives in and I crumble to the ground. My body can't take all the movement and I think my shoulder is still dislocated. Amera shares a look with Vail, and I'm not sure I'm going to like what is about to happen.

Amera kneels in front of me, placing her hand on my injured shoulder, and I wince in pain.

"What's wrong?" she asks, pulling her hand away from my shoulder quickly.

"It's nothing," I lie.

The look Amera pins me with reminds me of being scolded by my mom. I release a shaky breath and deliver a half truth.

"I must have dislocated my shoulder trying to reach for my grandpa after what happened."

I don't look at her, but I can tell Amera knows it's a lie.

"Mhm. Well, we'll fix you right up."

Amera stands and claps her hands and Vail approaches me slowly.

"Wait! What are you doing?" I panic and throw my hands up at Vail to push him back, but I remember these stupid shackles keep my powers in check, and I can't use magic.

"It's okay," Amera soothes. "Vail is going to carry you to your new room. You won't be able to make it on your own in your condition. Once we are in your room, I'll fix your shoulder."

I know she's right. I won't make it on my own. My body is weak and still recovering from the side effects of the drug I was injected with. Internally cursing myself for being in this situation, I nod at Vail, signaling he can approach me.

I'm shocked at how gentle he is when he reaches down to cradle his arms around my body, scooping me close to his chest. As brutish as he looks, he's rather tender with my frail body. I look over to Amera and she winks at me.

It's weird, but in this moment, it feels like there is a spark of hope and healing within me. I relax into Vail's arms as we make our way out of the basement and farther into the Vampire Court. We must be in the servants' hall because the hallways are empty as we head to the fourth floor. There are no portraits lining the halls or any kind of decorations filling the walls.

Once we emerge onto the fourth floor hall, we must enter the main parts of the castle. There are family portraits lining one wall and on the opposite wall are floating shelves with ancient vases, crowns, tiaras, and other relics. There are three doors in the hallway, two doors on one side, and a single door on the other side.

"My room is here," she points out as we walk farther down the hall, "and this is Colby and Kieran's room."

I nearly break my neck spinning to face her. "What! You know Colby and Kieran?"

Amera stops in front of one of the rooms and places a key in the lock. "Of course, Colby is my nephew."

I stare at her in shock.

Of course he is.

I know Kieran said he wanted to keep me safe, but his mission was to kidnap me and bring me here. Can I really believe that Amera and Vail are helping me out of the goodness of their hearts, or are they cleaning me up to present me to Antonio and collect their own prize?

She unlocks the door and flips on the light as Vail ducks through the doorway. I scan the massive room before Vail places me on the bed. I know whose room this is as I inhale the scent of summer rain.

The room looks exactly like I would expect from him. On one wall is a massive bookcase filled with tattered and worn books. On the opposite side is a record player with a massive stack of records next to it. Other than that, the room is in pristine condition.

I'm drawn back to reality when Vail closes the bedroom door and stands guard in front of it.

"And you'll be staying in Kieran's room." Amera smiles warmly.

I flop onto the bed as she disappears into the ensuite bathroom. I hear her start the shower and the sound of the water threatens to lull me to sleep. Before my eyes can close, the bed dips as Amera sits down next to me.

She lays a soft robe down and touches my arm. I hiss and pull my arm back from her touch.

"Let's fix your arm, then we will leave you to shower and get ready for tonight."

"What's tonight?" I question, as I gently place my hand in hers.

She slowly extends my arm, trying to straighten it. "Antonio wants to see you and apologize about what Bree did."

I wince internally and physically. I'm sure that's all he wants to do and not force me to do his bidding.

"Take a deep breath." Amera turns to me with my arm extended. "I'm not going to lie. This is going to hurt, but I'll count to three before we set it back in place, okay?"

All I can do is nod. My shoulder is already on fire. I take a deep breath as I wait for Amera to start counting. Instead, she throws me a curveball.

"I'm so glad you're Kieran's mate."

I turn and release the breath I was holding and stare straight at her. She yanks my arm back into place with a sickening snap.

"HOLY HELL!"

She laughs and releases my arm when she stands, then crosses her arms over her petite body. "I told you it was going to hurt."

"Yeah, and you also said you were going to count to three."

I stand, clutching my shoulder. Surprisingly, it feels a heck of a lot better already. Amera picks up the robe she left on the bed and hands it to me, turning me around and ushering me into the giant bathroom.

I turn to protest, but she places her slender finger over my lips, silencing me.

"I promise I will answer all your questions after you shower. We don't have much time before dinner starts. I'll be back shortly."

She exits the bathroom, leaving me completely baffled. I rest my back against the bathroom door, taking in the sight before me. To my left is the sink with a massive diamond shaped mirror hanging on the wall above it. There is a separate door, straight ahead, assuming for the toilet, and to my right the entrance to the walk-in shower.

I place my robe on the hook next to the shower and turn to face myself in the mirror. The person staring back at me looks like a stranger.

My hair is a knotted mess falling over my shoulders, but what stuns me is my face. I touch my cheeks as I see my reflection do the same. My dried tears have created a washed-out stream through my dirt covered face. My hands clench the end of the sink as I look at the dried tear marks and every bad memory from the last forty-eight hours comes flooding back into my mind.

With my emotions threatening to make me my own captive, I turn from the mirror and remove my dirty clothes. I throw the tattered clothes in the sink and walk into the welcoming shower. The warmth immediately surrounds me and I release a heavy sigh, but I'm caught off guard as I round the corner of the entrance.

The room is about ten feet wide on each side. In the center of the ceiling is a massive shower head with water raining down in patterns. On each side of the shower is a bench that sits right under six shower heads embedded into the wall, each one spraying to meet the mainstream above. I make my way to the middle of the shower and let every angle of water wash away the dried dirt, blood, and grief.

CHAPTER 32
LET'S PARTY

After triple checking all the dirt and blood is gone from my body, I turn the water off and wrap myself in the softest silk robe. I stroll back out into the bedroom and find myself drawn to the bookcase, amazed at the number of books that line the shelves, each one of them different in their own special way. Some of them are thick, with leather bounds, others small, with smooth covers.

I run my fingers across the spines of the books and it's clear they are all well looked after. Even the older books look as though they are in good shape, despite their age.

A knock on the door draws me away from snooping.

Amera appears around the door with a cart of supplies behind her. When Amera elegantly strolls past me to the bathroom, I glance at the contents it holds. The cart is covered in makeup, curling irons, and hair accessories. She surprises me when she exits the room again. This time when she reenters, she's pushing a rack full of beautiful gowns in all dark-colored tones.

I guess that's a theme around here.

"Are those for tonight?" I ask, stepping closer to admire the dresses.

"Antonio has invited a few guests to dinner tonight," Amera says indifferently, waving her hand as she beckons me into the bathroom.

When I see the counter covered in supplies, I know this isn't just any dinner. Something feels off, but I don't know what. I might be out of the dungeons, but as far as I'm concerned, I'm still a prisoner. I need to gather more information, and it seems by the way Amera talks about Antonio, she doesn't care for him. I need to figure out just how far that disdain goes and if she really is on my side.

Amera seems preoccupied with getting all her tools ready, so I leave her to it as I dry my hair. When I'm finished, she looks like she's about to explode with excitement. She slides a chair out from the vanity and urges me to sit.

"What are you so excited about?" I ask skeptically. Maybe she knows what's really going on tonight.

Her face softens as she runs her fingers through my long hair. "I've always wanted a daughter," she says softly.

My heart tightens as I look at her. She doesn't seem like the kind of vampire that is fueled by rage and insanity. She seems more maternal and sweet, which is why I find it hard to stay distant from her.

"As you know, the royal family are the only vampires that can have children. When my sister had Colby, we were all so excited. However, after years of trying, I found out that I couldn't have any of my own." She brushes a rogue tear from her cheek and smiles at me through the mirror. "After Antonio brought Kieran to the Vampire Court, I took him in and treated him as my own. He helped fill the void in my heart."

I smile, genuinely happy for her.

She smiles back, then grabs the curling iron. "But I am so lucky to have you here. So, let's get started, shall we?"

"I have to warn you, I don't really wear a lot of makeup and get all dressed up."

"Well, after I'm finished, you'll be begging me to be your personal stylist. Trust me."

As she starts to curl my hair, I figure it's a good time to question her on what she knows. "How did you know Kieran and I were mates?"

"Well, I didn't know for sure, but you just confirmed it."

I internally kick myself. "Okay, but how did you find out that we could have been mates?"

She grabs the clip holding my hair and releases the last section of hair for her to curl.

"Well, about a week ago, I received an encrypted hologram of Colby. He told me the person Antonio sent them after happened to be his mate's best friend and possibly Kieran's mate. So obviously he needed advice on how to proceed."

She reaches to unplug the curling iron and grabs a handful of bobby pins. As she starts twisting my hair, she hands me the rest to hold.

"Obviously, I told him to confirm that this person was indeed Kieran's mate first. He thought I didn't know who the target was, but I happened to listen in on one of Antonio's meetings and heard the description of the target."

As she twists my hair into intricate braids, I continue to hand her bobby pins while she answers my question.

"Imagine my surprise when I overheard there was a girl in the dungeon that matched your description." Her hands stop braiding for a moment and she meets my eyes in the mirror. "Had I known what was happening down there, I would have done everything in my power to stop Bree from hurting you and Artemis."

I reach for her with my free hand and grip her arm softly. "It's alright. Please don't think any of this was your fault. You have been nothing but kind to me."

She smiles and turns me around in the chair to face her. "Okay, enough of this sad talk. What do you want to do with your makeup?" she asks excitedly.

"Well, normally I just wear some tinted moisturizer and mascara."

Amera shakes her head and grabs the foundation sitting on the counter. "Do you trust me?" she asks.

Completely caught off guard, all I can manage is a nod. I still don't completely trust Amera, but my defensive walls are starting to slowly dissolve.

"Perfect!" She cheers.

After what feels like forever, Amera finally sets down her makeup tools with a wide grin on her face.

"Okay. As if you weren't beautiful before, you're going to bring every man to his knees tonight and we haven't even picked a dress yet!"

When she spins me around, I'm speechless.

Amera is right. I want her as my personal stylist.

My hair cascades down my back with two intricate braids on each side of my head, tied in the back. Somehow, she made it look like I have defined cheekbones, and my gray eyes are piercing with the brown smokey eye shadow she used. My eyelashes look like they've grown thicker, which brings my eyes out even more.

When I reach up to touch my plump-looking lips, Amera swats my hand away.

"Do not mess up my masterpiece!" she teases.

"Thank you so much. You truly outdid yourself."

"Don't thank me yet." She smiles, leading me out to the bedroom. "We still have to pick out your armor."

"My armor?" I ask skeptically as I follow her into the room.

She turns to me and grasps my hands softly. "Listen to me, Raven. I don't partially care for Antonio. He wasn't the kindest man to my sister. She and I tried our best to shield the boys from his wrath, but after she died, it became harder. There have been things that were done that are unforgivable. Antonio wants to parade you around tonight to show his court that he has stolen himself a prize and I will not let you go into that room feeling afraid. So," she says, dropping my hands and pointing to the dress rack, "whichever dress you chose will act as your armor tonight, showing everyone YOU should be the one they fear, not Antonio."

As I run my eyes over all the exquisite dresses, my eye keeps roaming back to the last dress. Amera smiles, pulling it from the rack and setting the hanger on the back of the door.

"I knew you'd like this one."

"It's beautiful," I gasp, touching the soft velvet material.

She hands me the dress and leaves me to change. After a few seconds, she emerges from the bathroom gasping. "Wow. Here, let me tie the back for you."

When I pull my hair up, Amera notices my necklace. "What a beautiful necklace."

I instinctively reach for the diamond and rub my thumb along the surface. Suddenly, an idea rushes to my brain. "Amera, do you still have your encrypted hologram?"

"Yes, why?" she asks, as she finishes tying my dress.

I turn to her and grab her hands. "Right before Bree kidnapped me, Kieran and I were arguing and I accidentally tele-ported to a coffee shop near my apartment. He doesn't know Bree took me back here to the Realm of Shadows." I feel bad leaving out that I was arguing with Kieran AND Asher, but she doesn't need to know the full truth.

She gently pats my hands and smiles. "I'm way ahead of you. I've already sent Colby an encrypted hologram, letting him know that you're here and to inform Kieran. Now," she says, releasing my hands, "it's my turn to go change. I'll be back shortly, dear."

When she leaves, I slowly walk over to look at myself in the giant mirror in the corner of the room. The dress hugs me in all the right places and the black tulle that cascades over my shoulder brings out my eyes even more. The A-line sweetheart corset makes it look like I actually have boobs, and the slit above my knee draws my attention to my once scarred leg.

When I sway back and forth, the dress gives the illusion that the flowing material changes colors from black to silver. With the finishing touch, I slip my feet into a modest pair of black heels. I'm still in shock at my makeover when Amera lets out a slow whistle and I laugh, turning to face her.

"Oh yeah, the men are definitely going to be drooling over you." She winks.

"Look at you! That dress looks amazing on you."

Amera does a little twirl as the Mermaid-style dress falls around her ankles. The silver dress is simple in the front, but the open back drops dangerously low. She reaches for my hand, and I follow her out the door. Vail nods as we pass and falls into step behind us. He doesn't look as scary tonight dressed up in his black tuxedo.

We don't take the servants' hall this time, instead Amera leads us down the hall to a private elevator. We step inside and as the doors shut, the self-doubt and what ifs start to take over my mind. I don't know Antonio, and I don't know what tricks he's going to pull. My magic is still being siphoned by these shackles on my wrists, so if things go south, I won't be able to defend myself.

Before I have time to tell Amera I changed my mind about making an appearance at this little dinner party, the elevator doors open, revealing a massive dining hall. Three giant chandeliers hang from the ceiling, the crystals reflecting light all around them.

There are round tables placed at the back of the room with a long table of assorted foods lining the back wall. A few finely dressed couples are dancing under the middle chandelier and at the front of the hall is an elevated stage, occupied by a few men in the most exquisite tuxes.

The hall is already filled with people. Mostly vampires, but I see a couple of golden auras mixed in, which means there are dragons here as well, who are most likely loyal to Antonio. As soon as I step out, all eyes fall on me.

Internally, my body starts to catch on fire and a bead of sweat threatens to run down my back, but then I remember the reason I'm here. I was kidnapped for my power. I will not be afraid of these people. Once these shackles come off, they will see what real power looks like.

I take a deep breath and muster all the badass vibes I can.

Amera senses my change of attitude and smirks as she starts to make her way through the crowd. I follow close behind, holding my head high. If they want to stare, go ahead. Get a good look before I burn this court to the ground.

We approach the front of the room, and the crowd parts for us as I hear whispers from the onlookers. Finally, we reach the front when Amera bows her head toward the man sitting in the chair before us on stage. He acknowledges Amera, then stands as the crowd immediately turns silent, waiting for him to speak.

He's tall and his salt and pepper hair sparkles in the chandelier above. But when he smiles, it doesn't quite reach his chocolate eyes. In fact, it makes me want to cringe, but I keep my composure and return his half ass smile.

"Raven!" he bellows, "how nice of you to accept my invitation."

Like I had a choice.

"Please, come sit next to me and let's have a little chat, hmm?"

When I walk up the stairs to meet him, the crowd returns to its previous state of drinking and chatting. He extends his hand and I reluctantly place my hand in his. He bows to place a kiss on my hand and when his lips touch my knuckle, an icy shiver runs through my body.

"And you must be Antonio," I grit through clenched teeth. I use all my strength to not pull my hand away.

"The one and only." He smirks, releasing my hand. "Come and sit. We have much to discuss."

As I pass by to claim the chair next to him, I remember what Amera said about my dress being my armor.

Alright, Antonio. May the best warrior win.

CHAPTER 33

PISSING OFF THE PARTY HOST NEVER
ENDS WELL

Sitting next to Antonio makes my skin crawl. Although he may appear good-looking to the eye, my senses tell me this man is not to be trusted. Antonio beckons a waiter over and takes two glasses of what looks like champagne. When he hands me a glass, I make sure to place my hands on the bottom, so his hands won't touch my own.

If he notices my tactic, he pretends not to be upset as he turns his gaze to me.

"I wanted to apologize for Bree's actions," he says, shaking his head. "She was only meant to bring you to me, nothing else."

I give him a tight smile as I take a sip of my drink.

His apology is void of any emotion, which makes me want to throw my sour drink in his face.

Calm down. The sooner you get through this, the sooner you can leave.

"Thank you," I manage to grit out.

Seemingly over the conversation at hand, Antonio finishes

his drink and switches out his empty glass for a new one as the waiter comes around again.

"Let me get right to it. By now you know why you've been brought here." He eyes the shackles cuffing my wrists and grins wickedly. "For too long, the Vampire Court has been forced to play a role in the Alliance's goal to keep all supernatural beings at peace with one another. I believe that if the Vampire Court could come to power over all other courts, we could break down the barrier that separates us from the humans. We could go back to the way it was before the barrier and use them as we wish."

That last sentence has chills running down my spine. The barrier was made to keep humans from the horror they endured from supernatural beings. They were hunted, forced to be slaves, and worst of all, killed for sport.

I'm careful to keep my face as neutral as possible as he takes my hand in his.

"You, my dear, will help me rise to power and take down the barrier once and for all."

"With all due respect," I say, pulling my hand away, "I decline your offer."

Setting my drink down between us, I rise to stand but am halted by Antonio's cold grip on my arm. His nails dig into my bicep; his wild eyes zero in on mine.

"Think carefully, girl. I'm not too keen on second chances."

"There is nothing to think about," I say, trying to tear my arm from his grip. "I refuse to help you enslave millions of innocent people for your claim to power. And, by the sound of it, you need me more than I need you."

If I can't use my power, at least I can use the defensive skills I learned when Leah and I took a self-defense class two years ago. With one swift move, I twist my arm from his grip and bring my other hand up into his nose. A gasp escapes many of the onlooking guests, but I don't have time to see the look on Antonio's face.

I grab the front of my dress and run as fast as my heels will allow me to. I barely make it off the stage before three of Antonio's guards surround me.

Stupid vampires and their stupid vampire speed.

The guard in front of me lashes out to grab my arm, but I drop down and kick his feet out from under him, catching him off balance as he falls into the guard behind me.

Two down, one to go.

Antonio fades to where I am and grabs a fist full of my hair with his bloody hand, pulling my head back to face him.

"ENOUGH!"

I gaze up into his wild eyes and smile.

"It doesn't matter if I didn't escape. Me, a defenseless little girl, was able to get the upper hand on you in front of your guests. What does that say about you, Antonio?"

His hand tightens in my hair, releasing a small whimper of pain from my lips. "You WILL help me." He seethes, blood still spilling from his nose. He throws me at the guard in front of him. "A couple of months back in the cells might change your mind."

Before I have time to fight back, there's a quick pinch on the back of my neck. This time, the drug takes a little longer to work through my body, threatening to lull me to sleep. The guard behind me is joined by another, and both of my arms are propped up over their necks. I hear Antonio usher his guests to the dinner table and try to cover his tracks by assuring them that I, the tiny human, had too much to drink.

The crowd's laughter fades into the background as the guards shuffle my limp body behind the stage and into the hallway. My vision is starting to blur, but our journey to the cells is halted by a mystery man. He's taller than both guards, and his suit must have been custom tailored to fit his massive arms.

Before either guard holding my body can react, they both become immobilized and fall to the ground. The mystery man reaches out and cradles my body before it can hit the ground, which I'm thankful for because my body doesn't need any more bruises. The drug is coaxing my body to sleep, but for some reason, my mind is putting up a real good fight. The mystery man stands with me cradled in his arms, and I swear I hear a growl rumble through his chest.

The sound startles me and, with my last ounce of effort, I stare up into my savior's golden eyes. That's all it takes for me to be pulled under by the drug.

I have the strangest dream.

I'm in a grand ballroom, dressed in the most exquisite dusty blue ball gown that follows behind my every step. My hair flows freely down my back, and a heavy, golden, jewel encrusted crown lies atop my head. The room is empty except for a massive fountain in the middle of the room.

Cautiously, I approach the fountain and see the detail carved in the sides. It shows all five species: vampires, mages, dragons, shifters, and humans standing side by side in harmony.

Circling the fountain, I find a man on the other side. His back is facing me, giving me a glimpse of his strong shoulders he hides under his tailored black suit. His hair is as dark as night and his skin looks like it's been kissed by the sun. As I slowly approach, he turns and I'm gifted with the most amazing, yet familiar, golden eyes staring back at me.

Instantly, my heart rate quickens and when he graces me with a soft smile, it feels as though the air has been stolen from my lungs. Suddenly, my body straightens and somewhere deep down, a missing piece finds its place in the puzzle that is my heart.

When he extends his hand toward me, a single golden thread appears from his chest. It swirls down his arm and aims right at my heart, piercing through it. The warmth that fills my body leaves me wanting to jump in the fountain behind me to cool my rising body temperature.

My extended hand is swallowed by his strong and calloused hands. He pulls me close and softly lays his hand on my back above my hips. I hear a foreign melody echo through the empty hall. In a daze, I place my hand on his shoulder as he gracefully leads us around the fountain in a dance I don't know, but somehow feels familiar.

With his molten eyes drawing me closer, I can't help but return his smile. As the music fades, a cold metal object is placed in my hand. Confused, I look down and unfold my hand from his. Inside is a small, simple looking, black key.

"What is this for?" I question softly, inspecting the key in my hand.

"You'll know when you wake up."

When he leans down and brushes a soft kiss on the top of my head, I swear I hear his deep voice whisper, "Mine. Mate."

The last word he whispers has my body burning from within.

When I look up to question him, the room goes black. Blinking rapidly, I inspect my surroundings only to find I'm back in the familiar cells that I first started out in.

"What a weird dream," I mumble to myself.

As I bring my hands up to my neck to rub out the sore spot from the needle, I hear a soft clang of metal hit the concrete floor. Frozen in place, I turn my gaze to my left, and there, sitting on the blood-stained concrete, is the black key from my dreams.

CHAPTER 34
PRINCE UNCHARMING

I don't hesitate. I quickly scramble to grab the key before someone can interrupt my escape. Praying this is the key I need to unlock my cuffs, I hold my breath as I jam it into the lock. I turn the key and the first cuff falls to the ground with a clank. I release a triumphant laugh and take the key from the cuff on the ground and do the same with my other wrist.

Realizing the key probably doesn't open my cell, I summon my fire element and melt the lock. My fire blazes hotter than ever, melting the door completely. I take a step back, slightly stunned at my own powers. I don't have time to waste dwelling on this new surge of power, so I shrug off my shock and step over the small smoldering pile that is left of the door.

Still wearing my dress from earlier, I find a knife on the table outside my cell and use it to cut the fabric around my knees. I have two seconds of regret for cutting the elegant fabric, but I can't have anything slow my escape, which is why I also ditch the heels and take my chances going barefoot.

I have my powers back, but I keep the knife just as an extra precaution. Hesitantly, I pull the outside door open that now sits between me and my freedom from the basement and peer around the corner, listening for any sign of guards. I don't hear any voices, so they must be up at the party and they probably assume I won't be escaping anytime soon.

I love it when people underestimate me.

I head the opposite direction from when Amera and Vail took me last time I was released from the cell. Hopefully, this path leads me out of the basement and to an exit. I move as fast as my still battered and bruised body will allow, which is surprisingly faster than I thought I could travel. I find a flight of stairs and follow the winding pathway up to another door. I place my ear on the door and carefully listen. All I hear is silence.

When I open the door, I freeze. I must be in the servants' hall because the walls are barren, except for an exceptionally dressed vampire, with his fangs plunged into one of the female servants. My gasp draws the man out of his frenzy. He pulls away from the woman, blood still dripping from his lips, zeroing in on me. I snap out of my trance as he fades toward me. He lets out an ear-piercing scream as I hit him with a fireball straight to the chest.

His body crumples to the ground, but I don't have time to celebrate this small victory because there's no way any of the vampires at the dinner missed hearing his scream. I race over to the servant still riding the high from being fed on. Grabbing her shoulders, I force her to look at me.

"Where is the exit?!" I plead, shaking her back to her senses. For a moment, I think all hope is lost, but then she blinks and points down the hall.

"Where? What way do I turn?!" I don't have time for this, so I shake her a little harder.

She bows her head, not meeting my eyes. "Down the hall, take a left and it's the last door on the right." She then looks up and I can see the apology in her eyes. "It's locked and I don't have the key. I'm sorry."

"Thank you!" I yell over my shoulder as I race in the direction she pointed. I take a left like the servant said and spot the door. She wasn't kidding when she said it was locked. I approach the door with a giant black padlock attached to the handle. I'm almost to the door when I hear voices coming from the hall I just fled from.

Shit.

Without breaking my stride, I raise my hands and blast the door with fire in one hand and throw a strong gust of wind with the other hand. The door reluctantly falls with a loud thud just as I reach the doorway.

Okay, there's no way that wasn't heard.

I scramble over the fallen door and the cold mountain air blasts into my body, knocking the breath out of me. When the smoke and dust clears, I finally catch my breath and stand; it's pitch-black outside. The only light that touches the ground is from two windows above, but not enough to illuminate a pathway out of here through the forest.

Escaping wasn't even the hard part. It's making my way off the mountain where the Vampire Court is located. The layout of all four courts in the Realm of Shadows is engraved into my memory from my studies my grandpa forced upon me after my family moved to the Human Realm. If I remember correctly, the Vampire Court is the most difficult to escape from.

Picture if you will: a remote mountaintop, mile high mountains, exceptionally beautiful lakes, and waterfalls that are encompassed by thickly packed trees. Now, place a centuries-old castle on the top of the highest mountain.

The only way in and out as a vampire is to fade to the entrance, or if you're any other supernatural being, invite only through a portal hidden within the town at the base of the mountain. No one has ever survived the hike up the mountain on foot.

I have no intention of finding the hidden portal. My only two options are to teleport out of the Vampire Court, or trek my way down the mountain, hoping my powers are enough to fight off any supernaturals that dare follow me. Since I don't know how to teleport on my own free will, it looks like I'll be hiking down this mountain in the dark. With no shoes and a skimpy velvet dress to keep me warm.

Great.

I pick up my pace as I head toward the edge of the giant stone wall as fast as my bare feet will take me. Creating a gust of wind to propel me up and over the six-foot wall, I fly through the air and land gracefully on the other side.

"Took you long enough," says a deep male voice from my left.

I swallow a scream and nearly fall back into the stone wall with my hands up, prepared to blast this mystery man off his feet. I'm about to demand who the hell he thinks he is when familiar golden eyes lock with mine. I immediately recognize him from my dream. My body starts to heat up and the faint golden string between us slowly appears.

He kicks off the wall and walks past me, making the string disappear as he throws a pair of leather pants and a cloak at my face. He places the boots on the ground before looking me dead in the eyes. "Put these on," he demands, walking away toward the forest.

I'm completely dumbfounded. One, at the rude way he just chucked the clothing at my face. Two, at how he even knew I was going to be out here and in need of warmer clothing. And three, by how he didn't even seem to acknowledge the mating bond.

When he walks by me, I notice his elegant outfit is now replaced with tight, black pants tucked into leather bound boots. His brown leather jacket is open, revealing a relaxed white undershirt. The material is so thin I can practically see the outline of his abs. It takes me a minute to remember that most of the supernatural species tend to dress like a character from

Outlander or *Game of Thrones*. They didn't evolve their fashion as the humans did when the barrier went up.

I quickly shimmy into the leather pants, stuff my feet into the boots, and throw the cloak around my shoulders, pulling the hood around my face.

The mystery man stops his retreat to the forest and turns to face me. "Are you coming or do you plan to be captured? Again."

The annoyed tone in his voice sets me off. I march right up to him, one hundred percent ready to knock him onto his ass with a gust of wind, until I hear shouting from the castle. I turn away from the mystery man and toward the castle. "Took them long enough to figure out I was gone," I say with a smug smile on my face.

"Unbelievable," he says to himself, but loud enough for me to hear.

"Oh, I'm sorry my delayed escape put a damper on your plans," I say, placing my hands on my hips.

The mystery man pins me with a death glare. "You know what? We don't have time for this."

He closes the distance between us within a few steps. Before I can even react, he grabs me and throws me over his shoulder. "Hold on," he says over his shoulder. That's the only warning I receive before two massive, scaly, golden wings shoot out from his back. The long golden wings sweep the ground, but I have little time to admire them before he launches himself in the air. Caught off guard, I close my eyes and scream, not prepared for what is happening.

We ascend higher and higher; the castle becoming a small dot on the ground. The frigid night air whips through my cloak, freezing my body from my toes to my head as I scream at my capture to release me. He either doesn't hear me or doesn't care because he starts flying faster.

To where? I have no idea. But I don't intend to find out.

I know it's a bad idea. Actually, it's a terrible idea, but I will not be captured again. I wiggle one hand that is tucked between my body and this man's back and heat my hand, placing it right on his ass. He screams and his flight falters, but not enough to drop me.

I guess I'll have to try harder.

I lift my heated hand and place it where his golden wing meets his sculpted back. This time, he releases me to grab for the burned skin. Instantly, his menacing face cracks as he sends me free falling back down to the ground.

I don't scream as I fall. It's now or never to figure out how to control my teleporting power. I take a deep breath, close my eyes, and visualize where I want to be. I can't teleport back to the Human Realm since I don't have a talisman, but I can teleport to where I've been before in the Realm of Shadows. Once I think of a safe place, I focus all my energy teleporting to the spot.

Suddenly, I hear my name whispered in the sky. I open my eyes to find the mystery man falling to meet me. His wings are tucked behind him as he barrels toward me with outstretched arms. His tan face is as white as a sheet as he reaches for me.

"Raven! Grab my hands!" he shouts over the deafening sound of wind rushing by my ears.

Confused at how he knows my name, I try with all my might to visualize the place I want to escape to, but not before his arms encompass my body. The second his hands touch me, his wings unfurl to their full length to catch the wind, slowing our descent. The sudden motion startles me and I close my eyes and scream.

Suddenly, the air turns muggy and thick. I think I even hear waves crashing in the distance. When I open my eyes, I'm speechless. The sun is rising in the east, just barely breaching the blue horizon. A vast ocean sprawls before us as we descend onto a small island in the middle of the ocean.

I have no idea how we ended up here, but as soon as my feet

touch the sandy beach, I rip myself out of the mystery man's arms and put some much needed distance between us.

"How did you do that?" the mystery man demands, shaking out his wings. Gone is the tender-hearted man who called out to me in the sky. His stony, grumpy attitude is back in full.

"No. Nuh uh. I get to ask the questions," I say as I watch him tuck his wings into his back. I remember from when I was little, my dad used to tell me stories of royal family members of the Dragon Court who could partially shift into their dragon form. Their wings, permanently inked onto their backs like a tattoo.

"Who are you? How do you know my name?" I demand.

The mystery man holds his hands up, as if to surrender. "My name is Nakoa Kahle, Dragon Prince of the Royal Family. I know your name because I was tasked with helping you escape the Vampire Court."

He takes a step closer, and I take a step back.

"So that dream I had was real?" I ask, hoping for him to confirm my suspicion.

"What dream?" he asks, taking another step forward. I take another step back, and he growls in frustration, but doesn't take another step forward. "When I knocked out the guards after your little scene with Antonio, you were barely conscious, but when we locked eyes, the mating bond was sealed. I couldn't just carry you out of the Vampire Court with no one noticing, so I carried you back to the cells, but before I left you, I concealed the key to your cuffs in your hand."

"Oh, so now you want to acknowledge the mating bond AFTER kidnapping me. Solid plan," I say, giving him a thumbs up. "Not."

I start to pace in the sand, trying to stop my mind from having a mental breakdown. I don't even know what to think right now. Another mate? This has to be some kind of joke, right? I was starting to come around to the idea of having two mates, but three?

After the mystery man, I mean, Nakoa, fills in the missing time of how I woke up back in my cell, he thinks it's his turn for answers.

"How did we get here?" he demands again, watching me pace the sand.

"I don't know, okay? I was hoping to teleport to my old home back in the Mage Court, and somehow ended up here. Which is weird because I've never been to this island before."

"No one has been here but me. I found this island on patrol two years ago. Wait," he says, realizing what I just revealed, "did you just say you were trying to teleport?"

I halt in my tracks, looking down at my feet and draw a line in the sand before answering. "Um, no?" I laugh, trying to throw Nakoa off. I don't know anything about him. Yes, we are mates, but for all I know, he could try to use my power for his own gain. "No witch can teleport. That's just crazy."

I slowly start to back away, but Nakoa's commanding voice halts me in my tracks.

"Raven, I'm not here to hurt you. I'm here to help you." A small piece of his grumpy exterior softens, trying to bribe me into trusting him, but I don't buy it and throw my defensive walls up.

"I don't trust someone who dropped me out of the sky." I smirk, crossing my arms, hoping to poke holes in his grumpy exterior.

"You burned me!" he shouts, the fallen piece of grumpiness quickly falling back into place in his hard exterior.

"Only because you kidnapped me!" I shoot back. It's kind of fun trying to get under his skin.

"Screw this. Good luck teleporting your way off this island, since it sounds like you don't even know how to do that properly." He turns and the morning sun reveals intricate wings inked onto his back. He unfurls his wings from his skin, getting ready to launch into the sky again.

"Wait!" I call out in a panic. I hate that I'm about to ask him for help and apparently, that's exactly what he wanted, as he tries to hide his smirk when he turns to face me.

"Yes?" he coos, taking a step closer.

"I might need your help getting off this island," I whisper into the breeze.

He takes another step closer, his smirk forming into a full on smile. "I'm sorry. I didn't hear that. Can you speak up?"

I puff out a frustrated sigh and stand straighter, looking directly into his beautiful golden eyes. "I said, I need your help getting off the island."

He raises his eyebrows, as if I'm forgetting something.

"Please," I add bitterly.

"With pleasure, Princess." He closes the distance between us and scoops me into his arms, bridal style, then shoots straight into the morning sky.

CHAPTER 35

THE APPLE FELL FAR FROM THE TREE

Once Nakoa levels out and we start to coast over the ocean, I can't help but admire the view. The sun rises higher in the morning sky, painting shades of yellow on the water below. He said he found the island we landed on during patrol, which could mean we are on the farther side of the Dragon Court's boundaries.

A wave of excitement washes over me. I've always dreamed of visiting the Dragon Court and strolling through the cobblestone streets, bouncing from vendor to vendor in the marketplace. My dad used to fill my head with stories of when he visited his friends here. After he died, I vowed I would visit here. I just never imagined I would be flying here in the arms of a dragon prince.

Nakoa leans down, bringing his face close to my ear so the wind doesn't catch his voice. "We will be back to the Dragon Court in twenty minutes." His low voice is like a soft blanket, wrapping around my body as he speaks.

I nod and pretend to take in the sights over his broad shoulders, hopefully being discrete as my eyes roam over his body. The wind has opened the collar of his white shirt, exposing a muscular, tanned upper body. My gaze slowly works its way up to his face, where his strong jaw is peppered with a five o'clock shadow. His cheeks are chiseled and defined, and his long, thick eyelashes would make any girl jealous.

One of his eyebrows suddenly raises, and his arms tighten on my body. I have a feeling it was a warning to stop checking him out. Eager to push his buttons, I press my body tighter to his chest and playfully run my fingers up his arm. I feel the mating bond start to vibrate up my own arm, knowing he feels it, too.

"Knock it off," he growls.

Gotcha.

I remove my hand from his arm, cross mine over my chest, and look up to stare at him. I have to admit, he holds out for a solid minute before breaking.

"I swear, Raven, if you don't quit staring at me, I will drop you into the ocean and keep flying."

"You wouldn't dare," I challenge.

"Try me," he says, his eyes locking with mine. His arms start to loosen their hold on me and, for a second, I think he might be serious.

"Fine," I huff, turning my face away. He adjusts his grip, holding me even tighter than before. I smirk, knowing that deep down, he enjoys me challenging him.

Soon enough, the rising cliffs of the coast appear in the distance. As we approach, the waves below crash into the side of the cliffs, carving out their own patterns as centuries pass by. Nakoa dips his shoulder, gliding us along the coastline, flying us toward a grand castle near the edge of the cliffs.

Suddenly, the sun disappears above us and two enormous charcoal-colored dragons drop from the sky, falling in sync behind Nakoa. He must have known they were approaching because he graces me with a quick laugh when he looks down at my face.

"First time seeing a dragon, Princess?"

My words fail me, so I nod instead, astonished by the sheer size of the two trailing dragons. Just as fast as they descended on us, the two dragons veer off back toward a giant stone building at the edge of the city. The main city looks to extend around a mile in each direction and is made up of beautiful stone buildings of all shapes and sizes. The city tapers out along the edges, making room for farms and settlements.

My gaze returns ahead of us and that's when I notice the castle is perched on its own little island, with an intricate stone bridge connecting the city and the island. The castle isn't as big as the Vampire Court's, but it's still enormous. The main building is square shaped, made from solid stone pavers, and placed on each side are two tall towers. The front of the castle brandishes a canopy in which carriages can drive under to be shielded from the elements, and the gravel driveway leads back down to a solid iron gate.

As we approach the castle, Nakoa's eyes shine with pride. "Welcome to Dragon Court, Raven."

He picks a landing spot on the lawn near an expansive flower garden. Flowers and bushes of all shapes and sizes line the pathways that create a maze near the cliff. When he finally touches down, he gently sets my feet on the soft grass. The temperature is much warmer here than the Vampire Court and I feel a small bead of sweat make its way down the side of my forehead.

Nakoa seems to notice the flush of red on my cheeks. "C'mon. Let's get you inside and out of these clothes. I don't want you melting while you meet my parents."

"Wait," I say, stepping in front of him, placing my hand on his chest. "You mean the King and Queen of the Dragon Court?"

He gently pushes my hand off him. "Yes. Otherwise known as my parents. Mom and Dad."

He turns and heads around the flower maze, clearly ending the conversation. The door he leads us to is shaded by a wooden canopy overflowing with grape vines. He picks a few grapes and pops one into his mouth before sharing a few with me.

"Here. Eat some grapes and chill."

I stick my tongue out at him behind his back, but the second I pop a grape in my mouth, the taste has me moaning internally. I've never tasted any grapes this sweet back in the Human Realm.

The door we enter through leads us down a long hallway. As we approach the end, voices flutter through the air, bouncing off the hallway walls. We emerge into a large circular room with three giant floor-to-ceiling windows overlooking the ocean. The ceiling immediately has my full attention, with its painted mural of dragons soaring through the air in the clouds. Yellow, white, gold, red, and blues, all painted together brilliantly. I'm too captured by the ceiling to notice that Nakoa has stopped walking.

When I look ahead of me, it's too late. My face, particularly my nose, smashes into his muscular shoulder blades.

"Oh, dear!" I hear someone in front of Nakoa gasp.

I take a step around him, rubbing my nose, when I see the most beautiful couple. I quickly release my hand from my face and bow.

"Raven," Nakoa says, with a devilish grin. "I'd like to introduce you to King Kalino and Queen Nani."

"Otherwise known as your parents," his mother corrects playfully as she approaches, enveloping him in a tight embrace. Nakoa stiffens in her embrace, then slowly relaxes.

Apparently, he's not much of a hugger.

"I'm so happy you're back safe," she says, releasing him and turning her full attention to me.

Queen Nani is the most stunning woman I've ever seen. Her long black hair flows freely around her body and her gold dress cinches at her waist, then fans out to sway around her ankles.

Her golden eyes scan my mismatched outfit, but there is no judgment passed. Her red lips part and she flashes me a brilliant white smile.

"I'm so pleased you're here," she says, taking my hands.

"That's enough, dear," King Kalino says, placing a hand on his wife's shoulder. "Let the girl relax and change before you try to win her over."

Queen Nani releases my hands and steps back into her husband's open arms. "You're right, dear. Nakoa, will you please take Raven up to the room we prepared?"

Nakoa nods once then turns to leave, however, I, for one, was raised properly.

"Thank you so much for your hospitality, Queen Nani and King Kalino. You truly have a beautiful kingdom, and I am so pleased to meet you both."

Queen Nani reaches for me again, this time bringing me in for a hug. "Oh, sweet girl, anything you need, we are here to help with." She releases me, but keeps me at arm's length. "And please, just call us Nani and Kalino." She hugs me one more time before releasing me to meet Nakoa in the doorway. "We'll see you two at dinner!" she announces just before we exit the room.

"You're a suck up," he says, rounding the corner to another long hallway.

"And you're a dick," I throw back at him, matching him stride for stride. "You knew I was meeting your parents first, didn't you? And dressed like this!?" I shout, pointing at my clothes.

He points at my hair, his stony face never cracking a smile. "Don't forget about your messed up hair."

I stop dead in my tracks and turn toward the floor-to-ceiling window. My reflection is a bit distorted by the glare of the sun, but it clearly reveals the complete mess I appear to be. Loose strands of hair have fallen from my braids and now zig zag across my forehead. The cloak is positioned sideways on my shoulder, revealing the shredded dress underneath, and one of my leather pant legs somehow untucked itself from the boot and sits below my knee.

Freaking wonderful.

Pretending to be unbothered by my appearance, I turn and shoulder check Nakoa with my uninjured arm as I walk past him. I don't make it very far before he calls out after me.

"Your room is actually this way."

I release an annoyed sigh, then turn on my heels and head back toward Nakoa, stopping right in front of him.

I playfully bow. "Lead the way, Your Highness."

The mating bond wrapped around my arm suddenly sends a zing up to my shoulder. I take a quick breath in and note that it didn't come from my end of the bond, which means my nickname must ruffle some of his feathers. Or scales?

When I look up to tease him, he's already turning the corner in the hallway. I jog to catch him and find him standing in front of two massive doors that must lead to my room.

"This is my room, and yours is the last one at the end of the hall. Dinner is at seven. Don't be late." He opens one massive door, steps inside, and shuts it behind him, leaving me in the hallway on my own.

What a dick.

CHAPTER 36
WE HAVE TO STOP MEETING LIKE THIS

I contemplate being late just to spite him, but since we are dining with the King and Queen, I think otherwise. Making my way down to the only other door on this floor, I twist the handle and welcome myself into my new room. The room is spacious, with a canopy bed positioned in the middle. The color scheme is completely opposite from the Vampire Court.

The sheets, curtains, and walls are dusted a golden hue with complementing blues and silvers placed around the room. It reminds me of the ocean, which is visible through another set of floor-to-ceiling windows. I untie my cloak and set it on the table next to the door as I saunter over to look at the view. Our rooms are on the third floor, giving the perfect vantage point to look over the cliff the castle is perched on. I can see the spray of the water as it crashes against the towering cliff.

As I look out at the water, I can't help but remember what my dad's letter said about visiting our spot by the river. I know the exact location he means, but I have no idea how I'll get there.

The Mage Court is at least a four-day ride from here. Although, maybe I can convince Nakoa to fly me there.

Yeah, right.

Unfortunately, this means relying on my unreliable teleporting skills. Frustrated, I lean my forehead against the cool glass, trying to calm my nerves after everything that has happened the past two days. Unconsciously, I reach for my necklace and remember that Amera sent a hologram to Colby, letting him know I was at the Vampire Court. Oddly enough, I've let myself be kidnapped and whisked away yet again to another court.

I close my eyes and try to focus on my mating bonds. Slowly, a vibrant magenta string appears in the darkness, followed by a stunning deep blue string. I reach out my arms and run both hands over each string before bringing them close to my chest. I hug both strings in hopes Asher and Kieran can feel that I'm alive and okay. As I release their strings and watch them fade, another string slowly forms. The glowing golden string wraps up my arm and settles on my skin, sending vibrations through my arm and up my body.

I can feel the strength of Nakoa's mating bond and it's unworldly. I'm tempted to reach out and run my fingers over it too, but I think twice about it. I know he's seen the mating bond, and even felt it, so why does he choose to ignore it? Tomorrow, I'll work on finding out why. I let the string unwind from my arm and watch it fade off into the darkness.

With nothing I can do about my predicament now, I push off the glass and head toward the bathroom, sending up a silent prayer that Amera sent another hologram to Colby to hold off on making an appearance to the Vampire Court. When I open the door to the bathroom, I can't help but stare in awe.

There's a circular cutout in the floor right in the middle of the bathroom. Stepping closer, I realize this is the shower and there's no curtain surrounding it to contain the stray splashes from the shower head that hangs from the ceiling like a chandelier. The floor of the shower is carved out, with five stairs leading down to the base. The last stair circles around the wall creating a bench. I've never seen anything like it, but I'm totally in love.

There are two paths around the shower that lead to a giant walk-in closet. Although it is devoid of clothing, I spot extra pillows and blankets occupying one wall of shelves. Coming back out into the main area, I discard my cut-up dress, leather pants, and boots, then slowly descend into the shower. The water is cold at first before it warms to the perfect temperature. The layout of the shower creates a funnel effect, trapping the steam around my body and keeping me warm and toasty.

Oh yeah. I could get used to this.

After washing and spending a decent amount of time letting the water roll off my body, I decide it's probably best to leave before my fingers and toes turn into prunes. I reach for the towel I set out on the sink and wrap it tightly around my body, looking at my discarded clothes.

There is no way I'm putting this outfit back on.

I exit the bathroom, intent on donning the cloak over my towel and heading to Nakoa's room to ask for new clothing, when my eye catches something draped over the bed. I change direction and head for the bed instead, finding a beautiful soft pink gown sparkling up at me. Holding the dress up for further inspection, it's clear this dress is just as beautiful as the dress I recently cut up.

The sun is starting to set out the window and I realize I've spent too much time in the shower. I lay the dress back on the bed and head back into the bathroom, hoping to find something that resembles a hair dryer. With no luck, I towel dry my hair as best as I can and use the brush I found to comb out the knotted mess. I take two jewel encrusted hairpins I found in the drawer and pin a section of my hair behind each ear flat against my head, creating a sleek, smooth look.

Satisfied, I head back out into the bedroom and step into the dress. The strapless corset pulls in at my waist and hugs my body all the way down over my hips, fanning out slightly past my knees. I slip one arm through three slender beaded straps that fall just above my elbow and notice they match the hairpins in my hair.

I search the room for a pair of shoes that aren't the old muddy boots I arrived in, but find nothing. Running out of time, I give up my search and head for the hallway, hoping to ask Nakoa if he can find me a pair of shoes. When I open the door, I almost smack right into the man waiting outside, but two strong hands stop me before I do.

"You're late. Again."

Without looking up, I can tell his face is going to be scrunched up into a scowl, but I throw on my best smile anyway, hoping to blind him with affection.

"I'm not late. I'm right on time," I say, stepping closer. I can't tell if it's the mating bond buzzing in my chest that wants me closer to him, or just purely for my enjoyment to watch him squirm.

The dark blue velvet jacket he's wearing is open and his white undershirt is tied right above his collar bones, revealing his bare chest. There are intricate gold patterns sewn on the lapels, which bring out his golden eyes. Nakoa drops his hands from my arms and takes a step back. He leans down and picks up a pair of heels from the floor, shoving them into my hands. "If they don't fit, just go barefoot."

He doesn't even wait for me to try the heels on before he turns and heads down the hallway, giving me time to admire his fine backside. I quickly slide my feet into the heels; they're a perfect fit. When I look up again, he's stopped at the end of the hallway, tapping his foot in annoyance.

I straighten and slide my hands slowly down my dress, working out any wrinkles, making sure to make eye contact with

Nakoa the whole time. His eyes follow my hands all the way down my curves, and desire dances in his golden eyes. The sound of my heels on the tile floor snaps him out of his trance, returning his scowl.

"Alright, lead the way," I say, winking at him.

He growls, then extends his arm for me to take. "There are no railings on the stairs, so place your hand on my arm. As much as I'd enjoy watching you tumble down the stairs, my mother wouldn't."

To defy him, I link our arms, but the second our arms touch, the golden mating bond appears and intertwines around us. Nakoa pulls his arm away so fast the motion sends me tumbling forward, just like he originally wanted.

As my body falls forward, he quickly slides his arms around my waist, pulling me closer against his chest. I can feel his fluttering heartbeat through my back and when he turns me to face him, I catch a quick glimpse under his stony mask. His eyes are wide with fear and remorse, but quickly shift back to their calm, uncaring state.

"What is wrong with you?" I push him away from me. "One minute you hate me, the next you look like a lost, lovesick puppy. Seriously, what's your deal?"

Nakoa opens his mouth to say something, then retreats into the hallway as I hear his door slam. Frustrated and confused, I grab the hem of my dress and march over to his door.

"Open the door, Nakoa!" I shout, pounding my fist on the wood.

"Or what?" I hear him challenge me from the other side.

I let out a frustrated cry, then conjure my wind element. I roll it in my hands, gaining speed and power until I have enough, then I slam it right into the door. With a deafening crack, the two doors snap off the hinges and crash into his room, revealing Nakoa leaning up against his bed with his arms crossed, one eyebrow cocked as if to say, "impressive."

I step over shards of splintered wood and walk right up to him, poking my finger right in his chest.

"What. Is. Wrong. With. You?"

"Don't push it, Raven," he warns, trying to step around me.

"No. Don't give me that shit!" I yell, stepping back in front of him. "I know you feel the mating bond. I know you see it just as I do." Calming myself, I take a step back, giving him the space he requested. "Do you really find it so repulsing to be mated to me?"

Nakoa looks up at me, his eyes softening. He takes a step forward, his arms reaching out to comfort me, when someone gasps behind us. We quickly jump apart and turn to find Queen Nani standing in the doorway.

"What happened? I came to check on you two since you weren't at dinner yet and heard a loud crash." She places her hand over her heart, and fans herself with the other hand. "I never expected to see this."

I open my mouth to apologize, but Nakoa steps in front of me. "I was teasing Raven and bet her she couldn't knock over the door. I lost."

The Queen pins him with a look. "Nakoa, have I not raised you better than this?"

"Sorry, Mother."

The Queen lingers another moment inspecting the damage, then turns to leave but halts near the doorframe. "Nice work, Raven. I expect to see you two down at dinner shortly."

When she exits the hallway, I turn to follow her, but Nakoa grabs my arm.

"Let go of me," I growl back in his face.

He lets go and I stride down the hallway after the Queen by myself. I follow the winding stairs down to the main floor and stop at the bottom to compose myself, wiping a stray angry tear away from my eye. Out of nowhere, a white handkerchief appears from around the corner, startling me.

"I give you my permission to punch him if you want," the King says, stepping around the corner to meet me. I laugh lightly, taking his handkerchief and dabbing away the stray tears. "Or you could turn him into a cat. Dragons absolutely HATE cats."

"If I had the ability to do that, I definitely would," I admit, folding the cloth up and handing it back to him.

He extends his arm with a smile, and I interlock mine with his. He leads me down another hallway and into a workshop. The smell of pine, cedar, and hickory bombard my senses, reminding me of my dad. The King releases my arm and reaches for a smooth piece of wood. "The Queen and I are so happy you're here, Raven. We were good friends of your father's and were so caught off guard when he passed."

My attention snaps over to King Kalino. "I didn't know you knew my dad."

"Yes, Lucas and I were very close. We used to hate going to meetings, so we made a game counting how many times Antonio would try to bring up the way things used to be before the barrier. The loser had to buy the first round of drinks after the meeting." He laughs, shaking his head.

That statement sets me on alert. Internally, I question if I should reveal Antonio brought me here to use me to bring the barrier down, but looking at King Kalino, I can tell he's a genuine person and has no ill intentions toward me.

"Antonio had me and my grandpa kidnapped. He wanted to use me to bring down the barrier, but I rejected his offer." The thought of my grandpa brings fresh tears to my eyes.

The King stands, offering me his handkerchief again. "And your grandfather?" he questions.

"He was killed by someone I used to call a friend."

"I'm so sorry, Raven," he says, pulling me into a hug. "I will inform the Mage Court immediately. This will not go unpunished and if need be, the Dragon Court will ally with the Mage Court."

I look up through teary eyes at this caring man who reminds me of my dad. He gives me one more tight squeeze, then takes a step back, holding my chin up with his hand. "Give Nakoa time to come around to the mating bond." Surprise falls across my face at his words and he laughs and continues, "Yes, I know about your bond. When you two entered the waiting hall to greet us, it was like you both became the sun and the room got brighter. Plus," he says, bumping his hand under my chin, "I'm the King. Nothing gets past me in my own court."

We leave the workshop and the King leads us to the dining room. The servants bow as they open the door for the King and me. When I enter, my eyes lock with Nakoa standing at the table and I can feel his uneasiness through the bond. The King pats my arm and releases me to take his seat next to his wife, while I make my way to the open seat next to Nakoa.

He lowers his head and pulls my chair for me, pushing it in as I sit. I smile politely in his direction, but don't thank him. He can sulk and feel sorry for himself all he wants. I have come to the conclusion, after talking to the King, that if Nakoa wants to feel out our bond and see where it could go, he has to come to me. I can be just as stubborn as him.

My eyes roam the table at all the delicious foods laid out in front of us. As soon as the King fills his plate, we begin adding food to our own plates. I must look like a complete fool loading my plate up with all kinds of foods, but I don't care. It's been over two days since I've had a proper meal and I'm going to take full advantage of the display in front of me.

"Raven, I'm so sorry about your grandfather."

Nakoa snaps his fork next to me, and my head swivels toward the Queen as I nearly choke on my wine. "How did you know?"

The Queen looks between Nakoa and I and smiles. "The King shared with me through our mating bond."

"I didn't know mates could do that?"

"Of course. Only the strongest connected mates are able to do this."

The King reaches for the Queen's hand, holding it lovingly. "I told Raven anything she needs, we will provide."

"He's right, dear. Anything at all, and we will be the first to help."

I set my glass down before my shaky hand spills it all over my gorgeous dress. I hardly know these people, but I feel like I've known them my whole life. I sense Nakoa shift and his fingers brush the back of my hand under the table. He gives my hand one quick squeeze, then retracts his hand. Even though it was small, the gesture still warms my heart.

Dinner goes by relatively quickly, with the Queen trying to embarrass poor Nakoa and pelting me with questions about the Human Realm until the King steps in.

"Alright, dear. Let the poor kids get some sleep. They're going to need it before Raven's training starts tomorrow."

"Training?!" Nakoa and I question at the same time.

The King smiles wide. "Yes, Raven needs proper training on how to defend herself if her powers fail her," he shifts his gaze toward his son and finishes, "and Nakoa will train you."

Nakoa lets an annoyed laugh slip from his lips, clearly not caring that I'm sitting right next to him. "Father, I have more pressing matters to attend to. I can't just drop everything and train her."

"Fine, if you won't train her, then I'll have Kai train her. Raven," the King says to me, "meet me here tomorrow morning and I'll take you there myself."

"Father!" Nakoa shouts, shooting up from his chair, knocking it over in the process.

He looks back at Nakoa with a stern look. "End of discussion."

The King kisses the Queen and leaves the dining room and Nakoa quickly follows him, leaving me with the Queen. She takes a long sip of her wine, then stands before I question, "Who is Kai?"

She looks at me and smiles. "The Captain of the Dragon Army and only the most handsome, eligible bachelor at the Dragon Court." She turns and glides out of the room, leaving me thinking that I've just been set up by the King.

I don't see Nakoa for the rest of the night. When I pass by his room, the doors have been replaced and the mess from our fight has been cleaned up. I quietly enter my room to find a lovely, lightweight nightgown waiting on the bed. Feeling exhausted, I change and crawl into bed. Nuzzling my face into the pillow and with a sigh, I wonder what Asher, Kieran, Leah, and Colby are doing back in the Human Realm. It doesn't take long for the sounds of the crashing waves to lull me to sleep.

CHAPTER 37

WHAT A PAIN IN MY NECK

ASHER

My neck is killing me. Leah and I crashed at Kieran's in case there was any news from the Vampire Court. Kieran retreated to his room around midnight and Leah never left Colby's room after he left yesterday morning, which means I had to sleep on the living room couch. Kieran at least gave me a pillow, but there was no way of being comfortable since the couch was too small for me. I had to curl up in a ball or have my feet hang off the side.

I sit up and stretch my neck, checking the clock on the wall. It's nearly six in the morning and I haven't heard as much as a toilet flush. I grab my phone and head out the door, sending a quick message to Kieran, letting him know I'll be back soon. When the cool morning air rushes my skin, I take off running. The pace is quicker than my normal morning jog, but I have a lot of pent-up emotions that I've been shoving down the past two days.

Elation at the fact that I finally had enough courage to take the leap of faith with Raven and let her know how I feel, revealing the mating bond between us. I knew she always felt the same about me, but hearing her say it out loud made me feel like I was on cloud nine. Until I found out she is also mated to Kieran. The anger and betrayal I felt in that moment fuels my jog into a full on sprint.

I know it's not her fault for being mated to two people, but what does that mean for our relationship? Not that we can talk it out because she's currently being held hostage at the Vampire Court by a psychopath. Which is partially my fault because if Kieran and I didn't push her to her limit yesterday, her powers wouldn't have gone haywire, and she wouldn't have teleported.

I push my legs harder, carrying me faster down the street. My blood is pounding in my ears and I'm so deep in my head that when I turn the corner and cut across the street, I don't see the car barreling straight for me. Within a fraction of a second from being hit, I jump, hoping that my momentum is enough to carry me across the car before it can hit me. The driver honks and swerves, giving me the finger out of his window as he continues down the street.

I lay sprawled out in the grass, catching my breath. The dewy grass seeps into my clothes and the sun is just starting to peek through the trees. With a heavy sigh, I stand and realize I'm right outside my apartment. I must have run here unconsciously, but I'm glad I did. I need a shower and a change of clothes.

Unlocking the door, I quickly set the keys on the counter and head for the fridge. I reach for a bottle of water and chug nearly the whole thing, taking the bottle with me to my room. I undress out of my damp clothes and chuck them in the hamper in the corner of my room next to the dresser.

A picture catches my eye as I walk toward the dresser and pick up the wooden frame. It's a picture of me and Raven at our high school graduation. She has the stem of a rose in her mouth with a huge smile on her face. I've got my arm around her shoulders, holding my rose out for her to take. It's one of my favorite pictures of us, considering Raven framed it and gave it to me for my birthday last year.

I smile as I set the picture down and head toward the shower. My shower is quick, as I've been gone for almost thirty minutes. My phone dings as soon as I exit the shower and my body takes control as I dash for my phone on my bed.

VAMPIRE PRICK

Got news. Need you here ASAP.

I throw my towel off and quickly change. There's no time to run, so as soon as I exit the apartment building, I shift into my hawk form. It feels like forever before I finally reach Kieran's, but when I slam the door open and glance at the clock, it's only a little past seven.

"What's the news?" I pant, watching Kieran pace the room. I look at Leah and she just shrugs and continues to sip her coffee on the couch. Her eyes are slightly puffy, which tells me she probably spent the night crying. I make my way toward her and plop down, sliding my arm around her shoulders. She sighs and leans into me, placing her head on my shoulder.

"We received a message from Colby's aunt, but Leah convinced me to wait until you returned to open it," Kieran says, still pacing.

I squeeze her leg gently with my hand. "Thank you."

"No biggy." She shrugs. "Now you can open it, Kieran."

He rolls his eyes and grabs the hologram device from his pocket, setting it on the table. He places his finger on the top and I hear all three of us take a collective breath, preparing for whatever message we are about to receive.

"Kieran, I have to be quick. I just overheard that Antonio has locked Colby away in one of the towers after he arrived at court."

Leah tenses beside me, and she grabs my hand and squeezes. Kieran stiffens but doesn't take his gaze from the wall.

"Raven has escaped, or was kidnapped, I'm not exactly sure. Antonio seems to think it was one of the dragons that he invited to the dinner. I'm so sorry that I failed, but if Antonio finds Raven first, I fear it might not end well. I'm monitoring Colby, but Antonio has forbidden me from seeing him. Vail was able to talk to one of the guards, and he said Antonio hasn't harmed Colby. He just wants him locked up so he can't get in the way of any plans. I'm so sorry, but I have to go now. I'll contact you if I find anything else."

The hologram is cut off and Kieran slams his fist into the wall. "I will kill Antonio." Kieran seethes, pulling his hand from the drywall.

I'm not sure if he is upset about Colby getting captured or Raven escaping and or getting kidnapped again. I know Raven is smart enough to escape, but if she was captured by someone else, who knows what could happen. I reign in my own emotions and focus on calming down Kieran.

Leah sets her mug down on the coffee table and stands, placing her hands on her hips. "You need to calm down." She points at Kieran. "Colby knew the risks of going back to the Vampire Court. At least he isn't being harmed. Be thankful for that."

I stand, walking around Leah. "I agree. He knew the risks."

Kieran narrows his eyes and turns to pace the living room again. "We're going to have to portal to the Dragon Court and hope they don't kill us on the spot."

I'm not happy about barging into the Dragon Court since dragons are very territorial creatures, but I am looking forward to seeing their territory again. I've only been there once with my uncle right before my family moved to the Human Realm, so my memory is a little foggy, but I'll never forget seeing the giant castle perched on an island. I was mesmerized by the waves crashing up against the cliffs, spraying iridescent rainbows in the sun behind the castle.

"When do you think you'll be able to withstand sunlight again?" I grumble.

Kieran stares at me for a moment, then answers. "I should be able to travel tonight. Our night should match up with the Realm of Shadows night tonight, so we will be able to travel after sundown."

"Great. That gives us time to figure out the safest place to open a portal."

"What should I do?" Leah pipes up.

Kieran and I share a look, thinking the same thing.

"You're staying here," Kieran says.

"The hell I am!" Leah shouts. "I'm going on this rescue mission to save my best friend and my boyfriend. You can't just leave me here," she says, throwing her hands up. "What if someone comes for me, too?"

I sigh, shaking my head. "She's right," I say to Kieran. "The safest place is for her to be with us, unfortunately."

"It's settled then," Leah says, grabbing her coffee mug. "Tonight, we travel to the Dragon Court."

CHAPTER 38

'IS IT HOT IN HERE, OR IS IT JUST ME?

Waking up early the next morning, I feel extra refreshed. This is a major improvement from the first time after I teleported and woke up with a massive magic hangover. And since I pretty much slept off the magic hangover the second time I teleported since I was drugged, I prefer waking up this way much more.

The bed is unbelievably soft, and I fell asleep within minutes of my head hitting the soft, lavender scented pillow. Not wanting to be late to training, I throw the covers back and take a minute to stretch my muscles. My shoulder is still sore, but instead of the intense pain, it's more of a small nagging pain. Annoying, yet bearable.

I finish my stretches, then make the bed before there is a knock at the door. Not expecting anyone this early, I'm surprised when I see a pleasant-looking, middle-aged woman looking back at me. "Oh, good morning!" I say, cheerfully.

She curtsies and holds her arms out to me, handing me a pile of clothes. "Morning, miss. Here are your training clothes for the day."

I stare at the clothes in my arms, then back at the woman. "Thank you . . . um . . . "

"Liza, miss."

I smile brightly back at Liza. "Thank you, Liza."

She curtsies again, then she turns and heads back down the hallway. I quietly shut the door and lay the clothes on the bed. I reach behind me to braid my hair as I stare at the black outfit in front of me.

I remove my nightgown and put on what looks like a black, skintight sports bra then pause to figure out the next article of clothing. It's a long, slim, very soft piece of fabric, with a thick black belt sitting on top of it. Confused on how I'm even supposed to wear it, I instead grab the pair of high-waisted, black leather leggings and slide them on. Just as I shimmy into my pants, there's another knock at the door.

I open the door, and my face falls. "Oh, it's just you."

"Why are you opening the door not properly dressed!?" Nakoa questions, turning around quickly.

"Uh, I am dressed."

"No, you're standing there in your training undergarments." I try to walk around him, but he turns to keep me behind him.

"Where is your training shirt?"

"I couldn't figure out how to put it on."

"Oh, for the love," Nakoa growls. He turns around, marching straight into my room, avoiding eye contact all together as he grabs the apparent "shirt" and holds it out. "Come here."

"What are you doing?" I ask, bewildered.

"I'm going to help you dress so you're not late," he says, annoyed, but still not making eye contact with me.

"I thought you weren't training me?" I question, placing my hands on my hips.

"I'm not, but the King had important business come up and

assigned me to escort you to the training grounds. After that, I'm gone."

I saunter forward and step in front of him. "Well then, how are you going to help me dress if you can't even look at me?"

Slowly, his eyes meet mine and my insides feel like they're on fire. The desire reignites in his eyes as he lets his eyes roam away from mine and over my body. I take a tentative step closer, feeling the mating bond pulling us together.

Nakoa clenches his eyes shut and releases a heavy sigh. When he opens them again, the desire is tamed, and his expression hardens into the all too familiar grumpy face. He loops the garment over my head and drapes it over my shoulders, criss-crossing the material in front of my body. His strong hands take my hips and turn me around, grabbing the excess material and tying it behind me. He then takes the thick belt off the bed and secures it around my waist, cinching the back and tying it off.

His hands trail over my back for a split second, flaming the fire inside me where his fingers brush against my exposed skin, then he retreats to the door.

"Come, Princess, let's get this over with. I have things to attend to."

After stopping by the kitchen to grab a quick breakfast to go, we're off to the training grounds. Nakoa helps me into the waiting carriage and follows quickly behind, taking the seat opposite from me. We eat our breakfast in silence, but it's not because I'm giving him the silent treatment. I'm too busy with my face pressed up against the window, taking in the beautiful sights.

When the carriage passes over the stone bridge that separates the town from the castle, I gaze at the clear blue water below. Instead of driving through the city, we take a road leading us around and out to the giant stone building that I remember the two dragons flew to. As we travel farther from the castle, the tall buildings of the city start to taper out, becoming smaller and more spaced out until we reach a wide-open field. Colorful flowers are sprinkled within the knee-high grass that rolls over the hills.

Before we reach the large building, Nakoa finally breaks the silence. "How is your room? Did you sleep okay?" he asks, shifting uncomfortably. Small talk doesn't suit him, but I spare him a soft smile.

"The room is great and yes, I slept just fine; thank you." I fix my gaze back out the window and that's the end of our conversation until we pull into the entrance of the building.

Nakoa clears his throat as if to draw my attention back to him. "Once we enter the building, I will leave to attend my meetings. You'll meet Kalena and follow her to the training arena where she will drop you off with Captain Ahe and pick you up again once training is over."

"Is Kalena your assistant?" I ask curiously. *I feel bad for her if she is.*

"No. She's the Commander of the E.D.O."

"E.D.O.?"

"Elite Dragon Operatives. They're the best of the best and she's the first female to make the group, let alone become commander." He leans forward, resting his elbows on his knees. "I suggest not messing with her." This is clearly meant to be a warning.

Noted.

The carriage pulls up and stops just under a walkway connecting the two buildings. Nakoa opens the door and exits, then turns to lend his hand as I step out. Three uniformed men stand at the entrance of each building. To the left is a plain two-story building where I'm guessing Nakoa will be retreating to, and to the right is a massive four-story arena where I'll be.

A fierce-looking woman emerges from the arena on the right. Her tall, lean body is dressed in an outfit similar to mine, except she has on a silver breastplate. Her long, honey-colored hair is pulled into a tight ponytail, with one small braid streaking through the right side of her hair. Her chocolate eyes lock on mine as she approaches.

Nakoa wasn't kidding when he said not to mess with her. She looks like she could rip me in half with one hand tied behind her back. I stand straighter, not letting her intimidate me. I expect her to completely ignore me and walk straight past me. Instead, she stops right in front of me and smiles, leaning in so Nakoa can't hear her.

"So, you're the girl who has put our little prince in his place?"

I'm so shocked at the words, I huff out a nervous laugh. "That'd be me." I smile, winking at her.

She leans back and laughs at the ceiling. Stepping forward, placing one arm over my shoulders, she starts to lead me to the arena. "Oh yes, you and I are going to be good friends."

"Be quick, Kalena!" Nakoa yells after us. "The meeting is starting soon."

She waves her middle finger at him as she leads me farther into the arena. "Don't mind his terrible attitude. His parents' wonderful personalities skipped right over him."

I can't help but laugh with her. "You must get on his nerves as much as I do."

"Hell yeah I do. Someone's gotta be the fun one and it's definitely not Mr. No Nonsense Nakoa."

She's a bad ass battle chick, but she's also down to earth and funny as hell. She retracts her arm as she opens the door for us, leading into a small room overlooking the main floor of the training grounds.

"I want to be just like you when I grow up," I say wholeheartedly as I walk past her, holding the door. She laughs again and shakes her head.

Someone clears their throat and we both look over to a man dressed similarly to us, but instead of the intricately wrapped shirt, he wears a tight white tank top. I hear Kalena sigh in annoyance behind me.

"You must be Raven," the man says, extending his hand.

I shake his hand as I nod. "You must be Captain Ahe?"

"Oh, please," he laughs gently, "just call me Kai." He looks up at Kalena and gives her a tight smile. "I've got it from here, Kalena. I'll see you after training."

"Yes, Captain." She turns to leave but hesitates at the door. "Raven, if you need anything, we will be just over the walkway."

"Okay, thanks, Kalena," I say, taking my hand from Kai's. I can certainly see what Queen Nani was talking about when she said he was handsome. He's just as tall as Nakoa, but his eyes are light brown whereas Nakoa's are gold. His dark hair is cut short, but it looks good on him. He really is handsome, but I feel nothing when I look at him. My only objective here is to learn to defend myself if my powers fail me.

"Alright," Kai says, clapping his hands together. "Let's get down there and get started."

He leads us down the stairs and out a door to the arena. The field is huge and the whole third level is lined with windows overlooking the field. Half of the roof is open to allow the morning sun to light up the space. Our section is gated off, with an octagon ring in the middle. It reminds me of a UFC octagon, except this one has padded walls. There are elevated bleachers on either side for people to observe as well.

There is a small group of soldiers practicing fencing in the corner, another group working on hand to hand combat, and on the far side it looks like the men and women are doing sprints.

Yep. Definitely going to avoid the far side at all costs.

"Okay," Kai says, walking farther into the arena, "first, we are going to test your stamina. We're going to warm up with some running exercises."

Yay me.

As we walk to the far side, everyone in the arena spares a

quick glance at me. Obviously, they can tell from my aura that I'm a witch, but they're probably wondering what I'm doing here. Honestly, right about now, I'm asking myself the same thing.

There are cones set up on one half of our side, which are currently being used for short sprint drills by the soldiers. On the other half are flat ladders for footwork. I groan internally; this is going to suck. I played soccer all the way up until college, but after that, there were only a few times I decided to go for a run just for the heck of it. This? This does NOT look like fun.

Kai closes the distance between him and his soldiers currently running through the drills. He stops to chat with a few soldiers who are waiting for their teams to finish up. Once the teams are done, half of them pack their things and head to a different station in the arena. The one remaining team lines up and waits for further instructions.

"Team," Kai says, addressing them, "this is Raven. Today, she will be training with us per the orders of the King and Queen."

Some eyebrows raise in surprise, but they quickly return to their neutral state. "Raven, why don't you break off with the ladies, and they can run you through the warmup."

The men break off to join Kai by the cones to run through more sprint drills. I'm left with three women, two of which look like they're annoyed to have to babysit me. The other girl is shorter than me, with light brown hair that's pulled into a tight pony like Kalena's. She seems friendlier than the other two that are now making their way to the beginning of the course.

"Hi, I'm Faya," she says, leading me toward the bench. She catches me looking over at the other two girls, eyeing them suspiciously. "Don't worry about those two. Their permanent R.B.F. is a natural deterrent for new people." She laughs.

"Oh, thank goodness," I sigh. "I thought they were plotting

my demise," I joke. Faya laughs again as we sit, stretching out our limbs.

"So, what brings you to our side of the world? You must be pretty special if the King and Queen are letting you train with us. Normally, no one other than dragons are allowed to practice with us," Faya says. The question is meant to be an opener for small talk, but I must be careful on how much information I divulge.

"The King just thought it would be fun to have me brush up on some training regimens to help me with my powers."

"That's cool!" she says, standing. She leads us over to the other girls and introduces us. "Leera, Amalla, this is Raven."

"We know," Amalla says, rolling her eyes.

"Just don't get in our way," Leera adds.

Faya shrugs and gets in line in front of me. "Just watch us run through a few times, then, when you feel comfortable, jump in. We usually go for two minutes with a thirty-second break. Then repeat five times."

I nod as I watch them start. And this is just the warm up?

Yep. I'm definitely going to die today.

After watching the girls run through twice, I think I have the hang of the pattern. First, we sprint to the ladder, the first round is a one step, in which we run through placing each foot in each box, then jog back to the start. The second round is a side step, where we start facing sideways, then tap our feet on the inside of each box. The third set is crossover, which is a sideway run through the ladder with each foot touching the inside of each box. Once you're done with those three, the whole cycle repeats itself.

I make it through the first two sets and feel pretty good about myself. In the third set, my calves start to burn and by the last set, Leera and Amalla lap me. Finally, when Faya calls time after the last round, I crumple to the ground with my eyes closed and hands above my head. Leera and Amalla snicker at the water table, but I don't care. A shadow appears to block the scorching sun and I look up to see Faya bending down to hand me a cup of water.

"It's better if you stand straight up with your hands on your head. It'll expand your lungs and help you breathe better."

I take the cup from her hand and down it after getting to my feet. "Thanks," I say, wiping my mouth with the back of my sweaty hand.

I jump when I hear Kai's voice right behind me. "How was the warmup, ladies?"

Leera and Amalla stand at attention behind me, and Faya stiffens beside me.

"Good, Captain," the two girls behind me say in unison.

"Lovely, let's switch and move to sprints then."

All three girls make their way to the other side of our half and stretch out again, getting ready for sprints. Kai walks with me as I follow behind the girls.

"You can be honest. How was it?" he asks, smiling down at me with his hands behind his back.

"Well, let's just say I won't be running any marathons anytime soon."

He chuckles and checks his watch. "Alright, I'll let you get back to it."

We depart as he heads toward the group of men setting up for the ladders. When I glance back at Faya, she's frowning.

"Okay. What's with the face? Are you plotting my demise now, too?"

She laughs lightly, bringing the smile back to her face like I intended. "I would never."

"Okay, then what is it?"

She sighs and slides closer to me. "Captain Ahe is great, don't get me wrong, but he favors the men more than the women."

I scrunch my eyebrows and look back at Kai. He's joining in the warmup and laughing with his men. He catches me looking and gives me a small wave. I nod back at him, then turn to Faya.

"Not too long ago, women weren't allowed in the Dragon Army, but now that we are, some men still believe our places are at home with the family." She pauses to take a drink, then continues, "When Kalena rose through the ranks and passed the E.D.O. exam, it opened so many more doors for us. She's pretty much our hero," Faya says, placing her hand over her heart as she smiles at me.

"So, Kai is like our very own Gaston."

"Gast-who?" Faya says confused.

"Nothing." I laugh to myself. I grab Faya's shoulders and peer right into her eyes. "To hell with those men, then. Show them that you're just as good of a fighter as they are. If not better!" I say, punching her lightly on the shoulder.

She laughs and shakes her head. "You would fit in just fine here, Raven. Now, let's get you in shape."

"Round is a shape," I point out, which has her laughing again.

I watch again as Faya explains the drill. This one doesn't seem to be that bad. Faya and I are partners, and Leera and Amalla are partners. The first person sprints to the last cone, then sprints back, then sprints to the middle cone and sprints back, then sprints to the first cone, then sprints back, and the next partner does the same. When your partner is running, that's your break time. We do this for ten minutes and I swear when the timer goes off, I could be a dragon myself with the way my lungs are on fire.

Instead of collapsing to the ground, I take Faya's advice and stand straight with my hands on my head. I'm able to catch my breath quicker and slow my breathing, trying to cool off my burning lungs. Just when I think I am starting to catch my breath, Kai sneaks up behind me again.

"Ready to show me your fighting skills?" he asks, scaring me so badly that I jump and dump my water cup all over Leera. Amalla laughs until Leera throws dagger eyes at her. I swear if she had an actual dagger, it would already be embedded in Amalla's leg. Faya just laughs and tosses a towel at Leera as she passes by.

Faya pats me on the back, leading me behind Kai to the other end of the arena. "I can't wait to see your powers," Faya adds excitedly.

"Doesn't the Dragon Court have an open territory?" I ask. I remember before my family moved to the Human Realm that the Dragon, Shifter, and Mage Courts all had open borders, meaning any supernatural being could come and go as they pleased.

"We do," Faya confirms, "but ever since the Vampire Court started gaining more supporters to Antonio's plan to bring down the barrier, things have become rather tense. Most people find it more comforting to stay within their own courts rather than risk traveling and running into rogue vampires."

"That's terrible. People shouldn't be afraid to be free," I argue. Have things really declined so much since my family left? I make a mental note to ask Nakoa if there is any way to contact Amera and find out if Colby received her message. Okay, scratch that. Maybe I should ask Queen Nani instead.

Kai allows me to wander around with Faya while he sets up what he needs for the sparring lesson. After a short break, Kai strolls up to the side of the octagon and nods to a few people in the ring already. They quickly finish their training and exit, bowing their heads as they pass by Kai.

"Alright, Raven," Kai says, turning toward me, opening the door to the octagon, "let's see what you got."

CHAPTER 39

THAT'S GOING TO LEAVE A MARK

I enter the ring and walk around the perimeter, stretching my neck, shoulders, and legs. Kai follows behind me, latching the door shut.

"So, am I allowed to use my powers now?" I ask.

Kai circles me slowly, keeping me opposite from him. "I would prefer that you refrain from using your powers. This is about teaching you to physically defend yourself if your powers fail you."

I nod my head, channeling all the things I learned from my self-defense class. Kai doesn't know anything about me, so this should give me a little bit of an element of surprise to hold off his attacks. We continue to circle each other as more soldiers gather around the outside of the octagon on the bleachers. My nerves build as the crowd grows. I'm either going to do decently with the skills I already know, or this is going to end up with me horribly embarrassed.

Kai is the first one to make a move, striking out to grab my wrists. I sidestep him easily and spin away, facing him again. He quickly turns and attacks again, this time snatching one of my wrists. I use the move that I was taught and smash my heel into his toe, bringing my free elbow down on his wrist and breaking my other hand free. Faya cheers from the bleachers, along with some whistling from a few soldiers.

Kai takes a step back, smiling in surprise at my counterattack. "Nice moves, Raven. It looks like you're not helpless after all."

I smirk at him as we circle each other again. This time, I strike first, dropping low to swipe his legs. He jumps over me just in time and lands behind me. He rolls as he lands, giving me enough time to get back to my feet. I see him calculate his next move and I'm ready for it. He lunges forward, grabbing my wrist again, but this time I lean forward, letting him take my wrist as I drop my shoulder and ram it into his chest. His momentum carries him over my shoulder as I throw him to the ground.

There's a beat of silence, then the crowd erupts. I'm so caught up in my small victory that I don't realize Kai shifting below me. He swings his feet out, catching mine, and I fall face first on the mat. Kai quickly takes advantage and pins me to the ground. I'm able to spin around so my back is on the mat, unfortunately putting myself in a compromising position with Kai on all fours on top of me.

Frustrated at my lack of awareness, I bring my knee up to jam it into his stomach. Unfortunately for me, his reaction is to crumble inwards, causing his forehead to collide with my cheek just below my eye.

Pain instantly radiates throughout my head, but all I can do is laugh. Of course, this would happen to me. Just another bruise to add to a quickly growing collection. Kai recovers and crawls over to where I'm sitting.

"Raven, I'm so sorry," he says, removing my hand from my face. He winces as he stares at my face. I'm sure the bruise is already starting to show through my fair skin.

"It's fine, really." I wave him off. "It's my fault, anyway," I say, standing. "I shouldn't have taken a cheap shot on you."

Kai jogs over to the door and unlatches it for Faya. She's already grabbed an ice pack and is heading my way. "You're such a badass. Even without your powers." She smiles, slapping the ice on my face. "Who taught you how to fight like that?"

"My best friend and I took a self-defense class together. Best hundred bucks I ever spent," I declare proudly, as we walk out of the octagon.

Kai stops me just outside the cage. "Raven, are you sure you're okay?"

"Pish posh, it's just a black eye." My blood is pounding under my cheek, but I'm not about to show any weakness in front of these soldiers.

"Why don't you take the rest of the day off and we can start again tomorrow. I'll have Faya escort you back to the castle."

I give a mini salute as I walk past him. "Sure thing, boss man."

Faya leads me out of the arena and up the stairs into one of the rooms that overlooks the training arena. "Okay, why don't you just lay back and relax. I'm going to call Kalena and see if the meeting is over."

I make my way to one of the couches and plop down with my ice pack. "You don't need to bother them, and I certainly don't want to take you away from your training."

"Captain Ahe said that I am to escort you back to the castle, and that's what I'm going to do," she states matter-of-factly.

"Faya, I'm fine. It's just a silly black eye. I'm not dying," I say, standing up and making my way to the door, but the look on her face tells me she's not convinced. I sigh in frustration, removing the ice pack from my face. She tries to conceal her gasp. "That bad, huh?"

"At least it brings out your eyes," she says sarcastically, opening the door for me.

We both fall into a fit of laughter as she leads me out to the carriage. We leave a note for one of the guards to give to Kalena after the meeting, informing her I've gone back to the castle for the day. Our ride home is filled with questions from both of us. She asks me about moving to the Human Realm and I ask her what her favorite things are about the Dragon Court. Before we know it, the carriage comes to a halt, and the door is opened by one of the guards.

"Thank you so much for riding back with me," I say, genuinely happy even though my cheek is still throbbing.

"Of course! See you tomorrow!" Faya waves as the carriage pulls away down the drive.

It's just about midday, and the sun is shining brightly. I head toward the kitchen to see if I can find some bread and meat for a sandwich. Luckily, the kitchen is empty of workers and there is a plethora of bread, cheese, and meats. I quickly whip up a sandwich and head back to my room to shower and decide to explore the grounds a bit while Nakoa is gone.

When I open the door to my room, I'm surprised to see a fresh vase of flowers on the table next to my door. The deep red roses are beautiful, and the baby's breath compliments them perfectly. I snatch the note from the stand and notice it's from Nakoa's parents.

Welcome Raven, we are so thrilled you're here with us and even more thrilled to invite you to your welcoming ball tomorrow.

See you at dinner, Kalino and Nani.

I'm excited for two whole seconds before I remember the marvelous shiner I'll be sporting tomorrow. No amount of makeup will be able to cover this one, I'm afraid. I groan and place the card back on the table, heading right for the shower.

After a relaxing shower, I wrap my towel around myself and walk back toward the closet and stop short. While I was gone, someone filled the closet with all kinds of clothes. Giddy with excitement, I do a little happy dance, then charge into the closet, running my hands over all the different materials.

I change into a pair of black leather leggings and a dusty blue button down, then grab a new set of black boots and head back out toward my room. As I finish looping the last button on my shirt, I look up to find Nakoa leaning against the door frame. When our eyes meet and he sees my face, his nostrils flare as he kicks off the door frame and marches right toward me.

Oh shit. He's mad.

CHAPTER 40

I'M IN TROUBLE

NAKOA

I'm furious.

When our meeting ended, I sent Kalena to retrieve Raven, but instead, as we exited the office, one of the soldiers passed a note to Kalena. Her smirk told me all I needed to know, even before I snatched the note from her hands.

"Who did this to you?" I demand, marching right up to Raven.

"Is that a love letter in your hand?" she jokes, trying to deflect my question.

"You know damn well what this is," I say, shoving the note into her chest.

She smirks and takes the note, unfolding it gently. She reads as she steps around me.

Dear Kalena, there was a little incident today, so Faya and I left training early. Don't let Nakoa yell at you for losing me, since this isn't your fault.

She lifts her gaze and smirks as she continues to read the note.

P.S. Nakoa, I know you've snatched this note from Kalena. I'm okay. I promise.

She finishes the note and smiles as she folds the finished letter. "See. I'm fine."

"How can you say you're fine! Look at your face!" I practically yell.

"What? You don't think it makes me look bad ass?" She pouts, crossing her arms over her chest.

"What happened at training?" I demand again, a little nicer this time.

Raven turns on her heel and walks over to the window, her hips swaying in a way I can't help but notice. "Kai and I—"

"Captain Ahe," I correct her, redirecting my eyes quickly to her face as she turns to scold me. I hate the idea of them getting close. Especially when my blood boils when she says his name.

Kai and I used to be friends, but when Kalena signed up for the E.D.O., I found out that Kai intentionally tried to sabotage her in the first round. Well, not him, but he sent his recruits to do it on his behalf. I didn't have any proof, of course, but I cornered him and warned him if he did it again, he would have to answer to the King and Queen.

It's no secret that most of the men in the Dragon Army don't like that women can now join the ranks, but being a captain means getting over yourself and dealing with it. To say that I'm actively looking for Kai's replacement is an understatement.

"Yeah, sure." She eyes me. "Captain Ahe wanted to see how well I could defend myself in the ring without my powers. I surprised him by taking him down, but he recovered and pinned me instead."

My blood starts to burn my body, hearing someone else was putting their hands on her. She must feel my growing rage when she glances at me from the window.

"Don't worry, after he straddled me, I shoved my knee in his stomach, but unfortunately his head jerked forward and smashed into my cheek."

I'm seeing red.

"I'm going to kill Captain Ahe for touching what isn't his," I bite out, striding for the door.

Raven quickly jumps into action, practically sprinting across the room to throw her back against the door, trapping me inside. "It was an accident, Nakoa!" she pleads, placing her hands on my chest.

"He touched you," I manage to say with my jaw clenched tight. I reach for her, grabbing her wrist gently. "He touched what wasn't his."

Her eyes narrow in a challenge as she tries to pull her hands from my grasp. "I. Am. No. Ones," she bites out in my face. Oh, how wrong she is.

"You're mine," I demand.

The next thing I know, my lips crush against her soft pink lips. I've caught Raven off guard because her lips purse under mine. Finally, she sighs and returns my kiss. When her mouth parts and my tongue dances with hers, I see fireworks. My body feels like I've been hit by lightning and I'm buzzing with energy.

I drop her wrists and she doesn't hesitate to snake her arms around my shoulders, grabbing a fist full of hair in one hand. I moan as our bodies crash together against the wooden door. She pulls on the fist full of hair to pull me back from her slightly, letting us come up for air.

"I'm not yours, Nakoa. You haven't earned me," she whispers against my lips.

I didn't know words could make me so crazy. The challenge to make her mine has my heart racing at a million miles a minute. I crash my lips onto her again, nipping at her bottom lip. She moans with pleasure and the sound has me wanting to spend every day winning her over. My hands trail down her soft blouse and land on her hips. I want to explore where this could go, and the realization hits me so hard it almost knocks me over.

I loosen my grasp on Raven and soften my kiss. When I pull away and look into her eyes, I can tell she's trying to figure out what just happened. I take a deep breath and gently kiss her bruised and swollen cheek.

"OW!" she cries sarcastically, pushing my chest. "It's still tender."

I take another step back and smile.

"Woah. So that's what it looks like seeing you smile," Raven teases.

Wait. I'm smiling?

Shit. I'm in trouble.

"Don't get used to it," I say, replacing my smile with my signature scowl as I straighten my shirt. "I still have a reputation to uphold. Speaking of," I gently place my arms on Raven's shoulders and move her out of my way so I can exit the door, "I need to speak with Captain Ahe about your training."

Raven grabs my arm before I can leave. "Nakoa, please. It really was an accident."

"Sure, it was." I smirk. "But I'm going to inform him that I will be training you tomorrow instead."

Raven's face lights up like I've never seen. Even the stars don't shine as bright as her. I quickly take advantage of her surprise and lean in, leaving a small kiss on her forehead, then retreat down the hall. Before I hit the stairs, Raven shouts something along the lines of, "Can't wait!" and the smile that feels unfamiliar to me tugs the corner of my mouth again as I race down the stairs.

"Is that a smile? From MY son? Oh, no. The world must be ending," my father jokes as he fans himself against a wall.

"You didn't see anything," I say, wiping the smile from my face and raising a challenging eyebrow at him.

He motions to turn the invisible lock on his lips. "You're right. I didn't see anything."

I turn and head down the long hallway to the study. Unfortunately for me, I'm not alone like I'd hope. As we enter the study, my father sits down on the fireplace as I take my seat at the desk.

"But if I did see something, what might cause my son to grace us with a genuine smile that has been lost for so long?"

I sigh deeply and thump my head against the desk.

"Ah, I see," my father chuckles. "What is so wrong with finding your mate? She seems like a lovely girl, son."

"She's amazing, Father."

He waits a few seconds before interjecting. "But . . . ?"

"But we aren't the same. How can a dragon and a witch rule together?" I ask, bringing my head up to face him. "Our people will judge her for not being one of us."

"Since when do you care what people think about you?" my father questions, rising to stand at the edge of the desk.

"I don't, but I care what others' harsh words might do to her self-esteem. I care about how she feels."

"This may surprise you, but I think Raven is stronger than you give her credit for."

He's right. From the moment I laid eyes on her, I knew she was a fighter. She may act tough on the outside and knows what buttons to push to annoy me, but I know she's sweet and tender-hearted.

"I just want what's best for her." I sigh, leaning my head back against the chair's headrest.

"I know, son, but give her a chance to prove she's capable of handling this before you make the decision for her." My father turns to leave after bestowing his relationship knowledge, but not before reminding me of the ball tomorrow. "I hope you're prepared," he says, exiting the room.

Just then, an idea takes shape. Raven said she wants me to win her over.

Okay. Game on.

CHAPTER 41
LIVING A DREAM

My face is no longer pounding because the throbbing has worked its way into my heart from that kiss. I lay on my back on the bed, looking up at the golden canopy and its intricate designs. Nakoa's kiss was hot, passionate, and needy, whereas Asher's kiss was tender, sweet, and loving. I grab a pillow and smash it into my face, suffocating an uneasy scream.

I've never known someone with more than one mate before, and the fact that I have three is incomprehensible. I've watched a few episodes of *Sister Wives* and I have no idea how the women don't fight each other. At least Asher and Kieran both know, but how am I supposed to tell Nakoa?

A knock at the door brings me out of my pity party quickly. "Come in," I announce, placing the pillow back in its rightful place.

"Hello, dear. I hope I'm not bothering you," Queen Nani says as she pops her head around the door.

"Not at all!" I smile, hopping down from the bed.

"Great!" she beams, stepping into the room. "Would you like

to join me this afternoon? Our Modiste will be arriving shortly with a new batch of dresses and I thought you could pick a few for the remainder of your stay."

"I would love that!"

"Perfect! Let us go wait then."

Queen Nani leads us out of my room and down the hallway. "I hope this is alright. When I heard from the King that Nakoa was off to speak to Captain Ahe, I wanted to make sure you were not left alone."

"Thank you," I say as we enter the room that I first met the King and Queen in. The room has been transformed since the last time I was here. The couches are pushed together in the center of the room, with a tall dressing curtain panel positioned in the corner. In the opposite corner, there are three racks of beautiful dresses of all shapes and colors.

Queen Nani nudges me with her shoulder as I scan the dresses. "Go ahead and pick whatever catches your eye."

"You're not going to look?" I question as she finds a spot on the couch.

"Not right now, dear." She smiles.

I return my gaze to the dresses and head for the first rack. This rack is coordinated by reds, pinks, and yellows. The dresses are lovely, but none of them appeal to me as I skim over them. The next rack contains purples, whites, and greens. My eye catches on a green sequin top. Gently, I pull the dress from the rack and hear a gasp behind me. Turning to assess the danger, I find nothing but a short, older woman with pink hair and a nose ring, sporting a light blue jumpsuit.

"What a lovely choice!" she squeaks.

"Thank you?" I raise an eyebrow toward Queen Nani, silently asking who this is. The little old woman practically glides over and takes the dress from me, turning her back to glide over to the empty rack next to the dressing panel.

"Modiste Cleed," Queen Nani whispers.

I nod in realization. "Got it," I mouth back before Modiste Cleed turns around.

"Anything else tickles your fancy?" she asks, gliding back over to the racks.

"Not yet."

Modiste Cleed nods and makes her way over to Queen Nani. The two dive into details for the ball tomorrow night, leaving me to browse some more. I move on to the last rack, which contains blacks, blues, and grays. Combing through the rack, nothing sticks out to me until the very last dress.

"Excellent choice," Modiste Cleed whispers from behind me. She snatches the dress off the rack and ushers me over to the dressing panel. There's a full-length mirror hidden from view.

I strip down to my undergarments and slip into the first dress. My first reaction is that the slit in the side is impossibly too high, but I don't have enough time to think about anything else before Modiste Cleed pushes me out for Queen Nani. At first, her eyes roam to my exposed legs and just when I think this is the wrong choice, she surprises me.

"Oh, yes. This will do just fine." She grins at me, then looks at Modiste Cleed. The two share a look and I'm not quite sure what it means, but I don't have time to think before I'm shoved back behind the dressing panel.

I carefully remove the green dress and place it over the panel for Modiste Cleed to take. As I finish putting on the last dress I selected, I can't help but admire how it fits me perfectly in the mirror. The spaghetti straps crisscross in the back, dipping low to expose most of my back. The deep blue velvet dress cascades to the floor with a much smaller slit in the side, only revealing my leg to my knee. Silver sparkles scatter across the bodice and tapper out at the bottom. The dress reminds me of the midnight sky on a clear night.

Modiste Cleed smiles in the mirror behind me, leading me around the dressing panel. Queen Nani's eyes grow wide with excitement. "I take it back. This," she stands, motioning to the dress, "this is the dress."

"I couldn't agree more." Modiste Cleed nods.

I eye the two suspiciously, but disappear behind the panel to change into my day clothes. When I emerge, Queen Nani is instructing Liza, the maid from earlier, to place this in my closet for tonight.

"Okay," I say, walking up to Queen Nani. "What is going on?"

"Nothing!" She giggles. "I just want you to look exquisite for dinner tonight, that's all. Now," she says, turning me around and guiding me out the door, "let's see what we can do about that cheek of yours."

After Queen Nani summoned her personal makeup artist to my room, the bruise is no longer visible. I assured them both that I didn't need a full face of makeup for dinner, yet here I am, staring at my rosy, contoured cheeks and smokey eyed, wispy lashes. Queen Nani told me I look like a dream, but I feel as though I'm the one who is living in a dream as I stare at my gown for tonight.

Something is off about tonight's dinner, but I can't figure out what. Queen Nani was peppier than her usual self and it didn't help that she insisted we do the full makeup. She claimed it was to test out how to cover my bruised eye for tomorrow night's ball, but when she left my room, she was practically skipping with excitement.

Yeah. Something is definitely up.

Liza finishes up tying the back of my dress and leaves me a pair of silver lace up heels. When I'm done lacing up the heels, I exit the closet to find Liza standing beside the bedroom door.

"Oh, hi Liza. I thought you had already left?"

She curtsies as I approach, opening the door for me. "No, miss. The King and Queen wanted me to escort you to dinner tonight."

"Is it not in the dining hall?" I question, following behind her.

"Tis not, miss."

I follow in silence as Liza leads me through the castle and to the back wing. As soon as she opens the door to the patio, I stop in my tracks. Candles line the pathway on each side to the garden, illuminating the stepping stones in the darkness.

"Sorry, miss. I was told not to tell." Liza smiles as I take a step forward.

"Who planned this?" I ask, still in shock.

"Can't say. But follow the path and you'll find out."

She pushes me gently out the door and I'm left on my own in the candle-lit darkness. I suck in a deep breath and let it out slowly, relaxing my nerves. I gently grab my dress and lift the hem to the side so I can find the stepping stones. Even though the candles are beautiful, they don't give off very good light and I really don't want to misstep and twist my ankle in these heels.

I travel farther into the maze garden and the candles start to burn brighter as I approach my destination. "Please don't let me be murdered in this dress," I whisper to myself as I round the corner. "Please don't let me be murdered in this—" my gasp cuts my mantra short as I stop in the entrance to the open courtyard before me.

Standing in the center by the fountain is Nakoa, looking just as he did in my dream when I first met him. His tailored black suit hugs his muscular arms, and his jet-black hair is tousled over to the side. His eyes roam my body, taking in the sight before him as a smile plays at his lips. He meticulously makes his way to where I am, always keeping his eyes locked on mine.

When he reaches me, he extends his hand, waiting for me to place mine in his. My heart skips a beat before my brain finally catches up and extends my hand to his. He bows, eyes never leaving mine, and places a searing kiss to the inside of my wrist. Gently, he tugs me into his chest, whispering into my ear, "You look like the midnight sky."

Shocked at his words, I lean away slightly, still entrapped in his arms. Whatever I was going to say is quickly silenced by his lips delicately meeting mine. It's not a fiery kiss like before. This kiss is like testing the water to see if it's warm enough to swim in. I lean into his kiss slightly, letting him know the waters are safe. He pulls back, leaving me with one last kiss before leading me through the courtyard.

"I saw this fountain in my dream," I say as Nakoa leads me to a table next to the fountain.

Nakoa nods as he pushes my chair in and rounds the table to his seat. "Yes. I know," he says, placing his elbows on the table and interlocking his fingers.

"What do you mean, you know?" I ask, confused. "When I told you about my dream when we landed on the island, you pretended to know nothing."

"I apologize about that, but I needed to know that I could trust you," he says quickly. "Finding you is the best thing that could have happened to me, Raven. I needed to get you out of the Vampire Court and to safety."

I relax a little at his confession, letting go of any anger that was building.

"When you drifted off, I was able to enter your mind and create a dream for you." He smirks and points to my dress. "Although, I do believe your dress was a lighter shade of blue, but that hardly matters," he says, waving his hand.

"Why?" I ask, softly.

"Oh," he says, "I just thought the light blue dress suited you better, but clearly this color is the better choice."

"Not the dress!" I laugh lightly. "Why did you need to create a dream for me?"

His eyes soften and his mask slips, letting me see the real Nakoa. "Because when our eyes locked and the mating bond sealed into place, my number one concern was keeping you safe at all costs. The mating bond allowed me access to your subconscious mind, and I needed you to trust me when I left you that key. I needed you to feel safe with me."

His words strike me through my heart. I do trust him, but will he trust me after I tell him he isn't my only mate? I smile at him, and he returns mine with a true, genuine smile. For now, at this moment, I just want to be Raven and Nakoa with no problems following us around. So, I promise myself as Nakoa raises his glass in a toast with mine, tomorrow, after the ball, I will finally tell Nakoa about Asher and Kieran.

CHAPTER 42
DO YOU WANT TO BUILD A
SANDCASTLE?

Dinner was incredible. Somehow, the food in the Realm of Shadows tastes far superior to any food back in the Human Realm. I savor the last sip of my moscato and look up to find Nakoa staring at me.

"What?" I ask, gently dabbing my face with the soft napkin. "Do I have something on my face?"

"No," he smirks, leaning back in his chair, "I was just admiring you, that's all."

Wowza.

"Who are you, and what have you done to the old, grumpy Nakoa?" I ask playfully.

"He's taking a break for tonight," Nakoa says, standing. "Would you like to walk around the gardens?"

I nod, rising from my chair and meeting him by the fountain. Nakoa once again extends his hand, but this time, he laces our fingers together. "Oh, yes. I could get used to this version," I joke, nudging his shoulder as we make our way through the garden.

The garden is truly beautiful. Once we step around the eight-foot hedges surrounding the court where we had dinner, the lights dim out behind us and we venture to the outside portion that leads us to the cliffs. The roar of the waves crashing against the cliffs grows louder and I shiver when the ocean breeze sweeps between us. I start to protest as Nakoa drops my hand, but when he shimmies off his suit jacket and places it gently over my shoulders, all is forgiven.

We stand there in a comfortable silence, listening to the waves. Nakoa steps behind me, sliding his arms around my waist and pulling me in closer, resting his chin on my head. After another breeze sends chills running through my body, Nakoa lowers his head to my ear. "I think it's time to call it a night, Princess."

I nod and let Nakoa lead the way back to the castle, weaving us through the garden. The castle is quiet as we enter the far wing, and most of the lights have been dimmed. A rogue yawn escapes my lips and Nakoa chuckles in front of me as he leads us up the stairs. We walk hand in hand down the hallway to my room and each step echoes through the hall. Finally, we stop in front of my door.

"Thank you," he whispers, lowering his head.

"For what?" I ask, bringing my free hand to lift his chin.

"For letting me experience what it feels like to let go and just live in the moment," he says, his golden eyes shining brightly.

Ugh, be still my beating heart.

I drop my hand and step closer, wrapping my arms around him in a hug. I remember how he was timid to hug Queen Nani when I first met them, but there is no timidness with me. He envelopes me and sighs into my hug. I look up to him, resting my chin on his chest and smile sweetly at him. "You're welcome."

He smiles back at me, then places another soft kiss on my

forehead. "Alright, off to bed with you then," he says, smacking my butt as I open the door.

"Yes, Your Highness," I say, winking at him. "I'll see you for training tomorrow morning, yeah?"

"Don't be late," he warns as he takes a step back from the door.

"Annnd he's back." I laugh, rolling my eyes.

"Goodnight, Raven."

"Goodnight, Nakoa."

I shut the door and listen to his retreating footsteps until his door opens and shuts. I push off the door and head to the bathroom to change out of my dress and clean my face with the wipes Queen Nani's makeup artist gave me, wincing as I brush lightly over my still swollen cheek. Hopefully, by tomorrow the swelling is gone and all that will remain is my beautiful shiner. Exhausted from today's events, I crawl into bed and welcome sleep with open arms.

I'm stirred out of my slumber by a loud banging on my door.

"You're late, Raven," Nakoa's muffled voice says on the other side of the door.

"Go away!" I shout groggily. I must have slept on my bruised cheek because it feels as though I've been headbutted all over again.

I hear the door open and shut as I roll off my injured cheek; footsteps approach the bed, then stop. Then, they shuffle across the floor. I groan, peeling the covers off my face, only to be bombarded with sunlight from my curtains being thrust open.

"Ahh!" I yell. "What the hell?"

"You're not a vampire. Stop being so dramatic," Nakoa says, approaching the bed.

At the mention of vampires, I remember that I have to come

clean to Nakoa after the ball tonight. I groan again, but this time, Nakoa grabs my warm and cozy comforter and yanks it off me.

"Hey!" I shout, grabbing a pillow and tossing it at him. "I could have been sleeping naked!"

"Oh darn." He pouts, sitting on the edge of my bed. He tickles the bottom of my foot and I scramble out of bed. "Get dressed, Princess. You have ten minutes."

"I'm so happy you're back to your usual self," I say sarcastically, heading into my bathroom. I pause in the doorway before I slam the door. "Not!"

Eight minutes later, my teeth are clean, my hair is brushed and braided down my back, and I finally gave up on the training shirt and opted for a thin button down instead. I open the door to find Nakoa in the same spot waiting patiently on my bed.

Walking past him, I holler over my shoulder before going through the bedroom door to the hallway. "Let's get this over with."

"Oh, come on. At least I won't give you a black eye," he jokes, following me out the bedroom door.

"Yet." I turn, narrowing my good eye at him. The swelling has thankfully gone away, but it still hurts to squint on one side.

I let Nakoa lead the way, but he veers off path and instead, we head to the west wing. We descend into what I believe is a basement of some sort, but then Nakoa opens a giant wooden door, and the scent of salt water fills the room. The sunlight floods the small room as he steps out onto a vast sandy beach.

"Woah." My vision adjusts to the light, revealing the beach before me. I blink a few times, hoping the scene isn't a mirage because it's one of the most beautiful beaches I've seen.

"I know." Nakoa grins smugly.

"But I thought we were going to train?" I ask, puzzled at why I'm staring at a beach instead of the training grounds.

"We are." Nakoa nods as he peels his shoes and socks off,

placing them next to the door. He rolls his pants up to his knees before turning to look back at me staring at him.

"Are you going to stare at my ass all day, or are you going to join me?" he asks, crossing his arms over his body.

"Can't I do both?" I tease, taking my own shoes and socks off.

Nakoa leads the way onto the beach, and I can't help but stop and sink my toes into the warm sand. The waves gently flow over the sand, and I pause to close my eyes and lift my face up toward the sun, soaking in the moment. The last time I was at a real beach was with my dad just before he passed. I blink away the memory and follow Nakoa to a spot where two chairs are set up next to a table with an umbrella covering all the furniture from the looming sun.

As we approach, I don't see any kind of training equipment, which makes me nervous because I'm not about to run laps in the sand. "So, what kind of training are we doing today?" I ask nervously.

Nakoa stops just before the table and turns to face me, his usually grumpy mask nowhere to be found. "I want you to use your powers." He hesitates for a moment, then continues, "All of your powers."

"Excuse me, what?" I say, placing my hands on my hips. "Is it even safe out here to do that?"

"Of course it is," he scoffs, crossing his own arms. "I wouldn't have brought you here if it wasn't," he fires back. "This beach is only accessible through the door we came out of, or by flying down here. Which is impossible since the Royal Guard monitors who flies over the castle."

"And you're positive it's safe?" I ask skeptically. I can't risk others knowing that I can control all four elements.

"Yes," he says, taking a step toward me.

"Okay." I shrug, and Nakoa gives me a questioning look as I

roll my shoulders back, cracking my neck on both sides. "This is going to be fun."

Before he even registers what's happening, I shoot my hand toward the water, summoning a large amount of water, and drop it right over his head. He raises his head with a vicious look in his eyes as I smirk right back at him.

Yep. This is going to be real fun.

Nakoa reaches for me, but I'm faster than he thinks as I push a heavy gust of wind to knock him flat on his ass in the sand. I laugh as I run off toward the water and hear Nakoa grunt behind me. When I turn around, his shirt is ripped to shreds on the sand. His beautiful golden wings unfurl from his back and are carrying him straight toward me at a terrifying speed.

I scream as he dips down and plucks me from the water, coasting right over the ocean. "Put me down, you cheater!" I yell. I heat my hand and hold it in front of his face. "Or else," I taunt.

Nakoa pins me with a devilish grin. "Whatever you say, Princess." Within seconds, I'm falling out of his arms and into the shallow waters of the ocean. When I surface, Nakoa lands gracefully on the sand, doubling over in laughter.

I trudge to the edge of the water. "You think that's funny?"

With his wings still out, I create a gust of wind that pushes him from behind, closer to the water. When he realizes what's happening, he stops laughing and tucks his wings back into his back, just like I planned. I kneel, placing my hands on the sand, heating the sand to an unbearable temperature.

With his wings gone, it forces Nakoa to sprint toward the water. Unfortunately for me, I didn't plan on him tackling me into the water with him. We both surface, and I can't help but laugh. I don't think I've felt this free in a long time. My giggles must be contagious because soon Nakoa is laughing alongside me. And wow. It sounds good to hear him genuinely laugh. I splash him, which makes him laugh more. He lunges for me, wrapping me in his arms.

Not even a second later, his lips are on mine. I wrap my arms around his neck and he secures my legs around his hips. He pulls me closer to him as his lips trail down my chin to my neck. "You taste like saltwater," he growls into the soft spot between my neck and collarbone.

I pull back a little, raising my eyebrow. "Uh, duh."

He places another fleeting trail of kisses back up my neck and to my lips, leaving me with one last lingering kiss. When we break apart, our foreheads meet as the waves crash around us. Suddenly, an idea forms in my head.

"Want to build a sandcastle?"

Nakoa pulls back and turns his face away. I place my hands on either side of his cheeks and force him to look at me.

"Don't tell me you've never built a sandcastle before?"

"I've never built a sandcastle before," he grumbles, releasing me to my own two feet as he walks out of the water and onto the beach.

I quickly follow behind him, jumping onto his back. "We are totally building a sandcastle!" I squeak as he pinches my butt.

He dumps me back on the sand and I scamper in front of him, placing my hands on his chest and peering straight into his eyes. I don't beg very often, but this is worth begging for. "Pweeease, Nakoa!" I pout my lip out even more, making the saddest, most pathetic face.

He holds out for all of three seconds. "Fine," he caves, nudging me away to go sit on the sand under the umbrella.

"YAY!" I shout, throwing my hands in the air. I quickly follow him to the shade and plop down next to him. I grab one of the cups from the table and chug the contents. "Let's begin."

I first start digging a square shaped hole in the sand about an inch deep until I hit the colder, wet sand. I look up at Nakoa to see his eyebrows judging me. "Wipe that look off your face and take this sand," I say, pointing to the dry top layer I set to our left, "and mix it with that sand." I point to the wet sand I scooped to our right.

I dig a smaller, circular hole next to Nakoa's knee and summon my water element to fill it with ocean water. "And this is in case you need more water to add to the sand to make it easier to mold."

Nakoa rolls his eyes, but starts mixing the sand while I work on packing the sand down where we want to build our castle. Once it's packed down, I use the cup and start filling it with sand Nakoa has mixed, then carefully flip it upside down on the sand I just compacted. Nakoa joins in with his own cup, adding to our mini town.

With each refill of his cup, Nakoa lets go of his grumpy exterior more and more. Finally, when we start working on the main feature, the castle, his playful, happy exterior, shines bright.

"Okay, so how do we build the big castle?" he asks, clapping some sand off his hands.

"Well, since we only have these two cups, I think we should put the sand dumps as close as possible to each other, then come back in and fill in the remaining space with sand."

"Good idea!" He smiles, which in turn makes me smile.

We work in concentrated silence for the next five minutes, placing our sand cups, and carefully filling in the empty space with sand. Finally, our castle is finished.

It's not the best sandcastle I've built. Normally, I use my earth element to help better shape the castle, but with Nakoa, I wanted this to be made by just us. No powers involved.

"It looks like shit." Nakoa laughs as he stands.

"But did you have fun?" I ask, placing my hands on my hips, looking up at him.

He rolls his eyes and extends a hand to help me up. "I suppose I did."

I wipe my hands together, shedding the excess sand. "Good! Then it doesn't matter if it looks lumpy or off center."

With all the fun we were having, we didn't notice Liza standing behind the table until she clears her throat.

"Excuse me?" she asks.

Nakoa is so caught off guard he jumps back toward our ugly, lopsided sandcastle.

I freeze him in place before his giant foot can come crashing down on our masterpiece.

"What the hell?" he shouts, unable to move his body. He almost looks like he's doing the Heisman pose, but without a football. "Raven?"

"Oh, yeah," I say, crossing my arms behind my back and rocking back and forth on my toes. "I forgot to tell you that I can also kind of freeze people in place?"

His mouth falls open for a fraction of a second, then his grumpy attitude is slingshotted into place. "Cool. Now unfreeze me."

"Right." I unfreeze him and he leans back a little more, narrowly missing the sandcastle. "Sorry." I shrug.

"Anything else you'd like to tell me about your powers?" he asks suspiciously.

I make a show of pretending to really think about the question by crossing my arms and tapping my index finger on my lips. "Mmm, nope!" I smirk.

"Okay then." He turns to Liza, and I see her trying to hide her smile. "How can we help you, Liza?"

"I've been sent to fetch Miss Raven to get ready for the ball."

"That's my cue," I say, patting Nakoa's shoulder. "See you tonight."

I follow Liza around the table, then pause to throw a wink back at Nakoa. "Your Highness." I catch his smirk before following Liza as she leads us back through the door we came through.

CHAPTER 43
IF LOOKS COULD KILL

After making our way back to my room, Liza informs me I have an hour to myself before the hair and make-up team find me. I peel off my damp and sandy clothes and toss them in the basket next to the bed. Unfortunately, my shower takes longer than I expected since I have to rinse out all the sand that lingers in my long hair from the ocean water. When I'm finally satisfied, I exit the shower and throw my robe on, heading for the closet.

The green dress that I selected from Modiste Cleed is hanging in the corner, sparkling back at me. Just as I reach for it, there's a knock at the door. "Coming!" I yell, making my way through the bathroom and back to the bedroom. The sun has begun to set, but it illuminates my room with the curtains still open from this morning.

I open the door to find Queen Nani's personal makeup artist smiling back at me with four other women behind her smiling just as bright. Each has a different cart or tote with different items inside.

"Mina! Come in!" I open the door wide, ushering her and her group inside.

Mina's thick Russian accent fills the room as she and her group head for the bathroom. "Good to see you again, Miss Raven."

I shut the door and follow them into the bathroom, waiting at the entrance as they all set up their belongings on the counters. Mina was born in the Realm of Shadows but grew up in Russia before being hired by Queen Nani. Mina said it was a chance of fate that brought Queen Nani to Russia that fateful day.

Mina looks back at me and sighs. "I see the swelling is gone, da?"

"Yes," I nod, "but hopefully you can work your magic again and hide my bruised eye?" I ask.

"Nyet," Mina says, shaking her head. I don't know Russian, but I do know she just told me no.

"Um, what?" I ask, tilting my head.

"We are going to use your black eye and incorporate it into the makeup. Pover'te mne."

"Sure." I nod slowly and I walk over to the makeup chair. "I literally have no other option than to trust you." I laugh.

Mina pats my shoulders and smiles. "Good girl."

While the ladies work on my makeup, they speak in Russian most of the time, only switching to English to give me directions. An hour later, Mina and her stylist spin me around to face the full-length mirror.

"Wow," I gasp.

"Told you." Mina smirks, high fiving one of the women that worked on my hair. "You look fabulous. Now," Mina pauses, crossing her arms, "let's get you dressed."

"My dress is in the closet." Before I can even take a step out of the chair, two of the other hair stylists step in my way, blocking my path to the closet.

"What's going on?" I turn to ask Mina, confused.

"You're not wearing that dress," Mina says, crossing her arms. "Liza!" Mina yells toward the bedroom.

Liza pops her head around the bedroom door from the hallway. "Is she ready?" she asks excitedly.

"Da," Mina confirms.

Liza pushes the door open and carries in the most beautiful dress I've ever seen. She shuts the door as I exit the bathroom, muffling my gasp with my hands.

I look between Liza, Mina, and her stylists. "Is this for me?" I whisper.

"Yes!" Liza squeaks. "And here!"

She passes me an envelope with my name written in cursive on the front. I look down at the note, then to the small audience in my room.

"Open it!" Mina urges as everyone else nods in agreement.

I open the envelope and slowly unfold the note. When I finish reading, my heart drops into my stomach. How am I supposed to break the news to Nakoa about not being my only mate after he has been so sweet to me?

I look up to multiple eyes staring back at me, waiting for me to relay the message that's on the card. I plaster a smile on my face before clearing my throat to read the letter aloud.

Dear Raven, I hope you'll do me the honor of wearing this dress tonight. The color of the dress reminds me of getting lost in your eyes and the flowers signify the bloom of life you have brought back into my world for the last three days.

Yours always, Nakoa.

The girls all sigh in unison as I place the note back in the envelope. "Okay, where do I get a man like that?" Mina jokes while walking toward the dress.

Mina unzips the side of the dress and slips it off the satin hanger. Liza holds the other side of the dress as I step into the gown. Before I view myself in the mirror, Mina grabs my hand and turns me toward her. "You're a vision, Miss Raven. Have fun tonight and enjoy the festivities with your man." Following her stylists out the door, she pauses and throws one last wink my way before vanishing down the hallway.

Liza is the last to leave the room, pausing before shutting the door. "I'll be right on the other side when you're ready." She smiles, then shuts the door, leaving me to myself. I take a deep breath before turning to view myself in the full-length mirror.

Wow.

I hardly recognize the person looking back at me. Mina was right when she said to trust her to incorporate my bruised eye into my makeup. If I didn't experience getting headbutted in the face myself, I wouldn't even know that I had a black eye with the way she blended the blues and purples together. I feel like she knew I wasn't going to be wearing the green dress all along.

The hairstylist must have been in on the secret too because my long hair sits in a low messy bun at the nape of my neck with two Dutch braids weaving around the edges, revealing the beauty of the back of the dress.

Nakoa is right. The silvery blue tone of the dress matches my eyes almost perfectly. The one shoulder, A-line dress flows to the floor, trailing slightly behind me and the bodice is outlined in beaded dark blue flowers that flow to the one shoulder cape behind me.

Both arms have a sheer covering, with the same blue flowers sewn into the mesh, making it appear as though the flowers are tattooed on my arms. When I admire the back, it's just as beautiful as the front. The dress is backless, with the same sheer mesh covering and blue and silver flowers sewn into the fabric.

I turn back around, shaking my nerves away. This is my first ball and I couldn't imagine anything more perfect than this. With one more deep exhale, I slip my feet into my heels and exit the bedroom, finding Liza just on the other side, like she promised.

She smiles brightly as she approaches. "You truly do look beautiful, Miss Raven. Are you ready?"

I smile back at her, straightening my posture. "Thank you, Liza. I'm ready."

The sound of my heels clicking on the granite floor makes me nervous again as we descend to the ballroom. Soon enough, the sound of my heels echoing is drowned out by the cheerful sounds of the awaiting guests. When we round the corner to the ballroom doors, Liza stops short, whispering to one of the guards on either side of the doors. He nods, then clicks his staff to the floor twice, inviting the attention of the guests.

Liza leans in quickly before the guard speaks. "Knock his socks off, miss." Then she's off, dashing around the corner, leaving me all by myself.

The guard steps forward, addressing the crowd. "May I present the honored guest of this evening, Miss Raven Montclair."

I step through the doors and catch my first glimpse at the ballroom. The walls are wrapped in beautiful golden wallpaper, with silver flowers and vine designs painted on. There are two massive golden chandeliers hanging from the ceiling, each designed differently. The one closest to me is dripping in different colored jewels that melt perfectly with the golden frame, and the second one holds ornate candles to help light up the room.

As I peer down the steps into the very fashionably dressed crowd, all the auras are the same, which means all the guests are dragons, and each one of them has their eyes pinned on me. Except, the only pair of eyes I can focus on are the sparkling golden eyes weaving their way through the crowd to the bottom of the stairs. I take each step carefully, never looking away from them.

I feel like I'm the leading lady in any movie where the main character makes her grand entrance to a ball, which should make me feel ridiculous, but I can't make my mind think of anything else but the way Nakoa is looking over my body. It's really hard to concentrate on not tripping down the stairs. Finally, we meet at the last stair as he extends his hand, bowing in front of me.

I scan the room quickly and find Nakoa's parents grinning ear to ear at the stage in the back. Redirecting my attention to Nakoa, I slide my hand in his as he places a gentle kiss on the inside of my wrist. He stands and the smile he gives me melts my heart and my nerves. I take the last step as he tucks my arm in his.

"You look absolutely divine," he whispers in my ear.

"You clean up nice as well," I whisper back as we make our way through the parting crowd toward his parents. Nakoa must have had his suit tailored to match my dress because his dark suit is complemented by a silvery blue tie embroidered with dark blue flowers.

I can hear whispers in the crowd, but I tune them out until I catch a glimpse of Faya and Kalena. I silently laugh when Faya mouths, "Oh my god" and fans herself as she wiggles her eyebrows and Kalena gives me two thumbs up. I smile even brighter when we approach King Kalino and Queen Nani.

King Kalino steps forward, and his strong voice hushes the crowd as it carries across the room. "Welcome, everyone! We are so excited and honored to be with you all tonight."

Queen Nani smiles down at Nakoa and I before joining her husband's side, taking his hand. "We hold this evening's ball in honor of something special. Our son, Nakoa, has found his mate!"

The crowd erupts in cheers and applause all around us. My body freezes as the reality of the moment sets in. This is going to make telling Nakoa the truth so much harder. I'm so caught off guard by the announcement that I don't realize Nakoa is trying to talk to me until he gently squeezes my arm interlocked with his. I snap out of whatever shocked state I was in as I finally hear what he is saying with a worried expression on his face.

"I'm so sorry. I didn't know they were announcing this tonight."

I squeeze his arm back, comforting him as I shake off my shock and smile back up at him. "It's okay. I was just caught off guard. That's all."

"I'll talk to them tonight about it. I swear."

"Hey," I say, dropping his arm and grabbing his hands. "It's okay. Really. Let them enjoy seeing their son happy."

Nakoa raises his eyebrow, questioning me silently.

"Seriously. It's okay."

His expression lightens a little as we turn back to the King and Queen.

"Please enjoy yourselves and let the party begin!" King Kalino shouts over the cheers of the crowd.

The crowd disperses around us and Nakoa pulls me off to the side and up the stairs of the stage toward his parents. Queen Nani is the first to greet me with a hug and a massive smile on her face. "I'm so happy for you two." She steps back, admiring both of us. "You both look stunning, by the way."

I playfully elbow Nakoa in the ribs. "Thanks to your son. He designed our outfits."

"Wow. I like this new, smiling version of my son." King Kalino laughs, joining our side. "You're definitely a keeper, Raven."

Queen Nani laughs and swats her husband's arm. "Oh, and now who is trying to win her over?"

"Hey," King Kalino laughs, holding his hands up in surrender, "any woman who can melt Nakoa's icy personality and challenge him is a keeper in my books."

"Alright. Alright. That's enough of this," Nakoa says, shaking his head and leading me past his parents.

"It was nice to see you both again!" I shout over my shoulder as Nakoa drags me through the crowd and toward the middle of the ballroom. The crowd slowly backs up as the dance floor clears. Suddenly, Nakoa drops my hand and turns to face me with a devilish look on his face as he slowly circles me.

"Care to dance?" he asks, as his eyes roam my body. My skin is practically scorching under his gaze.

"I don't know how to dance," I admit as he takes my hand and pulls me closer to him.

"Yes, you do," he whispers in my ear, placing my free hand on his shoulder.

Just as I'm about to refute, a familiar melody plays as Nakoa starts to lead us around the floor. The whole scene feels as though I've already lived it as we gracefully glide across the tile. My feet somehow move on their own, as if I've known this dance my whole life.

Nakoa spins me out and brings me back in, dipping me elegantly. "This is even better than the dream," he says with his lips brushing my neck.

The second his lips leave my neck, snippets of images flash in my mind, reminding me that we danced like this in the dream he created for me when I was trapped at the Vampire Court. He pulls me closer, leaning his forehead against mine as the melody comes to an end.

"Mine," he whispers, lowering his lips to mine briefly. "Mate."

Suddenly, the ballroom doors burst open, and the moment is broken by the crowd gasping as we all turn to see what the commotion is. The two guards that were manning the doors when I entered are shouting at something or someone when they are suddenly thrown against each door, crumbling to the ground, unconscious.

Nakoa steps in front of me, trying to protect me from whatever threat may be coming as the crowd shuffles to the back of the room. Kalena and Faya yell at people to move out of their way, trying to reach me and Nakoa as they collide with retreating guests. Time slows as I peek around Nakoa's shoulder and lock eyes with two ocean blue eyes and instantly freeze as I see two emerald green eyes following quickly into the room. A second later, the ocean blue eyes are standing right in front of us.

"What did you just say?" Kieran snarls, his fangs extended in a warning to Nakoa.

"Who the hell are you?" Nakoa growls, shuffling in front of me again.

Ohhh shit. Oh shit. Oh shit. Oh shit.

Asher's green eyes grow wide as he sees me, then narrows his sights on Nakoa as he and Leah run down the stairs toward us.

Wait. Why is Leah here?

I grab Nakoa's arm and step around him as he growls and tries to pull me back. "It's okay!" I say to all three men and Leah as I step in between all of them.

"Raven, who are these intruders?" Nakoa demands, as Kalena and Faya join his side.

"Nakoa," I say, turning to smile at the three people standing in front of me. "This is Kieran and Asher. And my best friend Leah?" I say, confused, as I look at Leah. She only smiles and mouths, "Good luck" as I turn back toward Nakoa.

Kieran and Asher both step forward. "We're her mates," Asher states coolly, interlacing our fingers.

"Who the hell are you?" Kieran demands, throwing a protective arm over my shoulder.

Nakoa crosses his arms, glaring at me, then looking at both men at my side. "I'm Nakoa Kahle. Prince of the Dragon Court, and Raven's mate."

CHAPTER 44
CAN'T WE ALL JUST GET ALONG?

Before I can even begin damage control, or wonder how Asher, Kieran, and Leah found me, a loud blast erupts in front of us, shaking the whole castle. The beautiful chandeliers sway viciously above us as the crowd starts scampering toward the stairs, falling over each other to flee for safety. Another loud blast echoes through the ballroom, causing the attendees to panic even more as the stone walls start to crack.

"What the hell have you done?!" Nakoa snarls at Kieran and Asher.

Asher steps in front of me as Kieran slides me behind him, next to Leah. "It's not us," Asher grits out.

A guard skids to a stop at the top of the stairs, breathing heavily as he doubles over trying to catch his breath as people rush past him. "The castle," he shouts down to the ballroom in between gasps, "has been breached," he gasps again, holding the side of his neck, "by vampires!" he finishes as his hand falls and blood spews from his neck onto fleeing guests. He drops to the tile floor, unmoving.

Screams fill the ballroom and Nakoa zeros his gaze on Kieran. "You!" he yells, lunging for Kieran. I freeze Nakoa in place before he can lay a finger on Kieran.

"This wasn't them, Nakoa!" I shout angrily as I step around Kieran and get right in Nakoa's face. I know Kieran and Asher are here for me. They wouldn't attack the Dragon Court just to retrieve me. This has to be some kind of planned attack.

"Unfreeze me, Raven!" Nakoa shouts. "Now!"

"Wow, you really know how to pick 'em, don't you, Tesoro?" Kieran jokes, stepping next to me.

"Not now, Kieran," I sigh, annoyed at the situation.

"I'll unfreeze you, but I promise that they aren't here to harm anyone. This is someone else. Please believe me," I beg, unfreezing him.

He turns his back to me, grabbing Kalena's shoulder. "Take my parents and make sure they get down to the bunker."

Kalena looks at me with sympathy before Nakoa shoves her away. "That's an order!" he shouts, turning his icy gaze to me as another blast erupts again.

This time, the blast is too much and the beautiful, jeweled chandelier above us snaps from the ceiling, falling right where we stand. Nakoa dives for me, pushing me out of the way as Asher dives for Leah. Faya hesitates for one second too long before Kieran fades over to her side, scooping her up in his arms and to the far end of the room, out of the way of the crashing jewels and metal.

"What the hell is going on!" Nakoa shouts as he unfolds his body from on top of mine.

I don't have time to reply before a loud roar echoes through the halls followed by gut-wrenching screams. I catch a glimpse of Kieran fading up the stairs and into the hallway before another round of screams rip through the hall. Faya, Asher, and Leah are now running to my side as Nakoa helps me up, dropping my hand as soon as I'm upright.

I'm going to pretend like that didn't sting a little because right now we have bigger things to handle at the moment. Instead, I reach for Leah and hug her tightly. "We don't have time to catch you up on everything." I step away from her and turn around. "Faya, I need you to get Leah out of here."

"What, no!" Leah protests, grabbing my shoulder.

"I can't have you here, Leah. I need you safe," I say, taking her hand. "Please," I beg.

Nakoa turns toward Faya, giving her instructions. "Take her to the bunker under the castle where my parents and Kalena are and lock the door until one of us comes to retrieve you."

Leah nods once, then Faya takes her by the hand, leading her to the back of the room by the stage where there is a hidden emergency exit door.

That leaves me, Nakoa, Asher, and a crowd of scared guests until Kieran fades back down the stairs. "I counted at least thirty vampires in the hall. I redirected the fleeing guests to the back of the castle, giving them an alternative exit," Kieran says to us before fully turning to face Nakoa. "Your soldiers won't be able to hold them much longer. What kind of emergency strategy do you have in place?"

"Who the hell do you think you are?" Nakoa says, stepping closer to Kieran.

"He's trying to help you, Nakoa. Stop being an ass!" I say, punching him hard in the shoulder.

He turns to me, narrowing his icy gaze on me. "This is all your fault," he accuses in a clipped tone that somehow sends a sharp pain shooting through my chest.

Asher places his arm around my shoulders, turning me away from Nakoa and laying into him. "Cut the shit, man. I don't care if you are her mate or not. You don't talk to her like that."

The crowd has grown thin, leaving a few guests left scrambling up the steps before one last massive explosion crumbles the already cracked eastern wall to the room. I cough as the dust circles around us, creating a thick blanket of darkness. As the dust starts to clear, I stand to view the mess left from the explosion and see a lone figure's silhouette standing on the rubble. I create a gust of wind to dissipate the remaining dust, only to be stunned to see Bree grinning wildly on the top of the rubble with a large group of vampires behind her.

Oh hell.

"Who is that?" Nakoa questions in a hostile tone.

"A pain in our ass," Kieran and Asher both say simultaneously.

"The person who killed my grandpa," I grit, preparing my powers for what's to come next.

Asher's attention snaps to me. "She did what?" he questions softly, taking my hand in his as Kieran swears under his breath.

I let out a shaky breath and squeeze my eyes shut before the tears can fall.

"Oh, I'm sorry," Bree says, pouting her lip. "Did I interrupt your little reunion?"

Asher gently drops my hand and steps forward when a hiss erupts from the vampires behind Bree.

"Oh, hello Asher!" Bree waves to him. "I see you've officially met Kieran." She laughs as her eyes roam over Nakoa's body. "And who is this fine-looking man?"

Nakoa takes a step forward to shield me as Asher and Kieran join in on each side of him.

"Oh dear," Bree says, tilting her head. "You're the lucky man who stole Raven away from the Vampire Court, aren't you?" Suddenly, Bree gasps sarcastically. "Don't tell me you're also Raven's mate? What a lucky girl you are, Raven."

"What the hell do you want?" Nakoa questions.

"I'm here to bring Raven back to Antonio. He was so sad when you took away his prize."

"I am no one's prize or possession," I demand, stepping around my mates.

Bree purses her lips and crosses her arms. "We'll see about that." She looks over her shoulder to the waiting vampires, raising an eyebrow at us. "Attack," she commands.

The vampires behind Bree suddenly lunge forward as I create a gust of wind to push the first line of them back. Kieran fades to the rushing line of vampires and collides with two of them, ripping each of their hearts out instantly. Asher shifts into a giant rhino and barrels forward into the left side of the attacking vampires, sending a few flying into the sky. Nakoa sheds his jacket and extends his golden wings, launching into the sky and sweeping into the remaining vampires, slicing their heads off with a sword he picked up from the rubble.

My mates all know I'm capable of handling myself, which is why I trust them to take care of the remaining vampires while I make my way toward Bree. She descends the rubble with a sinister smirk on her face as we approach each other. The electric current of my powers comes to life with the chance to seek revenge for my grandpa. A rogue vampire makes his way to my side and before he can come any closer, I lash out with my fire element and turn him to ashes.

Bree raises her eyebrow in surprise, but quickly recovers and cools her expression. I generate another gust of wind and use it to propel myself off the ground and right toward Bree. She rolls to the left as I narrowly miss hitting her with a fireball. She's quick to get back to her feet, launching herself at me as I sidestep her fist before it can make contact with my already bruised face.

We circle each other as the fight rages on around us. I catch sight of Nakoa fighting hand to hand with two vampires as Kieran rips out another heart next to him. I focus back on Bree, but it's too late to sidestep her kick as it collides with my knee, making it buckle under me. I quickly create a gust of wind to push her back, giving me time to stand again.

As soon as I stand, a searing pain slashes through my back as a vampire licks my blood from his blade. Nakoa is the closest one to me as I fall back to my knees. He swings the sword through the air, killing both vampires in front of him, then throws his sword directly at the vampire who just cut me. The sword cuts through the vampire's heart and sends the heart and the sword flying right toward Bree.

She quickly dodges it, rolling out of the way and closer to me. Asher's rhino form charges toward me and as he approaches, he quickly shifts back into his human form, kneeling at my side, covering my back with his shirt as I scream out in pain.

Bree stands quickly and brings her fingers to her lips, letting out a high whistle. The remaining vampires fade to Kieran on the far side of the room, circling him. Three of them lash out with small daggers and my mind goes back to Kieran fighting Sven on the mountain as I watch one knife sink into his shoulder.

"No!" I scream through the pain of the pressure Asher has on my back to stop the bleeding as Nakoa joins us. "Help Kieran!" I scream out as I start seeing black stars cloud my vision.

But it's too late. A second later, another vampire has elbowed him in the side of the head, knocking him unconscious as Bree sprints over to the group of vampires. She jumps on the back of one vampire as another scoops Kieran's limp body off the ground and they fade out of view.

That's the last thing I see before the stars fade and a black curtain falls over my vision, ending the searing pain in my back.

CHAPTER 45
FRIENDLY REUNION

It's still dark when I come to, but the moonlight fills my room enough for me to see Asher sprawled out at the end of the bed by my feet, sleeping soundly. My head is pounding as I scrunch my eyes shut, trying to sit up, careful not to wake him. I expect my back to be throbbing from the knife wound, but as I lay against the pillow, there's barely any pain.

"There's my girl," Leah whispers from her chair by the window. I huff out a sigh of relief seeing she's safe as she makes her way to the bed. "They've got some pretty crazy healing drugs here. You're practically good as new, except I told them to leave your black eye. Makes you look badass," she jokes, sitting down carefully next to me, laying her head on my shoulder.

A sob escapes my throat as I rest my head on hers. "I'm so sorry, Leah. This isn't how any of this was supposed to go."

Leah's smile fades slightly. "You don't have to be sorry, Rave. I'm just happy you're okay," Leah soothes, lacing her fingers through mine.

We're quiet for a few minutes, listening to Asher's soft

breaths before Leah speaks. "So, how long have you been holding out on me that you've acquired not one, but three fine ass men?"

I lift my head, looking right at her, and try to hide my smirk. "Well, I was going to tell you, but then I went and got kidnapped. Sooo not exactly my fault."

Leah tilts her head to the side, poking her finger in my side. "Touché. Speaking of fine ass men. What did Asher mean by mates?"

My stomach tightens at her question. Apparently, Colby never got around to telling Leah about their situation. I smile at Leah, hoping to glaze over the subject. If I make this conversation super vague, maybe she will just figure out she and Colby are mates by herself.

"Well, for supernaturals, being mated to someone is like finding your one true love." Leah raises her eyebrow at me as if to add some snide remark, but I quickly continue. "It's different for everyone when the mating bond solidifies. For Asher and I, it took sharing a kiss to cement our bond. For Kieran, it was when I saved him and he had to drink from me, and with Nakoa, it was instant. The moment our eyes connected, the mating bond sprang to life."

Leah's silent for once when I finish, but it only lasts a minute before Leah laughs, bringing my attention back to her. "Damn, girl, your life is a mess."

I can't help it. I burst out in laughter too, for how spot on Leah's assessment is. We both smother our giggles in our hands so we don't wake up Asher. With our laughter fizzling out, Leah turns to face me with tears glistening in her blue eyes. "I'm sorry about your grandpa," she whispers as a tear slides down her cheek.

I turn from her, wiping fresh tears from my own eyes. The pain is still raw and real, but being reunited with my favorite people has helped lessen the hurt for now.

"Thanks, Leah. I'm just glad you all are okay." I sigh, wiping my tears with the comforter. Another comfortable silence passes before something nags at me.

"Where's Colby? Why didn't he show up with you?"

Leah's silent for a moment before taking a shaky breath. "He went to the Vampire Court after Amera sent an encrypted hologram that you were kidnapped by Bree and taken to Antonio. He decided it was best he traveled to the Vampire Court alone under the guise of seeing what his father was up to, but instead, his father captured him as soon as he entered the castle."

I shake my head in disbelief. "Nakoa is right. This is all my fault."

Leah huffs out a laugh. "I mean, yeah, it kind of is." My mouth falls open in disbelief as I turn toward her before she continues. "Buuut, not really. Don't let that grumpy, tan, golden god ruin your mood. We all knew what we were getting into when we decided to come here and rescue you. It's not your fault you're like the hottest commodity right now because you can control all four elements, teleport, and zap lighting from your hands." Leah shrugs.

My mouth is still hanging open when Leah pushes my chin shut. "Yeah, I knew you could control elements, but Asher filled me in on the rest."

"I'm sorry! I really wanted to tell you, but I didn't know how, and I didn't want you to hate me. I just wanted to keep you safe." I whine into my hands.

Leah gently removes my hands from my face, her sweet smile breaking my heart. "I could never hate you, Raven. I know why you and Asher kept this a secret, but I'm happy I know now, considering everything."

I pin her with a look, wiggling my eyebrows. "Oh, you mean considering the way Colby looks at you and you look at him?"

Leah gently bumps my shoulder. "Yeah, something like that." She smiles. "You know, Asher hasn't left your side all night. I finally convinced him to catch a few hours of sleep while I looked over you."

I sigh, gazing down at Asher's ruffled blonde hair. "I don't deserve him. I don't deserve any of them."

"Yeah, speaking of. Kieran was ready to rip off Antonio's head after he heard what happened. Asher had to convince him otherwise. And Nakoa's been a Grumpy Gus outside your door all night, practically pacing a hole in the floor. He finally left after his mom pretty much threatened him to get a few hours of sleep."

"Oh no." I shake my head. "That's just his personality."

Leah and I share a look and can't help but giggle again; this time, waking Asher up in the process. He jolts up, practically tackling Leah and me. "Is she up?! Is she okay?" he pants.

"Yes, we're both fine, but we'd be better if you weren't pinning us to the bed," Leah jokes, shoving his arm from her legs. "Get off me, you crazy man."

Asher laughs as he sits back at the edge of the bed. "Sorry, Leah."

"Yeah, yeah," Leah grumbles, hopping off the bed. "I'll let you two catch up. See you in the morning."

Leah shuts the door quietly behind her, leaving Asher staring right at me.

"Hi," I say shyly.

"Hi," Asher says, prowling toward me. His green eyes shining with mischief. "I missed you," he whispers before placing a delicate kiss to my lips, lighting up my whole body.

"Thanks for saving me," I say, wrapping my arms around his neck.

"I told you. I'll always find you." Asher sighs, leaning his forehead against mine. I gently tug on his neck, causing him to fall next to me on the bed, turning my body to face him.

"I know, but thank you for taking care of Leah and Kieran as well. I know it must have been hard to be placed in that situation."

Asher smirks, pretending to bite my hand as I reach up to brush a stray hair from his face, causing me to laugh as he tucks my hand into his chest. "It wasn't that bad. Leah pretty much kept us both in check."

I roll my eyes, because of course she did. "How did she take the news of us being supernatural? Was Hurricane Leah in full force?"

"Well, we took every precaution, but turns out she already assumed you were a witch. She literally laughed in my face when I asked her if she believed in supernatural beings, Rave."

"What?!" I shriek.

"Yeah," Asher continues, "so, when I told her I was a shifter, she put two and two together that I was the collie from our childhood. And she knows Colby and Kieran are vampires, but that's it. I don't think Colby told her they are mates yet."

"Hmm," I draw, rolling back to stare up at the ceiling. I'm sure Colby has a good reason for not telling Leah, and I certainly won't be the one to break the news. Asher props himself up on his elbow and stares down at me.

"How have your powers been? Any unexpected things happen recently?"

I pause before answering. Now that I think about it, my powers haven't acted out since I've been in the Realm of Shadows. "Actually, no. The only issue I still have is teleporting."

"Interesting." Asher nods before peppering me with questions. "No unexpected thunderstorms? Ground shaking? Windstorms?"

I turn back to him and smirk. "No, no, and," I reach out and poke him on the forehead, pushing him back against the bed, "no."

I laugh as Asher pulls me in for a warm, cozy hug. Being with him like this helps to melt some of my stress away, but my heart still aches when I think of everything that's happened. "We have to save Kieran. I know it's not my place to ask and you have every right to hate me, but we have to save him, Asher."

"Hey," Asher says, turning my face up to him. His green eyes scan my face with no hatred or disgust. Just love. "I will do everything in my power to get him back safe. Him and Colby both. I promise."

"Thank you," I whisper, placing a gentle kiss on his lips before pulling away and snuggling into his chest.

His arms tighten around me before he speaks again. "I'm taking Leah to the Shifter Court with me tomorrow to talk to my Uncle Tobias. We are going to need more help to fight against Antonio. I want you to stay here with Nakoa."

"But—" I begin to say before Asher cuts me off.

"Please, Raven. I know you'll be safe here with him and his family. He won't let anything happen to you. Leah and I will be back in a day, which will give you and Nakoa time to figure out a plan to get us all into the Vampire Court and save Kieran and Colby."

I want to protest, but this gives me the perfect opportunity and most likely my only chance to sneak off to the Mage Court to the secret spot my dad mentioned in his letter and finally find some answers. "Fine."

"Thank you." He smiles, snuggling in closer. "Now, let's go back to sleep. Leah and I are leaving as soon as the sun's up," he says, kissing my cheek.

"Goodnight, Shifter."

"Goodnight, Witch."

CHAPTER 46

ANYONE UP FOR TWISTER?

sher's side of the bed is empty when I roll over, reaching out for him. Instead, my hand brushes over a piece of paper. I rub the sleepiness out of my eyes and sit up, hugging my knees before opening the note.

> Dear Raven, you looked so peaceful, and I didn't want to wake you. Leah and I are heading to the Shifter Court. We will be back tomorrow afternoon. Be safe.
>
> XO Asher.

I flop back against the pillows, looking out the window. The morning sun is shining brightly, and the sky is clear. Suddenly, an idea forms as I toss the covers off me and dash toward the closet. I rummage through the clothes, grabbing a pair of boots, leather leggings, a lightweight olive green button down, and a black cloak.

I quickly dress and crack open my bedroom door, peeking down the hallway. Nakoa's door is still shut and I don't hear any voices downstairs as I make my way to the kitchen. Poking my head around the corner, I find the kitchen empty. Taking a kitchen towel, I wrap up three croissants and some grapes and shove them in my cloak pocket. I swipe a water canteen as well, heading to the basement door. The same door Nakoa said is the only way on and off the beach.

I have one shot to teleport to the Mage Court and the beach is where I felt the best connection with my dad in this entire place. Just as I round the corner, I stop dead in my tracks when I see a shadowy figure leaning against the same door that leads to the beach.

"Good morning, Raven."

"Good morning, Nakoa," I grumble as he looks up from peeling a peach. "I was just going to walk along the beach."

"Mhm." He hums, wiping the excess peach juice on his thigh. "I'm sure you were," he says, popping a slice of peach in his mouth.

"Yep. So, if you'll just," I try to sidestep him to grab the door handle but he doesn't budge, "excuse me."

"You're not going anywhere unless you tell me where you're really going."

An annoyed sigh slips from my lips. I don't have time for this. I could easily freeze him in place, but my power only holds if I'm able to see the object I'm holding, so that won't work. Grabbing the bridge of my nose, I exhale as I slouch against the wall.

"I need to go to the Mage Court. My dad left something there for me to find."

Nakoa raises an eyebrow, contemplating my statement.

"It's important," I plead, staring into his golden eyes.

His expression softens for a half second before he takes a bite of the peach. "Well then, let's go."

I tilt my head to the side, narrowing my gray eyes. "Uhm, no. I'm going by myself," I say, reaching for the door handle again.

Nakoa places his hand on my wrist and shoves a piece of peach in my mouth with his other hand. "If you leave, I'm coming with you. Besides, Asher told me we need to create a plan to infiltrate the Vampire Court to get your friend back."

I chew on the delicious slice, contemplating on telling him off or not after hearing him refer to Kieran as my "friend" when Nakoa knows for a fact that Keiran is my mate. "Fine," I snarl, deciding to take the high road this time. I wipe my mouth with my sleeve and take a step forward toward Nakoa, staring him down. "Now get out of my way."

Nakoa steps to the side, letting me finally open the door to the beach. As soon as my feet hit the sand, I envision the memory of me and my dad at the beach. The vision slowly morphs into a different scene, revealing the willow tree by the river at the Mage Court.

The connection builds, getting stronger with each passing moment. I sense Nakoa right behind me, so before I can tell him what's about to happen, I reach out and grab his wrist as we're suddenly thrust into the sky. His scream fades out as our bodies meld together, jetting across the beautiful landscape.

Suddenly, the bright colors of the Dragon Court turn darker as we land on a dense forest floor. Nakoa rolls out and lands on his knees while I gracefully land right on my ass, laughing.

"I did it!" I shout, throwing my hands in the air.

"What the hell? Where are we?" Nakoa asks, walking over to help me up.

"Well, from what I can remember, we are near the territory line between the Mage and Dragon Court," I say, brushing leaves and pine needles from my butt.

"Did you teleport us here?" Nakoa asks, surprised.

"I certainly did." I nod smugly. I finally figured out, well, somewhat figured out, how to teleport. Even though we aren't at the exact spot I hoped for, this is just as good. "Come on. From here, it's about an hour's hike."

The Mage Court is on the opposite side of the Realm of Shadows and there is a four-hour time difference, which means the sun is just starting to rise, giving us a head start on anyone who might be wandering this part of the territory.

Just as we begin our journey, a bright flash of lighting streaks across the sky, followed by a loud clap of thunder that startles me. I turn to see Nakoa lifting his head up toward the sky as rain begins to fall. I remember a small cave just up ahead and start sprinting toward it. I know what these clouds are and it's not looking good. The sky darkens even more, and Nakoa races to catch up to me as the wind picks up. The trees shake violently and the rain is now falling harder than before.

Veering left, I spot the small opening I remember from my childhood and peel away fallen branches from the entrance. Nakoa catches up with me and quickly helps move the larger branches enough for us to climb over and seek shelter. We fall into the cave entrance just as another bright flash of lightning paints the sky.

"I hate twister season in the Mage Court," Nakoa grumbles.

Twister season works differently in the Realm of Shadows. Instead of a twister that may last a few seconds or even minutes, these twisters last hours and circle around, generating massive amounts of damage before fizzing out. It's typical that every season there are a total of two or three twisters, and we just so happened to be caught up in one of the rare occurrences.

Weather in the Human Realm is much easier to control since there isn't an abundance of magic in their world, which is why I was able to manipulate the weather back home. However, here in the Realm of Shadows, there is magic all around. The environment has adapted and evolved to resist any magic being used to manipulate the current weather patterns.

I make quick work to break off some of the fallen branches before the rain can totally soak them, placing them in a pile in the middle of the floor for kindling. Channeling my fire element, I light the fire and throw more dead sticks on the pile, making sure to keep the fire going as the wind picks up even more.

Nakoa paces the cave. He's not a fan of being caught off guard like this. I remove my wet cloak and hang it from a rock that juts out near the fire, hoping to dry it off a little before we continue on our journey. I watch Nakoa pace some more before deciding to plop down next to the fire as the temperature outside grows colder.

"Well, we might as well hunker down and wait it out. It's not like we have any other choice," I say, looking out at the dark sky. "Let's just hope the twister doesn't come anywhere near us."

Nakoa eyes me cautiously, like I'm the dangerous one and not the raging storm outside. The more he stares at me, the more I feel like he might really think that I'm actually the dangerous one.

"What's your problem now?" I ask, annoyed.

"You, Raven," he says as he starts pacing again. "You're my problem."

I stand quickly, making my way around the fire, halting him from pacing. "What the hell is that supposed to mean?"

Nakoa shakes his head, stepping around me. "Never mind."

I grab him by the arm, my anger now bubbling to the surface. "No. Tell me what's going on. You're practically glowing with hatred right now."

"Because I am!" he shouts, causing me to step backward. He runs his hand down his face before stepping back. "I'm sorry. I didn't mean to shout. I'm just so frustrated."

"Why?" I ask cautiously.

"Because you lied to me. You made me believe I was the only one when, in fact, somehow, you have two other mates."

I cross my arms defensively across my chest. "I didn't lie. I was going to tell you after the ball, but then everything happened and I couldn't. I just wanted one more day with the two of us before I had to break the perfect bubble you created for us."

I watch Nakoa's eyes soften. "Those three days were the best days of my life. I fell in love with you, and now I have to share you. How is that fair to me? To any of us?"

I turn away to spare him from seeing the physical pain his words cause me. "I don't know," I whisper, but I know he heard it.

Nakoa sighs and crosses the distance between us, wrapping his strong arms around me. His warmth envelops me on the ever growing cold day.

CHAPTER 47

CONFESSIONS IN THE DARK

Eleven hours later, the storm seems to start easing up. After our little fight this morning, Nakoa stayed toward the entrance of the cave, watching the storm with hardly any glances back at me. I gave him his space to work out his frustrations in his mind while I stared at the fire and worked on strengthening my elements to pass the time.

We have no plan to save Kieran and Colby yet, but now that I can teleport, I feel as though I could get us close enough to the back door that I escaped from. The only thing holding me back is, what if I accidentally teleport us somewhere we aren't supposed to be or nowhere close to the castle at all. I can't take that chance, so it looks like we're back to square one.

I'm so in my head I don't hear Nakoa approach behind me. "We should get some sleep. We can leave here before sunrise tomorrow to make up time."

I nod, pulling out the food from my cloak. I unwrap the kitchen towel and hand Nakoa two of the croissants I saved.

"Thanks," he says, taking the food. I munch on the grapes,

saving my croissant for last. It's not much, but it'll have to hold us over until tomorrow.

I stand and place the last sticks I've saved onto the fire. They won't get us through the night, but my cloak has dried, so I'll be able to use it as a light blanket. Tying the cloak around me, I sit on the opposite side of the fire as Nakoa.

He stares at me through the fire, his eyes glowing in the firelight. "Why are you sitting over there?" he asks in a low voice.

I shrug and stare into the fire. "I'm just giving you your space." A gust of wind whips through the cave, causing me to shiver in my cloak. Nakoa sighs and stands, walking over to where I'm sitting. "What are you doing?" I ask skeptically.

He sits down next to me, and I yelp when he pulls me into his lap, wrapping his arms around me. "Dragons have a higher body temperature than other supernatural beings. We're never cold."

As he speaks, my body heats up under his touch. My shaking hands slow as I relax into his chest.

"Why do you need to go to the Mage Court so bad?" he asks after a moment.

"To find answers."

"Answers to what?" he asks.

I sigh, taking a deep breath before explaining myself. "Everything, I guess. When my dad died, he left a note for me to open on my twenty-first birthday. Unfortunately, the note went missing the night of my birthday and when I was kidnapped by Bree, she revealed that she took the note. She read it to me and then killed my grandpa."

"Raven, I'm so sorry," he says, gently tightening his hold on me.

"It's okay. The letter said to return to our special place and find the answers I seek. I'm hoping there will be some sort of explanation for my extra powers and why I have more than one mate."

"Hmm," Nakoa says, placing his chin on my head. "Let's try to get some sleep."

I nod as Nakoa lays down, opening his arms for me to cuddle close. I take the cloak off and drape it over us as a blanket, but I have a feeling I won't be needing it since my body is nearly sweating from being trapped in Nakoa's arms. He wasn't kidding when he said dragon's bodies give off some massive body heat.

We lay by the fire in silence, and just when I thought he fell asleep, Nakoa laces his fingers in mine. "I don't hate you," he whispers in my ear. "I could never hate you, but I hate myself for falling in love with you, even when all my senses told me not to. I couldn't help it."

I squeeze my eyes shut, listening to his confession. I didn't mean to fall in love with him, either. It's different from what I feel when I'm with Asher and Kieran. This love is dangerous and exciting. Nakoa drives me crazy, but at the end of the day, I know we both push each other to be our best version of ourselves.

I'm still trying to navigate having three mates. I don't expect these guys to accept this right away, but eventually, they are going to have to. I can't imagine what it would feel like to lose one of these three amazing men. My heart felt like two big pieces were missing while I was here at the Dragon Court. When I saw Asher and Kieran emerge at the top of the stairs, those pieces instantly slid back into place and I felt as though everything was right again in the world.

I just can't bring myself to tell him what he wants to hear. Instead, I roll over and crash my lips onto his. It's hot, passionate, and wanting, and over too quick as Nakoa pulls back, placing a soft kiss to my forehead. "Get some sleep, Princess."

My heart aches as I snuggle into his chest, listening to the wind howl outside the cave. The leaves bristle and a stray branch scratches somewhere on the outside of the cave as Nakoa's deep breaths pull me into a sorrowful sleep.

I wake up when I roll over onto a sharp rock, trying to jab its way into my shoulder. Opening my eyes, the sun is barely up, creating a deep orange sunrise shining on the entrance of the cave. Movement catches my eye as I turn to see Nakoa entering the cave.

"Morning," I greet him, sitting up, running my fingers through my morning hair.

He nods and waits for me to finish braiding my hair before we head out of the cave. Even though it's the wee hours of the morning, the destruction from the storm is visible. Trees are thrown against each other, streams are rushing faster, almost breaching their banks, and the trail up to the secret spot where my father and I used to visit is caked in mud.

This should be fun.

Less than an hour later, I've fallen more times than I can count. My boots are covered in mud, along with my knees and hands. I'm pretty sure I heard Nakoa stifle a laugh the last time I fell, wiping fallen hair from my face and smearing mud along my cheek as I dragged myself to my feet once again.

Finally, the familiar boulder emerges, letting me know the spot I'm looking for is just at the top of the hill. I stop next to the boulder, grabbing the water canteen from my cloak and taking a long pull before handing the rest to Nakoa. He takes it graciously, drinking the last of the water.

"I appreciate you coming with me, but I need to do this last part on my own," I say as he tucks the canteen in his own cloak.

He nods and for once I'm thankful he doesn't argue with me. "I'll go refill the canteen in the waterfall we found earlier. Then, I'll wait right here for you so I can see you at all times."

"Thank you." I nod, turning to make my way up to the familiar willow tree. As I approach the tree, memories bombard my mind from visits here with my dad. I wipe a stray tear as I place my hand on the trunk of the tree, tracing the carving of our initials in the tree. I turn, looking out at the wide riverbank as I remember all the times we hiked up here to watch the sunset over the water.

"I'm here, Dad, and I wish you were too," I whimper, sinking down into the grass, leaning against the massive trunk. I spread my hands out on the grass, relaxing into the tree as my pinky rubs against something harsh. I look down and brush the grass from the rough object, discovering a weathered, slim rope. I sit on my knees as I try to dig up the rope, but it seems to be buried too far into the ground.

I place my hand over the grass, accessing my earth element. The ground shakes as I pull my hand away, the rope and dirt below it falling away, revealing a small blue box. I untie the rope and gently lift the lid to the box, and find a silver disc. I vaguely remember my dad using holograms, but I have no idea how to work it. I flip it over a few times in my hand, looking for some kind of an "on" switch when my finger finds a slight indent in the back of the disk. I place my thumb there and the whole disc lights up a bright green color.

I drop the disk on the ground, taking two steps back just in case I accidentally engaged the self-destruct button. Instead, a screen flickers on the tree trunk and my dad appears before me. I gasp, covering my mouth with my hands as he smiles right at me.

"My beautiful Raven." He smiles even brighter as tears stream down my cheeks. His brown eyes sparkle back at me through his circular framed glasses. He looks exactly as I remember with his signature khaki pants, dark blue cardigan, and his hair slightly longer than usual, in desperate need of a haircut. He must have recorded this right before we left for the Human Realm because he's in his office at the Mage Court.

"I hope you find this message when you need it most and I'm sure you have plenty of questions, but first, if you're seeing this,

I want to say happy twenty-first birthday. I wish I was there to see the woman you grew up to be, but I have no doubt you are still as perfect as ever," he pauses, wiping a stray tear away from his own face before continuing.

"Your powers are something to be proud of and I hate that you have to hide who you are. I did everything I could to keep you safe and I hope one day you forgive me for what I've done." He pauses again as I brace myself for what comes next.

"When we first learned that you could control all four elements, I searched the realm for answers. Finally, as I was about to give up hope, I came across something hidden away in the Seneca Library. It was a spell to create a mating bond. I knew it was wrong, but we were running out of time when Antonio started kidnapping young mages.

"I stole the scroll and brought it home for deciphering when Tobias showed up to the Mage Court with his nephew. The second you and Asher laid eyes on each other, I knew the mating bond was sealed for you two. At that moment, a plan was formed. There is no one who could keep you safer than your mate, and when I realized this, I told Tobias of my plan. He was hesitant at first, but after some convincing, he finally agreed."

"Agreed to what?" I ask myself skeptically.

"Tobias and I traveled to the Dragon Court, knowing they had a son who was your age. We told King Kalino and Queen Nani about the delicate situation, and after some heavy bargaining, they agreed as well. We couldn't risk traveling to the Vampire Court, but that's when Queen Nani revealed they had a vampire prisoner in the basement cells. Queen Nani assured us he was harmless, as he was caught at an illegal gambling ring on the edge of the city. So, I did what I had to do."

"What did you have to do!" I ask desperately.

"Your grandparents helped me perform the mating spell. We took Nakoa and Kieran and temporarily severed their own mating bonds and recreated them to be mated to you in order to keep you safe when the time came."

I gasp in horror at what my family did.

"We wiped all three boys' memories, of course, so that they wouldn't know they were mated to you until the time arose. We wanted the mating bonds to feel real when you all met for the first time. The feelings you all have for each other are real and genuine. We just helped strengthen those feelings. Let them protect you when you need it, but when the danger is over, you must pick who you want to spend your life with. Once you do this, the remaining two bonds will be reinstated, letting each man find their true mates."

I shake my head, not believing a word that I'm hearing. How could he do this to them?

"I'm not sorry for any of this. I would do anything to keep you safe, little bean. I need you to be strong and fight this evil with your mates. You're stronger together." It feels as if he's really looking right at me when he smiles the truly mesmerizing smile I remember from my dreams. "I love you, Raven. I will always love you."

The hologram ends, the light retracting back into the disc as my shock brings me to my knees. His words echo in my mind like a song stuck on repeat when Nakoa's scream breaks me from my daze.

"Raven!" he shouts, sprinting toward me. "RUN!"

CHAPTER 48

DON'T BE DRAGON ME DOWN

I scramble to my feet as Nakoa practically barrels into me. Before I can ask what the hell is going on, a giant, charcoal-colored dragon emerges from the clouds above.

"Who the hell is that?" I shriek, as Nakoa grabs my arm, hauling me down the other side of the hill.

"I don't know, but I would rather not stick around and find out. Get us out of here."

My mind is so fogged over from the overload of information my holographic dad threw at me that I can't clearly visualize somewhere to teleport to. Nakoa's patience is growing thin when the dragon sweeps down, aiming its claws right at us. "Now, Raven!"

"I can't!" I shout back, pushing him away with a gust of wind and out of the way of the dragon's claws.

Nakoa throws off his cloak and without skipping a beat, a bright golden light emerges from where he's standing, completely showering him in light. A second later, a massive, golden dragon surfaces from the light, shooting straight at the other dragon. Nakoa's dragon is beautiful. His body zeroes in on the other dragon and I can see slightly different brown tones on his back as his scales shimmer against the sun. He is at least double the size of the other dragon, but when they collide in the air, the charcoal-colored dragon finds the soft spot under Nakoa's wing and pierces his skin with its claw. Nakoa lets out a tremendous roar, causing me to cover my ears.

Suddenly, I catch movement on the edge of the hill near a downed maple tree. Two vampires stalk toward me and another movement causes me to turn as two more vampires make their way from the woods. With the battle continuing in the sky, the two vampires in front of me fade toward me, seemingly unfazed by what's going on above us.

I quickly create a gust of air to push the two vampires back as two vampires behind me circle me. One rushes toward me and without thinking, I throw a fireball at him, narrowly missing as he steps out of the way. I quickly channel my earth element and reach for the buried tree roots to wrap around his ankles, pulling him into the ground. That buys me a little time before the female vampire rushes at me, throwing a punch right to my stomach.

She steps back laughing. "So weak," she hisses.

I bring my head up before she realizes what's happening and headbutt her right in the nose. Blood instantly pours from her face, but this just brings a sinister laugh from her. She reaches out and grips my throat, her hand tightening to the point where I see spots. I choke on a breath before throwing my arm out toward the river, bringing a giant water ball toward us.

The water douses us both, but I bring my other arm down on her wrist, breaking her hold on me as I step out of the water vortex. I watch as she chokes on the water, unable to escape as she falls to her knees. Only when her body hits the ground, do I release her from the funnel.

I turn to see the male vampire struggling to dig himself out of the ground that has swallowed him up to his shoulders. He won't be much of a problem now, but I have to figure out a way to tele-port me and Nakoa out of here. I look up briefly to see Nakoa and the other dragon locked in an air chase, with Nakoa hot on the other dragon's tail.

I turn to run back up to the willow tree when the two vampires I blew away with the wind gust reappear in front of me. Nakoa spots me and changes course, flying toward me instead. If I can stall for just a while longer, he can take out the vampires. Thinking quickly, I decide to aim a fireball at each of them, firing each one in rapid succession to throw them off balance. My plan seems to work because when the female vampire hesitates, my fireball hits her in the leg, causing her to drop to one knee as she screams in pain.

I fall to the ground, flattening myself into the grass as the male vampire lunges for me, but before he can reach me, Nakoa plucks him from the ground. I don't have time to see what Nakoa does with him, as the female vampire is back on her feet and seriously pissed.

"You're going to regret that," she seethes.

"We'll see," I taunt her as we both circle each other.

The charcoal dragon is nowhere to be seen as Nakoa barrels right at us again. Just as I'm about to create a gust of wind to knock the female vampire back into Nakoa's clutches, the other dragon plows into Nakoa's side. My eyes grow wide as they both crash into the river, but that's all it takes for me to lose my concentration. The next thing I know, the female vampire lunges for me, her elbow cracking against my face.

CHAPTER 49
SHOW NO MERCY

NAKOA

My dragon hits the water hard as the other dragon lands on top of me, submerging us both. I'm temporarily stunned as we both sink farther into the river. I struggle to free myself from under the other dragon, but I use my last breath to shift into my human form and kick with all my might, using my dragon wings to help propel me to the surface. I suck in a deep breath, launching myself into the air, my now human body being carried to the riverbank by my wings.

I fall to my knees, exhausted on the riverbank, and tuck my wings back into my body. I pick my head up, searching for Raven, but she's nowhere to be found. I suck in another deep breath as I scan the tree line.

"Raven!" I shout. My gaze narrows in on a male vampire buried in the ground, squirming to break free of the earth and tree roots. Next to him, a female vampire lays unmoving and soaking wet.

As I drag myself to my feet, a wave of water floods the riverbank momentarily. I turn to see the charcoal dragon land not even thirty feet from where I am. Before I can even move, the dragon shifts, leaving a wheezing redhead splayed on her back, clutching her chest.

"You!" I snarl as I close the distance, reaching for my knife, ready to attack. Except, when I finally reach her, her face is pale, and her breathing is ragged.

"Go on then," Bree wheezes. "Finish the job."

My mind is caught in an internal battle as I gaze upon her. This is the woman that kidnapped Raven, killed her grandfather, and tried to kidnap her again on MY territory. I should have no trouble killing her. So why can't I bring myself to drive this knife through her heart? Maybe it's the way she's looking at me now. Scared and even regretful, maybe?

I sigh loudly, sheathing my knife. "No."

"Do it!" she yells, her teeth stained red. She doesn't have long before she drowns in her own blood. The puncture on her chest is deep. Even if I wanted to save her, she wouldn't survive the flight back to the Dragon Court.

I turn, stalking toward the two vampires, ignoring Bree's muffled cry. I shove my foot into the side of the female, rolling her over. She's passed out. The male vampire spits on my shoes, looking up to me as he struggles to free himself.

"You'll never get to her in time for what Antonio has planned." He grins sadistically up at me.

Rage fills my body as I realize the vampire I had been aiming for before I was tackled into the water most likely knocked Raven out and took her back to the Vampire Court. I raise my boot and bring it down right into the male vampire's face, wiping away the smug look as I break his nose.

I crouch down, grabbing his hair and forcing him to look at me. "You better hope nothing happens to her because the way I see it, your life now depends on her safety." I bring my fist back and land another hard blow to his face, knocking him out.

I manage to dig out his body to his waist. From there, I'm able to drag his body the rest of the way out of the ground. Turning on my heel, I throw the unconscious vampire next to his accomplice on the forest floor. With one last look back at Bree's limp body, I shift into my dragon form and collect the two vampires in my claws, flying faster than I ever have back to the Dragon Court.

The sun has almost set by the time I land near the castle entrance. I make it back to the Dragon Court in three hours and when I land, Asher, Leah, Kalena, Faya, and my parents all wait for me near the flower garden. Kalena and Faya run toward my dragon, crouching under my body and collecting the two vampires. They secure shackles around their hands and feet, then haul them off to the dungeon.

I shift as Asher approaches, his eyes wide with fear. "Where is she?" he demands, stepping in my way.

"Move. Now!" I shout in his face.

"I trusted you to look after her. Where is she?" Asher demands again.

"She tried to sneak out to go to the Mage Court for some stupid thing from her dad! I went with her and we were attacked by Bree and those vampires," I snarl, pointing in the direction Kalena and Faya dragged the vampires.

Leah stomps over and moves in front of Asher, pushing him back and poking me in the chest. "It wasn't stupid! Anything from Raven's dad was precious to her, so she must have had a good reason to leave now and try to retrieve it."

She's so close that when I try to take a calming breath, all I smell is her lavender perfume. "Get out of my face, human," I grit out. I don't have time for this senseless arguing. I have to rally our troops and get Raven back.

Leah must think this is a joke. She throws her head back and laughs right in my face.

"You're crazy," I say, stepping around her as I walk away.

Asher grabs me by the arm, halting me. "Is Bree dead?"

I nod my head as Asher sighs, lowering his head. "All differences put aside; we need to talk. I found out some interesting things from my uncle."

I shake my arm out of Asher's grip and stalk toward the castle. "Meet me in the dining hall in fifteen minutes."

I enter the castle, leaving everyone outside as I head straight to the infirmary. I was able to stop halfway and pack my wound, but I can tell I've lost too much blood. I barely make it into the doorway before my step falters, collapsing into Kalena's arms.

"Woah there, big guy," she huffs, catching me before my body can hit the floor. "Let's get you fixed up."

I grunt as she practically throws my body on the exam table, no gentleness in her touch. "I get that you're mad," I say, as she cuts my shirt open, exposing a nasty-looking wound under my armpit.

"I'm not mad," Kalena says, reaching for the antiseptic. "I'm just disappointed," she continues as she dowses my wound.

"Ahh! I get it!" I yell as she cleans the wound, throwing bloodied gauze to the floor. "Remind me to just bleed out next time instead of coming to you for help when you're mad."

She stops sewing my wound mid-stitch, looking up at me with raised eyebrows, and retorts, "But who else would put up with your angry ass?"

I chuckle as she starts stitching again. Kalena's the only one who isn't afraid enough to push my buttons besides my parents, and now Raven. I hang my head, thinking about her. "It's my fault she was taken again. I should have made sure we weren't followed."

Kalena slaps a bandage over my now closed wound, making me wince. "You did your best. Now, let's go get our girl back."

Everyone is gathered in the dining hall hunched over the table when Kalena and I march into the room. As we get closer, I can see a detailed map of the Vampire Court sprawled out.

"Where did you get this?" Kalena says, running her hand along the ancient-looking scroll.

"My Uncle Tobias had this in his archives. When I told him everything that's happened, he had his historians dig it up." Asher straightens, focusing on me. "He also said that the Mage Court is in chaos with Artemis now gone. Raven's Aunt Melody is in charge, but barely holding things together."

"We were able to convince Asher's uncle to provide some of his best soldiers to help us retrieve Raven, Kieran, and Colby," Leah chimes in.

"You're not going anywhere near the Vampire Court," I say, turning back toward Asher. "She can't come. She'll be a liability."

"Hello! I'm right here," Leah says, waving her hands in my face, "and yes, I'm coming."

I raise my eyebrow at Asher and he shrugs.

"I'll keep an eye on her," Kalena offers, winking at me. I swear this woman lives to provoke me.

"Fine. Then you both can stay at the edge of the barrier and wait until the fighting is over."

Leah and Kalena smile at each other and I hope I didn't just make a huge mistake teaming those two up together. I shake my head and focus on the map. "So, how do we break into the Vampire Court?"

CHAPTER 50
THE FEELING ISN'T MUTUAL

Once again, my face is throbbing as I roll over on the cold, hard ground, prying my eyes open to see a vaguely familiar room. My wrists feel heavy as I raise them above my face, revealing the siphoning shackles from my first stay at the Vampire Court.

Shit.

"Good morning, sleeping beauty," Kieran whispers through the cell bars. I tilt my head to the side to see his bloodied and bruised face as he leans against the stone wall, his arms resting on his knees. I glance at his wrists; he also has his own set of shackles.

I suck in a quick, deep breath as I prop myself up on my elbow. "You look like shit." I try to joke, but my emotions reveal the truth of what I'm feeling as a tear rolls down my cheek. I wipe it away swiftly, but not before Kieran sees it fall to the stone floor.

He reaches his shackled hand through the cell bars, and I

crawl closer to him, taking his hand in mine. "Don't cry. You should see your face," he jokes, drawing a soft laugh from me.

I can only imagine how I look. That vampire elbowed me on the non-bruised side of my face, so I'm sure both eyes look like I just smeared mascara all over them. "I was going to say I'm happy to see you, but never mind."

He chuckles as we both lean against the cold stone wall in our own cells.

"How are you, really?" I ask, studying him. His face and arms look like they haven't healed very quickly from the slash marks.

Our shoulders brush against each other as he shrugs. "Nothing that I can't handle."

The guilt slowly starts creeping its way into my mind. He's here in this situation because of me. He was kidnapped because of me. I lean my head against his shoulder as best I can through the bars. "I'm sorry," I whisper, "this is all my fault."

Kieran turns slightly and tucks his knuckle under my chin, angling me to face him, his ocean blue eyes drowning me into their endless sea. "This isn't your fault. Antonio is a fool if he thinks he can use you to bring the barrier down. I'll never allow him to use you, Tesoro."

I nod once, looking over Kieran's beaten frame. "Let me give you some of my blood. It'll help you heal and give you your strength back. Whatever they did to you, you're not healing like you normally do."

He shakes his head, dropping his hand. "I won't ask you to do that. You need your strength more than me if we get the chance to fight Antonio."

I turn my body and throw my hands out through the bars and grab his face, crashing my lips to his. He's hesitant at first, but then I feel him relax against my lips. I quickly deepen the kiss. I only have one shot at this, and I can't mess it up. I pull away for a millisecond, biting the inside of my lip hard as I bring my lips on his again.

He instantly tries to pull away, but I wrap my hands around his neck, locking my fingers together. I run my tongue over the cut on my lip, then slip my tongue inside his mouth. He moans as he tastes my blood, leaving the metallic taste on my lips. I know he didn't want to take my blood, but if even a few drops can help him heal and regain some strength, then it's worth it.

I unlink my hands and rest them on his shoulders as he continues to kiss me, slowly sucking on my bottom lip. Kieran's kiss is playful and sweet, just like his personality. He cups my chin and runs his tongue over my bottom lip and a moan escapes from me as I feel Kieran's lips turn up into a smirk at the sound. He pulls back, piercing me with his blue eyes. As I look at him, the cuts on his face slowly start to mend together. His cheeks regain some color and the wounds on his arms start to disappear.

I smile triumphantly. "You're welcome."

"If I knew that's how to get a kiss from you, I would have had Colby beat me up long ago."

We both laugh quietly, returning to rest against the cell wall.

"What do you think they did with Colby?" I ask cautiously, but before Kieran can answer, four guards appear on the outer door, unlocking it and stepping inside the room where our cells are.

"Time to go." One of the guards smirks, flashing his fangs at me.

"Leave her alone, Simon. Antonio wants her alive," another guard says, stepping forward and unlocking my cell. I stand as the third guard enters my cell, grabbing the chains on my shackles, pulling me behind him. The guard, Simon, opens Kieran's cell and punches him in the face. Kieran wipes his bloodied nose on his arm as he stands. I pull against my chains, trying to step back toward Kieran, but my guard yanks my chains, almost knocking me over as I shuffle to keep up with him. I hear

Simon's sinister laugh as he spits in Kieran's face before tugging Kieran behind him.

The guard leads us through a maze of hallways before stopping in front of a set of familiar doors. He knocks twice and the doors open, revealing the same ballroom from my first encounter with Antonio. The room is void of all the beautiful decorations from last time, except the sparkling chandeliers. As the guard steps to my side, he kicks the back of my knees, forcing me to kneel. I look up to see Antonio perched in his crimson red chair, grinning wickedly from the elevated platform as Kieran is forced to his knees beside me.

"Hello, my dear," Antonio purrs. It sends a cold chill up my spine, making me straighten as his eyes shift to Kieran. "And hello, Kieran. Such a pleasure to see you again."

Kieran spits at the floor in front of Antonio. "I can't say the feeling's mutual. We know you kidnapped your own son. Where's Colby?"

Antonio lets out a harsh laugh. "That's not the only person I've kidnapped." Antonio claps his hands and two guards haul in Colby by his chains. He looks relatively unharmed as the guards shove him to the ground next to Antonio. I hold my breath, waiting for the other shoe to drop as the guards pull someone into the room with a brown hood over their head. The guards force the new person to the ground, just as they did to Kieran and me. We watch Antonio slowly stand from his chair, prowling around to the front of the newcomer, grinning at me like the maniac he is.

"I thought it was time for a little family reunion," he says, snatching the hood away from the person in front of us.

"You son of a bitch!" I shout at Antonio as I stare into my mom's worried and bloodshot brown eyes. "Release her now! She has nothing to do with this!" I try to stand, but the guard next to me plants a firm hand on my shoulder, keeping my knees on the ground.

"On the contrary, dear," Antonio says, tossing the hood to the ground, "your dear old mom is here to make sure that you do exactly as I say."

"Don't help him, Raven!" my mom shouts.

Antonio's hand strikes her face lightning fast. "Shut up, bitch!" Antonio hisses, returning his gaze to me. My body thrums with power as I feel it start to swell, even with the siphoning shackles on. "You will help me, or I'll start by killing your mother, then Kieran, and even my own son, if that's what it takes."

Antonio slowly walks off the platform, making his way to me. He grabs a fist full of my hair, tilting my head back to face him. Kieran tries to lunge out for him, earning him a hard kick in the stomach from Simon. "Then, if that doesn't work, I'll hunt down the dragon who stole you away from me and kill him, then find your little shifter and human friend and kill them, too. Do you understand?" he growls.

I nod my head slightly, careful not to move too much, as Antonio still has my hair fisted in his hands. "Now." He nods to the guard next to me. The guard grabs my arms and inserts the key to the shackles, hesitating for Antonio's command. "I'm going to release these shackles and you are going to accompany me to the barrier between our world and the human world."

Somehow, he tightens his grip on my hair, causing me to whimper. "And if you try to escape, or use your powers on me, I will not hesitate to rip out your mother's throat. Got it?"

Before I agree, a guard rushes in through the main doors, but halts quickly as he scans the room. "What is it?" Antonio snaps, beckoning him forward with my hair still wadded in his hand.

The vampire guard whispers in Antonio's ear and he grinds his jaw in frustration at whatever news is being relayed. Antonio turns to the guard and grabs him by his chest plate with his other hand, growling in his face. "Take care of it."

As we wait for the guard to leave, there's a slight movement in the corner of the room. I narrow my gaze to see Amera and Vail in the shadows by the hidden door I was taken through after I caused a scene the last time I was here. Amera brings her finger to her lips, nodding at me. A tear escapes the corner of my eye from how tight Antonio's grip is, but I fix my gaze right at him.

"So, no tricks then?" he asks.

I blink away another unintentional tear and nod.

"Good. Wonderful!" he cheers, releasing my hair harshly.

Just as the guard is about to turn the key to my shackles, Amera and Vail fade toward Antonio, weapons aimed right at his heart. Simon and another guard next to Colby intercept Amera as they fight to disarm her. She's able to slash the neck of one vampire, but not before Simon has her in a choke hold, nearly breaking her neck. We watch in horror as Vail is able to decapitate one of the guards, fading right toward Antonio.

Antonio anticipates the move and ducks, spinning away from Vail as he falls to the ground. Antonio stands to his full height and drops Vail's heart to the floor. The whole incident took less than ten seconds, but the damage that remains is permanent. Amera's shriek pierces the ballroom, shattering the crystal chandelier above as glass rains down on us.

Antonio's hand flies across Amera's face, silencing her. "You ungrateful piece of trash! After everything I've done for you, this is how you repay me?"

Colby's eyes go wide and Kieran tries to break free while another guard comes to hold him back.

"Let her go!" Kieran shouts.

Antonio runs his tongue across his teeth, looking right at Kieran. "You want me to let her go?" he says, tilting his head. "Okay then."

In a flash, Antonio plunges his hand into Amera's chest as she screams. He bends down, whispering something into her ear, and her eyes grow wide before he yanks his hand from her chest with her heart in his hand.

Kieran, Colby, and I all scream, watching her lifeless body fall to the granite floor. My powers surge from within, burning me from the inside as Kieran shouts and fights against the hold of his guards. My eyes cloud over and Colby lunges for one of the guards near Amera before Simon kicks him hard in the face.

The electrical buzz from my powers fills my ears, drowning out the sounds around me as an explosion erupts behind us. My mind is fizzling as I barely register nearly two hundred vampire guards flooding the room preparing for a fight. All I see is Vail and Amera's lifeless bodies on the floor next to my mom. Her brown eyes latch onto me as I succumb to the infinite power rising within my body.

I feel intense heat, as if I'm melting into the floor, and suddenly, I feel a cooling sensation, like being doused with water, spreading through my body, making me take a deep breath. I feel light and my mind is clear as my powers harmonize beneath my skin, intertwining and becoming one.

Kieran and Colby fight against their guards, and Antonio continues yelling at the other guards to form a barrier as they try to barricade the door from the incoming intruders. My mating bonds send an electric spark up both of my arms, causing the hair on my arms to stick straight up. I hold my shackled wrists in front of my face and notice a faint shimmering golden string appear around my right wrist, snaking up toward my elbow.

I look at my other wrist and a vibrant magenta string is doing the same. I watch as a stunning dark blue string intertwines around my fingers. All three of my mates' strings vibrate with power as my body starts to surge with more power than I've ever felt. It's almost as if my body is using them as an amplifier for my own powers.

Another loud explosion erupts from behind me, this time causing the ballroom doors to completely shatter from their hinges. Battle cries fill the room. I spare a second to peer behind me toward the crumpled doors. The strings around my wrists zap me with energy as I see Nakoa and Asher leading an army of dragons, shifters, and mages through the doors, colliding with the Vampire Guard. I turn back and watch Antonio vanish into the fight, leaving eight guards surrounding us, presumably to stand guard over me in particular.

I smile to myself as I channel my powers. Only my mom notices when my shackles suddenly disintegrate into ashes in my hand. My mom and I are still stationed on our knees, which helps my plan come to life. I slide my arms in between my knees, making sure the guards don't notice my now free wrists as I channel my fire element to my hands.

I tilt my head to point toward the guards on her left, cluing her in on my plan. She nods, slowly pulling one knee close to her chest. I nod as she kicks out her leg, catching the vampire to her left off guard. Her distraction causes the other seven guards to take their eyes off me and instead focus on my mom.

I pull my hands from my knees and jump to my feet, swinging my arms from my back and clapping them in front of me. I watch as my fire element turns all eight guards into a pile of ash in front of us. My mom glances up at me, her eyebrows nearly touching her hair line in surprise.

I quickly bend down and place both of my palms on her shackles, disintegrating her own chains and freeing her to use her powers. "Help Kieran and Colby. I'll go find Antonio," I say, guiding her to her feet as the fight roars behind us.

My mom quickly rushes off to handle the guards trying to hold back Kieran and Colby as I turn to scan the ongoing battle. I catch a glimpse of Nakoa's golden armor and run to the far wall, hopeful to miss most of the fighting. I duck behind each of the long velvet curtains that cover the windows.

CHAPTER 51
HUMAN IN TRAINING

LEAH

Kalena and I are at the edge of the barrier, hidden amongst the forest, just as we promised Nakoa we would be. A loud explosion echoes through the dense forest, signaling our troops have breached the castle. I know I promised Asher that I wouldn't join the fight, but I can't sit here and twiddle my thumbs while everyone fights to save Raven, Colby, and Kieran. I know I'm human, but I can handle myself if I need to. Besides, I have Kalena and no one's going to want to mess with her.

"So, what's the plan?" I ask, cozying up to Kalena as she lounges on the trunk of a fallen spruce tree. She smirks at me and I can practically see the wheels turning in her big brown eyes.

She leans forward, elbows resting on her knees, as she points through a layer of trees with her jeweled dagger. "See that long stone wall over there, just outside the castle?" she asks, turning her face to mine. I nod, scanning the surrounding area. "We're going to scale it and go in through that door on the far side."

"But won't there be guards?" I ask, skeptically.

Kalena flips the dagger in her hand, catching the hilt as she stands. "Nope. I tasked my two best fighters to dispose of any vampires patrolling the wall. We're all clear."

"Nice!" I cheer quietly, jumping up from the tree trunk. Kalena flips the dagger once again, this time catching the blade as she extends the hilt toward me.

"Here," Kalena says as I accept the dagger, "in case you need to protect yourself."

"Thanks," I say, tucking the dagger into my belt, hoping I won't have to use it.

"Now, follow my lead and do exactly as I say. Understand?"

I nod again, watching Kalena's fun and easygoing expression shift into a hard, determined glare. *Holy shit.* I feel bad for the poor sucker who gets in her way.

Kalena crouches lower to the ground, weaving in and out of the trees until the forest meets the edge of the stone wall. She signals me to hold my position as she quietly approaches the wall, listening for any sign of someone patrolling the other side. She's only gone a few minutes, but it's as though time has stopped when I look out into the pitch black forest. I kneel on the ground, peeking a glance toward our entrance; even the castle is enveloped in darkness, except for two poorly lit windows above the door.

Kalena pops her head around one of the trees, surprising me as I crumple to the ground. "Jesus, Kalena! A little warning would have been nice!"

She laughs and her warrior mask fades for a moment in the darkness. "Yeah, but then I wouldn't get the chance to see you nearly piss yourself."

"Har, Har," I tease, holding the dagger a little closer to my chest. I hadn't noticed I snatched it out until now, but thank goodness some of my reflexes still work.

"Come on," she urges, helping me to my feet. "There are no

guards and it's a pretty easy shot to the main ballroom through that door." She halts me before we break our cover. "Once we're inside, find Colby or Kieran and stick by their side. Do not hesitate to use the dagger. Do you understand me?"

Again, I nod. I'm sure by now I probably remind her of a bobble head. *Wait, does she even know what that is? Do they have those here? Oh, forget it.*

Kalena nods too, but surprises me when she places her palm on my collarbone, leaning her forehead to mine. I don't know what's happening, but it feels like she needs this more than I do. "Be safe, my friend. I'll see you on the other side."

Kalena pulls away and laces her fingers together so she can help boost me over the wall. I hurry and scan the other side for any guards but find none, just like Kalena said. I haul myself up and swing my legs under me and over the other side, pausing before I jump to watch Kalena take five steps back from the wall.

Kalena tosses her braided hair behind her shoulder before running straight at the wall. She kicks off the wall with incredible speed and hoists herself up and over the wall, flipping through the air like a gymnast, landing perfectly on her feet.

"Show off," I whisper under my breath as I land hard and awkwardly on my feet.

"I heard that," Kalena throws back over her shoulder.

We sprint across the open space, approaching the slightly open door. Kalena retrieves two daggers of her own as she kicks the door open the rest of the way, finding an empty hallway. I make sure I'm always two steps behind Kalena as we follow the hallway deeper into the castle.

Quiet voices grow into loud shouting as we come to the end of the hallway. Kalena stops, flattening her back to the wall and I do the same, waiting for her next command. She peers around the corner for half a second, then straightens back against the wall. "Nakoa and Asher are still fighting their way through the crowd of vampires to our left. Colby and Kieran are in shackles on the stage, fighting their guards. There's a smaller lady with short brown hair casting spells at the same guards."

I'm stunned. "How could you possibly see all that for the one second you looked?"

Kalena shrugs like it's no big deal. "After I leave, I'll create a distraction to lure any remaining vampires from the area so you can enter safely. Turn right and you'll find Colby and Kieran."

Without another word, Kalena vanishes around the corner into the crowd of supernaturals. Now that I'm alone, merely steps from battle, fear and doubt creep into my mind. I take a deep breath, mustering all my strength and push that fear deep down inside me. My friends need me. I won't let them down.

I glance at Kalena for a moment, watching as she slices her bicep, causing any vampires around her to turn and assess where the fresh blood is flowing from, and I watch as her daggers slice through each vampire that approaches. I'm totally making her train me after this is over.

I refocus and look to the right and sure enough, Colby and Kieran are fighting their guards. There are bodies piled on the floor around them, some of them dressed in the same Vampire Guard armor and some in plain clothes. Colby and Kieran still have shackles on their wrists and as I glance at one of the bloodied guards on the ground, I notice a similar looking black key chained to the hip of a guard on the side of the stage.

A shiver races through my body at what I'm about to do. I slide my way around the corner and drop to my knees, crawling to the body holding the key. Thankfully, his body is positioned toward the back of the stage and mostly out of the eyesight of anyone. Unfortunately, when I reach my hand out to grab the key, the guard I thought was dead snatches my hand, pulling a bone chilling scream from my lips.

He lifts his head, revealing his fangs and a brutal, bloodied gash on the side of his head that extends from his forehead to his chin. He's weak, but still strong enough to yank me nearly on top of him as he tries to sink his fangs into my shoulder. I throw my elbow into his nose, just like Raven and I were taught in our self-defense classes, causing his head to jerk back, giving me enough time to grab my dagger and plunge it into his stomach. The vampire snarls, his fingernails still digging into my shoulder.

He lunges his head forward again, aiming at my neck this time. I close my eyes and wait for the excruciating pain, except the bite never comes. When I open my eyes, the vampire has his fangs sunk into Colby's arm. Colby swiftly retracts the dagger from the vampire's stomach and drives it into the vampire's heart. Instantly, the vampire falls limp as his body turns into an ashy gray color. Colby pushes the vampire off him, turning to face me. "Next time, aim for the heart, love."

I sit up and cross my arms over my chest, pouting. "I had the situation under control."

"What are you even doing here?" Colby asks, standing and plucking the dagger out of the now deceased vampire.

I stand and unfold my arms, holding my hand out toward him and dangling the key I snatched with my index finger. "Rescuing the damsel in distress, of course."

Colby smiles at me, and my heart warms. It feels as though I can breathe easier now that he's closer to me. He grabs my outstretched hand and pulls me in, his lips melting into mine briefly. "I supposed that makes you my princess charming?"

I push off him and try to hide my smile by reaching for his cuffs and unlocking them with the key. The cuffs fall to the floor as Colby takes the key out, yelling to Kieran. Kieran kicks the vampire he's fighting off the stage and looks up just in time to catch the key. His eyes widen briefly as I wave to him, then he smiles and unlocks his cuffs.

I take a step toward the stage and Colby grabs my hand. "Oh, no. You're not going anywhere near the fight. I'm locking you in my secret hiding spot until this is all over."

I dig my heels into the ground as Colby tries to tug me along. Unfortunately, while we were reuniting, neither of us saw Antonio fighting his way through the crowd toward us. We only take notice when a fire ball flies over our heads to where Antonio is standing. Colby shoves me behind him, and I turn, expecting to see Raven standing on stage. Except it's not Raven. It's her mom, Moriah Montclair.

I'm sure my eyes nearly pop out of my head when I see her forming another fireball in her hands. *What the hell is she doing here?* There's no time to ask her as Colby pushes me backward, causing me to dive onto the stage at Moriah's feet.

"Hello, dear," Moriah says, smiling down at me with her fireball still in her hands.

I scramble up to see Colby and his dad entangled in a quickly escalating fist fight. They each exchange a few good punches before Colby lands a solid punch to Antonio's side. Antonio uses his disadvantaged position to bring his fist up, right into Colby's nose. For the brief second Colby takes to regain his wits, Antonio fades to the stage.

Moriah launches her fireball straight into Antonio's shoulder, causing him to stumble backward a step. His stumble gives Kieran and Colby time to fade to where Moriah and I are, ready to fight. When Antonio regains his position, four vampires appear behind him, awaiting his orders to attack. Kieran steps in front of me, pushing me behind him as he slowly retreats near the corner.

"What are you doing?" I demand, trying to halt his retreat.

"Saving your ass," Kieran shoots back.

"But you're leaving them outnumbered!" I shout.

"No, I'm not. Asher is nearly here."

Just as I'm about to refute, I see a beautiful white snow owl flying overhead. A sudden bright light flashes, revealing Asher standing next to Moriah, ready to fight. Kieran has me nearly to the hidden exit door when Antonio gives the signal and his vampire's attack. Moriah creates a gust of wind that knocks over the two vampires charging at her. Colby and another vampire are locked in a fight, fading from side to side, causing me to just see a blur of colors.

Antonio hangs back as the last remaining vampire lunges at Asher. The vampire is sloppy and untrained, which is what I expect Asher to be, except I watch as Asher sidesteps the vampire with ease, slashing his dagger along the vampire's back. The vampire turns and lashes out again. This time, Asher spins out of the way, slicing the inside of the vampire's thigh. Once more, I watch the vampire attack Asher, but Asher grabs the vampire's arm, twisting it backward behind him as Asher plunges the dagger into the vampire's heart.

I stand behind Kieran, stunned at what I just saw my best friend accomplish. I had no idea he was so skilled in combat. There's no time to celebrate as the moment the vampire's body hits the floor, Antonio takes this opening to fade right to where Asher is. Asher regains some of his composure, but not before Antonio snatches the dagger from the fallen vampire and thrusts it into Asher's stomach.

I scream as Moriah hurls a fireball at Antonio. He falls, and Colby fades back to the stage, landing a surprising punch to Antonio's face. One of the vampires that Moriah pushed away earlier grabs Colby by the throat. The two of them are locked in another fight as Asher tries to stand and protect Raven's mother, but it's too late. Asher has already lost too much blood and is too weak to fight off any attack.

I watch in horror as Antonio fades back to the stage and practically throws Asher out of the way, leaving Moriah nearly defenseless. I grab onto Kieran's arm as he tries to push me through the door, obviously trying to block my view of the oncoming scene. The last thing I see before Kieran pushes me through the hidden door is Antonio's hand around Moriah's throat.

CHAPTER 52
LOVE AND LOSS

Reaching Nakoa, I find Kalena fighting by his side. "Where's Asher?" I ask, throwing a fireball straight at a vampire about to attack Nakoa.

"I don't know," Nakoa grunts, throwing a dagger at another vampire.

Kalena sprints by, grabbing the dagger from the dead vampire and returning it to Nakoa. "I thought I saw him fly toward the stage. It looks like Antonio is up there now." She points toward the stage.

Through the path of fighting supernaturals, I see Antonio fade to the stage and, without hesitation, he sinks the blade into Asher's stomach, his face scrunching in pain. I realize I won't make it in time if I try to fight my way through the crowd, so my only option is to try and teleport. I close my eyes tight, willing myself to be on that stage with him. Hoping with all my might that this works, I take a step. When I open my eyes, I step out onto the stage, right next to Asher. He reaches out in shock, his blood-soaked hand shaking as I grasp it. Antonio turns his head, a murderous smirk on his face as he tightens his grip on my mother's neck.

I'm too late.

"Well, well, well. Look who decided to finally join the fight. It's a shame you're too late." Antonio turns back to face my mother as a tear rolls down her cheek.

"I love you," she whispers, before Antonio lashes out, fangs sinking into her neck as he rips out her throat.

My breath leaves my body as Asher's hand falls from my grasp. His eyes roll into the back of his head as Antonio tosses my mother's lifeless body off the stage like a rag doll. Kieran emerges from behind the stage, only to be stopped in his tracks at the scene before him. I watch as anger flashes in his eyes, burning hotter than the sun as he fades to where Antonio stands. Kieran catches Antonio off guard and knocks him to the ground as Colby fades to the stage to help hold Antonio down.

I rise slowly, pulling energy from Kieran and Nakoa through our mating bond and generating as much energy as my body can hold. I look at Antonio's bloodied smirk and raise my head to the ceiling, letting out a heartbreaking cry as I force the energy to my fingers, letting out a bright, blinding flash of lightning that cuts through the ballroom. My body instinctually creates a protective barrier as I'm engulfed in a strong wind funnel.

My body feels electric as I hover mere inches above the stage. My mind is blank, except for the purple, gray, green, and golden auras floating in the darkness. I weave my powers around all colors except for the gray auras with red hues, striking through every vampire that has rallied against us in the ballroom. The allied vampires immersed in blue hues are spared from my wrath. When the light fades and the energy leaves my body, I fall, kneeling on the floor next to Asher as tears fall from my eyes.

Nakoa approaches me from behind, placing a comforting hand on my shoulder. The sound of battle has stopped, replaced with the sound of shuffling feet and murmurs from the surviving supernaturals.

"Holy shit," Kalena whistles. "She's incredible. She just cut through every vampire like it was nothing. How did she do that?"

"Her powers are even stronger than I thought," Antonio whispers to the ground.

Kieran punches him in the back of the head. "Shut the hell up, you piece of shit."

Kalena bends down, lifting my face to meet hers. Her brown eyes are filled with sorrow and awe. "Let me take Asher to the infirmary. We can still save him."

I nod, glancing at Asher's bloodied body. Kalena reaches down and softly cradles Asher's body in her arms, as Colby gives her directions to the infirmary. I take a second to compose myself, wiping my tears from my face.

Finally, I stand and straighten my shoulders, peering down at Antonio's face. "You don't deserve to live, but I will not be your executioner."

"You don't know the power you have! I can help you reach your full potential!" Antonio yells, fighting against Kieran and Colby's hold.

"No thanks," I say, turning to Colby. "Do with him as you see fit."

I turn to leave through the hidden door at the back of the stage as I hear Antonio's cry for mercy cut short. I walk through the door, and Leah nearly sprints into my arms, her blonde hair tickling my nose; I inhale her calming lavender scent. My knees give out as a sob escapes me, racking through my body. Leah softly brings us to the floor, and she holds me while we both cry.

Leah's crying subsides as she pushes back from me slightly, brushing a stray hair behind my ear and wiping away my dried tears. "I am so sorry, Raven."

I nod as Colby and Kieran emerge from the door. Colby

extends his hand to help Leah up and I don't protest when Kieran bends down and scoops me into his arms, carrying me away to his room. When we arrive on the boy's floor, Kieran stops in front of his door and nods to Colby as Leah and Colby enter his room.

The room is in the same shape as I left it, and Kieran's head tilts slightly as he inhales my lingering scent, placing me on the bed. We both crawl under the covers, snuggling close to each other as Kieran holds me.

He huffs out a deep sigh, kissing the top of my head. "Kalena and Nakoa have taken charge of disposing of the bodies. They will burn Antonio's corpse and they will bring Amera, Vail, and your mother's body to the waiting hall. You can go when you're ready."

I have no tears left to cry, but if I did, they would be for his loss. I look up into his big blue eyes and see an ocean of sadness. "I'm so sorry about Amera and Vail," I say, cupping his cheek.

He leans into my touch, bringing my hand away and kissing my palm gently. "And I'm sorry about your mother and your grandfather."

I nod, snuggling into his chest once again. With all the loss around us, this next part is sure to break my heart even more. I take his hand in mine and play with his fingers. "There's something I need to tell you."

"Ohh kaay . . . " he draws out.

I take a deep breath, trying to calm my nerves. "I discovered that in order to protect my powers and myself, my father curated a plan before he passed away. Before we left to live in the Human Realm, my father found out that I was mated to Asher, which sparked this insane idea. He searched the Seneca Library and finally found the answer to his plan."

"And what was that?" Kieran asks, rubbing my arm.

"He found a spell that can temporarily sever someone's true mating bond and reform it with someone else."

Kieran's hand stops trailing my arm as I turn, sitting up in bed to face him. I reach for his hands and place them in my lap with my hands interlocked around his.

"My father went to the Dragon Court to ask King Kalino and Queen Nani if they would offer their son as my protector, temporarily mating him to me."

"Okay, but what does that have to do with me?" Kieran asks, not sure if he wants to hear the answer.

"You were their prisoner at the time and my father couldn't just walk into the Vampire Court since he was trying to protect me from Antonio. Queen Nani offered you instead, in exchange for a large treasure."

"Why don't I remember any of this?" Kieran asks, skeptically.

I look away, ashamed, but Kieran brings my face right back, his eyes focusing on mine.

"Why, Raven?"

"Because my father had your memories of this event erased. He erased Nakoa and Asher's, too. He said he needed our bonds to develop naturally so that when the time came, you all would protect me out of love and not because you were forced to."

Kieran's quiet for a while, but then he pulls me close, lowering me to the bed. "It's not your fault, Tesoro. And for the record, he was probably right. My feelings for you are real; it's not just the mating bond drawing me to you."

I smile at his confession, but gently push him back. "There's one more thing I need to tell you."

"Oh," Kieran sighs, tilting his head back toward the ceiling, which makes me scrunch my nose, trying not to cry. The realization must dawn on him because he takes my hand and squeezes it. "It's okay, Tesoro."

"None of this is okay!" I cry. "He had no right to do what he did, even if it was meant to protect me."

"Look at me," Kieran commands softly.

I shake my head, refusing to look at him. He tucks a piece of fallen hair behind my ear and tilts my chin to force me to look at him. I see the sadness in his blue eyes and it kills me. He just lost two people that meant the world to him, and now, after finding his so-called mate, he realizes that I'm not his true mate. That this whole thing was just a fabricated lie.

"I regret nothing. You and me?" He smiles, motioning to the space in between us. "It was real, and I will cherish every moment I was able to spend at your side. I will always be here for you, no matter what happens. Do you understand?"

I nod because that's the only thing I'm capable of doing in this moment after my heart has been shattered yet again.

"Good," Kieran says, kissing my knuckles.

I inhale deeply, leaning my head on his broad shoulder. "I'm so sorry," I plead, looking up into his glowing blue eyes, "but I'm glad we can still be friends."

"Hey," he smiles, poking my nose with his finger, "of course we can. What would I do without my little bird?"

I jab him in the stomach, which causes us both to laugh. "I love you, dork."

"And I love you, Tesoro." Kieran laughs, releasing me from our hug. "Well, I better go bring Leah in here and save her from her queenly duties that Colby is probably trying to force on to her."

I laugh, knowing he's probably right. "Thanks, Kieran," I say as he opens the door.

"Anytime, babe," he says, blowing me a kiss as he shuts the door.

I fall back onto the bed and wait for Leah.

One down, one to go.

CHAPTER 53
THE FINAL ROSE

I hear a soft knock at my door as Leah pops her head around the door. I wave her over as she steps inside the room, closing the door and leaning on its solid wood frame. "I'm screwed," she half-heartedly laughs.

"Come, come," I say, patting the spot next to me. "Let's wallow in our pity together."

Leah smiles and launches herself at the bed, landing next to me in a heap of giggles. She rolls over, clutching a pillow to her chest as she stares up at the ceiling. "Colby asked me to stay at the Vampire Court with him."

"Wow," I say, rolling onto my back, mirroring her with a pillow clutched to my chest as well.

"Yeah. I know," Leah sighs.

"I found out that my dad found a spell and temporarily severed Nakoa and Kieran's real mating bonds and mated them to me only for my protection."

Leah rolls over facing me, throwing her pillow off the bed. "WHAT?!"

"Yeah, and the worst part is, now I have to pick who I want to stay mated to so the other men can reinstate their original mating bonds."

"What. The. Actual. Hell." Leah lets out a low whistle, laughing to herself as she flops back down on the bed. "Okay. You win."

We both fall into a fit of giggles, realizing our lives will never be the same. "Wait. Is that why Kieran looked like a sad puppy when he came into Colby's room?" Leah asks, sitting up.

I sit up, placing the pillow on the bed. "Yeah. And he took it surprisingly well. I, on the other hand, am a hot mess express."

"Damn, girl. How are you holding up?"

"The best I can, I guess," I say, shrugging. "I suppose now I know how every bachelorette feels when she sends one of the final three men home. It feels like a part of me walks out the door with them."

Leah reaches out and takes my hand. "It's all going to be okay."

I look at her skeptically. "Are you saying that for me, or are you trying to convince yourself as well?"

"A little of both. Colby confirmed that we are mates, and he wants me to stay here at the Vampire Court. He wants me to just give up my life in the Human Realm and live here. I mean, I can't do that, right?"

I shrug, hopping off the bed. "I can't make that decision for you, babe. You have to make this choice on your own. But whatever choice you make, I've got your back."

She flops back on the bed, huffing and kicking her feet, obviously not happy with my vague answer. When she hears the door open, she props herself on her elbows. "Where are you going?"

I flip my hair over my shoulder, giving her a sad smile. "To break the news to another great guy."

I wander down to the main level of the castle and pass by the ballroom, stopping briefly to survey the mess. Most of the bodies have been removed and members of the Dragon Army have started cleaning up the mess of broken furniture, while the few remaining vampires that allied with Colby help in healing the wounded. Before I leave, I spot a familiar face in the crowd.

As I approach the group of dragon warriors, whispers from curious onlookers hush the crowd. Appreciative nods from some, but mostly quiet glances in my direction. Silence falls over Faya's small group as I tap her on the shoulder. Her eyes grow wide as she throws her arms around my neck.

"I'm so glad you're alright!" she says, pulling back. "You had me worried sick!"

"Sorry," I shrug, "I'm sure the rumor mill is in full swing, then?"

"Oh, yes." Faya laughs. "I heard that you incinerated Antonio with just a snap of your fingers."

My eyebrows raise as another warrior, a dark-colored woman with long wavy hair and one dreadlock tucked behind her ear, chimes in. "I heard that you slayed four vampires with one hand behind your back with one simple word whispered."

"Now that would be cool," I say, laughing to myself. Faya excuses us from her group as she walks me back to the entrance.

"I saw what you did in here. It's something people are going to be talking about for a long, long time."

I nod, not knowing what else to say. After a brief beat of silence, Faya pulls me into another hug. "I'm so happy we met. May the gods bless your new journey."

I squeeze her tighter, realizing I don't know when I'll see her again. "Thank you, Faya. For everything."

We pull away smiling, each of us nodding and understanding the unspoken goodbye. Faya returns to the ballroom as I make my way down the hall, stopping a passing vampire to ask where the infirmary is. After being pointed in the correct direction, I take a second to calm my nerves.

When I enter the room, I find a middle-aged male vampire

checking over Asher's vitals. He's unconscious with an IV in his hand and his shirt has been cut off to reveal a large bandage wrapped around his abdomen.

The vampire looks up from his clipboard, smiling at me. "Ahh, you must be Raven. I'm Dr. Sage."

"Yes, sir. How is he?" I ask, taking a seat next to Asher's bed and reaching out for his hand.

Dr. Sage flips through papers on his clipboard, checking over notes before he replies. "He lost a decent amount of blood by the time he arrived. We had to inject him with a vial of vampire blood just to help stop the bleeding."

I wince, knowing this is all my fault.

"He just finished with his blood transfusion, so hopefully he will be awake soon."

"Thank you," I say, smiling briefly.

"You're welcome. I'll leave you two alone, but I'll be back soon to check on him again."

When the door closes, I drop my head onto Asher's bedside. "I'm so sorry, Asher. All of this is my fault."

I close my eyes, listening to the heart monitor and Asher's deep, steady breaths. The emotions from the past week pick this moment to come to a head and once the tears start falling, it's as though the floodgates have opened. I grieve for my grandpa and for my mom. I grieve for Amera and Vail and the kindness they showed me when I arrived here. And even though my dad has placed me in an impossible situation with this whole mating mess, I grieve for him too with the sacrifices he had to make and live with to protect me. Minutes pass as I silently let the sadness run its course.

A knock breaks me out of my trance as I drop Asher's hand and wipe my sleeve over my eyes. "Just a moment!" I call, trying to pat dry my cheeks.

"It's just me," Nakoa whispers from behind me, shutting the door.

I stiffen in my chair as Nakoa slides into the chair next to me, his arm wrapping around me, pulling me into his strong chest. "He's going to be okay, Princess," he whispers into my hair.

I squeeze his bicep, looking back at Asher. "I hope so."

We sit peacefully, watching over Asher as Nakoa strokes my hair. I savor this moment and commit it to memory before breaking the spell. "Can I be real for a moment?"

"Of course," Nakoa says, dropping his hand from my hair. I turn toward him, crossing my legs in my chair.

I sigh, rethinking the painful memory before I continue. "Remember how I told you my dad left a note for me to return to the Mage Court to find more answers?"

"Yes, to find the willow tree by the river," Nakoa finishes for me.

"Yes. When I went back, I found a hologram he had left for me. He explained he needed to find a way to protect me and my powers from Antonio. Unfortunately, my dad did something I don't agree with that changed our lives without us knowing."

"What did he do?" Nakoa asks, taking his hand from mine.

I try not to let the hurt flash in my eyes as I swallow back my emotions. "My father found a spell that can temporarily sever your mating bond and remate you to someone else."

Nakoa jumps to his feet, glaring at me. "What!?"

"I know, Nakoa. I don't agree with what he did. He went to your parents and asked permission first, which they gave. Then, he had your memory wiped so that our bond would develop naturally." I reach out to grab his hand, but he turns away.

"Am I the only one?" he asks, running his hand through his black hair.

"No. My father did the same thing with Kieran."

"So, Kieran knows?"

"Yes. Kieran knows," I say calmly.

Nakoa paces the small space as I give him time to process

everything. "What am I supposed to think now?" he asks, stopping to cross his muscular arms over his body.

"There's one more thing you should know," I say, standing to my full height. Nakoa turns, mere inches away from me, as his eyes shimmer in the lights. "After your protection is no longer needed, I'm supposed to choose who I stay mated to so the other men can find their true mates."

Nakoa's eyes grow wide as he shuffles backward, as if my words pierced his armor. "So, who is it then?" he asks desperately, as if he knows the answer already.

My eyes drift to Asher, softening briefly.

"I see," Nakoa says, clearing his throat.

I return my gaze toward Nakoa, our eyes locking as I speak, "Everything I felt for you was real, but Asher has always had my heart. It's always been him."

I step closer to Nakoa; relief floods through me when he doesn't make a move to step away. I gently take his hand and bring it to my chest. "My heart will always have a place for you, but it's time that you find your true mate."

His grip tightens softly around my hand. "What if we didn't sever the bonds? What if we all agreed that you are who we want to be with?"

My eyes widen at his confession. When Nakoa first heard that I had two other mates, he was angry and hurt. That night at the ball, I thought all hope was lost for us. He looked so hurt and betrayed that it almost broke me to see him like that. And now, I don't know what to think as I stare into his molten eyes.

"I know I was a jerk when I first found out you had two other mates, but the time I have spent with you was incredible. You're a good person, Raven, and you make me want to be a better man." Nakoa pulls me closer, wrapping his arms around my hips. "I am willing to share you with Asher and Kieran, if that means I'm able to be by your side forever."

As much as I want to be selfish and say yes, I just can't.

"Nakoa, what about your true mate? Are you really willing to take away someone's chance at finding their true mate?"

Nakoa takes a small step back, lowering his head.

"I know it hurts right now," I say, tears sliding down my cheeks. "But one day, when you find your true mate, this will have all been worth it." I reach up and tilt his chin up so I can see those golden eyes again. "I fell in love with you, Nakoa, and your mate will too. You're truly a special person and I will forever treasure the time we have spent together."

Nakoa's forehead brushes mine softly as he dips down to place a brief kiss on my temple, wiping my tears with his other hand. "You're right." He sighs, a small, sad smile appearing on his face. "And my heart will always have a place for you."

He releases my hand and steps around me, reaching for the door.

"Nakoa," I say. He stops but doesn't turn to face me. "I wish you well, Your Highness."

I catch a glimpse of Nakoa's ears wiggle, keying me in on his rare smile, hearing his nickname that he hates so much as he shuts the door quietly behind him. I exhale deeply, turning to find Asher staring straight at me with the biggest, goofiest grin on his face.

"Wow. I can't believe he was willing to share you. That would have been awful. Kieran kind of grew on me, but I can't imagine getting along with Nakoa."

I laugh and run over to his bedside. "It would have been fun to see you all trying to get along."

Asher laughs, then takes my hand, his green eyes holding my gaze. "Is that true? Have I always had your heart?"

"Yes, you big dummy," I say, wiping newly emerging tears from my eyes.

"Come here." Asher smiles, scooting over in his bed to make room for me.

I slowly climb into bed with Asher, nuzzling into his uninjured side.

"So, did we win?" Asher tries to ask seriously.

I burst into laughter, causing more tears to fall from my eyes as Asher laughs, trying to wipe my tears away.

"Is it too late for you to change your mind? I'm sure Nakoa would love all this emotion you're throwing my way."

I pinch his arm as he laughs. "You're stuck with me now."

"That's all I ever wanted," Asher says, his fingers plunging into my hair as he brings our lips together. A surge of warmth fills my body as I deepen the kiss, shifting my body. Asher hisses in pain as I realize his wound is pushed up against the rail of his bed. When we break apart, Asher stares at my hand in awe, holding it in between us as a magenta string appears around my wrist, weaving through my fingers, leaving delicate tracings on my arm.

I look down at Asher's hand and see the same thing occurring on his wrist. I reach out and grab his hand, holding it with my own as the bond loops around both of our hands, lacing them together. Within seconds, the bond disappears, leaving a warm, tingling sensation. Having heard of the healing properties between true mates, I close my eyes and intertwine my fingers with Asher, sending some of my mage magic through the bond to Asher.

He gasps, then reaches out to his bandage, unwinding the material. Before our eyes, the scorching red wound fades slowly. Soon, the only remnants of the wound is a small pink area around the stab wound.

"Woah," Asher says, touching where his wound used to be. He looks up at me, touching my cheek. "You're amazing."

I lean into his touch as we lay back on his bed. Asher's voice wavers as he kisses my knuckles. "I'm sorry I couldn't save her."

"Hey," I say, turning his face to look at me. "This is not your fault. My mom loved you and would sacrifice anything to save you, me, and Leah."

Asher nods, looking away for a brief moment, wiping his eyes. I slide off the bed, giving him some space. "I'm going to find you a change of clothes and inform Dr. Sage that you're awake. I'll find Leah so we can go say goodbye to my mom. I'll be back shortly."

Before I can walk away, Asher grabs my hand, his green eyes holding me captive. "I love you, Raven."

"And I love you, Asher."

CHAPTER 54

GONE TOO SOON

I arrive on Colby and Kieran's floor, hoping to raid one of their closets for clothes for Asher, but stop short when I hear Leah laughing. I'm glad she and Colby are on better terms than when I left her earlier.

"Hi guys," I say, as Leah turns to face me. I catch a flash of sadness in her eyes, but when she blinks, it's gone.

"What's up, babe?" Leah asks, as Colby slings an arm around her shoulders.

"Well, I actually have a favor to ask Colby."

"Sure. What's up?"

"Would you mind me borrowing some of your clothes for Asher?" I ask, looking him up and down, but not in the "I'm checking you out kind of way". "You both seem to be about the same size."

"Yeah, no problem," he says, kissing Leah's temple. "I've got some work to start on downstairs, but Leah can help you pick something out."

"Thanks!" I call after him as he descends the stairs.

Leah turns and opens the door to Colby's room, which is very much the opposite of Kieran's room. Colby has every inch of his walls plastered with posters, paintings, and pictures of all different themes and genres. It's like a paint set exploded on his walls with all the different colors brightening his room.

"Cool, isn't it?" Leah smirks, opening up his massive walk-in closet.

"Totally," I agree, taking my time to walk around the room, admiring everything.

Leah rummages through the closet and comes back with a pair of dark blue jeans and a white crew neck sweatshirt. "Colby shouldn't miss these too much."

"Thanks," I say, taking the clothes in my arms. With one more glance around the room, I then follow Leah out into the hall. Before I can step toward the stairs, Leah tugs on my arm, causing me to peer into her watery blue eyes.

Gasping, I shuffle the clothes into one arm and pull her into a hug with my free arm as she sniffles. "What's wrong, Leah?"

"Please don't hate me," she hiccups into my shoulder.

So she's made her choice then. I gently pull back and wipe away one of her tears. "I could never hate you. You're my best friend."

"I've decided to stay with Colby here in the Vampire Court and help him clean up the mess from what Antonio left."

"Leah, that's great! I'm so happy for you!"

She takes a step back, wiping another tear. "Really?"

"Yes, really." I smile, resting my hand on her shoulder. "You deserve everything and more. Besides, if you need anything, just leave me a hologram and I'll be here ASAP."

She laughs, playfully bumping me with her shoulder. "You're the best."

"I know," I say, flipping my hair and flashing her my best smile. "But what are you going to tell your mom about school?"

She pauses for a moment. "I haven't thought that far ahead yet, but I'm sure I'll think of something."

"Tell her you're studying abroad!" I say excitedly.

Leah purses her lips, thinking about it. "That might actually work."

We giggle down the stairs, approaching the infirmary wing as Kalena steps around the corner, nearly knocking us over.

"Oh, hi Kalena!" Leah squeaks.

"Hi girls," Kalena grins down at both of us, "have you seen Nakoa?"

Leah's eyes nearly pop out of her head in surprise at the mention of Nakoa's name. I know Leah admires Kalena and doesn't want to keep secrets from her, but I'm thankful she keeps her mouth shut about this secret. If Kalena notices Leah's odd behavior, which I'm sure she does, she doesn't say anything.

"No," I say, "but we did have a particular discussion earlier that didn't go as he would have liked." I smile sympathetically at Kalena.

"Okay, well, if you see him, let him know that the Dragon Army is heading back to the Dragon Court. I just wanted to say it was a pleasure to meet you both. If you ever need anything, just give me a shout, yeah?"

"Of course, we will," Leah laughs. "I fully expect to be trained by you soon."

"Can't wait." Kalena smiles, turning to join her soldiers.

Leah practically swoons right there in the hallway. "She's so cool."

"Yeah," I smile, "she really is."

Leah and I continue down the hall, chatting about nothing in particular, as we step into Asher's room. He looks much better than when I left him earlier. His face has regained most of its color, showing off his tanned skin. His eyes aren't bloodshot any longer, and his wound is nearly impossible to spot.

"You can stop drooling over your boyfriend now." Leah

laughs, pushing me out of the way so she can embrace Asher. "It's a shame you didn't die. I really wanted your vintage records."

"Such a shame." Asher smirks, pushing Leah onto the bed as he stalks toward me, his firm hands gripping my hips as I throw the clothes at Leah on the bed. "Hi," he whispers in my ear, sending chills down my back.

"Hi." I smile shyly, looking up at him through my eyelashes.

Leah pretends to gag on the bed. "Get a room!"

Asher turns his head, laughing at Leah. "This is my room, in case you forgot. I was stabbed, remember?"

"You're never going to let that go, are you?" Leah challenges.

"Nope," Asher replies, popping the "p" in the word before turning back to face me. His hands move like lightning up to my face, cupping it softly before bringing his lips to mine. I swear the world turns upside down as I close my eyes and inhale his cinnamon scent. I don't think I'll ever get used to being in his arms. My mind is black except for the glowing magenta mating bond. Our mating bond.

Leah coughs. Signally, she is, in fact, still in the room. "You're annoyingly cute and gross at the same time."

"Thank you." Asher smirks, and Leah throws the clothes at him.

"Now, would you please get dressed? You're practically naked."

I take a step back, looking at Asher, and realize Leah is right. He's stripped down to just his boxers. Our little make out session made him just a touch excited, and he quickly covers himself with the clothes.

"Right," Asher laughs nervously, "I'll be right out."

He hustles into the bathroom and before he can close the door, Leah reaches out, grabbing my hand and pulling me onto the bed with her. "Oh my gosh. Did you see the size of that thing?"

"Leah!" I chastise, but still giggle. *Of course I did.*

"What?!" Leah whines sarcastically, winking at me.

"Not the time or the place," I remind her.

"Okay, but when you do get together, I want every juicy detail."

"Do you really?" I ask, knowing full well she will not want to hear about her two very best friends getting it on.

"Absolutely not!"

"That's what I thought." I smirk, turning to see Asher exiting the bathroom. My eyebrow arches in approval as I scan Asher from head to toe. I knew that Colby and Asher were around the same size, but damn. Asher looks like an absolute dream boat with the way those jeans hug his hips.

Leah nudges me, bringing me out of whatever fantasy I was trapped in as Asher repeats the question; his eyes soft with sympathy. "I said, are you ready to see your mom?"

I blink and the memory of her lifeless body being thrown off the stage comes barreling back into my mind. I can't believe I was just sitting here fantasizing about Asher when my mom is laying in a wooden box down the hall. I inhale in a shaky breath and nod, swinging my legs off the side of the bed.

Asher opens the door for us, stopping to talk to Dr. Sage as Leah leads me out of the infirmary. "You know it's okay to be happy and sad at the same time."

I shake my head, turning toward Leah. "What are you talking about?"

"I saw how quickly your mood changed when Asher brought up seeing your mom. You can be sad for your mom," she says, taking my hands in hers, "but you can also be happy for yourself that you finally found your true mate and have a chance at happiness."

I know she's right, but right now, I can't accept it completely, so I nod and slip one hand from hers as Asher approaches, taking his hand with my other one. We may look ridiculous walking down the hallway hand-in-hand, but I wouldn't want anyone else by my side as I say farewell to my mom.

We turn the corner to find Kieran standing in between Vail and Amera's bodies, his hands holding each one of theirs under the white sheet. He doesn't see us enter the room since his head is down, but I can tell he hears us as his head turns slightly to the side, listening to our approaching footsteps.

Leah and Asher wait just on the inside of the room, giving me time to console Kieran. I slowly approach him, waiting for him to acknowledge me as he gently tucks their hands back under the sheets. He reaches up to wipe his tears, but I step around him, peering into his bloody blue eyes as another blood-stained tear rolls down his cheek. I reach up, wiping it away as I draw his head down onto my shoulder.

He's stiff at first, but then, slowly, he sinks down into my embrace. His arms snake around my waist as I rub circles on his back. "I'm here," I whisper through my clogged throat. Kieran nods into my shoulder as I peek through blurry eyes at Asher and Leah, beckoning them over to us.

"Thank you for everything," Kieran whispers, standing straight as he wipes his last tear away. I release his hands and gaze at him as Leah slips her arms around Kieran's waist from behind. His eyes show surprise, but then he scoots her around and embraces her properly, nodding to Asher as he comes to stand by my side.

"Thank you. To all of you," Kieran says, releasing Leah as he takes a step back. "I'll leave you here to see your mom. She's just around the corner."

I nod, not trusting my voice as I blink back more tears. Hopefully, these will be the last tears for a very, very long time. Asher leads the way, tugging me gently around the corner as Leah takes my other hand. When we enter the next room, Asher stops and turns to face me, his arms bracing my shoulders. "Are you ready?"

I close my eyes for a brief moment, channeling all my strength to help me through this before stepping around Asher. He takes my hand again as all three of us approach the altar she is on. A beautiful embroidered black sheet has been laid over her body and folded down at her neck, hiding the gash in her throat. Silent tears seep from my eyes as I release Asher and Leah's hands, reaching out to brush my knuckles on her cheeks.

"She looks so peaceful," I whisper to no one in particular. I take my time scanning her face, committing it to memory. It shouldn't be too difficult since we share the same button nose and full lips.

My mind races with everything I wish I could say to her. All the birthdays and holidays that won't be the same without her. How to bake a proper pie after I already burned the crust on the first one. What cleaning product to use to remove mascara from my favorite sweatshirt? How can I continue life without her when my heart hurts so bad from the pain of losing her?

I smooth out her hair, fanning it around her face as I lean in to kiss her forehead. "I love you, Mom." Blinking away my last tear, I straighten, turning toward the door and leave Asher and Leah to say their goodbyes.

A few minutes pass as I wait outside the room for Asher and Leah. My back rests against the stone wall with my eyes shut, trying to ward off the headache from crying when a sudden breeze fills the hallway, carrying the faint scent of lilacs, which was her favorite flower.

My eyes shoot open as I look around, hoping to determine where the flowery smell came from, when I spot a hummingbird outside the window, hovering above the windowsill. Just as quick as the hummingbird appears, it's gone in a flash, but deep down, I know it was my mom sending me a sign that she's alright, wherever she is.

CHAPTER 55
HOME SWEET HOME

The next hours fly by in a blur as Colby and Leah help arrange for a convoy of soldiers still loyal to Colby to escort my mom's body to the Mage Court. Asher and I plan to teleport while the convoy travels on foot. I've already said my final goodbye and I don't think my heart could take seeing her be lowered into the ground next to my dad, Grandpa Artie, and Grandma Elaine.

We couldn't leave the Realm of Shadows before making sure there is a plan in place at the Mage Court for proper succession laws. I have a tentative idea on how to work out a plan of action for my Aunt Melody to step into a temporary role as leader of the Mage Court while Asher and I figure out things in the Human Realm.

All too soon, it's time for me and Asher to leave as we find our way to Colby's new office. I reach out and knock twice, waiting a moment before Leah opens the door with a sad smile on her face.

"I'm going to miss you," she says, pulling me into a warm hug.

"I'll see you soon. I promise." I smile back as I hold my hand out to Colby. He reaches for my hand, but pulls me into a hug as well.

"I promise I'll take care of her," he whispers in my ear.

I step back, pointing my index finger at his chest. "You better."

Colby cracks a smile as Leah joins his side, and Asher joins mine.

"I'm sure I don't have to warn you about keeping her safe, do I?" Asher says, sounding like an overprotective brother raising one accusatory eyebrow at Colby.

"Asher," Leah whines, "I'll be fine."

"Still, if anything happens, you know how to reach us," Asher reminds them and smiles at Leah.

I'm really going to miss her, but Colby will do everything in his power to protect her. Before we depart, someone clears their throat behind us. I turn to see Kieran leaning against the door-frame with a playful grin playing on his lips.

"I know you weren't about to leave without telling me goodbye."

"I would never." I smile, closing the distance as he tucks his arms around me.

"I'll see you soon, Tesoro." He smiles, his bright blue eyes crinkling in the corners as he looks at Asher. "Keep her safe."

"Always." Asher nods, reaching his hand out for me.

I pat Kieran's chest and turn for Asher's hand. Kieran steps into the room near Colby and Leah as Asher and I take three steps back into the doorway. I close my eyes and envision my first home at the Mage Court with the reception hall and its giant stained-glass windows. Just before I take a step into the room, I open my eyes and glance at my friends one more time. "Try not to get yourselves into too much trouble while I'm gone."

I close my eyes and step forward, tugging Asher along with me as our feet touch down on the black shiny tile of the reception hall in the Mage Court. The receptionist gasps and I step forward, freezing her as her chair nearly topples to the floor with her in it.

"Sorry!" I say as Asher runs around the side of the desk and steadies her shoulders moments before I unfreeze her. "We didn't mean to startle you. I'm here to meet with Melody Montclair."

The receptionist, Teela, as her name tag reads, smiles at Asher as she runs her hands through her short black hair. "Thank you." Asher nods and rejoins my side. "And you are?" she asks with a friendly smile.

"Raven Montclair and Asher Beaumont."

Teela's eyes widen for a moment, then she picks up the phone and calmly informs whoever is on the other end that we have arrived. She nods once, then places the phone down. "Would you like anything to drink? Melody will be with you shortly."

"No thanks." I smile, turning to admire the beautiful stained-glass window. This used to be one of my favorite places to come when I was upset. I would spend hours lounging on the couch and staring up at the image of the women who created the barrier between our world and the Human Realm.

Although most of our records of her were lost in the Great War after the barrier was created, her image will be forever preserved by this amazing work of art. It's almost as if the person who created the glass was right there with her at the end of the creation of the barrier. Her slender hands are raised in front of her, creating the invisible barrier while her long white hair flows in the wind behind her. Her green eyes burn with intensity and her high cheekbones are speckled with freckles as she concentrates on the world in front of her.

My concentration is broken when my name echoes in the hall. "My dear, Raven. It's been too long."

I glance to my left as Aunt Melody approaches with her arms open wide. I smile, looking at the woman in front of me who is a spitting image of my dad, even though she was a few years younger than him. Her brown eyes shimmer in the light behind her glasses and her shoulder-length brown hair sways with every step.

Turning, I meet her the rest of the way as we lock in a warm embrace. Asher smiles at us as we let go and Aunt Melody's warm brown eyes focus on Asher for the first time. "And you must be Asher? Such a pleasure to finally meet my niece's true mate."

Asher blushes as he takes her hand, bowing low as a sign of respect. "The pleasure is all mine."

Aunt Melody shoots me a quick, cheeky grin as she mouths, "I like this one" before Asher rises.

I muffle a laugh, taking Asher's hand and following her down the hall to the office that used to be my dad's. As she closes the door behind us, Asher and I sit in the two chairs, waiting for her to take her seat behind the desk.

"First off, I just want to say how sorry I am for the loss of your mother. Moriah was an amazing woman. Furthermore, losing my dad has thrown this place into chaos for sure, but when that lovely woman from the Vampire Court brought his body back home, things seemed to be looking up."

"Amera was here?" I ask softly.

"She was. She and that scary, yet good-looking fellow brought his body back after you were taken away from the Vampire Court. She asked if you had been here, but sadly, we didn't have any information on your whereabouts." She tilts her head to the side, curiosity getting the better of her. "Where were you?"

"Oh," Asher squeezes my hand with reassurance, "I was taken to the Dragon Court for safekeeping."

Aunt Melody's eyes squint for a millisecond before softening again. "Well, regardless, I am so happy you're here and healthy. When can we expect your mother's remains to be here?"

"In two days. However, we won't be here when she arrives."

"What?" Aunt Melody says, shocked. "Where will you be?"

"Back in the Human Realm," Asher offers for me. "We have things we need to finish before we can come home, back to the Realm of Shadows. We've already been gone for over a week and people will start to wonder why three students have gone missing from the university."

"Yes, and so I need you to remain the temporary leader of the Mage Court." I shift forward in my chair, reaching across the desk to take one of Aunt Melody's hands. "I know I'm asking a lot of you, but I can't just abandon the children my mom was teaching magic to in the Human Realm. I need to find a proper replacement teacher for them before I assume my role as leader of the Mage Court."

Aunt Melody nods. "I understand, and I respect that."

"We won't be leaving you completely alone," I say, standing. "Asher will be able to travel between realms and help with anything urgent if I am not able to attend. Hopefully, we will be able to permanently settle in the Mage Court at the beginning of next summer."

Aunt Melody stands, meeting us around the desk, placing her hand on my shoulder. "I look forward to having you home, Raven."

"I look forward to coming home." I smile.

After saying our goodbyes, Asher and I step outside and onto the pebbled path that leads down to the gate entrance to the Mage Court headquarters. It's a crisp fall evening and the leaves swirl at our feet in the gentle breeze.

"Are you ready to go home?" Asher asks, clasping my hand in his.

"I'm ready," I say, stretching up and kissing his cheek.

Once again, I close my eyes and envision the two-story, ivory home that sits on the hill overlooking the lake. I see the giant island in the kitchen and the breakfast nook where I shared the last embrace with my mom and grandpa. I also see Asher, Leah, and I as children, racing around the kitchen in our pajamas. And I see my dad and I making chocolate chip pancakes in the morning before tearing into our Christmas presents.

Happy memories that I will forever cherish as I smile and take one step forward into the new chapter of my life with my true mate at my side.

THANK YOU

Your thoughts and feedback are immensely valuable to me and other readers. If you'd be so kind as to leave a review to share your thoughts with others on Amazon and/or Goodreads, I would greatly appreciate it. Your insights not only help fellow readers but also guide me in my ongoing work.

ACKNOWLEDGMENTS

Big thanks to my sister, for always joking that reading for fun is a waste of time. Obviously, she doesn't read for fun, so she'll never know this exists. LYLLB

Shout out to my husband, who is most definitely NOT an avid reader, for actually reading my first draft and fan-girling over it. Also, thank you for supporting the idea of me shaping a character's personality after Roy Kent. We love you, Roy.

To my mom, who would text or call me wanting to know what was going to happen next, even when I hadn't written the next chapter. Your support means everything.

For Barb, who put in the time and effort to edit my first draft. I will forever be grateful for your help and guidance.

For the teacher who shares a name with one character (you know who you are), I swear it was a total, but cool coincidence. Your editing notes had me cracking up and your critique helped whip this bad boy into shape.

And finally, shout out to my hype girl and book bestie, Angela. Your inspirational, but mostly comical, GIFS fueled my desire to keep the story going. Thank you for enduring all my crazy plot twists and filtering through my suggestions and ideas. You've helped me more than you can ever imagine.

ABOUT THE AUTHOR

Nicole Moore is a proud Midwesterner who loves traveling and exploring new and exciting destinations. If she isn't hopelessly cheering on her favorite football teams on the weekends, you can probably catch her curled up with another book from her never ending TBR pile. Her most honorable trait is never turning off reruns of New Girl, Friends, Ted Lasso, or Lord of the Rings.